A Furtherance of Hell

A Furtherance of Hell

A Harry Webster Mystery

John Seeley

ALSO BY JOHN SEELEY
  A Pale Horse Passing By
  What the Ashes Bring Forth
  Webster's White Devil

For Maggie & John

The Devil pulls the strings which make us dance;

We find delight in the most loathsome things;

Some furtherance of Hell each new day brings,

And yet we feel no horror in that rank advance

(Baudelaire)

We are each our own devil and we make this world our hell

(Oscar Wilde)

1.

The bar of the Tanglewood Inn was as quiet as a mime festival in a Trappist monastery. It was six thirty on a raw Monday evening in late March and most of the world was at home with the wife or still in the city getting stuck into the Happy Hour with somebody else's. Up here, on the edge of the Pennines, it was too early in the year for the heavy walking trade; too late in the day for the boss and his secretary. Apart from the bored-looking barman in a frilly shirt and 'Rocket' Ronnie's second-best waistcoat, there were only two other people in the bar. One of them had to be my prospective client and I didn't think it was the old guy dozing behind the evening paper at a table in the corner. That left the solitary punter at the bar who looked prosperous enough to afford the prices and old enough to enjoy the peace and quiet.

Nursing a glass of whisky, he sat with his head at a slight angle, as if listening to something beyond the range of other ears. He wore a royal blue Armani suit and a bright yellow shirt, and he smelt of money and Ralph Lauren Polo Red. The look was too young for him, and for the lounge bar of the Tanglewood Inn, but he had the lack of self-consciousness of someone at ease with the image he projected. My first impression was that I wasn't going to like him.

The barman offered me a stern "Good evening" and I asked for a Miller. He looked as if he disapproved but training won out and, with a minimalist nod, he turned to the beer cooler to serve me. I paid him with a fiver and took a long drink, savouring the sharp, clean taste of the day's first beer.

I looked along the bar. The man in the blue suit had lost the faraway look and was eyeing me speculatively. He sucked whisky through his teeth as if it was so much cheap mouthwash. Ye Olde McListerine.

"Are you a resident?" he enquired. "Or a just poor, benighted traveller who mistook this place for somewhere interesting?"

The barman looked affronted. He began vigorously polishing a glass, as if trying to summon a vengeful genie to make this brightly-coloured dissenter disappear.

"Neither." I said. "I'm supposed to meet somebody here."

"Are you Webster?"

I took another drink of my ice-cold beer and nodded.

"Well, then, I guess I'm the guy you're supposed to meet." he said.

Somebody shouted off set and the barman mooched through a tasteful, rococo archway out of sight. The man in the suit eased himself off his stool and stuck out a hand to show me his gold Rolex.

"Callum Jensen. It's good to meet you."

He sounded English but not quite, his hard, local vowels abraded by the mid-Atlantic twang of someone who had spent a lot of time stateside.

The barman returned, bearing a plate of pallid roast beef sandwiches. He slapped them on the bar in front of Jensen and drifted away again to his tea towel. The only sound he made was the barely perceptible susurration of his shiny waistcoat.

Jensen cast a baleful stare after him.

"Service with a snarl, huh?" he said.

He lifted a corner of one of the sandwiches and peered at its contents. He had the look of trepidation of a Victorian chambermaid making up Oscar Wilde's bed. It turned into an expression of grim satisfaction, as if his worst suspicions had been confirmed.

"You ask for a beef sandwich, you get a beef sandwich." he said. He made it sound as if a beef sandwich was the last thing he was expecting to get. "Back in the States you'd get this with lettuce, tomato, pickle and the best damn mayonnaise you ever tasted!"

"The women knead the bread on their naked thighs too, so I've heard." I said.

He didn't smile. Two nations separated by a common sandwich.

"Let's sit."

He jerked his head towards an empty table and set off towards it with his drink and sandwiches. When we had settled, he took another sip of his scotch and gave a thin smile.

"Thanks for coming all the way out here. I would have come to you, but I had some people to see earlier and I fly to Ireland first thing. I didn't want to leave this business hanging till I got back."

He glanced balefully towards the bar again and sighed.

"Not the oasis of rural charm you expected?" I suggested.

"You can say that again! You want 10-year-old malt, they only got 8. You want a sandwich? The kitchen's closed. And room service? You think they've heard of room service?"

I tutted in sympathy.

"Maybe you should buy the place and fire the lot of them."

"It crossed my mind!" he said matter-of-factly, which would teach me to be flippant with the seriously rich.

I reviewed what little I knew about Jensen from my brief phone conversation that afternoon with Don Charles, the solicitor who had hired me on his behalf. Jensen was in his mid-forties. He'd been born in this country but spent most of the last twenty-five years in America. After working for one of the big games software houses he'd used that experience as the platform to launch his own company, Dragon's Tail. It proved to be a big success, producing a string of top selling fantasy games. The most well-known of them was *Dungeons of Spite*, which sounded as if could have been inspired by an earlier visit to the Tanglewood Inn.

Jensen had sold Dragon's Tail in 2005 for enough to have bought himself a small country on the proceeds. On the evidence so far, I'd guess Albania. His wealth did not seem to have noticeably softened the edges of a deeply inherent disappointment with life. Money doesn't always buy you happiness – or even a decent roast beef sandwich.

It was unlikely that he'd brought me out there to listen to him lamenting the Tanglewood's poor customer service, though, so I reached for my notebook and shifted into professional gear.

"Don Charles said you wanted me to find your wife for you." I said.

Jensen nodded absently as if reluctant to pull back from the narrow focus of his trivial grievances with the hotel trade.

"Or I could slip through to the kitchen and give the chef a slap?"

He looked at me as if I'd slapped him, then broke into a rueful smile.

"Sorry. Just venting. The psychiatrists call it displacement, don't they?"

I thought that if anyone knew that it would be him. I drew a smiley face in my notebook.

Jensen sighed again and withdrew a postcard sized photograph from his inside jacket pocket. From the look of pensive nostalgia on his face it was either his favourite New York deli or the missing wife, I guessed.

He passed it over and I saw it was the latter. I could also see why he went all dewy-eyed over her. She was a stunner, all right. Just as I remembered her...

"Hi, I'm Jill." she said.

"Hi," I answered. "I'm Jack. You want to come up the hill with me?"

Okay, so nobody was more surprised than I was that a line like that got me anywhere but, hey, it was late, and we were both a drink or two past the pint of no return. With the benefit of hindsight, I believe she'd made up her mind she was going to have me before I even opened my mouth. I was more than happy to meet her halfway. When she laughed, the sound ran down my back like electric rain and quickly invigorated other parts. It didn't take me long to recognise it wasn't going to be a meeting of minds and after another couple of drinks we made it to the nearest taxi rank on the pheromone rush. We arrived at her place in a haze of alcohol, and kisses, and over-tipping. Shortly afterward,

Jack and Jill went up the hill indeed, and stayed there until dawn came tumbling after.

In the morning we said our half-sheepish farewells over lousy coffee and burnt toast, rumpled as the bed we'd recently left. We murmured the usual platitudes with stale breath but whatever spark we'd kindled had been no more than that. A brief ignition that had got us up that hill before the feeling stalled. We had coasted down on the fumes of designer beer and loneliness, the exhilaration of the sex pouring past us like the wind. There were no regrets on either side but we both knew it wouldn't happen again. The knowledge brought with it a curious sense of relief.

As I rose to leave I had the strangest urge to shake her hand. I settled instead for a quick, uneasy peck on the cheek before I slipped gratefully out of the door.

I didn't look back, and I got the feeling that she would have forgotten all about me by the time I reached her front gate. It was only then that I realised that I didn't even know her real name – or she mine.

"Her name's Jennifer." Jensen said.

I flashed back to him with what I hoped was a neutral expression, wondering if my face had betrayed me when I'd first seen the photograph. If so, he gave no sign that he had noticed anything amiss. He looked at the cool blonde in the picture with a sloppy smile that sat as uneasily on his face as a crash helmet on a nun.

"My Jen Genie, I used to call her." he said wistfully,

Bet that rubbed her up the wrong way, I thought, but I kept that one to myself.

"She's very attractive."

"She's beautiful!" he said defensively.

I shrugged. "Yorkshire understatement." I said. "How come you're not still together? You look as if she still means a lot to you."

"She's the love of my life." he admitted. "We met at Durham University. She was a leading light in the drama club, never thought she'd look at me twice, but somehow this humble spear carrier got lucky! We were inseparable through the last two years of college and got married soon as we graduated. We were a real partnership. I was struggling to get a break in the software industry and she was my rock. Unpaid secretary, chief cheerleader and all-round inspiration. I wouldn't be where I am today if not for Jen."

"So, what happened?" I asked.

He shrugged fatalistically.

"Until I met Serena – that's my current partner – I used to ask myself that two or three times a day. I never really came up with an answer that made any sense. I suppose, in a strange way, being successful screwed things up. Everything was fine when we first moved to America, I had a steady gig with Raven Software and we brought this great little place in Shorewood Hills. That's up in Madison, Wisconsin, right by Lake Mendota..."

"*By the shining deep-sea water, near the wigwam of Nokomis?*" I suggested.

"Huh?"

"I get the picture, Mr Jensen. Good job, nice house, happy marriage. You lived the American Dream for a while. I'm suitably envious but skip to the bit where it fell apart."

"Sorry. They were such good times! I guess I'm feeling a little nostalgic, is all."

"It's okay but I don't need that kind of detail right now. Broad strokes will do."

"Of course. Well, where did it all fall apart? It started when Activision acquired Raven back in '97, I suppose. That's when myself and a couple of other programmers decided to try striking out on our own rather than taking the safe path and sticking with the big boys."

"That must have taken some guts." I said.

"Indeed – and Jen was not happy about it. We had a great lifestyle going and she wanted to keep it that way. Dragon's Tail was a risk she didn't want me to take but I had to follow the dream, you know? I won't deny it was hard at first. I hardly dared look at the company accounts for the first year! We managed to stay afloat, but it put terrific strain on my marriage. Jen knew what it was like to live on the edge, but that's a lot easier to handle when you're two young graduates struggling to get a toe hold in the real world. Not so much when you're pushing thirty and your partner wants to take everything you've worked so hard for and gamble it all on a single bright idea in a field already awash with them."

"Dungeon of Spite." I acknowledged. "A chop and shop classic."

He smiled modestly. "If I do say so myself. The game 'Diablo' wanted to be."

"But its success didn't save your marriage?"

He smiled ruefully.

"Damage had already been done. We both lost faith in each other for a while, I suppose, and we couldn't get back to where we used to be. Oh, we tried, believe me. A few months after Dungeon was released, Jen's mother got sick. That's when she decided she had to come back to England. I came with her, figured we could make a fresh start, rebuild what he had, but we never really got the chance. I had to be away from home a lot pushing DoS and doing all the other shit that comes with running a breakout software company. Meanwhile, Jen's stuck at home worrying about her mother and rattling around in a house that was probably too big for a couple, let alone a woman on her own. I came back as often as I could but the distance between us seemed to grow with every absence. By the end it came as a relief when I had fly back to America. It was pretty obvious that Jen started to feel the same."

"Things finally boiled over when her mum died, and my flight home got delayed. I missed the funeral and I guess I didn't seem too sorry about it. Not sorry enough anyways. This would be about five years ago. We had a flaming row that brought everything to a head and I walked out for good. Or she threw me out. A bit of both, if I'm honest. We've lived separate lives ever since, other than the occasional communication through our lawyers. Neither of us was particularly bothered about getting a divorce so we stayed married, if in name only. I made sure she was well provided for. The house is hers and she gets a generous allowance that keeps her in the style to which she's grown accustomed. It's an arrangement that suited us both until recently. I met

Serena a year ago at a political fundraiser in Maine a year or so back. We moved in together six months ago and I proposed this Valentine's Day just gone. That was my last contact with Jennifer - when I rang her to ask for a divorce."

"And how did she take it?"

"She was fine about it. It was all very amicable. We agreed to let our lawyers get things moving and speak again when things were sorted."

"Is that what brought you home?"

He shook his head. "Not exactly. These things move at their own speed. We were both cool with that. This visit was a spur of the moment thing. I'm a guest speaker at Warpcon in Cork this coming weekend so I thought, what the hell, I'd stop over here on the way and see Jen face to face. It's been a while and, well, I guess I hoped that we could get to sit down together and talk without screaming at each other."

"Was she expecting you?"

He shook his head. " I did try to let her know. I couldn't get an answer on her land line and her cell always went straight to voice mail. I've also emailed Jen and her solicitor. Got nothing back from Jen but the lawyer sent this."

He reached into the inside pocket of his jacket and pulled out a folded A4 sheet. While I read it, he picked up his sandwich again, looked at it dubiously and took a hesitant bite. The paper was a printout of an email.

Dear Mr Jensen,

Thank you for communication concerning your forthcoming trip to England. I have tried to contact your wife about your request for a meeting in respect of your ongoing divorce proceedings, but I regret that I have been unable to contact her. There have been no answers to my phone calls or emails and on enquiring at her place of work I am informed that she is no longer employed at the offices of Stentor Alarms, having left that post at the end of December. Since receiving her letter of resignation her former employer has had no further contact with her though I understand that, prior to ending her employment with the company, she had spoken to work colleagues of her intention to spend the remainder of the winter in a more hospitable climate.

Be that as it may, I am sure that her current elusivity is disconcerting news to you given your hopes of progressing your mutually agreed divorce. Regarding this matter, please feel free to contact me when you arrive in the country irrespective of whether you can reach your wife in the interim.

yours sincerely
Roger Carver

I folded the email printout in half again and passed it back to him.

"Elusivity?" I said

"Lawyers, huh?"

"And you've still not been able to contact Jennifer?"

"No. I tried calling again before I left the States and soon as I landed on Saturday evening. When I got no answer, I drove over to the house yesterday."

"To find what?"

"Not much." he shrugged. "Nobody at home but I've still got a key."

"Where exactly is the house?" I asked

"Oh – yeah, it's at Loxley Green, well on the fringe of it. Big old place in its own grounds, nice for the price."

Something that would always matter to Mr Jensen, you imagined. Loxley Green was a ruggedly pretty, little village up on the edge of the Moors, where buying a converted Victorian labourer's cottage would cost a Victorian labourer an arm and a leg these days. The house he described was a cut above that level and it didn't sound anything like the place that Jennifer had taken me back to that night.

"And what did you find behind the Loxley Green door?" I said

"Nothing." He shrugged, amending hastily: "Nothing untoward, I mean."

"No body?"

"Nobody at all – oh, I see! N-no, thank goodness." He grinned sheepishly. "Though it did occur – well, all sorts of things go through your head, don't they?"

I conceded that they do indeed.

"No signs of a struggle or anything like that?"

He shook his head firmly. "No, everything was as it should be, I guess."

"Did it feel like anybody had been there recently?" I asked.

He looked puzzled. "Sorry? I don't -?"

"You can usually tell when someone is living in a place – empty cups and half-read magazines on the coffee table, for instance, dripping taps, the tick of cooling radiators – and then there's the Hum."

"The – Hum?"

"It's always in the air when someone's been there not so long ago. It's a subtle vibration in the air, a residue of body heat maybe, kinetic energy, unresolved emotion. Fragments of them all, really. I call it the Hum."

"What are you? Some kind of psychic?" he said with a wary laugh.

"No. I would have warned you not to touch that sandwich if I was. So – no Hum then?"

"Not that I heard – felt – no. Although, now you mention it I don't think anybody had been there for a while. There was dust on the furniture, like the place hadn't been cleaned lately."

"Okay. Did anything else catch your eye?

"I checked the garage to see if her car was there. It wasn't – or at least the garage was empty. I suppose she does still drive but I wouldn't know for sure." He pulled a rueful face. "Don't know much, do I? I didn't really hang around once I realised no one was home. I haven't been there for five years and it felt wrong being in the house when Jen wasn't. I just scribbled a brief note asking her to call me. Then I left."

"Did you try speaking to the neighbours?" I asked.

He shook his head around another tentative mouthful of bread and meat, swallowed hastily and washed it down with a swig of malt,

"Aren't any." he elaborated. "Not adjacent, anyway. The place is detached and some ways from any other houses. That's what first appealed to us when we saw the place. We both like our privacy."

That didn't exactly jibe with the party girl Jen I remembered from our brief acquaintance. People change in five years though, I suppose. Maybe stepping out of his shadow had brought her out of her shell.

"Do you or your wife own any other property?" I asked, thinking back again to the night I'd spent with Jennifer.

"Not over this side of the pond, in my case. Jen did inherit her mother's house back in the day. I always assumed she would have sold it, but I couldn't swear to that."

"What about friends or relatives?" I asked.

"Jen's an only child and her father died when she was still at school. You know about her mother. I wouldn't have a clue who her friends were these days."

"Anyone she was close to back in the days before you first went stateside?"

"That was over twenty years ago." he said dubiously. "We kept up with one or two of our old college friends for a while. I could probably come up with a list of names if it might help."

"It's probably a long shot but make the list anyway." I took a business card out of my wallet and passed it to him. "My email's on there."

He nodded and took the card.

"So, I guess that means you'll take the job?" he said, almost surprised.

"I rarely turn down offers of work from people with six figure bank accounts." I assured him

He chuckled at that. The truth was I didn't really need his money and his clothes made my eyes hurt. I thought Jennifer was most likely off drinking mojitos on a beach somewhere, but the coincidence of her appearing again so unexpectedly in my life was enough incentive for me to spare at least a couple of days looking for her.

"Hey, I hope she is just chilling on a beach somewhere with a twenty-year-old stud." he said presciently." I'm okay

17

with that. The thing is, I'm getting a lot of heat from Serena to move the divorce along, so we can tie the knot. I need to catch up with Jen as soon as possible. If I didn't have this commitment for Warpcon I'd be looking for her myself, but I don't want to waste another week hanging around for her to show. That's why I need you to be looking while I'm tied up in Ireland. I'm hoping by the time I get back next week you'll have been able to pin her down, so we can get through this divorce crap and all move on without regrets."

If not without alimony, I thought.

"When exactly do you expect to be back from Ireland?" I asked.

"Next Monday or Tuesday. After the convention I'm staying with some old friends in Cork for a couple of days. I'll let you know soon as I get back."

I made a note and asked a few more questions while I finished my drink and he worked his way through the last of his uninspiring snack.

"I don't think there's anything else for now." I said. "I'll look around the house first thing tomorrow and let you know anything I find."

"I just want your honest assessment." he said. "Am I over-reacting or should I be genuinely worried for Jen?"

He handed me the keys to Moorside, along with a printed note with his contact details, Jennifer's email address, and her cell phone number. When I mentioned the delicate matter of the usual, up-front retainer he paid me in crisp new twenties from a hallmarked silver money clip.

"If this turns out to be a false alarm, you'll get it back less whatever time I put in on it tomorrow." I said

"The money doesn't matter. I just want to know that Jen's safe." he reiterated.

As we shook hands one final thought occurred to me.

"Just as a matter of interest, why did Don Charles send you to me? He doesn't use me normally."

"It was my idea – and you can blame the power of the press." he grinned. "That White Devil business? You nailed a serial killer inside a month that a specialised task force couldn't catch in three years. That makes news even in Coon

Rapids, Minnesota! Once I decided to hire somebody to look for Jen, it was a no-brainer. You're the man."

Yeah, the man who's famous in a place called Coon Rapids, I thought. I returned his smile half-heartedly. I could have told him that all the above was mainly luck – and bad luck at that. I might just as easily have ended up in the obituaries as in the headlines. I had a nasty scar near my right shoulder to remind me of that fact from time to time, usually when there was damp or trouble in the air.

The familiar dull ache started virtually the moment I left the warmth of the Tanglewood Inn and stepped out into the cold March night.

2.

Moorside lounged in opulent seclusion at the end of a
narrow, tarmacked farm lane flanked by bare, untilled fields.
It was prime building land, but Loxley Green doggedly
defended its green belt status. I don't suppose it hurt, either.
that one of the city's MPs had a house there, complete with
moat and ornamental bird house no doubt.

The Jensen house stood at least a quarter of a mile from the
main road, sealed off by electronic gates in a seven-foot-high
boundary wall. The fob Jensen had given me controlled the
gates, which opened onto a gravelled courtyard. The house
itself was a south-facing, two-storey build of pinkish, pitch
faced sandstone.

To the left of the house stood a double garage built of the
same material and the fob remote also operated the garage
door. It slid up noiselessly to reveal that the garage remained
as empty as when Jensen had checked it two days before. I
had a quick scout round the interior, but nothing caught my
interest. There were no bloodstains on the concrete floor,
only a few tyre scuff marks and the odd oil stain. A set of
aluminium ladders hung on the back wall above a mini
workbench on which the usual detritus of grimy rags, oil
cans, a tub of Swarfega and a few basic, ill-matched tools
were scattered. A green hosepipe, coiled on a hook stood to
the right of the bench beside a standing tap. In the far-right
corner a connecting door led through to the house. I tried it
but found it locked. None of the keys on the fob fitted the
lock.

I left the garage and walked around to the front door which
opened onto a wide vestibule with polished wood flooring
and a central staircase leading up to the second floor. As
Jensen had warned me, the house was fitted with an intruder

alarm and I turned off its warning beep with the four-digit code he had provided. The keypad, just inside the door, had the distinctive logo of Stentor Alarms, the company that Jennifer had worked for.

Silence resumed, and I paused for a few seconds to listen for the Hum; the indefinable pulse of the house. It could hear it but only very faintly, like the merest whisper of vermouth in an Extra Dry Martini, and it may only have been a lingering trace of Jensen's recent visit

I looked around, counting four doors off the hallway to downstairs rooms. To the left of the front door a large alcove served as a boot room and general depository for wet weather gear. I noted a pair of navy Hunters with a flash of lipstick pink down the back and a couple of expensive outdoor jackets. I checked the pockets, found nothing but a scrunched-up tissue and the stub of a cinema ticket for 'Love and Friendship'.

The only other item in the alcove was a small, pine table, covered in a thin, tell-tale layer of dust. Inside the table's single drawer, I found a pile of unopened mail, junk for the most part. I stuffed it into my jacket to check later.

I climbed the stairs to a short landing that gave access to two large, front facing bedrooms. At the rear, a third bedroom stood next to a communal bathroom. The smaller of the two large bedrooms housed a Queen-sized bed and matching pine dressing table, wardrobe and chest of drawers. A few small ornaments stood on the dressing table and a framed photograph of Whitby Abbey, brooding gothically in a winter sunset, hung on the wall above it. A bowl of pot-pourri sat on a small lamp table by the bed, giving a pleasant, mildly fruity fragrance to the room. The wardrobe and all the drawers were empty, suggesting that this must be the guest bedroom.

The small, rear bedroom housed various boxes and plastic skips containing everything from unwanted clothes and household miscellanea to old seed catalogues and holiday brochures. Neatly packed and stacked, the rooms contents appeared to have remained undisturbed for some time. I left them that way.

The master bedroom yielded a little more to go on: the lack of a toothbrush in the en suite bathroom and visible gaps amongst the plethora of beauty products marshalled on the big oak dressing table. No sign of a Vanity or make-up bag, either. Apart from a tan leather overnight bag on the floor of the walk-in closet I couldn't locate any suitcases or other hand luggage. Add that fact to the noticeable number of empty hangers in the closet and the odds were stacking up that my client had overreacted. He must also be one of the least observant men I'd ever met.

That fact niggled at me a little, but I ploughed on. After a quick search of the formidable array of clothes remaining in the closet, I turned over the bedroom's sundry drawers and cupboards with equal lack of result. At this point I sat on the bed to draw breath and take a closer look at the pile of unopened mail.

It consisted mostly of unsolicited pleas for Jennifer to sponsor a donkey, donate to cancer research, take advantage of 0% balance transfers or subscribe to a never-ending collection of hideously twee decorative plates featuring characters from Disney films. Amongst the re-cycling fodder, however, I came across her latest bank and credit card statements and the picture I had in my head began to change.

The credit card bill showed that the card had last been used a fortnight ago, though the transaction related to the automatic renewal of an Amazon Prime subscription. No other charges had been made to the card in the period.

The bank statement told a similar story. It showed the state of her account up to the previous Friday. There were many sizeable deposits, representing regular investment dividends, and a healthy monthly funds transfer from her estranged husband. The only money that had gone out, however, was in payment of standing orders and direct debits. No cash withdrawals or debit card purchases appeared.

She might have more than one bank account and multiple credit cards, of course. Until proven otherwise, though, the statements raised anomalies. I kept hold of them when I returned the rest of the post to the Boot room.

The four doors downstairs led to a living room, a dining room, a small office and a kitchen-diner that gave access to the garage. There was also a rear extension containing a drained and covered swimming pool. Everything seemed neat, tidy and well-ordered in the slightly unnatural way that some people always tend to leave their homes when they plan to be away for any length of time.

The office was the only room that proved fruitful. It was not a large space and contained only a pinewood work station on which sat an all-in-one PC and a laser printer. I switched on the PC and, while it booted, I went through the lower shelves of the work station. They held stationery, three or four well-thumbed computer manuals and a thick, dark blue concertina file. In the single drawer there were a few pens, a stapler and some spare staples, a pair of scissors and a green leather key fob from which hung two tumbler lock keys. I examined them but there was no indication as to what they might fit. I left them where they were for the time being.

The PC screen was demanding a password, but I ignored it for the moment. I pulled out the concertina file from its niche. Its plastic pockets bulged with assorted paperwork that Jennifer obviously felt the need to keep at her fingertips. The tabbed pockets were alphabetized, and items filed by their first letter. Working my way through from A to Z, I found a stack of older bank and credit card statements, all representing the same accounts as the two I now had in my pocket.

As I worked my way back through the statements the same pattern of minimal use emerged for the first two months of the year. Before the turn of the year, however, a more normal pattern of expenditure presented itself. One large money transfer caught my eye on the statement for the previous December and the months preceding. They showed regular payments of £300 on the 15th of every month to someone called Janet Lazenby. I pulled the latest statement out of my pocket to double check. There was no payment this last month, nor on the January or February statements.

Jennifer kept two years-worth of financial statements in her file. As I combed through the credit card bills I noted several payments to travel companies or airlines. Jennifer liked to take regular holidays, up to three times a year according to her card statements. Her destinations on each of these trips were easily traced by the transactions on her card. If she was on one of her trips now, then the same pattern should have been observable from her most recent credit card statement.

I finished going through the statements and filed them back in their respective pockets. I worked quickly through the rest of the file until I got to the letter I, confirming that Jennifer had a very healthy investment portfolio and drove a 2011 Nissan 370Z. In the same pocket, I found current Home Insurance policy documents for Moorside and another property: 17 Old Willow Lane in West Bretton, a former mining village about twenty minutes' drive from the city. According to Jensen, Jennifer's mother had lived there. It looked as if Jennifer had indeed kept the property and I wondered if that might have been the house to which she had taken me back for our one-night stand.

I found nothing else of interest until I got to the P section. It contained only a small, red, spiral notebook. On closer inspection it proved to contain a neatly tabulated, handwritten record of the various passwords that Jennifer used for the computer, her router and the various websites she visited.

All the remaining pockets were empty apart from the one labelled W. In this I found a clutch of wage slips from Stentor Alarms going back over the last twelve months. Under the company name in slightly smaller print it said: 'A division of Delphic Security'.

The name prompted a frisson of recognition that almost matched that I had felt when Callum Jensen had shown me his wife's photograph. Delphic were the biggest security company in the city and about five years ago they had bought out the small but profitable agency run by my friend and mentor Ben Cross. As part of the deal Ben insisted that his staff were kept on, but the resulting experience was not one I remembered with fondness. I lasted less than six months before I clashed one too many times with my arrogant boss and walked out – or got fired. Opinions vary but let's say my knuckles were bruised more than my ego.

As I put the wage slips back into the folder, I reflected on yet another unexpected connection between myself and my client's wife. I couldn't help wondering at what point coincidence became something else entirely.

I turned back to the notebook. The first entry read: PC - killerh33ls. I typed it into the login box and hit enter. The cursor disappeared, and a line of dots chased each other in a circle for a few seconds before the screen dissolved into the sparsely populated desktop It contained only the icons for the Chrome browser, Microsoft Word and the Recycle Bin. These were also pinned to the task bar, along with File Explorer and Outlook. I clicked on the latter and opened Jennifer's email account. A flurry of new mail downloaded into the Inbox. It consisted largely of spam or newsletters from sites like Groupon and Wowcher. There was nothing of a personal nature and nothing older than a couple of days. This suggested that Jennifer, or somebody, was checking and weeding her mailbox on a regular basis.

I expanded the Folder pane but could see only the usual defaults. It seemed a bit surprising but easily enough explained by the possibility that she used a laptop or tablet as a main point of access to her mail and Internet.

I turned to File Explorer. It proved to be a similarly fruitless exercise, except to provide confirmation of previous suspicion. There were no personal documents or other files on either hard drive but at the bottom of the Navigation window, icons for 'My Laptop' and 'My iPad' were listed under network devices.

I checked the little red book again and, sure enough, found relevant passwords. All I needed now was the devices themselves. I looked in all the work station drawers but found no sign of either.

Her Internet browsing history only reinforced the conclusion that the PC was her line of last resort. Only a handful of sites were listed going back the default ninety days. Without exception they were auction or shopping sites. I could only conclude that she only turned the PC on when she was working in the office on her accounts or other paperwork.

I checked the Recycle Bin, found it empty, but this reminded me I hadn't checked the deleted items folder in her email. There were about a dozen discarded mails in there, most of them just acknowledgements of orders or despatch of items she'd bought online. The only mail that looked as if it might be something different had been received in mid-December. It came from dash@gmail.com and had the subject heading: Friars of St Francis. There was an attachment to the mail, the body of which consisted of the brief, cryptic message:

Friday 19th, 19.30.
Fais ce que tu voudras!
Venue to follow.

I opened the attachment, which revealed a full colour picture of a naked man and woman engaging in rear entry sex in front of a log fire blazing in a stone fireplace that was bedecked with mistletoe and holly. Both participants wore black domino masks covering their faces and the man in the driving seat wore a Santa Claus hat at a jaunty angle. Whether this was a by-product of the strenuous physics of intercourse, or deliberate insouciance, who could say? In a similar seasonal vein, the raven-haired recipient of Santa's imminent Christmas delivery wore headgear in the shape of a pair of sparkly, silver antlers, though it clearly wasn't just her bells that were jingling.

I forwarded the mail to my own email address then powered down the computer. I wasn't sure if the invitation had any relevance to finding Jennifer Jensen, but one thing was certain: I would never hear Rudolph the Red Nosed Reindeer again without seeing that picture in my head.

In the kitchen, the polished, wooden floor and grey marble worktops were dulled by the now familiar patina of dust. A separate utility room contained the usual appliances and provided access to the garage and swimming pool through separate doors in opposite corners. Although the pool had been drained, a faint odour of chlorine still lingered.

The back door opened onto a stepped flagstone terrace, descending to an immaculately tended lawn dotted with flower beds in which early daffodils and narcissi were already in bloom. As I stepped outside the earthy smell of compost wafted from a nearby rose bush. Neglected though the house may be someone had been taking good care of the garden in its owner's absence.

I sat on the top step and lit up a cigar, savouring the first smoke of the day. The warm Spring sunlight had driven the chill from the stone but a fragment of it pierced the spot near my right shoulder where the knife scar was. I massaged it absently, a mannerism acquired during physiotherapy and never quite discarded. I'd picked up the wound in my confrontation with Rocky van Dorn, a psychopath responsible for thirteen murders during just one, brutal month. He was also linked to a series of murders attributed by the press to a serial killer they dubbed the White Devil, and to a group of wannabe mercenaries/terrorists called The Templars. They were all dead too, the only upside of the nasty business that had so impressed Callum Jensen on my behalf.

The final act of violence in Van Dorn's blood-soaked career came when I emptied most of the clip of a Desert Eagle Mark XIX into him. I did it to save my own life, though nobody could argue that he didn't deserve his fate. I certainly hadn't lost a moment's sleep to regret, though I'd lost plenty through the warped flashbacks that still surfaced from time to time in vivid nightmares of our violent face-off.

A psychotherapist might tell me the dreams are part of the price I paid for killing a man. If so it was a price I was happy to pay considering what the alternative outcome would certainly have been. The combination of blood loss and hypothermia almost killed me anyway, but the emergency services got to me just in time. I was hospitalized for a couple of weeks and in physio for six, but I refused to talk to a shrink despite the plentiful advice I got from the hospital staff, police, parents, friends and anyone else who gave a damn. That included my ex-girlfriend Mattie, though her concern for my mental health may have had more to do with the fact that I'd knocked out two of her new boyfriend's teeth during that same crazy weekend.

I felt more guilt over that than I ever did about shooting Rocky van Dorn.

In the aftermath I was a hero for a little over the standard fifteen minutes, though the police were a bit sniffy about it. I had a certain amount of sympathy for them. They only had an elite team of detectives, cutting edge forensic backup and unlimited feet-on-the-ground man power going for them. I had malign fortune on my side, which had dumped me into the middle of one psychopath's plan to thwart the equally deranged plan of another.

Still, the official response was less than gracious. If the new licensing rules for private investigators had been in force at the time, I would probably have been out of a job by now. Such, at least, was the considered opinion of DCI Jarvis, head of the so-called White Devil Squad. Threats were made concerning prosecution for obstructing a police enquiry and there was even the suggestion of a manslaughter charge. Nothing came of either. Smoothing Jarvis's ruffled ego wasn't worth the bad publicity that would have ensued, I suppose.

I came out of the whole mess better than I probably deserved, all things considered. Not that everybody saw that as a positive outcome, though I did receive plenty of 'Get well' messages and letters of general good will, including a handful of marriage proposals and an offer to shoot a US TV commercial for MRI. On the down side, the usual run of trolls, cranks, racists, misogynists and Daily Mail readers also came out of the woodwork. Their letters and emails were never signed with the senders' real names, of course. They hid behind tags such as 'A Patriot' and 'A True Englishman' or obvious pseudonyms that paid homage to the heroes of the morally bereft such as 'Timothy McVeigh' and 'Anders Breivik. The most literate rant I received came from someone who signed themselves 'The Smiler with the Knife', who may have been my old English teacher Mr Parkinson. He never liked me.

I passed on the overt death threats to the police, but nobody was ever arrested and since I was still walking around I guess they were just from posers. The mail, good and bad alike, soon dried up once the press circus moved on to the next big story. When my moment of fame expired no one was more pleased about that than I was.

Not that life went back to normal overnight. For one thing, my various injuries meant I couldn't drive for several weeks, which was a definite drawback for someone in my line of work. Thanks to my friends Eddie Snow and Tommy Clegg the business kept ticking over nicely though. It kept Eddie off the streets and out of Trading Standards' hair and the publicity generated by the White Devil case certainly didn't hurt me professionally. As the current job testified, it was still blowing the occasional client my way over a year after the event. On balance, though, I still found myself wishing that none of it had happened. I didn't feel guilty about the shooting, but it had changed me in some way. Van Dorn's life was not all that was lost on that night.

3.

I got to my feet, crushed out the remains of my cigar and
dropped the stub into the packet. As I turned to go back
inside I heard tyres crunching onto the gravelled drive at the
front. I allowed myself the tentative hope that it might be
Jennifer, returning home from her holiday with an all-over
tan and a two-fingered salute for her mithering husband.

That brief hope soon faded as I walked quickly round the
side of the house. Jen Genie had not materialised - unless
she'd magically transformed into a scruffy looking middle-
aged guy wearing dark brown cargo pants and a tatty camo
jacket. As I came around the side of the garage he had his
back to me, leaning into the side door of a red VW van. He
was whistling some unrecognisable tune that faltered as he
straightened up and turned from the van, holding a black,
plastic bulb tray.

The man appeared startled but no more than I was when I
got my first glimpse of his face, which looked like something
out of a horror movie. The right half belonged to a normal,
almost handsome, brown-eyed man in his forties. The left
side, in contrast, was just a wreck of red, ruined flesh that
almost seemed to be melting before my eyes in the warm
sunlight. He could not have helped but catch the sudden
intake of breath I was unable to completely stifle. He reacted
with no more than a stoic smile and dismissed my attempted
apology with a quick shake of the head.

"It's okay, it gets most people that way the first time." he
said, defusing the moment with an unexpected chuckle.
"Imagine how I feel having to look at this ugly mug in the
mirror every morning?"

There was not a lot I could say to that. He laughed again.

"Relax. I'm messing with you. My shrink says I've got a fucked-up sense of humour, I tell him it goes with the fucked-up rest of me. Name's Louis Sifer. I'm the gardener, case you've not guessed."

"Harry Webster." I said. He had his hands full, so we settled for a brief exchange of nods. The ensuing silence was on the verge of becoming uncomfortable when he spoke again.

"IED just outside Fallujah." he said. "Just in case you were wondering. I was in a three-man patrol. I'm the lucky one, believe me."

It sounded weird hearing him echoing similar thoughts to those that had recently occupied me. I wondered if he believed it, or if deep down, he wished that someone else had caught all that luck.

I nodded again and explained what I was doing there. He listened attentively, the right half of his body angled towards me. I wondered if the bomb had done some damage to his hearing too, forcing him to favour his good ear.

"Well, there's not much I can tell you, really." he said when I had finished. "Last time I saw Mrs Jensen would be the beginning of January, I suppose. Said she was shooting off for a while but would I stay on top of the garden and keep my eye on the place." He delved his left hand into the pocket of his camo jacket and fished out a key fob identical to the one Jensen had given me. "My usual days are Wednesday and Friday – just for three or four hours depending what jobs there are to do. It's mainly the garden but I do her windows too and any little odd jobs around the place. She's one of my regulars. The genial village handyman that's me! It's been a godsend, I'll tell you! It supplements my pension and I like being out in the fresh air without having to worry that some mad bastard's going to take a shot at me."

I asked him a few more questions but he had little more to add.

"Honestly, I've never seen much of her to speak to." he confessed. "She answered my ad in the Parish Magazine last summer and she interviewed me for about five minutes. Other than that, she'll pass the time of day if she's around, but I've never been asked in for elevenses or anything like that. Not that'd I'd mind if she did." he added with a sly smirk that did nothing to improve that irredeemably disfigured face.

Some of my sympathy for him ebbed away and he seemed to sense as much. He cleared his throat and, with another brief nod, made to move past me. I stepped aside and let him go but, after a few steps he paused and turned back to me.

"Tell you who might know more." he said. "You should talk to Janet, her cleaner."

Janet. I remembered the standing order on Jennifer's old bank statements.

"Would that be Janet Lazenby?"

He shook his head slowly. "I don't know her surname. She usually works the days when I don't, but I've bumped into her occasionally when one or other of us has swapped our days for some reason. Mrs Jensen's pretty flexible that way."

At least this time, he didn't smirk when he said that.

"Well, best get on." he said. "I've got Mrs Robshaw's gutters this afternoon and it'll take a while to plant these." He nodded at the tray in his hands. "Purple Irises." he added. "Her favourites. These are called 'George, I hope she likes them."

Now the disturbing smirk did return, and he ambled past me with a final nod. I noticed that he dragged one leg slightly as he walked. Another legacy of Fallujah, I supposed. I watched him thoughtfully until he reached the corner of the house and turned out of sight.

I wandered back to the rear of the house in his wake. As I climbed the steps back onto the terrace he was kneeling by one of the freshly turned flower beds, the tray of bulbs by his side. I watched him for a few seconds as he produced a trowel from his jacket and began to dig in the iris bulbs. He started to whistle again, a cheerless threnody that seemed to chill the very air.

Back inside the house I did a quick sweep of the kitchen, finding nothing of relevance in any of the drawers or cupboards. There were a couple of notes pinned to the refrigerator door with fridge magnets, but these turned out to be just recipes. The fridge itself was empty apart from a few non-perishable condiments, and the bottles of gin, vodka and Hunter Valley Chardonnay in the door rack.

The living-room, overlooked the rear garden, where Louis Sifer worked steadily at his planting. It was a large, airy room, minimally but expensively furnished with matching black leather couches, a marble-topped coffee table and a couple of elegant standard lamps. A mahogany unit took up almost all of one wall, showcasing a variety of small antiques that included a Clarice Cliff vase and a Henri Jacot carriage clock. A second set of shelves on the opposite wall was filled with books.

More prosaically, a 50in flat screen television was fixed to the chimney breast, hooked up to a DVD player that sat on top of a media stand in the adjacent alcove. The second shelf housed her DVD collection, a mix of classic tearjerkers and modern Rom-Coms.

I opened the third-tier storage drawer. At first glance the contents appeared innocuous enough: a trio of remote control units for the media devices and a gold-coloured Christian Louboutin shoebox containing more DVDs.

My first thought was that they were just overspill, but it struck me as odd that they were all without cases. I picked up a couple of discs at random to take a closer look. They were both classic weepies: *Now Voyager* and *Titanic*. I checked them against the cases filed in alphabetical order on the shelf above. Both titles featured amongst them. I pulled out the case for *Titanic* and checked the contents. The disc inside lacked any of the usual title details found on either a legal or expertly pirated copy. The only identifying mark on it was a six-figure number – 061115 – scrawled in black marker pen. Likewise, the second DVD, albeit a different number: 210316.

Every one of the DVDs in the shoebox could be matched to a case containing a similarly marked recordable disc. It didn't take Stephen Hawking to work out that the numbers were a simple date notation. The earliest was 7th September 2015 and the most recent 15th October 2016.

Curious, I reached back into the drawers for the TV and PVR remotes and turned on both devices. I slid the disc from the Now Voyager box into the machine and pressed play. The TV screen came to life with two people, who were clearly not Paul Henreid and Bette Davis, having at it on a bed with mutual fervour. The video had been shot from above and behind the man, whose face was never in camera as he toiled away doing what a man's got to do. His partner, as I recognised at once, was Jennifer Jensen.

Equally familiar to me were the sexy, curved leather headboard and the distinctive pale blue and gold wallpaper that went so well with the mustard coloured carpet. I may have been drunk at the time, but I still had my eye for detail and a good memory. The raunchy scene I was watching had been recorded in the very same room where I myself had capered with my client's missing wife

The other discs repeated the scene: same wallpaper, same bed, same Jennifer. Only her partner changed, and they came in a variety of shapes, sizes and colours. The vigour with which they performed varied though they all shared a complete lack of self-consciousness that suggested they were unaware of being filmed. Jennifer appeared likewise uninhibited and immersed in the moment. There were no knowing looks or sly winks at the camera, or any other signs she knew of its presence. Still, I couldn't imagine her keeping these recordings in her collection if she hadn't been a knowing party to their content.

I'd soon seen enough. I switched everything off and returned the discs to their cases. Before filing them back in the sequence, I checked the rest of the shelf for more unexpected content, particularly a disc marked 18/08/16, which was when Jennifer and I had so briefly connected. I found no such disc, which came as a relief, attended by an odd twinge of disappointment. It was akin to hearing the nominations for the Oscars and realising your name didn't feature on the list.

A glance at her bookshelf confirmed Jennifer's more than cursory interest in sex. *Jane Eyre, Pride and Prejudice*, and other classics rubbed up against contemporary chick lit novels and a whole section of erotic novels. These titles ranged from *Fanny Hill* through scandalous Victoriana on the lines of *The Lustful Turk* and *Night in a Moorish Harem*, to more recent genre heavyweights such as *Nine and a Half Weeks* and *The Bride Stripped Bare*. A few non-fiction titles, dealing with aspects of female sexuality and modern sexual attitudes, rounded off the sequence. Step forward Nancy Friday and Betty Dodson.

In amongst this section I found the copy of the book about the Hellfire Club referred to in the email I'd found on Jennifer's PC. There were other titles on the same subject, one of which being Daniel P. Mannix's 1959 eponymous classic. I flicked through it wistfully, recalling the long ago, rainy afternoon in my febrile teenage years when I'd first read it. Jennifer's copy was a recent re-issue and looked new, the spine barely cracked. There was a hand-written dedication on the title page.

To the Midnight Lady
Fais ce que tu voudras!
Dorian

This was the second time I'd come across this phrase from Rabelais' bawdy masterpiece, *Gargantua and Pantagruel*. It was the motto of the Abbey of Theleme, the fictional utopia where men were free to indulge their most ardent desires. The notorious 20th century occultist Aleister Crowley appropriated it as the founding principle of his Book of the Law, the personal magical system he devised with the chief aim of getting into the pants of any woman he fancied. Before Crowley it had similarly inspired the original Hellfire Club and its various imitators in pursuit of their libertine philosophy. Do *Who* Thou Wilt might have been a more honest declaration of intent but, either way, the evidence of this morning confirmed Jennifer to be an enthusiastic convert. She had an itch for sex and no inhibitions about scratching it with whoever took her fancy.

I must admit that her chosen lifestyle made me uneasy, though not in any moral or judgemental sense. I was broad-minded enough not to care what consenting adults do to each other in private, whilst not being unaware of the inherent dangers in laissez-faire sex. Apart from the obvious risks to individual health and safety that might accrue from casual sex with strangers, the DVDs added an extra dimension of risk. Not many people would react with equanimity if they discovered their unwitting starring role in an uninhibited skin flick. I dare say I wouldn't have been too happy myself. As a single man with no current significant other vague embarrassment would probably be the extent of my reaction. Someone with a wife or long-term partner at home might have a more volatile response, however. As, indeed, might the wife or long-term partner should they learn that they'd been two-timed.

What had motivated Jennifer to make and keep a record of her most intimate relationships in this way? Did she enjoy reliving her conquests, peremptory as they might be, over a glass or two of chilled Hunter Valley? This seemed more like something a man would do – and a shallow, sad kind of man at that.

There was the darker possibility, of course, that the discs represented prime blackmail material. Certain individuals would pay dearly to ensure their lurid infidelities didn't reach the wrong audience. Possibly that was why I wasn't part of her video scrapbook, I reflected. My relationship status offered no opportunity for serious financial gain.

Of course, she might have a 'Best of' disc stashed somewhere. Yeah, I bet I'd be on that one.

Back in the real world, meanwhile, I was wary of forming premature conclusions, but I couldn't help wondering if Jennifer's secret video diaries had somehow rebounded on her.

The rest of the room threw up no further surprises, though on the shelf of the coffee table I came across a small pile of well-thumbed holiday brochures for Australia and the South Pacific. This seemed to suggest that, if nothing else, Jennifer had indeed been seriously planning a holiday, just as she had apparently mentioned to her workmates.

On the table top there was a single piece of printer paper with a brief scrawled message: Where R U? Call me asap. The note that Callum Jensen had left for his absent wife.

I looked in vain for a land line. Like so many people these days Jennifer seemingly relied on her mobile. There was no sign of an address book either, which might simply infer that she had taken it with her, or that she kept her contacts on her phone.

In the bottom cupboard of the wall unit I found a photograph album and skimmed through it with interest. Its pages took me on a rapid tour of faraway places, from the Golden Gate to the Hermitage Museum, from the Faroes to Bali. When Jennifer herself featured she was usually on her own but always looked smart and relaxed, a woman completely at ease in her own skin.

Towards the rear of the album the story changed. She still looked cool and confident, but she had at some point found a friend to share her wanderlust. In a variety of shots – the deck of a cruise ship, a sunny beach, a busy bar- Jennifer posed alongside a younger, red-haired woman who was in no way overshadowed by her older companion. I found a snap in which they'd both shed their designer shades and slipped it from its mounting. If I couldn't find Jennifer, then perhaps I could find the red-haired beauty and question her about her friend over dinner and a few drinks.

I put the snapshot into my wallet and returned the album to the cupboard. As I did so I couldn't help reflecting that it was alone in the cupboard. Where were the records of the rest of her life? Her student drama days, her previous forty odd years of birthdays, her twenty plus years of marriage? Where for that matter was her wedding album? Was that and all the other memories of a crowded life hidden away somewhere amongst the boxes in the spare bedroom or had it made a sad little bonfire in the back garden when her marriage had fallen apart?

I cast a last look around the room before I left, and my gaze settled on a vibrant print on the wall opposite the flat screen TV. It was an eye-catching tangle of brilliant blues and pale greens, which I recognised as Van Gogh's Irises. It's more

serene than most of his later work but you can still see the
turmoil inside him in those green leaves writhing up from the
ground. They lick around the bright blue blooms like verdant
flames, eager to devour them and then engulf the drabber,
earth-toned flowers in the background. I look at it and see
genius holding madness at bay with a fragile brush.

The print made me recall the comment made by Louis
Sifer, the unsettling gardener, about irises being Jennifer's
favourite flowers. I glanced out of the window to check if he
was still hard at his planting and found him staring straight
back at me, his half-ruined face unreadable. Then he smiled,
and Two-Face became the Joker. He raised his right hand,
still clutching his planting trowel, though whether the gesture
was meant as a curse or a valediction I wasn't sure.

4

Janet Lazenby lived at the end of a cul-de-sac called
Foxglove Row on the southern fringe of the village. It was
the last in a line of four bungalows on the right-hand side of
the un-adopted road, which terminated at the wrought iron
gates of a redbrick Victorian villa. An ornate metal sign atop
the gate identified this as:

The Foxglove Hall Preparatory School- *Aspirat Primo
Fortuna Laborat.*

If my Latin was still fit for purpose that meant something
like: Fortune smiles upon our first effort. Judging by the
gleaming silver Mercedes S parked in the otherwise deserted
school courtyard, fortune did more than smile on some
people. She rubbed her breasts in their face and French-
kissed them.

I pulled in behind a four-year-old blue Honda Civic parked
outside the address I had identified as the home of Jennifer
Jensen's former cleaner. I was scarcely out of my car when
the front door opened. A slim, refined–looking woman in her
early fifties regarded me unsmilingly from her step. She was
wearing a grey, herringbone skirt and a white blouse that was
buttoned all the way to the top and beyond if the look on her
face was anything to go by.

I introduced myself and flashed the smile that had broken a
thousand hearts. Janet Lazenby's cardiac pump kept beating
resolutely. Fortune had nothing to fear from me.

"Please come in, Mr Webster" she said, returning my smile
with one as prim and proper as you might expect. "I hope
you have not had a wasted journey. As I told you on the
telephone I'm unclear as to how I might help you."

"Thank you for inviting me anyway." I said to her
retreating back. Well: "Come if you must" was an invitation

of sorts. Ill-sorts, chiefly, which I quickly learned was her default setting when the subject of her former employer was raised.

"Flighty." Janet Lazenby said, sipping decorously from a fine China tea cup.

It was some time later. She may not have especially welcomed me being there, but she knew the obligations of a hostess and the Earl Grey was very good.

"Flighty?" I echoed, feeling even more like I'd fallen asleep and woken up in a Victorian novel.

"It's what my mother would have called her." Janet said in a tone that made it clear she was far too polite to tell me what label she herself would have stuck on Jennifer.

"Ah – a bit of a flibbertigibbet then, eh?" I said. "Something of a coquette?"

"Sarcasm is the lowest form of wit, Mr Webster." she said, smiling tightly.

"But it is the highest form of intelligence." I reminded her. She smiled again, less rigidly this time.

"So, Mr Wilde would have us believe."

"I think he was probably just being sarcastic." I said.

"You are not at all what I expected, Mr Webster."

"I get that a lot." I admitted. "I assume you mean that Mrs Jensen liked men?"

"That's certainly the impression she left me with." Janet said carefully, unbending slightly to add. "There are signs you can't help but notice when you're in someone's home regularly."

"Strange hairs on the pillow, raised toilet seat, that kind of thing?" I said encouragingly.

"Used condom wrappers in the waste paper basket." Janet responded deadpan.

"Ah! Still could've been worse. At least it wasn't the used condoms."

We both drank some more tea and contemplated that thought in a mutual silence that was almost cosy.

"This happened a lot, did it?"

"Only the once." she admitted. "But as you say, there were other signs – and people aren't blind to who comes and goes."

"They must have remarkable eyesight or very good telescopes." I reflected. "The nearest house must be half a mile away."

She smiled indulgently.

"I don't mean the village, Mr Webster. She doesn't bring them to Moorside - usually. I'm talking about her other property. I cleaned both places. Tuesday at Moorside, Friday at Willow Drive. It's a fair drive to West Bretton and I wasn't keen at first. To give her credit, though, Mrs Jensen was happy to pay me extra for petrol and travel time. The bungalow is in the middle of a row and directly opposite a public house. It's hard to be discrete in such a setting and you'd be surprised how eager the neighbours are to invite the hired help in for a cup of tea when they scent scandal."

I wasn't surprised at all and I expect she knew it.

Janet had worked as a part-time cleaner for Jennifer Jensen for the past couple of years. Her dismissal three months earlier had come completely out of the blue. Arriving for work on a Tuesday morning in early January she had found an envelope addressed to her lying on the kitchen table. Inside she found a month's salary in cash and a brief note thanking her for her good work. It went on to explain that her employer was taking an extended trip aboard and was uncertain when she might be returning.

Janet had kept the letter and after a brief show of reluctance for appearance sake she dug it out of one of the drawers of a solid looking dark walnut sideboard that stood against one wall of her small sitting room. She handed the letter to me and I skimmed over the first few lines, which Janet had already summarised for me. It continued:

Wherever I land, I anticipate that my stay will be a prolonged one. I am still relatively young, effectively single and lucky enough to be financially independent and able to pursue my sudden fancies wherever they might take me. I am tired of the seemingly endless English winters; the cold winds off the Pennines; the grey, threatening skies. I want my skies to be blue and full of sunshine, to feel hot sand between my toes and cool ocean breezes in my face.

I am fixed on my new course and I cannot wait to be away. In the circumstances, however, the open-ended nature of my plans makes it necessary for me to terminate our current arrangement. Please be assured that this is no reflection on the service you have given whilst in my employ, which has been exemplary, and I should be more than happy to re-engage you on my return – whenever that might be.

Please find with this letter four weeks' severance pay in lieu of notice.

Yours sincerely

Jennifer Jensen

The letter was printed on a single sheet of A4 and signed in black ink. The envelope was plain white with only the name JANET block printed on the front. With her permission I used my phone camera to take a photograph of the letter and envelope. It was at this point, mellowed perhaps by the opportunity to vent her feelings, that my hostess had excused herself to make the tea we were now drinking.

"These men – did you ever actually meet any of them?" I asked.

"Not at the West Bretton house. If Mrs Jensen had been there she was long gone – as were any of her 'guests'."

"Not at West Bretton?" I said.

"Pardon?"

"You said 'Not at West Bretton' – which suggests that you might have seen her with someone elsewhere?"

She frowned then nodded, almost approvingly.

"You have a sharp ear to match your sharp tongue, Mr Webster." she acknowledged.

"And all my own teeth." I added.

"That does surprise me." Janet Lazenby said, which made us both smile a little. "But – you asked if I ever met any of Mrs Jensen's ah – how to describe them?"

"Condom donors?" I suggested.

"Let us say 'paramours', shall we? or 'inamoratos', perhaps."

I could swear she was starting to enjoy herself a little.

"Let us." I agreed. And save the last waltz for me, I thought.

"I did not in fact meet any of them in the sense of being formally introduced but you are correct to assume that I have encountered one of her lovers in the flesh – so to speak." she added hastily.

I kept a straight face and sipped my tea.

"When was this?"

She thought about it for a moment or two.

"The first time would be about six months ago. I was a little before my usual time one day and I passed Mrs Jensen's car in the lane as she was just leaving. She had a man with her, dark curly hair, sunglasses. I didn't see much more than that."

"But you're sure it was a man?"

"Quite sure. There isn't room for two cars, so I backed up to a passing point to let Mrs Jensen pass. I got a long enough look to be sure of her passenger's gender, I can assure you."

"And you saw him again – the same man?"

"I do believe it was the same man who was at the house a couple of weeks later, yes. He was sitting eating toast in the kitchen when I arrived and seemed quite at home. I was a little surprised, I confess. As I mentioned earlier, Mrs Jensen was not in the habit of bringing men to *Moorside*. However, she had already left for work, so she obviously knew and trusted him well enough to leave him alone in the house."

It did sound like he might be more than just last night's Special, and I pressed Janet for more detail. Most of the frost had thawed by now and she seemed almost eager to share what she knew. Mollified, perhaps, by the realisation that Jennifer's abrupt departure might be more than just the whim of a beautiful woman with too much time and money on her hands.

"He's younger than Mrs Jensen, I think – or extremely well-preserved. In his late-twenties, perhaps. Tall, though not quite as tall as yourself, dark hair going mad to curl, as I said.

Eyes – blue-grey. Clean shaven and very good looking but not in a pretty boy way. His face has character. I don't know – a sort of knowingness I suppose you'd call it."

Knowingness would be good, I thought, wondering where I might pick some up.

"Did you speak to him?"

"We exchanged polite greetings, no more than that. He said his name was Dorian."

That made me sit up. That was the name of the man who'd written the dedication to Jennifer in the book about the Hellfire Club!

"He didn't mention a surname?"

She shook her head. "No."

"Anything else that you can think of that sticks out?" I asked, which sounded like something Louis Sifer might have said.

"He's local, I'd say, or he's lived in this part of the county long enough to sound like a native. I should think he'd be easy enough to find. Dorian isn't exactly a common name."

Not where I was brought up, certainly, unless your school uniform included a mandatory bulletproof vest. Once out of puberty you could probably get away with it, at least with the ladies. Mrs Lazenby certainly seemed as if she had a little stardust in her eyes after meeting him.

"He drives a black sports car, I couldn't say what type exactly, I'm afraid. I think Mrs Jensen was seeing him fairly regularly through last summer and autumn."

"What makes you so sure? I mean, if you only actually saw him twice -?"

"Eau Sauvage" she said. "I smelt it around the house a lot in the summer months. It happens to be my son's favourite too, so I'm very familiar with its fragrance."

I followed her eyes towards a silver photograph frame on the sideboard. It held a full-length portrait of a smiling young man in naval dress uniform.

"He's a warrant officer on board HMS Bulwark" she said with undisguised pride. Her gaze dwelt on the photograph for several seconds and when it snapped back to me her eyes were glistening slightly.

"You must miss him." I suggested.

"Indeed." she said, effectively shutting down any further conversation on the subject. She leaned forward in her chair and regarded me earnestly. "Do you think that Mrs Jensen may have come to some harm?" she asked.

"I hope not." I said carefully. "Everywhere I look I just seem to find a little more evidence that she's just decided to take a long holiday – but I find myself not quite believing that narrative."

"I think you are a man whose instincts are well honed." she said gravely. "I hope in this case they prove to be wrong. Mrs Jensen and I are not friends and I confess that losing my position was both unexpected and unwelcome. Irrespective of that, and critical as I may be of her lifestyle, I sincerely hope that she is safe and well."

She released my arm and stood politely to signal that my audience was at an end. I left her on her doorstep as I had found her, a handsome, ever-so-slightly-uptight woman whose better nature struggled constantly to wriggle through her defensive shell of rigid politeness. I wondered what her story was. She was hardly your run of the mill Hoover jockey and I guessed she just took cleaning gigs to get out of the house. I figured her for a retired professional type, a teacher or librarian. Someone more familiar with 'Mr Wilde' than Mr Sheen for most of her working life, I thought.

There didn't appear to be a Mr Lazenby anywhere in the picture. He certainly didn't merit a spot on the sideboard, where apart from the one of her son the only other photograph was a wedding day shot of a beaming bride and groom. It looked far too recent to be a memory of her own nuptials, though the bride looked enough like Janet to be her daughter.

Of Mr Lazenby there was no sign, which suggested to me that she was divorced rather than widowed. Not amicably, either, I thought, or there would surely have been some lingering, subliminal trace of him from happier days. As it was the room was determinedly, indeed aggressively, Janet's room: spotlessly clean and tidy, feminine but not flighty, an unabashed mash-up of Laura Ashley and John Lewis in

which a male presence would be tolerated only for so long.
My time was up and if I didn't leave now I could almost
believe that the room would release anti-bodies from its walls
to swarm upon and repel the unwanted invader.

5.

Stentor Alarms were based in a small business park that had sprung up on the former site of a long defunct steel rolling mill. It was a two storey, red-brick unit with a green tiled roof rubbing shoulders with a discount carpet warehouse on one side and a cash-and-carry grocery outlet on the other.

According to their web site the company had started life in the 1980s as a strictly local firm specialising in home security alarms. It had expanded in time to service the whole of South and West Yorkshire and had been bought out around the turn of the millennium by Delphic Security. This was a nationwide operation with its home base in the city. It was a voracious animal and over the last ten years it had subsumed several smaller outfits, amongst them Cross Security, the company owned by my friend and former employer Ben Cross. Delphic covered the whole spectrum of security-based work from the mundane (door and event security supervision) to the sexy (close protection, corporate security and counter-intelligence.) They even offered cleaning services through a sister company called Alpheus Solutions – though I thought Alpheus Ablutions had a better ring to it.

I didn't much care for Delphic or, to be more accurate, their founder and CEO Ellis Thatcher. Though I had only met him a handful of times during my short and not too sweet tenure with Delphic it was enough for me to work out that he was a man whose sense of self-importance was only matched by his apparent disdain for the abilities of anyone else. He would say he was a perfectionist, I guess, though anybody who had felt the sting of his usually unjust and self-serving criticism might disagree. 'Paranoid narcissist' is probably a more accurate description. Of course, when your business is selling security as a high-end commodity, paranoia is probably an asset and there was no doubt that as paranoid narcissists go he was at the disgustingly rich end of the spectrum. He also had a penchant for sexually harassing the more vulnerable female members of staff, which had eventually led to my fist hitting his jaw and my feet hitting the bricks.

Stentor Alarms was just a small part of Thatcher's ever-expanding empire. The building housed its Alarm Monitoring Centre, fitting and maintenance department and the regional sales team. I was met in the downstairs reception area by a middle-aged man who looked a little old to be the office gofer. He introduced himself as Gareth and shook hands limply. He was dressed in comfortable brown cargo pants and a grey cardigan. He wore this over a navy Minecraft T-shirt and the Office Nerd effect was completed by metal framed, tinted glasses and lank, greying hair, scraped back into an untidy ponytail. His inexpertly trimmed beard couldn't quite hide the acne scars beneath that spoke of a long, losing battle to escape from puberty.

Gareth seemed like a man who loved his job and he maintained a steady running commentary about Stentor as he escorted me to the lift. He was still talking when we stepped out into the large, open plan office space occupied by the sales team.

I tuned out most of what he told me, but I got the general impression that if Stentor was a woman he would have married her. Or, more likely, pined over her impotently from a distance while she ran away with the captain of the rugby team.

Only about a third of the twenty or so desks in the office were occupied by a mainly female staff tapping away at keyboards or talking into phones. The few bodies that were present interrupted their routines just long enough to assure themselves that I wasn't anybody important then went back to what they were doing. Only one person took more than passing notice of me – and I couldn't help but repay that interest. She was strikingly attractive, with deep chestnut-coloured haired and a quizzical smile. I recognised her at once as Jennifer Jensen's female friend from the holiday snap in my pocket. When I smiled back at her she seemed suddenly shy or nervous. Toying with her neckline she turned her gaze back hurriedly to her computer screen as if it had suddenly become an object of the deepest fascination.

We moved on, passing through a door at the far end of the office into a short corridor with several glass-panelled doors opening off it. The shiny name plate on the first of these announce that we had reached the office of Sharon Erickson, the Manager. Gareth rapped confidently on the door and opened it without waiting for permission, ushering me in flamboyantly.

"One private detective delivered as requested, boss." he announced cheerfully to the woman sitting behind the boomerang shaped desk that was the focus of her not over-large workspace. Apart from the desk there were a couple of faux walnut filing cabinets, a small printer table on which sat a laser printer and a fax machine. Behind her chair a small bookcase stood within a hand's reach, containing what looked to be mainly management texts and technical manuals. The only personal touches were a healthy-looking Philodendron, in a plain white pot on the window sill and a framed certificate stating that Sandra Erickson had successfully completed Office Management Level 3 with the Open Study College.

Sandra herself was an improbably tanned forty-something year old, who half-rose from her chair to shake my offered hand and wave me to a seat opposite. The smile she flashed along with the handshake was only marginally more genuine than her tan or her straw-blonde hair, cut in a stacked bob, which would have better suited somebody ten years younger and three shades paler. She was sturdily built but was probably not unattractive beneath the Sun Shimmer and the too young haircut.

"Thank you, Gareth." Sandra Erickson said.

"Mon plaisir, as always." Gareth chortled. "Can I get you a coffee before I trudge back to my little hobbit-hole?"

"That would be brilliant, Gareth. My usual please."

"Double tall hazelnut Moccacino, coming up! And for monsieur?"

I was impressed by his smooth transition from tour guide to barista, but I declined the offer. With a quick smile in my direction and a deferential nod to his boss, he left to do battle with the coffee machine.

Erickson smiled tolerantly at his departing back.

"Gareth." she said, with a fond shake of the head. "He's a pet."

"I wish I'd known; I would have given him a biscuit." I said.

She wasn't quite sure what to make of that, so she decided to leave it alone.

"So – Mr Webster, isn't it?"

"It is – and thank you for seeing me."

"Of course, anything that we can do – though I'm not sure what I can add to what I told Jennifer's husband."

"I'm really just gathering background. The more I learn about Mrs Jensen, the better my chances of tracking her down. That's the theory at least."

Ms Erickson accepted that logic with a brief inclination of her head and, flipping through my notebook, I went on:

"I'd just like a brief chat with yourself and then, if I could speak to – Molly - was it?"

"Molly Grayson. She was probably closer to Jennifer than anyone else here. They shared adjacent desks, sat together at social events and staff meetings, that kind of thing. I believe they even went on holiday together from time to time."

"So, I understand. Was your own relationship with Mrs Jensen good?"

She frowned in thought, one hand toying with a gold-coloured ballpoint that rested on a A4 pad that lay on the desk in front of her.

"Professional." she said finally, then: "Cordial, for the most part. She's an excellent saleswoman."

I could believe that. I'd seen some of her technique first hand. It was a good job she'd never tried to sell me one of their alarms or my office would have been wired up like Fort Knox.

"Her numbers were stellar really for someone who only worked part-time." Erickson continued. "I would have hired her full-time, but she didn't want to know. I gather she doesn't need the money and, good as she was at the job, I always got the impression that coming to work was more of a social outlet than anything else. She was clearly a people person."

"So, I'm finding out." I said. "Would you say she got along with everyone else in the office? Sales is a competitive area after all."

"Tell me about it!" she laughed, flashing perfect white teeth and the theme from 'Jaws' played softly in my head. "There are always tensions in any office environment and I've had to referee the odd cat fight from time to time, I'll admit. In general, though, we're a tight team and I'd say Jennifer was a good fit with her workmates."

"How long had she worked here?"

"Oh – well, let me see. I've been here three years this Easter and Jennifer was already on staff. I could check her personnel file if you wish but, from memory, I'd say she'd been here a couple of years when I started. She always gave me the impression she liked the job. Her resignation came right out of the blue. It's been a horrible winter and I can well understand her wanting a break. She needn't have made it permanent, though. If she'd talked to me, we could have sorted something out to suit both parties. Sales talent like hers earns you a lot of leeway in my book."

"Did you ever try to contact her and tell her that?" I asked.

"I rang her a couple of times – and sent her an email inviting her to come in and talk but my calls went straight to voice mail and she never even bothered replying to my email. I just took that to mean she didn't have any intention of letting herself be talked out of her decision to leave."

"So, nothing to set alarm bells ringing then?" I said.

She didn't laugh and that was about it for Sharon Erickson. When Gareth barged back in with her steaming Macchiato I shook her hand again and took myself of to talk to Molly Grayson.

Sometimes this job has its moments and she was one of them. Up close Molly was even more attractive than her photographs suggested, with clear, pale skin and hazel eyes that looked straight back at you without guile or artifice. Her chestnut hair shone with a thoroughbred's condition and hung almost to her shoulders. Her dress was office casual: cream-coloured trousers and an off-white blouse open at the neck to show off a simple gold chain with a heart shaped pendant studded with a single, small diamond. Her perfectly manicured hands, clasped lightly around a mug of lemon-scented tea, were devoid of any rings and her only other jewellery was a Michael Kors watch with a rose-gold case and bracelet.

As her manager had suggested we talked in the Meeting Room, a couple of doors along from Sandra Erickson's office. It was about twice the size, equipped with a single conference table, interactive white board, overhead projector and a forty-inch flat screen television mounted on the wall above a recess in which sat a slim DVD player. A single computer terminal sat on a work station to the left of the TV screen and twenty or so metal chairs, identical to those on which Molly and I were seated, were neatly stacked off in the corner near the window.

Molly and I sat at right angles to each other at one end of the conference table. She seemed relaxed and at ease but the way she would occasionally fiddle with the chain round her neck suggested she may not have been as sanguine as she appeared.

"I appreciate you taking the time to speak to me." I said "There's nothing to get stressed about. I just want to find out a bit more about Jennifer. No one seems to have seen her for a while and her husband is a little worried about her."

"Better late than never, I suppose." Molly said spiritedly, speaking with a smile that smoothed away any rough edges from her words. "Sorry, it's not you. Just the mention of Callum's name gets my hackles up. When he left he cut her out of his life completely. Never remembers her birthday or sends her Christmas cards. She always makes out like it doesn't bother her but, tough as she is, I think it still stings.

For him to suddenly start acting like he gives a damn now –
well – it just takes a little swallowing, that's all."

"I think his concern is chiefly for himself." I admitted.
"He's under pressure to rush through a divorce and re-
marry."

"That sounds more like it." she said, adding with a rueful
smile: "Listen to me? I've never even met him. He could be a
really nice person for all I know."

She looked at me as if I might know one way or another. I
realised that I didn't.

"I've only met him once myself." I shrugged. "He seemed
like a bit of a fish out of water, to be honest. Or, rather a big
fish whose just been tossed back into a rather small pond he's
long since outgrown."

"English by birth, American by inclination." Molly said.

"That's quite astute to say you've never met."

"It's what Jen says. She doesn't mean it nastily. He was the
love of her life – still is, I think, despite everything."

"Define 'Everything'?" I said

"Oh, you know – their separation, Jen's – flings." Our eyes
met for a moment then she looked away, uncomfortably. I
felt the heat rising in my cheeks.

"You were there, weren't you?" I realised. "The night we -
"I stumbled over the right word. It was probably 'Fucked' but
I found I wanted her to think well of me, so I settled for: "-
connected?"

She looked back at me, blinked, and then started to giggle
nervously.

"Yes – sorry – I seem to be doing nothing but apologise to
you! It's just, well, your face! You said 'Connected' but I
heard something else."

"You've got a good ear for subtext." I smiled.

"There's no need to be diplomatic on my account. Whatever
it meant to you it probably meant even less to Jen." she said
sadly. "That's how she rolls these days."

"Flings?"

"Yes. It's all she can handle. I'm not sure she's had a serious
relationship since Callum left her. As I said, I think she's still
in love with the – man."

We locked eyes again and both laughed.

"You heard something else too, didn't you?" Molly said.

With the ice well and truly broken I moved things on. Molly had worked for the company only for a couple of years, though she and Jennifer Jensen had been friends prior to that, having met at a gym where they were both members.

"It was thanks to Jen that I got the job, really." she admitted. "She was the one who persuaded me to apply and though she never said as much I'm pretty sure she put a good word in for me."

"Did she have that kind of influence?"

"She's hard to say 'No' to, put it that way."

"I'll second that." I said

"We were really close at that time. When we met I'd just come out of a bad relationship and Jen, well, I don't think she ever has come to terms with her separation. We bonded over the Cross-Trainer, she used to tell people. We just clicked. She was like my elder sister and best friend rolled into one lovely package."

"I've seen some of her holiday snaps. You two seem a good match."

"Yeah – we were BFFs. We had some really great times while it lasted."

"Have you had a falling out?" I asked.

"Hmm? Oh – no – not really. I mean, we're still good friends, at least I think we are. It's just that we don't we're not joined at the hip any more. Haven't been for the last year or so - even before I met the latest dickhead."

"No subtext there, I guess."

"Not a pet name." she admitted. "A whirlwind romance that turned into a shit storm."

"Has anyone ever told you, you have poetry in your soul?"

She laughed, a hearty, unaffected sound that fell pleasantly on the ear.

"Anyway, it was all pretty serious for a while, so Jen and I saw less of each other outside the office than we were used to. Still feel a bit guilty – especially given how things turned out between me and Mark - I don't think Jen resented it in anyway. When everything blew up in my face she couldn't have been more supportive – always there to put a comforting arm round my shoulder or to lend me hers to cry on."

"But?"

"It just wasn't the same between us. Jen seemed to have become more cynical, especially where men were concerned. I mean, I don't want to give you the idea that she was ever a candidate for a nunnery, but she never went out of her way to meet men purely for sex. That had clearly changed. The few times that we went out together after my breakup I saw a side of her I'd not seen before – and didn't especially like. Men always liked her, she had to beat them off with a stick sometimes, but she rarely encouraged their interest. Now, suddenly, it was the men who needed the stick! As soon as we walked into a place she'd be checking out the room, looking for somebody to take home with her – and if she saw something she liked she went straight for it; so blatantly available."

Molly shook her head sadly, looked down into her coffee mug as if peering into a muddy well of regretful memories.

"It wasn't Jen – not my Jen, anyway. When she was in her hunter-killer mode I felt like I barely knew her – and to be honest, I might as well have not been there. I'd end up sitting on my own fending off the 'chosen one's' drunken mates and going home alone on the last bus while she – well –. You know all about that, don't you?"

"I have some vague recollection." I agreed.

"I put up with it a couple of times but the third time it happened I thought 'Enough is enough'. After an hour and a half of being ignored by Jen and trying to make small talk with a drunken crowd of PE students I just went to the loo and never came back. Next time she suggested going out for a few drinks together I told her I didn't care to, at least not until she stopped trying to shag every man in town under 50."

"That must have stung." I said.

Molly shook her head.

"You would think so – but she just gave this nasty little laugh and said 'Sweetie, age is no barrier. Don't you know

55

the best wine comes in old bottles.' I said, 'You're not that old, Jen.' which probably wasn't very diplomatic of me."

"No, but it was quick." I assured her. "Did it get a response?"

"Oh, I think her exact words were 'Fuck off, you prissy, little bitch'. Then she just laughed again and before I knew it I was laughing as well and then, all at once, we're both crying our eyes out and hugging each other. Only it wasn't like two friends making up after a row, you know? It felt more like two friends recognising that something was broken that neither of them knew how to fix."

She shook her head at the thought and we shared a brief silence in memoriam before she shook herself and offered me a rueful smile.

"That would be last summer. Like I said, we were still friends at the office, but the phone calls stopped and the offers to go out on the town. Apart from a couple of office birthday parties the only other time I was in her company outside work hours was that night at The Barracuda."

"I've had worse birthday presents." I assured her.

"Jen recognised you, you know." Molly said.

"She recognised –?"

"From the newspapers and the television. She knew who you were."

"Ah – my fifteen minutes of unwanted fame."

"You shouldn't make light of what you did. It was heroic."

"It was mostly just about being scared and angry and wanting desperately to stay alive." I contended.

"I suppose you had to be there to look at it that way." she conceded. "But Jen was certainly impressed from a distance. I'll swear she was a little bit star struck."

"You mean she didn't love me for myself? I'm crushed."

"Were you looking for love, particularly?" Molly said archly.

"Fair point." I admitted. "They don't call that place Barracuda for nothing."

"I hate the place." Molly said, "But it was a leaving do for one of the girls at the office and I got outvoted. Jen goes there a lot. Well, I suppose you'll have guessed that much. I'm surprised you never bumped into each other before."

"It's not really my scene, either." I admitted. "It was just a fit of nostalgia that brought me there. When I first started drinking it was called The Prince of Wales and nobody in jeggings would have been caught dead there – if there'd been such things as jeggings back then, I mean. It's where I got falling-down drunk for the first time in my life. For some reason it struck me as a good idea to revisit the scene of the crime."

"You old sentimentalist." Molly said with a smile.

"How sad and bad and mad it was, but then how it was sweet." I said.

"Did you quote poetry to Jen? I think she would have liked that."

"Then I hope I did."

Our eyes met and beneath her playfulness I sensed her real concern.

"Jen will be all right, won't she?"

"I hope so. I just want to make sure, that's all. There's a possibility she's just taken off on a long vacation. She had a lot of brochures for Australia at her home."

"Jen does love to travel, and she can afford to take two or three holidays a year. She can be impulsive too." Molly agreed. "I hope that's the explanation - but something is telling me you don't think it is."

"One or two things just seem a little off to me." I admitted. "Apart from yourself is there anyone else she might have confided in?"

Molly thought about it, a sudden burst of sunlight through the window giving her pensive expression a Pre-Raphaelite glow.

"Not at Stentor. She got along with everybody, but she found most of them dull to be honest. Outside of work? If she has any close friends I never met any of them."

"Does the name 'Dorian' mean anything to you?" I asked. "He would be about my age, black hair and a roguish grin? Well, I'm making it up about the grin. He's been seen at her home, though. Jennifer's cleaner confirms that. He gave her a signed book as a present too, not the act of one of her casual one-night stands."

"Jen never mentioned anybody of that name to me." Molly said "As I said, our days of sharing such confidences are in the past, I'm afraid. I think I know who you may be talking about though. I just need to check something first?"

I nodded my agreement and she stood up and hurried from the room. While she was gone I settled back into my chair and savoured the scent of Molly's lingering perfume; a sensual hint of roses with warm citrus top notes that filled me with a sharp sense of longing. Or Lust, as Eddie would have said.

She returned a few minutes later, dropping back into her seat and thrusting a couple of sheets of printer paper at me.

"I knew I recognised the name from somewhere!" she said excitedly,

"What this?" I asked.

"The first sheet is a print out from Jen's calendar. We use Microsoft Office here and everybody's diary is online. It's mainly for the boss's convenience, so she can keep track of who's where and what leads they're chasing, but we all have access to each other's calendars. You're looking at Jen's appointments from last May. Look at this."

She leaned over and pointed to an entry dated the 19th May in the 10 a.m. time slot was the entry: Dorian Wilde – Heimdal? I scanned down the page. There were several more appointments listed and though there was no more mention of the name Dorian Wilde the initials D.W cropped up on the 28th and 29th.

"It has to be who you're looking for, doesn't it?" Molly said triumphantly

"It would be quite coincidence if it wasn't." I agreed. "Do you know what 'Heimdal' is?"

"Oh, that's our premium security package. It includes monitored alarms, CCT and a whole lot of other extras. If he was thinking about that system, he must have money to burn. Jen used to say it would be cheaper to just leave the front door unlocked and let the thieves pinch everything! Maybe she told him that too. He didn't bite, at any rate."

"You're sure about that?"

"Oh yes. If Jen had sold a Heimdal, if anyone had, Sharon would have made sure the whole office knew. Stoking up competition is her favourite motivational tool."

"Not free tanning vouchers, then?"

"Ooh -miaow!" Molly laughed. "Seriously, though. Jennifer didn't close the deal with Mr Dorian Wilde – not one she got any commission off at least. It looks like she tried hard enough, mind you. It's unusual to have more than a single meeting with a prospect. If you don't close first time you rarely get a second bite. I mean, it's not like they can take one of our systems for a test drive before they make up their mind."

"Surely some people have second thoughts?"

"Oh sure, it does happen – but that usually just takes a phone call."

"So maybe these other two meetings didn't have anything to do with alarm systems?" I suggested.

"Possibly – but if they were personal meetings why arrange them during office hours and put them in her diary?"

"For an extra kick, maybe? Some people might get an extra buzz from enjoying a little afternoon delight on the firm's time?"

She nodded thoughtfully.

"Yes, New Jen probably would, and she could probably have got away with it a couple of times, at least. Any more than that and Sharon would have been wondering why her best saleswoman couldn't close."

"So, I take it DW doesn't appear on her calendar again after the 29th May?"

"No – but look at this. Ta! Da!" With a theatrical flourish she whipped away the top sheet of printer paper to reveal a second printout. A standardised application form made out in the name of Dorian Wilde of 15 Maplin Road, Heronshaws.

"We ask every lead to fill in one of these. If they decide to buy and/or need financing, it saves time moving ahead with the credit check – and if they don't buy we keep them on file and cold call them every so often in case they've reconsidered."

I skimmed my eyes down the sheet in front of me. The form also included home and mobile phone numbers, and an email address (wildething@gmail.com).

It all seemed too good to be true, which meant it probably wasn't.

6.

On the way back to the office my mental auto-pilot steered me towards Friendly Street. Only when I saw the giant construction crane dominating the skyline up ahead did I realise my mistake, by which time it was too late to switch into the right lane.

To get back on track I had to drive past my old office building, or what was left of it. This amounted to not much other than a tumbled heap of rubble, surrounded by a temporary wooden rampart. The usual warning signs were plastered all over it, as was the logo of Phoenix Ventures: a builder's boot stamping on a human face forever.

Well, not really, but I had less than fond memories of that bird of ill omen. A couple of years ago the company appeared to crash and burn without hope of resurrection in the massive corporate corruption scandal that brought about the demise of its criminal parent company Allardyce UK. True to its name, however, Phoenix Ventures had risen again. Once the ashes had settled, it had been revived by the warm embrace of Grey International, a corporate giant that had weathered its own share of controversy over the years. I knew its founder and CEO Jack Grey better than I might have wished. He'd threatened to kill me a couple of times and ended up saving my life. It was an irony that I guess was pleasing to him. As would be the fact that one of his companies was the one to flatten the place where I'd hung my hat for the last five years.

Rising from the wreckage of my former place of business – and half a dozen other shops and offices - was a brand-new shopping mall: The Amity Centre. It was sentiment that had been nowhere in evidence on the day that myself and the other tenants of the building had received our landlord's

Notice To Quit. That had been nine months ago, six since I'd moved out, but my inner compass still tugged me back to the old neighbourhood on occasion, as it did that afternoon.

I drove through with only a brief twinge of nostalgia, working my way back into the one-way-system and navigating back through the city centre. The new office was on Minster Way, on the north side; a third-floor unit in Sir Thomas Fairfax House. This was a modern red brick facility that also housed the main office of the DWP, earning it its street name of the Kremlin. Conceived about during the years when the economy was booming, the development had been completed just in time for the 2008 banking crisis that blew up so many large and small business in the city and everywhere else. As a result, many of the new office units had remained empty since completion, which helped somewhat towards negotiating a reasonable rate for the new premises. Even so it would still have been a little steep if not for Clegg's bright idea of sharing office space.

Clegg, originally my neighbour in the old office building on Friendly Street, had become a good friend and had willingly pitched in to help keep my business afloat in the first difficult months after I left hospital. As a semi-retired accountant with a small and very select group of clients, all he needed to conduct business was a phone, a computer terminal and desk, for which, over my protests, he insisted on meeting half the monthly rent. As if that wasn't generous enough he was happy to act as the de facto office manager when I wasn't around.

He did my accounts too. Well, he likes a good laugh.

When I finally walked into the office I found him sitting at his desk in his shirt sleeves nursing a jumbo mug of tea strong enough to tap dance on. He was chuckling at something Eddie Snow had just said. He greeted me by raising his mug in an ironic, Falstaffian toast.

"*Oh now, who will behold the royal captain of this ruined band!*" he beamed. "Where hast been, Hal?"

"Bollocks, bollocks, bollocks." Eddie Snow said, barely glancing up from the PC screen he was scowling at.

"I see you've finally mastered computer language." I said.

"And you can bollocks as well – er – boss." he grumbled.

"That better not be porn." I said.

He looked affronted. "You always say that!"

"Your point being?"

"It's not always porn."

"Sorry. I forgot about the online poker and dating sites."

"Ha, ha! My sides are splitting here. You can relax, anyway. It's homework, isn't it?" He turned back to the screen and read from it: "Data Protection and Open Source Intelligence. Using the Internet as an investigative tool."

"To find porn, online casinos and Russian birds with big knockers?" I suggested.

"I'm not listening." he said. "I'm trying to better myself here. I've got my assessment in a couple of weeks. You should be encouraging me, not taking the piss. It would serve you right if I got my licence then set up on my own."

"Hmm – Man With A Van Investigations? I can see it! It could work."

"Sod off." he laughed.

Eddie waved me off and went back to what he'd been doing – mainly swearing under his breath and stabbing viciously at random keys like Dr Strangelove. From our brief exchange it was clear he was working through the latest module of the SIA Level 3 Private Investigation Course. Passing this, or a similar recognised professional training course was a crucial step to obtaining the SIA licence that would become compulsory for all legitimate private investigators in the very near future

I had taken a six-day intensive course in January to obtain the requisite qualification, but Eddie had opted to take the more sedate online route. He was no scholar, as he himself would readily admit, but he enjoyed helping me out and recognised that our ad hoc working relationship couldn't continue if he failed to measure up to the new standards.

Having to cut him loose would be a big loss – and still might be necessary. Even if he gained certification there was still the matter of what the new regulations called 'The Fit and Proper Person Test' to get over, which was by no means a foregone conclusion. To be fair he had no criminal record, though as an 'independent, freelance entrepreneur' (his words) he had certainly sailed closed to the wind more than once. It was a cause of concern, but I'd worry about that when the time came. He had to pass the SIA course first and the noises he was currently making weren't encouraging.

"If you're finding it too much Eddie, I'll understand." I told him. "You know I wouldn't have put you through it if I had any choice in the matter."

"Eh?" He looked up again, frowning. "What are you on about now?"

"The course -?" I explained patiently. "If it's too hard-"

"Who said that?" he demanded indignantly. "Look, I know I'm no Frank Einstein (sound of Clegg choking involuntarily on a ginger biscuit) but I'm doing okay. Ask Charlotte if you don't believe me."

"And Charlotte is -?"

"My tutor. She thinks I'm outstanding – and she says I'm doing okay in the course, as well!"

Unbelievable. I shook my head and busied myself making a cup of coffee.

"So, you're enjoying it then?" I said. "The course, I mean. I know it's not easy getting back into the habit of learning."

"For a natural thicko like me, you mean?"

"For any kind of thicko, really." I assured him.

He snorted and went back to waging war on the machines while I finished brewing my drink, snaffled a couple of Clegg's biscuits and sat down at my own desk. The ensuing coffee break passed agreeably in a companionable silence. Only when my cup was drained, and the crumbs swept into my waste paper basket did I gather the troops to bring them up to speed on how I'd spent the last couple of days. When I'd finished I invited their input?

"Sounds straight forward enough to me." Eddie said. "Fit older woman seeks hunky toy boy for fun and sun. Where can I get one?"

I bit back a comment and glanced at Clegg, who was massaging his double chin thoughtfully.

"Edward could be right." he observed. "But I sense that you have reservations?"

"There are a few anomalies." I agreed.

"Okay – then let's break it down."

He rooted around in one of his desk drawers and fished out a magic marker. Clutching it one chubby hand he advanced on the interactive whiteboard he had insisted we install. Down the middle of it he drew an impressively straight black line to make two columns. At the top of the first column he wrote:

INDICATORS THAT SUBJECT IS ON HOLIDAY

The second column he headed:

CONTRA-INDICATORS.

He turned to look at me expectantly and I flicked open my notebook and began to summarise my findings so far. As I spoke, Clegg entered information into the relevant column. When he had finished filling in the board Clegg returned to his desk. The three of us studied the results in silence for a few seconds as he tapped the magic marker thoughtfully against his chins.

INDICATORS THAT SUBJECT IS ON HOLIDAY

Stack of holiday brochures under coffee table

Told Louis Sifer the gardener that she was going away

Also mentioned it in the letter to Janet Lazenby

No sign of any suitcases in house

Empty hangers in wardrobe.

Missing toiletries.

Missing laptop

No car in garage

John Seeley

CONTRA-INDICATORS

Didn't tell Molly Grayson or anyone else that she was
planning a holiday.

No record of flight or hotel bookings

Lack of activity in bank account except for standing orders,
etc.

No credit card activity, unlike previous holiday periods

Not answering her phone or replying to texts. Why not if she
has mobile and laptop with her?

"Looked at in black and white, I can see why you have
reservations." Clegg said. "There's a lot of noise in column
A but most of it is details that could easily be
faked by another party. Anybody with access to the house
could have packed a suitcase, taken her laptop and car and
written the letter to Janet Lazenby. When it comes down to it
the only bit of verifiable proof is her conversation with the
gardener chappie. Is there any reason he would lie?"
    "He creeped me out a bit, it's true but I've no real grounds
to doubt his word. In any case, just because she told him that
she was planning on going away it doesn't mean that she did
so. Something could have happened to her between her
conversation with Sifer and the time she was planning to
leave."
    "You mean, somebody could have killed her and covered it
up by making it look as if she went ahead with her holiday as
planned?" Eddie chimed in.
    It wasn't a solution I cared to dwell on, but it was a worst-
case scenario that had occurred to me. As Clegg had
remarked, looking at the stark black and white facts on the
board didn't do anything to dispel my uneasiness. If most of
the perceived activity implicit in Column A could be
explained away by the intervention of a second person, the
clear lack of activity in Column B spoke even more loudly to

my anxiety for her safety. For whatever reason Jennifer Jensen was off the grid and it seemed to me that my client had been right to voice his concern.

With that thought on my mind, I wrote up a summary of my day's work and emailed a copy to Callum Jensen. His reply came back inside fifteen minutes. It consisted of just two words: FIND HER!

7.

There was a Word attachment with the mail entitled
Contacts, which I assumed was the list of Jennifer's friends
Jensen had agreed to compile. When I opened it, however,
the contents of the single page were as unreadable as
hieroglyphics. It looked as if the file had somehow been
corrupted in transit and I replied with a brief message asking
him to check the contents and resend the file.

Five o'clock came and went, taking Clegg and Eddie with
it. After they'd gone I lingered, fleshing out a copy of the
report I'd mailed to Jensen for my own files. There were
some things I'd chosen not to share with him, like the
pornographic DVD collection, the raunchy party invite and
Jennifer's apparent fascination with the Hellfire Club. I
added these details in but left out the bit about my own brief
encounter with her. When I'd done I emailed copies to Clegg
and Eddie then locked up and headed out into the teeth of the
evening rush hour.

When I got home I showered, cracked open a bottle
of Miller and called Callum Jensen. In response to his email I
told him I was happy to keep looking for Jennifer if he really
wanted me to. In fairness to him I suggested that he might
get quicker results by handing the matter over to the police.
Jennifer had been gone long enough for them to have to take
notice if he reported her missing and my preliminary
investigation had raised enough questions to get them to take
his concern seriously. He didn't much care for my suggestion
but, after we'd gone back and forward a few times, he
accepted a compromise. I'd stay on the job until he returned
from Ireland. If I hadn't found Jennifer by then, or assured
myself that she was safe, he agreed to escalate the search and
bring in the police.

He sounded more resigned than anxious, I thought, but maybe I was letting personal feelings colour my impressions. He ended our conversation by apologising for the corrupted attachment to his email and promising to resend it.

When we had hung up I sat and finished my beer, smoked a cigar and thought about my next move. That involved opening a second beer and settling myself on the couch with my phone, my tablet and my notebook, opened to the page where I'd written down Dorian Wilde's details. Despite Molly Grayson's enthusiasm, I didn't share her confidence in the value of the information. Quick calls to the landline and cell phone numbers he'd given seemed to confirm my scepticism. The only response to both calls was the unobtainable signal.

I turned to my tablet and logged on to one of People Finder sites I subscribed to. A quick Electoral Roll check proved as fruitless as the phone calls. There was nobody called Dorian Wilde listed at the address Molly had shown me or anywhere else in the city or county. I tried a few other professional sources with the same lack of result.

I had only slightly better luck on social media. There were several Dorian Wilde's on Facebook, one of which seemed promising. He lived in the city and gave his profession as actor and model. His profile didn't list much further detail and his posts were mostly innocuous: reports of photo shoots, auditions good and bad and the usual run of humourous memes that gave an occasional glimpse of a left-leaning social conscience. There were, however, plenty of photographs of a handsome, dark haired young man who was a fair fit for the description Janet Lazenby had given me.

I printed off the best picture amongst them, then turned to Google Maps. The address he had provided on his registration form at Stentor was, at least, real. Street View showed it to be a neatly maintained property in the middle of a single row of terraced houses in the Heronshaws district of the city. Not the best of addresses but not the worst by a long way. It seemed a nice quiet area, helped no doubt by the fact that the opposite side of the street was entirely occupied by Maplin Road Methodist Church. It didn't look like the kind of place somebody called Dorian Wilde would choose to live but, then, all the signs were that he didn't.

Still, maybe it was a lead of sorts. While it was possible he'd just picked it at random to flesh out his fake persona it was a fact that people often throw in bits of truth to flavour the lies they spin. It might just be laziness or lack of imagination but incorporating familiar details into a fake identity made sense in case your phony CV was tested. If 'Dorian Wilde', whoever he was, fell into the latter category then maybe he'd chosen that address because it meant something to him – and if that was the case then maybe someone who really did live there might know why.

I spent another fruitless half hour or trying to find some trace of Jennifer herself on line but she did not have a presence on any of the usual social media sites and though I found a few mentions of Callum she was mentioned only in passing in his brief Wikipedia entry.

That left Dorian Wilde as my best bet and I was up early next morning to begin my search for him. Before doing so, though I found myself back at Moorside while the dew was still pearling the grass. It had been barely 24 hours since I was there last, yet a deeper layer of silence seemed to drape the house; the lengthening shadow of Jennifer's absence remorselessly deadening the pulse of the building. The 'Hum' was no more than a fading threnody.

I was there to see if I could confirm that the man in the picture was the Dorian Wilde I was looking for. I located the proof inside a DVD case that had originally housed *The French Lieutenant's Woman*. The date marked on the disc was 19/05/16 and featured Jennifer performing enthusiastically with a tight-bodied young man, whose dark Romany looks were framed by a fashionably dishevelled mane of jet black hair. There was no doubt that it was the same man in the picture from Facebook.

I ejected the DVD from the player and took it through to the office. Booting up the PC I loaded the DVD and spent fifteen minutes using the computer's photo-editing software to isolate and print-off a head shot of Dorian Wilde that might have more impact on him than the carefully posed Facebook picture.

When I'd done I shut down the PC, returned the DVD to its place on the shelf and left. It felt good to step out of the silence that was slowly possessing it and into the bright, March sunlight. The mocking chatter of a solitary magpie and the faint chug of farm machinery drifting from a distant field were a welcome discordance after the dusty stillness inside.

An hour later I was knocking on the door of number 15 Maplin Grove. The current residents proved to be a pair of slacker types who looked as if they lived on takeout pizza and only took exercise through a mouse and keyboard. They bore a resemblance to each other but none to Dorian Wilde. They didn't recognise his photograph either, shaking their heads in unison when I waved it under their noses.

"Don't know him." said the taller of the two in a nasal twang that emanated somewhere South of Watford but had been flattened somewhat by his sojourn in northern climes. He had long hair to his shoulders, more grey than brown and was wearing a Wolverine T-shirt and denims, faded nearly white with fond use.

The other man agreed with a shake of the head. He was younger, though not by much, and favoured a blue and white Hawaiian shirt and khaki-coloured crops

The two of them stood side by side in the doorway. Behind them I glimpsed a long, narrow hallway and a steep looking staircase. The carpet and walls looked clean and smart, but a funny kind of smell drifted down the hallway from somewhere deeper in the house; some unidentifiable miasma of all male house sharing.

"What's he done?" Hawaiian shirt asked.

"I'm not sure he's done anything." I said. "I'm looking on behalf of a mutual friend and I'm hoping he might know where to find them. Are you sure you've never seen him around here? His name might be Dorian Wilde?"

The pair of them exchanged puzzled looks.

"Might be? Don't you know?" 'Wolverine' asked.

"I think it might be an alias."

"Cool!" Hawaiian shirt said. "Like a User name?"

"Yes – though probably not quite in the sense you mean it."

"Well, he doesn't 'use' it round here." Wolverine re-iterated. "Not while we've lived here, anyway."

"And how long is that?"

They looked at each other again and Hawaiian shirt reckoned it out quickly on his fingers.

"Five – no, six years!" he said.

Wolverine nodded. "Yes, it was right after they shot Osama."

"Or so they say." Hawaiian shirt said cryptically. "Nobody ever saw a body."

"Maybe it's in your spare room." I said, sniffing the air pointedly.

Wolverine laughed but his partner looked affronted.

"Hey, that's our lunch, man."

"Tofu Dahl." Wolverine said. It sounded a little like a curse the way he said it.

"My condolences." I said. "I don't suppose you know who lived in this house before you?"

"Not a clue. We only rent. The guy from the property company might know. What do you say, Derrick?"

"What's wrong with tofu, anyway?" was his only response.

Wolverine rolled his eyes theatrically.

"Nothing." I assured Derrick. "As long as they're killed humanely.

Derrick did the eye rolling thing too and stomped off back to his kitchen without a further word.

"He's touchy about his tofu." Wolverine explained. "It tastes better than it smells." He lowered his voice briefly. "But not much."

He smiled and nodded to show that my time was up then stepped back and closed the door to make sure I really got the message. That seemed to be the end of that line of enquiry, but I had barely reached the front gate when the door opened again.

"Hey, wait a sec." Wolverine called after me. "I've just had a thought."

"I've already eaten, thanks." I said.

"What? Oh – ha! No – about your guy, I mean."

"I'm listening."

"You should ask 'Digger'." he said, gesturing vaguely up the street. "Him at number 1. Mr Digby. He's as old as two elephants and a tortoise and he's lived here, like, forever. I'll bet he can remember when Kermit was a tadpole."

"Thanks." I said. "I'll try him next. If you're right, he might save me some time."

I offered him my hand to show how grateful I was, and he shook it politely.

"Good luck." he said.

"Bon appétit." I said.

Digger's house was the last in the row, its façade distinguishable from its neighbours only by the differing styles of UPVC makeover that each had undergone. Every house had a small, front garden separated from its neighbour by a low brick wall. Most of them seemed to have been paved or concreted over at some time but No 1 retained its original character. A neatly trimmed square of grass was edged on either side by well-tended flower beds already putting forth a few precocious blooms. The low front wall at the front was topped by a wooden fence a freshly painted shade of green that matched the wooden gate and added to the well-cared for air of the property.

I rang the doorbell a couple of times and heard it buzzing faintly in the depths of the house. A couple of minutes passed but nobody came so I pressed the bell again, thumping my fist against the frosted glass panel in the door for emphasis.

"I'm not deaf, lad!" a stern voice said. "It's just that I'm not in at the moment."

The voice belonged to an unsmiling man, somewhere in the foothills of his seventh decade, who was standing behind me. He wore turned up jeans half a size too big for him and a Leeds Rhinos shirt that would have better fitted a prop than a hooker. He was wearing a backpack and carried plastic bags full of shopping in each hand and sharp brown eyes looked back at me from his interestingly seamed face with a twinkle that belied his severe expression

"Mr Digby?" I said.

"Might be. Not Jehovah's Witness, are you? You can save your breath if you are. I'm a Muslim, so I'll say good morning to you."

"Alhamdulillah." I said.

"Clever bugger." he snorted. "I don't vote, neither, so it doesn't matter if you're Labour, Tory or UKlux Clan. I'm not buying."

"I'm not affiliated with or represent any political party or religious group. Unless you count The Whisky Connoisseur Club."

"You got any samples with you?" he asked with interest.

"I was just kidding." I said." I'm looking for someone who may once have lived on the street – and I'm told you've been here since they put in the footings?"

"Who told you that? Bet it was Oscar and Felix at No 15! Here, hold these."

He thrust his shopping bags at me and grunted something that might have been 'Thank you' when I took them from him. He rummaged around in his jeans for his front door key, stepping past me to unlock the door. I followed him and down the hallway into a single, large living room, passing through that into an even larger kitchen.

"Put them bags on there." he said, nodding towards one of the work tops. Then, gruffly: "You prefer tea or coffee?"

"Coffee's fine." I said. "Does this mean we're bonding?"

He tried to scowl but his expression dissolved into a fruity chuckle and he stuck out a calloused hand.

"Eric Digby." he said. "Call me Digger, everybody does. Well, that's what they call me to me face, anyway."

We shook, his grip dry and firm, his hand rough with the callouses of manual labour.

"Harry Webster." I said.

He nodded an acknowledgement then busied himself filling the kettle and setting it to boil. While we waited for it he bustled about the kitchen unpacking his bags and rucksack and stowing away his shopping in the fridge and various cupboards.

"So? Was it the Odd Couple who sent you my way?" he asked.

I admitted that it was.

"Liam and Michael." he elaborated. "They're good lads, really, though they drive each other crazy half the time. When they kick off the whole street knows about it."

"Are they really a 'couple'?" I asked.

"Huh? No – they're not homos – well, I suppose they might be. Don't know, don't care. They're brothers. The Finucanes. Musicians. You might have heard of them? Finucanes' Rainbow? Not bad really, sort of the Everley Brothers meets Foster and Allen."

"That may be the single most terrifying thing I've ever heard." I said.

He chuckled as he put away the last of his shopping and moved on to making the coffee. When he'd finished he put two large mugs on a wooden tray along with a bowl of sugar, a milk jug and half a packet of chocolate digestives. He carried the tray over to a wooden table positioned in front of a sliding glass door that overlooked a short patio and a back garden as carefully maintained as the one at the front.

When we were settled Digger took a sip of his brew and sighed contentedly.

"Aah that's better! Really gives me a thirst dragging around the shops. I hate going into town, you can't move on the bloody buses for all the 'twirlies'."

He winked to show me that he was being consciously ironic and dunked a digestive into his tea like a gleeful six-year-old.

"So? Who's this finger you're looking for?"

"Dorian Wilde." I said. "Though the chances are it's not his real name."

"Doreen? You sure he's a bloke?"

"Dor-ian." I corrected, passing him the picture I'd printed off. "It's non-gender specific but more common for a man."

"If you say so." he said, peering myopically at the printout. "I'd better get me specs."

He retrieved them from one of the pockets of his rucksack and settled at the table again. He took a long hard look at the picture of Dorian Wilde and I thought I detected some faint glimmer of recognition behind the slightly grubby, finger marked lenses of his spectacles. He continued to ruminate over the image as he crunched his way through another biscuit. Finally, he lay the printout down on the table and removed his glasses. He belatedly started to polish the lenses with a small cleaning patch he took from their case. When he'd finished he regarded me thoughtfully, tapping the folded glasses against his stubbled chin.

"The name means nowt." he said at length. "Well – even an old fart like me's not likely to forget somebody with a name like Dorian Wilde, is he? On the other hand-" He tapped the printout thoughtfully. "- yon chap in your photo has the look of somebody I used to know. Wait here a sec."

He left the table and went through to the living room, from which the sounds of him rummaging through cupboards and drawers eventually filtered through, along with the odd muttered swear word. Whatever he was looking for came to hand eventually, however and he re-appeared, holding a plain, white cardboard box. Contained within were the assorted fragments of the old man's past in the shape of photographs, official documents and the odd newspaper clipping. Sifting through the contents he occasionally stopped to seize some item or other and stare at it with an expression that mirrored whatever emotion the discovery had kindled in him. If I had not been there I thought, he might well have forgot himself completely and wandered happily for hours through this ramshackle gallery of lost memories. As it was, he eventually found the item he was rooting for, pulling it from the box with a flourish that would have done credit to a member of the Magic Circle.

"This is it!" he announced.

'It' was a sheet of green newsprint, folded over several times to fit into the box. After clearing a space on the table, he opened the sheet out, taking great care not to tear it along the fault line of age that had worn through the creases. It was a page torn from a local, weekly sporting paper called, ingeniously, The Green 'Un. It had been rolling off the presses every Saturday night for almost a hundred years. The page that Digby unfurled was torn from a copy dated April

1969 and proved to be a report of a minor league football match.

"Mid-Yorkshire Sunday League Challenge Cup Final, 1969. The Cocked Hat versus The Brewery Taps" Digby elaborated fondly. "It was a right bloodbath! Two sent off, ten bookings. Taps won 3-1 and I scored the third – cut-in from the left, beat two defenders and leathered it past Ikey Summers in t' top corner."

He swelled with pride at the memory of his finest hour and I nodded encouragingly. He shook himself abruptly.

"Still, you're not bothered about that, I daresay, but this might be of interest."

He pointed to the picture that accompanied the match report. It was a photograph of the winning team, formed up happily around a trophy clearly modelled on the FA Cup. Including reserves and what they call technical staff, these days, there were about twenty people in the group and my eyes roamed over it quickly.

"Who am I looking at?" I asked.

"Well, I'm the good looking one kneeling down next to the cup, but I think you'll be more interested in the goalkeeper."

He was easy enough to pick out from his distinctive kit and the fact that he towered above the two players to either side of him – and almost everybody else in the picture. The quality wasn't great, but it was clear enough to make out his features and the mop of dark, curly hair that hung at shoulder length in the fashion of the times,

I set my printout alongside the newspaper photograph and compared them. Digby was right: the resemblance was obvious.

"You've got a good memory for faces, Digby." I complimented him. "Who is he?"

Digby frowned in concentration, then sheepishly took back the clipping.

"Good on faces, not so good on names." he admitted. "Least, not when they're a bit of a tongue twister." His sharp eyes quickly scanned the article again. "Ah - yes, here it is!"

I read the passage he was pointing at.

In the last ten minutes The Cocked Hat pressed hard but the Taps defence, aided by solid work by keeper Jerzy Walczak, kept them at bay as they ran down the clock to lift the trophy for the first time.

"Walczak." I repeated, reaching for my notebook to write it down.

"Polish." Digby said. "His father was a pilot, came over in the war, like a lot of them did. Brave men."

Indeed, I agreed, and not always receiving the gratitude that was there due for the role they played. Digby nodded in solemn agreement, smiling with remembered fondness.

"Jerzy was a good lad. Great keeper! Him and his missus – Stella, I think – lived at No 15 when me and my Rose moved in. Just after we won the World Cup, it was! They'd just had their first bairn then – a little girl. Called her Roberta after the two Bobbys in the England team!"

"You knew the family well, then?"

"Oh yeah, everybody knew everybody back then. Not like it is today. I couldn't tell you the names of half the folk who live down the street these days. Well, people keep themselves to themselves more, don't they? And half of them are only renting, anyway. No sense of ownership or community. Give 'em a fifty-inch telly and a six pack and they're happy as pigs in the proverbial. I tried to organise a street party when that old witch Thatcher died. Most of them didn't even know who she was. Or what damage she did. Lucky them, eh?"

"I suppose they have their own demons." I said.

"Happen." he conceded. "I miss that sense of belonging we had, though. Being part of something beyond your own four walls. You'd walk in the Taps on a night and everybody knew your name and what you'd had for your tea."

"Some people would hate that." I said.

"Yeah. I suppose I did at the time!" he chuckled. "Still, I do miss the old place since they pulled it down. Never think do they? Every time they pull down a pub they're pulling down somebody's past wi' it. Great old boozer, it was. Just flats now, full of druggies and dole wallahs. Time they brought in the bulldozers again. Good times, though, back in the day.

78

That's where I first got to know Jerzy. It was him and Jackie Lawrence who brought me into the team. He was at no 11, Jackie. Wing half. Died of liver cancer in 1990." he added sadly.

"And Jerzy?" I prodded gently. "You think the man I'm looking for could be related?"

"He's got a look of him, sure. Don't you think so?"

I agreed that I did.

"Did he have a son?"

"Hmm – Danny. Their third, the other two were girls. He'd be born – what? 1989 or maybe the year before. They'd both be past forty then, him and Stella. It was a bit of a shock when Danny popped out! Family flitted not long after, got one of the new builds at Town End Gardens. Moving up in the world we thought at the time but they're dropping to bits now and even the social workers won't go near it unless they're mob handed."

"Do the Walczaks still live there?" I asked, nudging him gently off his hobby horse.

"Couldn't tell you." he shrugged. "I hope not – but to be honest we lost touch when they moved. He was a brickie. Top boy. About six months after they moved from here he fell off some scaffolding on a job in Scunthorpe and broke his leg. Knackered him for football and without that he didn't have anything to drag him back over to this side of the town. I suppose I was a bit stuck in my ways too. You know how it is? You think: I'll give him a bell next week – or the week after – only you never do and before you know it best part of thirty years have gone by!"

It sounded like a lament for something more than just a single lost friendship, which added a sudden poignancy to the scene of this feisty old man sitting at his kitchen table with a box full of fading memories.

"I ought to sort these out." he said, as if he'd read my mind.

We chatted for a few more minutes as he began sifting through the ephemera of his life, sorting it into separate piles on the table according to whatever personal criteria he had decided. As he did so a soft, sad smile played at the corners of his mouth as something or other stirred a particularly fond reminiscence.

When I had finished my tea, I shook his hand warmly and got up leave.

"Thanks for your help Digger. I'll leave you to it." I said, nodding at his memories, scattered across the table, and the cardboard coffin he continued to exhume them from.

"Aye, lad." he smiled. "I think it may take me some time."

8.

Back in the car I checked the electoral register again. Walczak was not a common name in this part of the county. There were just seven listings and only one that seemed a likely fit. The address was Apartment 10, Lytton's Goit, a former industrial area of the city along the river that had undergone a process of gentrification earlier in the millennium. Most of the old industrial sites had been levelled and replaced with mixed use buildings housing apartments, bars and restaurants. A quick map search revealed that Walczak lived right in the heart of the risen Goit, which meant that he was probably doing very nicely for himself from what I knew about waterfront property prices.

A quick call to Directory Enquiries got me a phone number but his answer phone picked up. I left a brief message asking him to contact me asap then hung up and drove back to the office. When I walked through the door Clegg was sitting at his desk, Buddha like as ever, poring over columns of figures in one of his ledgers. He looked up and beamed at me happily, making urgent drinking motions with his right hand. Since it was too early for the pub I made straight for the coffee maker, earning a gracious nod of approval.

"No Eddie?" I said.

Clegg scanned his desktop and seized a yellow post it note.

"Serving papers for Gainsborough and Partners. Back Friday." he read. "I think that last bit is meant to be a joke."

"You haven't known Eddie as long as I have." I said.

"True – but long enough to know that Edward is a fine fellow."

"None finer." I agreed. "But easily distracted."

"Aah, the ladies!"

"Yes, some of them are I believe."

Clegg gave a snort of laughter.

"He does have a wandering eye."

"Not the bit of his anatomy that gets him into trouble." I said.

"You've been friends for a long time." Clegg said, a statement of fact not a question.

"Class 2, Tanner's Lane Infants. He pushed in front of me in the dinner queue, I pulled his hair, he bit my arm and we've been best friends ever since."

"Like David and Jonathan."

"More like Tony and Sid." I said with a smile.

"Still, close as you are, it's not always easy working together. Especially when you're used to being a lone operator."

"Tensions arise." I agreed. "I'm used to my own space, being my own boss."

"You're still the boss, Harry – and Eddie knows it. He'd probably never say it to your face, but he loves working with you – and he's deadly serious about getting properly licensed."

"I know – and don't think I don't appreciate what he brings to the table. What both of you have done for me this last year and before. It just takes a little getting used to, that's all."

"For all of us." he agreed. "But all in all, I think it's working pretty well so far, don't you?"

"Oh yeah? Then why is it always me who ends up making the coffee?"

Hr chuckled and toasted me ironically with the steaming mug I'd just placed before him. I carried my own drink over to my desk and booted up the PC.

"So, did you have any luck tracing Mr Dorian Wilde?" Clegg asked.

"Getting there." I said. "I met somebody who thinks he looks like a Polish goalkeeper he used to know."

I elaborated on my encounter with Digger. When I'd finished Clegg frowned at me in concern.

"Using a false name - that's not good is it?"

"Well, he describes himself as an actor stroke model, so it's not necessarily a red flag."

"I've been reading the notes you typed up from yesterday." Clegg continued. "Thinking about that book that Dorian gave her. The Hellfire Club? Not your typical lover's trifle, is it?"

"Makes a change from flowers and chocolates, though."

"Joking aside, reading between the lines of your report I think you fear that her pre-occupation with sex may have lead her into deep and rather dark waters."

"The possibility has occurred." I agreed.

"And that it might tie in with her taste in reading matter?"

I said nothing, letting him follow his thoughts where they took him, pretty sure they'd meet up with mine somewhere along the way.

"Do you know anything about the Hellfire Clubs?" he asked.

"The broad strokes – no pun intended - though what's with the plural? I wasn't aware that there was more than one."

"The name 'Hellfire Club' is actually a catch-all for several different groups that have popped up from time to time on the murkier fringes of high society. There's even a swinger's club today of that name with its own website though I suspect there probably more egalitarian in their membership."

"Tim Berners-Leigh will be so proud." I said.

"Ha! As far as I can gather the original model was founded by Philip, Duke of Wharton in 1719 and its main purpose was to provide a forum for trendy anti-religionists. I believe blasphemy was all the rage with the fast set at the time. The club didn't last long though, the Duke fell afoul of Robert Walpole and ended up being hounded out of parliament and forced to end the club's activities. Worked out well for him in the end, though. He joined the Freemasons and eventually ended up as Grand Master of England.

"So? You think the Freemasons have kidnapped Jennifer?"

Clegg pulled a face and took a drink of his coffee.

"Moving along – the next and probably most notorious incarnation of the Hellfire Club wasn't even called that at the time. It had several names in its lifetime, most memorably The Monks of Medmenham, after the old abbey where they conducted their bawdy business in the name of Bacchus and

Venus. Or so Horace Walpole maintained. Must say they seem to have been a real pair of killjoys the Walpoles, probably resented not being asked to join in the pagan frolics."

"Those pagans have all the fun." I said. "Sex and drugs and what – chamber music?"

"At the very least, though rumours circulated at the time – and ever since – that there was more than just casual depravity on offer. Black masses, orgies, Satanic worship. Nothing proven, of course, but their motto was Do What Thou Wilt after all. Whatever the truth of it all the club fizzled out in the mid-1760s but the Hellfire Caves in West Wycombe, where they used to meet are a big tourist attraction these days. Oh – and just in case you didn't know, the man who organised it all was called Sir Francis Dashwood."

"Dashwood? The pornographic party invitation on Jennifer's computer was from someone calling himself 'Dash'!"

"It is suggestive." Clegg agreed. "Especially when taken in conjunction with those volumes you found on the lady's bookshelf and the rather blatant dedication from 'Dorian'. It occurs to me – as I'm sure it has to you – that perhaps our missing client's quest for conscience free sex may have involved her in something rather more organised that simply trawling the local singles bars."

More organised – and perhaps more dangerous too? Clegg was right, it was a thought that had occurred me as soon as I saw the book and its inscription, though I had missed the 'Dash' connection. That seemed to make it even more likely that Jennifer Jensen had got herself involved in with some local re-incarnation of those notorious Monks of Medmenham.

"A modern Hellfire Club in our own backyard?" I said. "Just don't tell Eddie!"

Talking things through with Clegg only served to intensify my misgivings for Jennifer Jensen. I tried ringing Danny/Dorian again but there was still nobody picking up. I didn't bother leaving another message. A more direct approach was called for.

I left the office shortly afterwards, pausing only to pick up a piece of kit from the cupboard where the surveillance gear was stashed. I detoured briefly to pick up bottled water and some snacks from the nearest supermarket, then headed across town.

The Goit was bustling with the usual crowd of daytime drinkers and the bargain hunters who haunted the outlet shops that were clustered in the Moorview Centre. You would have needed the Hubble telescope to see the Moors from there but there already was a Riverside Centre further downstream in Longthwaite and the Goit Centre would have been too easy to vandalise into the Goitre. So, the Moorview it was.

Danny's apartment building stood downhill from the mall, on the south side of the Mill Run. This offshoot of the river gave the Goit its full name and was now home to half a dozen brightly painted houseboats. A steel bridge spanned the Mill Run just beyond that point, connecting the Goit to Farnham Quay, another recovered industrial wasteland elegantly scabbed over with trendy bars and restaurants. Not a Poundworld or BetFred in sight

The front of the warehouse conversion was protected by seven-foot-high walls of yellow brick topped with metal railings and enclosing a courtyard with covered communal parking spaces at opposite ends. Tall metal gates fronted the street, probably locked after a certain time and only accessible to residents with the necessary access code. At this time of day, they were thrown open for the usual comings and goings of any residential area.

On the other side of the street there was a row of shops and a pub called The Good Companion. It had somehow survived the onrushing tide of urban regeneration to stand defiant in the same space it had occupied for the last hundred years or so. Given the general attrition rate for pubs in these islands I thought that was an achievement worth drinking to. It also gave me a legitimate excuse to make use of the pub's tiny car park, which afforded an unobstructed view of the apartment complex.

I locked up the car and went into the bar. It consisted of a single L-shaped space, the long arm of which contained maybe half a dozen tables arranged in front of a long bench seat that ran two thirds of the lengths of the room. The last third was occupied by a pool table, a dartboard and a jukebox that was currently playing Top of the Pops by The Rezillos. An audience of half-a dozen middle-aged drinkers sang along raucously, even though the only words any of them actually seemed to know where the four that made up the title.

It made me think of a line from Coleridge.

Swans sing before they die— 't were no bad thing
Should certain persons die before they sing."

I gave the choir abysmal a wide berth and stepped to the bar. I ordered a Bud and carried it through into the quieter, carpeted space of the lounge bar. I took a seat as far away from the speaker as I could get and drank my beer stoically. The Rezillos eventually gave way to The Ruts who yielded in their turn to The Ramones. I began to think the jukebox must be stuck in the R section. It didn't seem to bother the old punks in the other side, though. They still appeared to be singing along to Top of the Pops. When one of them stood up and started to pogo to Sheena is a Punk Rocker I decided I'd had enough nostalgia for one afternoon and, headed back to the car.

It was a pleasant spring afternoon. Not quite short-sleeve weather but warm enough to go al fresco for lunch. I retrieved a packet of sandwiches and a bottle of water and wandered out of the car park. A bus shelter stood opposite the apartments, next to weathered wooden bench put there for the convenience of weary shoppers. I settled down there and ate a BLT that tasted marginally better than its cardboard wrapper, washing it down with fizzy water.

People came and went, flitting in and out of the shops or the 24-hour medical centre, getting on and off buses or simply wandering by on their way to somewhere else. Nobody gave me a second glance, but I didn't want to sit too long just the same. Call it tradecraft or simply occupational paranoia.

I ate a second sandwich, drank more water and smoked a cigar. Nobody went in or came out of the apartments. By the time I'd finished my smoke I'd been there about half an hour. Time to move on. I got to my feet, brushed off any lingering crumbs and dropped the detritus of lunch into an adjacent cast iron waste bin. I crossed the street, the stroll back to the pub car park taking me past the gates to the apartment precincts. I glanced idly in as I passed. A chrome yellow Honda Civic was the only occupant of the courtyard, clearly not the black sports job Janet Lazenby had described. I noted CCTV cameras mounted on the frontage of the building to monitor the courtyard and the street immediately beyond the entrance. The left-hand gate was adorned with a metal notice bearing a familiar logo and the declaration: 'This Building Is Protected by Stentor Alarms'.

The world was small indeed – but by no means always beautiful.

I walked back to the car and settled in to watch and wait. From the pub I could hear the faint boom of the jukebox and the rasping vocals of yet another forgotten punk classic. It was hardly a lullaby, but I felt my eyelids growing heavy and wound down the window to let in some fresh air. Beer at dinner time was a bad idea, I reminded myself...

The darkness is absolute, dark as the deepest, darkest part of the deepest, darkest night. It's dark's what I'm saying. I think I might be blind at first but after a few seconds subtle gradations develop, earth and water slide apart, fire dances against the frozen air and far away, like a gull lost at sea, a siren unwinds its moronic threnody.

Now I see the burning hulk of a once immaculate river cruiser spiralling slowly amidst the flames that are devouring it. I feel the heat across the distance between us and heavy, whirling flakes of ash and snow are slanting into my face. I feel the relentless trickle of blood flowing down my arm from the wound in my shoulder, the bite of cold steel embedded there and the drag of the Desert Eagle semi-automatic pistol in my hand, its dead weight pulling me down, down, even as I struggle to raise it.

My heart is thumping so loudly it's like it's moved from my chest to my ears, fuelled into turbo-drive by a nameless dread whose grip is more chilling than the piercing wind that howls and shrieks around me. I see it then: a sudden turbulence in the dark water. No more than a few ripples at first but growing apace until the surface is churning angrily, as if some unseen malevolence was wrestling with the water itself, eager and determined to break free of the black indifference of its clutches.

And so, it rises! A shock of white hair, like cold fire burning on the crown of a grinning, eyeless skull atop a skeletal body that hovers and sways above the boiling surface of the river. The ghastly head moves slowly from side to side, as if it were searching the darkness for the scent of some unseen prey, until it suddenly stops and seems to stare straight at me for a long heartbeat before the grisly figure begins to glide slowly and noiselessly towards the bank.

As it comes it raises bony claws that clutch, with awful familiarity, the squat, deadly shape of an Uzi sub-machine gun. As if in slow motion I raise my own weapon as the skeletal spectre steps onto the bank. My eyes are drawn reluctantly to the dark, empty sockets of its grinning, skull-face. Unswervingly the dark, abyssal holes look back at me and the grinning jaws articulate, words that echo to me faintly as a long white finger caresses fire from the brutish snout of the Uzi.

"Nothing of nothing: leave thy idle questions. I am i' the way to study a long silence."

I woke up with a jolt, as if those phantom bullets had administered a physical shock. I felt disoriented, dry mouthed and sweaty, my heart racing like that of a cornered animal. I sagged back into my seat and drew a long, shaky breath as the reality of still being alive sank in. In a couple of minutes my pulse was back to normal and I could smile sheepishly at myself in the driving mirror. It had been several weeks since my dreams had taken me back to that terrifying night on the frozen river bank. Long enough for me to start thinking I might be free of Rocky Van Dorn's malevolent shade. That was a premature hope, clearly.

To reinforce the point the nagging ache in my shoulder had

started up again. I massaged the spot gingerly as the last of the dream trickled from my consciousness. I drank some water to wash the last bitter taste of it from my mouth then checked my watch. I'd dozed off for only a few minutes, but it was unprofessional. Boring as surveillance could be it was often an important part of the job and I thought I had comfortably mastered the art. That was clearly not the case and I was both embarrassed and angry with myself for nodding off. When I'd finished calling myself names, I reached for my phone and redialled Danny Walzcak's number. A terse male voice answered almost immediately.

"Hello?"

"Is that Dorian?" I managed, almost tongue-tied with surprise at getting an answer.

"Sometimes." he said, with a trace of mild amusement. "What can I help you with?"

"I have a message from Jennifer." I said.

"Jen -?" he said hesitantly. "O-okay, go on."

"Fay ce que voudras." I said.

9.

Danny Walczak, aka Dorian Wilde, had a two-bedroom apartment with lots of exposed brickwork, barrelled ceilings and industrial windows that overlooked the river. The large living space blended its original features with innovations like spot lighting, electric radiators and the obligatory 50" plasma TV with all the usual add-ons you'd expect for a thirty-something single man who clearly liked his boy toys.

On the polished wooden floor two burgundy sofas angled towards the flat screen, one to either side but the furnishings were otherwise Spartan: a computer desk with PC and printer, a couple of standard lamps, a dining table and wall unit - both of Swedish pine – and a matched coffee table that stood between the two sofas. That was about it, other than a few framed movie posters that softened the look of the stripped back walls. All in all, it was well maintained and wouldn't have cost much more than £300,000, I guessed.

"Nice place." I said, settling into one of the sofas. "Business must be good."

He smiled tightly and gave a little shrug.

"I get by." he said.

"How do you get to be a gigolo, anyway?" I asked.

He looked confused, then angry.

"What the hell do you mean by that?"

"I mean, are there courses you can take or do you just put a card in the window of the local corner shop?"

"I'm not a gigolo." he said frostily.

"Really? It seemed a fair bet. Expensive apartment, flash motor, home at three o'clock in the afternoon – a taste for older women. The name. Dorian Wilde? Got to admit you're eminently qualified."

"It's my stage name." he grated. "I'm a model – and I do

some acting work."

"Ah, right! Now you mention it, I think I may have seen something you were in."

He continued to scowl at me, but his expression couldn't mask the uneasiness that I'd sensed in him from the minute I'd given him Jennifer Jensen's 'message' on the phone. When I'd asked for five minutes of his time to talk about Jennifer I'm sure he would have liked to turn me away with an easy lie but his unguarded reaction to her name had already made it clear that he knew her. It would have been hard to pretend ignorance after that and putting the phone down on me would have only made it more obvious that he had something to hide. Which, having now met him face to face, I was sure would prove to be the case.

His very posture said as much. He stood facing me, his arms crossed defensively in front of him as he tried, unconvincingly to look the master of his own home. He was wearing black jeans and a short-sleeved, green Lacoste polo shirt. The dark curly hair described by Janet Lazenby had been cut short and tamed by industrial strength hair gel into the 'Don Draper' look that was all the rage that year. His face and arms were naturally tanned, and he had the ripped look of somebody who worked out regularly and liked it. Still, for all his brooding looks and tight abs he was about as intimidating as Johnny Bravo.

He obviously didn't like me being there but whether his nervousness was because of a guilty conscience or just down to a natural mistrust of strangers, was a matter of conjecture. Maybe if I asked him for his autograph he might relax a little.

"It's mainly adverts." he said, responding to my last remark with a sullen reluctance. "I've done Emmerdale though – and I was an extra in Spectre."

I snapped my fingers in recognition.

"Of course! Corpse with gelled hair – that was you!"

"Fuck you." he said.

"Just kidding – no, the thing I saw you in was on a bit smaller scale. A 'two-hander' I think they call it in the business? Though it looked as if you had more than two at certain moments, I have to say."

"I haven't got a clue what you're talking about. If you're just here to take the piss-"

"No – that's purely an entertaining diversion. Does this ring any bells?"

I passed him the head and shoulders shot I'd captured from Jennifer's home movie of the two of them. He frowned at the image for a few seconds then threw me a questioning look.

"Where did you get this?" he demanded.

"All in good time. It's you though, isn't it? Before you watched Mad Men?"

He conceded that it was.

"So? Do you want me to sign it?" he said, which wasn't a bad recovery to be fair.

"I did think about it." I admitted. "Ebay would go mad for it when your next catalogue comes out."

"Fuck you."

"You say that a lot, Danny. I'm concerned. I don't think we're bonding."

"Where did you get this?" he repeated, waving the printout in my face for emphasis.

"I've told you – it's a still from one of your films – though I don't think you actually realised that the camera was rolling on this one and it was no easy job finding a still with just your face on it, let me tell you!"

He studied the image again and thought about what I'd said. The dawn of realisation brushed its rosy fingers across his cheeks.

"Jen -? She – filmed us?"

"Don't know. She was definitely in the frame with you, though, if you know what I mean? Nudge, nudge, wink, wink – and please don't say 'Fuck you' again. It won't solve anything."

"What do you want – Webster, was it?"

"Still is." I agreed. "Though you might be onto something. Maybe I should change it. How does Crash O'Brannigan sound? No? Too much? You're right. Dante Rabelais? Yes, I think I could carry that off."

His expression doubted my judgement – and my sanity.

"Okay, enough kidding around, promise. To answer your

question, as indeed I told you when we spoke on the phone all of ten minutes ago. I'm trying to find Jennifer Jensen and your name came up – well, your nom du theatre, at least. The photo's just to save you the trouble of lying about your relationship. Unless you have a stunt double for your sex scenes?"

He merely shook his head irritably, his attention focused on the printout again, still trying to process its implications, perhaps.

"Fine – yes, it's me." he admitted at length. "So, we had a relationship. We're both adults, unattached, what can I say? We had fun – while it lasted – but she's too old for me. I couldn't see a future in it. I'm easily bored."

"Ah – so she dumped you!"

"Screw – that. It was mutual."

"You mean: she dumped you and you accepted it?"

"Think what you want."

"I think she was probably the one who got bored." I said. "But it doesn't really matter. When did you decide to go your separate ways?"

He thought about it, relaxing enough to finally sit down on the other sofa, albeit perched at the edge as if ready to spring to his feet again if provoked.

"About three months ago, I'd say – just before the New Year. Fresh start and all that. No hard feelings either side."

It made a kind of sense when put alongside the notion of her quitting her job and taking off for the sun; breaking the cocoon of old habits and old relationships to soar above them on brand new wings.

I wished I could believe it.

"And you've had no contact since? No phone calls or emails?"

"No." He shook his head. "It was a clean break."

I nodded. "Did that include the Club too?"

That caught him by surprise, as I'd hoped it would. He recovered quickly not so quickly that I didn't register his initial reaction.

"Club? I'm not sure what you mean."

"A group of like-minded people who gather to pursue

mutual interests in concert." I said.

"I know what a fucking club is!" He was back to being aggressive again. "I meant: what club exactly?"

"The Hellfire Club, naturally." I said.

I didn't know how much he made as a model but on current evidence his acting career was going to be hand to mouth. He couldn't hide the shocked look, shading into panic, which flashed across his face before he could completely stifle it.

"You've lost me again." he managed.

"You've never heard of it?"

"No."

"And yet you bought Jennifer a book with that title, signed it with the very phrase I used to you on the phone earlier."

"Well, of course I know about that Hellfire Club – "

"So, there's another one, is there?"

"I wouldn't know." he blustered. "I was just going to say that I gave Jen that book as a laugh. We'd watched a film together – one of those old Hammer horror things? You know the kind of thing – so bad it's good?"

"Not Hammer, as it happens, but a fair enough copy." I said. "Good cast though. Peter Cushing, of course, Keith Michell and Adrienne Corri."

"Yes, yes, that's the one! A load of rubbish, really, but we got a laugh out of it – and Jen seemed fascinated by the fact that it was inspired by real events. I thought she'd like to find out more, so I bought that book for her. It's thought of as a classic on the subject."

"That's so romantic." I said. "I bet she went all weak at the knees."

"It was just meant as a joke." he scowled. "I don't know what else to tell you."

"Maybe this will give you a clue." I said, handing him another printout.

It was a copy of the raunchy party invitation that I'd run off at the office that morning. He stared at it as if he couldn't quite believe what I was showing him.

"Where did you get this?" he said, doing his best to bluff it out. His 'best' was more Golden Raspberry than Golden Globe.

"From Jennifer's computer. I said. "Did you get an invite too?"

He didn't reply. I tried prodding him again.

"Who's 'Dash'?"

"What? I – how should I know?"

He pulled himself together, shoving the printout back at me as if it had suddenly become radioactive.

"Look, I've told you the truth. I haven't seen Jen for months and when we were together we didn't live in each other's pockets. I thought she was just a lonely, middle-aged divorcee looking to have some fun. If she was into anything more – more – edgy I never knew anything about it."

He said it with an earnest sincerity just dripping with artifice.

"So, you didn't know that she was seeing other men, making secret home movies with them – and you? It would have come as a shock to find that out, I'm sure. Nobody would blame you for being angry. Maybe you just lost it a little bit – lashed out at her, not knowing your own strength …"

"No!" he almost shouted, "That's not what happened. The split was mutual and amicable. She clearly had another life that I knew nothing about – and I'll admit that it's a shock to learn about it. I had no idea what kind of shit she was into but even if I had known I would never have hurt Jen – or any woman. It's not my thing."

"It's not the kind of thing anyone would admit to, even it was." I said but, funnily enough, I more than half believed him. He was lying about just about everything else, mind you.

I lingered for a little while longer, explaining why I was looking for Jennifer and throwing a few more questions at him. I cut back on the cynicism, though, and he played a straight bat to most of them. After another five minutes or so I was struck by a sudden bout of coughing that turned my voice into a croak and when I asked him politely for a glass of water he was relaxed enough to oblige me without thinking twice about it. As soon as he was out of the room I fished the gadget I'd brought with me from the office out of my jacket pocket. This was a small but powerful listening device, no bigger than a twenty pence piece. I attached this to the underside of Danny's computer work station where it would sit unnoticed and inert until it picked up the sound of voices anywhere in its vicinity. At this point it was programmed to dial up my cell phone to allow me to listen in.

By the time Danny returned with the glass of water I was back in my seat again, pretending to check my phone for messages whilst actually turning it off, so it wouldn't ring when the two of us resumed our conversation. That didn't last much longer. I drank most of the water in one long swallow and put the glass down on one of the coffee tables. Then after a few more innocuous questions, I closed my notebook, stood up and thanked him for his time.

He was relaxed enough by now to give me an almost-sincere smile and assure me that it had been no trouble.

"Just sorry I couldn't be more help." he said, shaking my proffered hand without rancour. "I really hope Jen's okay."

I handed him one of my business cards, pretty sure it would end up in the bin as soon as I left. He agreed to get in touch if he thought of anything else, which was another lie probably. Whatever he knew he wouldn't give up voluntarily but that was okay. I'd find out what it was whether he liked it or not.

Dorian walked me to the door, barely able to disguise his relief that I was leaving. The door closed firmly behind me and as I headed for the elevator I turned my mobile back on and dialled in the four-letter pin number that activated the listening device I'd left in his apartment. It immediately picked up the sound of him moving about on the uncarpeted floor, followed shortly by what sounded like the clink of bottle on glass. I pictured him pouring himself a stiffener, pondering our conversation, which I hoped might have stirred him up enough that he'd feel the need to talk to somebody else about it.

The next thing I heard was the sound of him swallowing, then what might have been him putting a glass down firmly on a hard surface. A few seconds silence, followed by the unmistakeable sound of nervous fingers drumming out an indecisive rhythm on that same surface. There was a sharp, electronic beep as he picked up the telephone handset and a few more seconds silence in which to make his call and be connected. Then, his anxious voice launching into a breathless conversation with whoever had picked up.

'Dash, it's Dorian. I'm fine – you? Yeah, I know what you mean. Listen – it's Jen. Jen - that lost Nun we talked about? Yes, that Jen. Well, there's a husband, not been on the scene for years but seems he's been trying to get in touch and failing. He's hired a private detective and, well, he's just been sniffing round here."

Pause

"Well – I know – I know – yeah – look, I'm sorry but it seems she likes making secret movies. Movies, Dash, that's that I said. What? Put it this way, I don't think she filmed us playing Scrabble! No, of course I didn't know! I thought – well, it doesn't matter now. He's seen the film and he identified me from it. I didn't ask how! What difference does it make? He found me, that's what he does for a living – and the sarcastic bastard is obviously very good at it."

Pause.

"Look, I don't want to get into this on the phone, but there's more. He was asking about the Club. He was just fishing, and I blanked him, but he knows your handle."

Pause.

"No, I've said, I denied all knowledge - not that he believed me."

Pause.

"I don't know. I told you all about it and nothing's changed. I haven't heard anything since Christmas – I wish I had."

Pause

"Okay, if you think we should. Eight o'clock at The Kestrel? I'll be... Hello...Hello? Dash? Fuck you then!"

Sound of the handset being slammed unceremoniously back into its station.

"Fuck! Fuck! Fuck!"

Now there was one would-be thespian who needed a new dialogue coach!

10.

The Kestrel was high-end gastro pub ten miles out of the city, near the pretty Pennine village of Langstrop. It had a reputation for good food at slightly less than London prices and a wide selection of real ales that brought in plenty of transient connoisseurs who thought beer was food.

I'd been there a couple of times with Mattie, my most recent romantic mistake and enjoyed the old-style country ale house ambience right up until the moment I got the bill.

"So, make sure you eat before you get there." I warned Eddie.

He snorted derisively.

"I'd sooner have a curry, any road." he opined. "Pubs should be for supping and nowt else – except copping off with the barmaid, of course."

"And you can forgo that as well." I said. "Keep your mind on – work."

We were sitting in The Jackdaw, an avian hostelry of a very different feather to The Kestrel. It was one of the new, scruffy-chic places with bare brick walls and wooden floors and fifty shades of beer and lager to suit every palate. They did food too, though if you fancied anything more exotic than a double chilli burger you'd be out of luck.

Eddie and I were both nursing halves of Beck's Vier at one of the stripped back tables in the front window of the bar, looking out at the dwindling foot traffic as the city's offices and shops shut down for the day. I'd just finished bringing him up to speed on my encounter with Danny Walczak, aka Dorian Wilde and his subsequent urgent call to the mysterious 'Dash'.

My immediate thought had been to turn up at The Kestrel that evening and front the pair of them, but I'd soon ditched that idea. Dorian's end of their conversation that afternoon seemed to confirm that neither he nor 'Dash' had any idea of Jennifer's current whereabouts – or didn't want to let on to the other if they did. Dorian's reference to a 'missing nun' had, however, firmed up my suspicion that he and Jennifer were involved with a local incarnation of the Hellfire Club. The male members of the original club had mockingly referred to themselves as 'The Monks of Medmenham' and, by association, the women who shared or slaked their appetites were known as 'nuns'.

Even if Dorian and Dash were as clueless as they appeared to be there could be any number of other members who might be able to shed light on Jennifer's disappearance. If 'Dash' was their leader I assumed he would be able to identify these parties, but I decided I needed to know a bit more about him before I confronted him in person. It seemed like a good idea to stay well in the background that evening since Dorian had seen my face and I didn't want to risk being spotted by him before Dash made his appearance. This was where Eddie came in and he was loving it.

"Ha! Can you believe it? The Naughty Knights of Nooky in our own backyard" he enthused.

"Yeah, well, just don't be asking for an application form! Just keep an eye on Dorian and see who he meets. Try and get a photograph – but don't be too obvious about it. I don't want this 'Dash' character to know he's been sussed until I'm ready."

"Relax, H. They don't call me the Phantom for nothing."

"You misheard. That's not what they're calling you my roly-poly, ninja friend."

Eddie gave me the finger and drank his beer unconcernedly. Not for the first time I felt grateful for the easy bond between us, which the events of the last year or so had only strengthened.

"You know I love you really, don't you?" I said.

Eddie looked at me with surprise.

"Where's that come from? How long have we been friends?"

"Nearly thirty years."

"Exactly. You think I'd still be around if I didn't know that your backchat switch has been stuck in the 'on' position since birth? Man, what would really upset me is if you started being nice to me – so fucking cut it out!"

"I love you, Eddie, man." I said.

"Fuck off!" he laughed.

I ordered a couple of more beers and we nailed down the details for later that night. We would make our way to The Kestrel separately and while Eddie went in and acted like passing trade, I would wait in the car park. When Dorian met Dash, Eddie would observe them discretely and get a picture if he could. Either way he'd be able to identify Dash and, when he left the pub, I would follow him to wherever he went from there.

"That's cool." Eddie said, finishing what was left of his half and getting up to leave. "I'm off home now to get fettled. They have a dress code at this place?"

"Smart casual." I said. "But just do the best you can."

"You cheeky git – boss." he grinned.

"You don't have to keep calling me 'boss'." I told him. "I look like Springsteen to you?"

"Whatever you say, guvnor."

He gave me a mock salute and left. I sat for a while after he'd gone, finishing my own beer and checking my phone for any new emails or messages. I replied to those emails that were semi-urgent but left the majority for another day.

It was about twenty to six and time for me to head home too. I had a leisurely shower, changed clothes and made a quick sandwich of Danish salami, Maasdam and smoked red peppers. I ate sitting at the kitchen table, killing time reading Peter Ackroyd's biography of Shakespeare. It felt good to lose myself for a spell in the dangerous, vibrant first Elizabethan age. I never ceased to marvel how the greatest poet the world has ever seen could have flourished in the unpromising soil of lethal pandemic disease, religious intolerance and general human brutality and paranoia. It was a thought that always made me catch my breath in a kind of wonder.

At about half past seven I reluctantly put my book to one side and set off for Langstrop. It was dark now and the temperature had fallen so it felt more like the end of winter than the start of spring. It was a clear night, though, with no hint of the rain showers that so often swept down on the city from the Pennines. I pulled onto The Kestrel's spacious car park almost on the stroke of eight and parked well away from the brightly-lit pub entrance.

I had barely turned off the engine when my phone vibrated. It was an incoming text from Eddie enquiring where I was. I messaged him back to let him know I'd arrived and a couple of minutes later my phone rang.

"H? It's me." he said redundantly. "I'm in the bog."

"Well, thanks for not Face Timing me, at least." I said. "Any sign of Dash yet?"

"Don't think so. Danny boy's been here about ten minutes and he's spoken to a couple of people in passing but he's just sitting on his own at the bar right now and checking his watch every couple of minutes. He don't look happy. What if this guy doesn't show?"

"He'll show." I said. "He's the alpha dog, he's probably late on purpose just to remind Danny of the fact."

"Because that's the kind of thing you alpha dogs do, right?"

"Woof!" I said.

Eddie rang off and I settled in to smoke a cigar and study the coming and goings in the car park. A few more cars came in, but the occupants were all in multiples, couples or greater, making it unlikely Dash was amongst them. Just after quarter past eight the pub's front door opened and a single figure emerged. He was a middle-aged man of heroic girth wearing a tan shearling coat and matching trilby. Despite the warm coat he seemed to shiver in the cool night air and he thrust his hands deep into his pockets before walking briskly to a silver Lexus RX in the front rank of parked cars. I admired the coat and the car but forgot both them and their owner as soon as the Lexus left the car park. A couple of minutes later my phone vibrated again. Another text from Eddie.

He's here! And you'll never guess who Dash is!

101

Eddie was right. I could have sat there until Christmas and never have guessed that Dash was really Glenn Wood

"Glenn Wood? Get out of here! The Glenn Wood? I mean – Glenn...Wood?" I said. "Damn. Glenn Wood!"

"You've never heard of him, have you?" Eddie said accusingly.

It was about fifteen minutes later, and Eddie had joined me in the car to brief me on what he'd seen in the pub. He had been bristling with excitement at the big reveal he had for me, but it had all fallen a bit flat.

"You've never heard of Glenn Wood? Really? You're telling me the name means nothing to you?"

"Did you sleep with his wife?"

He seemed to hesitate then shook his head testily.

"They weren't married then." he said.

I think he was joking here but with Eddie who knew?

"Extreme Bouncers?" he continued.

"Don't know, I've never met the lady."

"It's a TV show." he explained patiently. "And not about what you're thinking. You sure you've never seen it? Glenn Wood's the compere, host, smirking git in a suit, whatever. He's done loads of other stuff as well. Reality TV shit, you know? He's Yorkshire's answer to Simon Cowell."

"So, not pepper spray then?" I said but a vague bell was ringing at last.

As if to amplify it Eddie thrust his smartphone in my face. I found myself looking at a middle-aged man with spiky black hair and a smile like the Cheshire Cat that got the cream. The camera seemed to like him, but I decided I probably wouldn't.

"He's certainly got Cowell's 'punch me hard in the face' look off to a T." I conceded.

Now I had seen that face that bell, which was at the bottom of a tea chest in the attic of my memory, got a little louder. I scrolled down to read the potted biography beneath.

Wood was a former DJ on Northwards Radio who had graduated to regional television via a souped-up pub quiz show called *This Rounds On Me*. It went out in the middle of the night to an audience of insomniacs and game show zombies. Wood had used this platform to show off his smooth, good looks and patronising wit to such effect that he was able to score a prime-time slot as front man for a peripatetic current affairs programme called *That Bloke in the Pub*. Every week he travelled to a different pub from which he hosted a Newsnight style panel of bar room know-alls, trivialising the burning issues of the day before an equally ill-informed audience of regulars. It was variously described as "pure comedy gold" (The Sun) or "a bunch of surly drunks shouting at each other" (The Daily Telegraph) but it didn't do Wood's career any harm either way.

Soon he was producing his own shows in a similar vein; TV for people who thought Big Brother was too cerebral. *Yorkshire's Smartest Whippet*, *Car Boot Treasure Trail* and *My Granny Can Fight Your Granny* (Don't ask!). His latest smash hit was, indeed, *Extreme Bouncers*, in which club doormen competed against each other in a series of Herculean tasks under jokey pseudonyms like Mad Max from Morecambe, Tony O'Hooligan and Ivan the Terribly-Dressed. It was lowest common denominator entertainment: crass and exploitative and making Wood a fortune through his production company Woodpecker.

I handed the phone back to Eddie with a sigh.

"Do you ever get the feeling we're living in the End Times?" I said to nobody in particular.

"You should watch it sometime." Eddie coaxed. "Bouncers. It's a laugh. I know one or two who've been on it.!"

I could just imagine. It wouldn't have surprised me in the least to learn that half the contestants had thrown Eddie out of somewhere at some time or other – or tried to.

"But you sure that Wood is Dash?" I persisted, though the names seemed to confirm it.

"Trust me." Eddie confirmed. "I recognised him straight off. I know my celebs, H. I've got a photogenic memory for the glitterati."

I glanced out of my window to hide a smile, but Eddie wouldn't have noticed anyway. He was too busy staring at the image of Glenn 'Dash' Wood on his phone.

"So? What happened in there?" I said, nodding towards the pub. "I don't recall seeing him go in while I've been sitting here."

"What? Oh – no, you wouldn't. He was already in there wasn't he? In the upstairs restaurant bit. He came strolling down about quarter past eight with this other guy – fiftyish, beardy face, bit on the 'stout' side. Nice whistle though and not off the rack either. His shearling coat must have cost a few hundred as well. Plenty of money there, I'd say. His agent maybe? Or another of his Hellfire pals?"

It sounded like the man I'd seen leaving in the Lexus.

"Possibly both." I said. "Possibly neither. We'll worry about him some other time. Let's get back to Dash and Danny

"Well you were right with that alpha dog bollocks. Danny did everything but sniff the guy's backside when Wood finally showed."

Thanks Eddie, another image I would struggle to flush from my brain

"How did Wood react?"

"He pissed on three chairs and two tables and then he was fine." Eddie said with a grin. "No, I mean he didn't chin him or anything. They were chill with each other at first. Even had a bit of a cuddle like some blokes do these days."

It sounded like Eddie would have had more tolerance for them if they had sniffed each other's backsides.

"Why do we never hug?" I said.

"Fuck off, H." Eddie said cheerfully, "Where was I? Oh yeah, well they were just like two old mates getting together for a couple of jars and a natter. Once Danny boy bought a fresh round they took their drinks off to a table in the lower bar. 'Fraid there was no way I could get close enough to try and listen in without them sussing I was swan-necking. Best I could do was keep an eye on them from a corner of the bar. Maybe you should send me to lip reading classes."

"Practice with this." I said turning to him and mouthing a short reply.

"Okay. A simple 'No' would have been enough." he said. "But – back to Maverick – Danny had plenty to say and he ended up getting pretty agitated. You must have really shaken him up."

"That was the idea." I said. "How did Wood react?"

"Well, he didn't look particularly happy about anything Danny was saying." Eddie conceded. "But then you wouldn't expect him to. Think what the papers will do to him if they get wind of his secret bonking club!"

We sat in silence for a few seconds, amusing ourselves by imagining how that scenario might play out.

"Not just him, either." Eddie continued at length. "Who knows how many other celebs might be involved?"

Who indeed? Though genuine celebrities were a bit thin on the ground in our neck of the woods to be fair. It's true that the city had thrown up a few successful rock bands over the years and its fair share of household names from TV, Film and the Bestsellers lists. Not many of them stayed local once they'd hit the big time though. Still, fame is relative, and the city had its social hierarchy like any other. Eddie was probably right to suggest that Glenn Wood might not be the only recognisable name on the Hellfire Club's roster. If so, that could certainly be a useful point of leverage to use with Wood.

"So how were things looking when you slipped away?" I asked.

"Pretty calm by then. There was a bit of verbals from Wood when Danny had said his piece but no major bust-up. I mean, he looked a bit pissed off, but he wasn't getting in Danny's face. Looked more like he was doing an Obi Wan on him, you know? Over-reacting you are, young Skywalker. Chill out you must."

"That would be Yoda." I corrected automatically,

"What, like deep breathing exercises to calm him down an' that? Yeah, could've been."

"Not – oh never mind. Carry on."

"Well – he was in control, that's what I'm saying. Soon got Danny pulling his neck in, you know? Alpha dog."

"Right – and now we've flushed him out of his kennel let's see if we can get him to fetch a stick for us." I said.

105

I told Eddie that he could head off home if he wanted but he opted to stay. He was living apart from his wife Maureen, who was currently at her sister's place in Doncaster with their two boys, Clint and Bronson. It had been almost two years now since Maureen had walked out but, though he rarely admitted it, I knew that Eddie still missed her – and he absolutely adored his kids. It had been an amicable split and it was by no means the first thanks to Eddie's roving eye and dodgy sinuses. (She still claimed that his gale force snoring was the ultimate deal breaker.) Neither of these anatomical shortcomings had noticeably improved since they split, though I think Eddie was still married in his heart. Going back to an empty house could sometimes be an unwelcome reminder of how much he missed his family.

He talked about looking for a smaller place but that was all he did – talk about it. Somehow, eighteen months and more down the line he was still paying the mortgage on the terraced house he and Maureen had moved into the night after their honeymoon. I think that deep down he still hoped that they might all end up back together again – and since she never seemed to hassle him about selling up or getting an actual divorce, I think Maureen did too. For whatever reason Eddie wanted to talk about it that night as we sat in the car waiting for Dash and Danny to appear and go their separate ways.

"I'm thinking about asking Mo to give us a second go." he said out of the blue. "What do you think?"

"I think your arithmetic sucks." I said.

"Seriously, H."

"Very seriously." I assured him. "Okay, seriously: be careful what you wish for. Are things going to be any different if you get together again? I'd think Maureen would want some pretty strong commitment to change from you."

"I could have an operation." Eddie said.

"Still leaves the problem of your snoring." I said.

It was about then that the pub door opened, and Dorian Wilde stepped out, closely followed by Wood. They paused outside the door to exchange quick 'Goodnights' and a brisk hug that seemed to suggest that the emotional equilibrium had been restored between them.

At my side Eddie muttered something that I didn't quite catch, though I expect it would have got pained looks from the PC Police. I ignored him and watched them go their separate ways to their cars. Dorian's black 2007 Porsche Boxster was already rolling before Wood even reached his vehicle, a brand new, royal blue Audi 8 coupe.

"Better hope he doesn't cut loose in that." Eddie said enviously. "He'll blow us off before we get out of the car park."

He had a point, but The Kestrel was a bit off the beaten track and I was banking on 'Dash' not burning it up too much on the narrow country back roads. I was right. His pace was almost sedate as he glided out of the pub car park, indicating left. I waited until he was out of sight and followed. The road dipped about a hundred yards past the pub entrance and I lost sight of him a few seconds before he came out of it, only to vanish again seconds later around the first of several bends. There was nowhere to turn off for at least a couple of miles though and when we hit a longish stretch of straight road he was only about fifty yards ahead of us.

I had no idea where Dash hung his hat, but I guessed it probably wasn't too far away. He had picked The Kestrel to meet Danny for a reason, probably because he had already arranged to meet his dinner partner there. It certainly wasn't convenient for anyone living in the city, where there were plenty of other gastro-pubs its equal or better. It was popular with people from Langstrop and the other local villages, though, and I hoped that Wood might be one of them. He didn't disappoint me. We were only a couple of miles past Langstrop when he turned left into the driveway of an imposing detached house with a mock Tudor frontage, which stood back off the road amidst spacious grounds. As we drove past, the lights of Wood's car were disappearing round a bend in the drive and the automated, metal gates were already closing behind him.

I drove on for perhaps a quarter of a mile before the entrance to a field came up where I could make a turn. Before heading back, I let the motor idle while I thought about what to do next. Eddie was all for getting in Wood's face there and then, but it was late, and he was by no means certain to let down the drawbridge for a couple of strangers at that time of night. I could also see the advantage to making him sweat a little bit more before fronting him.

I turned off the engine and switched on the interior light. Eddie watched me passively as I took out my notebook and tore out a blank page on which I scrawled a simple message: Dash, you're going to have to talk to me or the Press. You decide.

Eddie squinted at it dubiously, clearly unimpressed.

"What? Too prosaic?"

"It's hardly going to get him shaking in his shoes, is it?" he grumbled.

"You think if I added the skull and crossbones, it would elevate it?"

"It doesn't even say who it's from, H!"

"It's called 'deniability', Eddie. Nasty, suspicious policemen might construe a note like this as evidence of a crude blackmail attempt."

"He's hardly likely to call Babylon, is he? He's not stupid."

"You're probably right – but I'd rather not take the risk. He'll work out who it's from soon enough after his head to head with Dorian. He'll be in touch within twenty-four hours. He won't be able to resist."

Eddie looked unconvinced. It was all too subtle for his liking.

"How are you going to deliver this? "he said, waving the note at me. "Tie it to a brick and lob it through a window?"

"I expect he can afford double glazing." I said. "I thought you could just hop over the wall on our way home and poke it through his letter box."

"Likely! This is my best Paul Smith knock-off!"

"Kidding." I said. "I think I saw a mailbox on one of the gateposts as we went past."

I plucked the note from his fingers and he harrumphed and muttered while I rummaged in the glove compartment for an old envelope. I stuck the note in the envelope and held it out to him.

"Why me?"

"Your side of the car." I said, and he subsided as the logic of it sank in.

He took the envelope with a sigh and I turned the engine back on and moved off.

"And don't forget to smile for the CCTV." I said as I pulled up a couple of minutes later in the road opposite the big gates to Wood's home. "You never know: you might get talent spotted for his next show."

Eddie clambered out of the car, gave me the finger and slammed the door behind him louder than was strictly necessary. He darted across the road with surprising alacrity, dropped the envelope into the mail box and returned to the car within twenty seconds or less. He jumped in, breathing heavily and shouting: "Go! Go! Go!" as if he'd just robbed a post office at gunpoint.

So, I went.

11.

In fact, it only took Wood twelve hours to react to my note. It was almost lunch time the following day when a pair of ill-matched but tough looking types turned up at the office. They both wore black suits over white shirts with neatly knotted black ties. One was tall, maybe a couple of inches above six feet, with retro-styled black hair and an effortless swagger that recalled the younger John Travolta. He looked like he worked out a lot. By contrast his partner had a shaved head, barely came up to his companion's shoulder and looked like he ate out a lot.

They were polite enough to knock and wait to be invited into the office, where they found me deep in conversation with Eddie about the dire state of United's forward line and our chances of getting hired to help them detect where the goals where. The new arrivals looked at us dispassionately. Probably Leeds fans. Travolta flicked his eyes from one of us to the other, settling finally on me.

"You are Mr Webster?" he asked with an accent that came from Barnsley via Sarajevo.

"Yes. Was it my air of cool command that gave me away? Who are you? Mr Orange or Mr Blue?"

"You take piss?"

"Cash or cheques only."

Dr Evil looked pointedly at Travolta and said something I couldn't understand. It sounded like a Pentecostalist gargling with razor blades. Travolta shook his head and gargled right back at him.

"He say John Travolta was not in 'Reservoir Dogs'" he sighed.

"I know. I was free associating."

"What is all this Travolta shit, anyway?" he grumbled. "I don't get it. I don't look nothing like him, you ask me."

"Ah, but I can tell by the way you use your walk." I said. "Now, what's your problem? Strange noises over at the Frankenstein place again?"

He smiled expansively.

"I don't know these people." he said. "I am here to do favour for Mr Glenn Wood."

Up until this point Eddie had kept quiet but now he reared up, pushing back his chair and jumping to his feet.

"Yeah? You think you and Igor will be enough to do the job?" he enquired belligerently.

Travolta merely looked surprised.

"How you know his name is Igor?" he said, which seemed to throw Eddie. Some of the 'testy' drained out of his testosterone. Travolta laughed. "Ha! Is joke! Name is Bojan, really.

Stifling a grin, I waved Eddie back to his seat.

"Cool it, Eddie. Let's hear what Bojan and -?" I looked questioningly at Travolta.

"Jadran." he supplied, with a little bow. "Jadran Stojanovic – and this is my kolega – colleague, yes? Bojan Kovac."

"You look like a pair of 'bouncers' to me." Eddie said.

Travolta looked pained.

"Your friend is very aggressive. Is often so with short people. Bojan too. Like pocket rocket ready to explode."

We all looked at Bojan who mostly looked ready to fall asleep on his feet. Jadran shrugged philosophically.

"No worries. No work for short, angry persons today. We only want to do our job for Mr Glenn Wood. He wish to speak with you very much but want be sure you don't try no funny stuff. He very famous man, have much problem with journalist and papa-assholes all the time try to catch him with trousers down."

"A not uncommon occurrence, I understand."

"You may say it is so. I, Jadran, know nothing of this. Only that Mr Glenn Wood is very cautious man. He say we must make sure you not try to set him up. Is okay?"

As he was speaking his right hand dipped towards the corresponding pocket of his jacket. The action galvanised Eddie again and next thing I knew he was on his feet again, only this time, to my astonishment, he was brandishing a baseball bat, pointed warningly at Jadran.

The tall man reacted calmly. Immediately raising his hands in mock surrender, he seemed more amused than alarmed. Bojan's only reaction was to frown slightly then mutter something to me in his native tongue.

"What's he saying?" I asked Jadran.

"He say: Build it, they will come." Jadran translated with a grin. He shrugged. "Bojan love movies."

I shook my head, wondering just how the day could get any more bizarre. I waved Eddie back again.

"Take it easy, Eddie." I turned to Jadran. "Go ahead – but do it slowly."

Obediently he lowered his right hand to his pocket again, drawing out what looked at first glance like nothing more threatening than a slightly bulky mobile phone.

"What's that some kind of Taser?" Eddie said, seeing a more sinister possibility.

"It's an RF Detector." I said. "Though most people just call it a 'bug detector'. We've got a couple in the equipment locker. You must have seen them."

"Oh! Right." Eddie said. He lowered the bat but remained watchful and suspicious. "Unless it's a Taser designed to look like an RF Detector?"

"Is that even a thing!" Jadran said, sounding impressed. "No worries. Is like boss say. Is just bug finder. What good Taser anyway? If I shoot boss, you break my face with bat before I can reset."

"Your pal could have one as well." Eddie said, not giving ground easily.

"Bojan? He cannot even work TV remote."

Bojan said something that might have been 'Fuck you' in Serbian but he was smiling as he said it.

"Okay – enough. Put that thing down Eddie." I nodded to Jadran. "Fine, if it will make Mr Glenn Wood happy you can sweep the office. He has nothing to worry about though. It's illegal for me to record any conversation with him unless I ask his permission first."

"Is also illegal to plant sneaky bug in apartment of Mr Dorian Wilde." Jadran pointed out, suggesting his little bug sniffer had already been busy that morning.

"So that's where it got to!" I shrugged. "Go on then Jadran – have at it!"

With no further exchange beyond a curt nod he switched on the detector and began the painstaking process of sweeping the place for bugs. He wasn't going to find any – not active at any rate – and he probably knew that as well as I did. He had a job to do though and I gave him credit for doing it thoroughly, while Eddie, Bojan and I looked on in various states of interest or boredom.

Apart from the front office the suite consisted of a kitchenette, toilet and a smaller room that was nominally my personal office. I only used it for meetings and phone calls that needed a degree of privacy. After scanning the main room without result Jadran checked them out dutifully with similar outcome. When he was satisfied he switched off the device and returned it to his jacket. From the other pocket he then produced a genuine mobile phone and made a call. It was answered and Jadran listened for a moment then spoke.

"Yes, is Jadran. All is clear. No buggies here – just two guys and big-ass bat. Best you leave Taser in car."

He broke the connection and grinned at us.

"Not have Taser, really."

"Is joke?" I said.

He grinned again, made a gun with two fingers and the thumb of his right hand and pointed it at Eddie and me in turn.

"Shoot you later guys." he said and, with a quick jerk of the head in Bojan's direction, he ambled towards the door. Bojan trailed behind him obediently, an oddly superfluous sidekick to the end but probably a big help at quiz nights.

The door closed on them and I glanced at Eddie. He still clutched the bat loosely across his chest, but all the aggression had leaked out of him and he looked a little sheepish.

"A baseball bat?" I said. "I didn't know you even had a baseball bat!"

"eBay." he shrugged, adding with a touch of pride. "It's a Louisville Slugger!"

"Because every office should have one." I said.

"Does that mean I can claim it as a legitimate business expense?" he said hopefully.

Before I had chance to respond we were interrupted by another knock on the door. I gestured for Eddie to lose the bat and he scurried back to his desk and laid the Louisville Slugger on the floor out of sight. Through the frosted glass panel of the door I could make out the shapes of two people waiting patiently in the hallway for someone to invite them in.

"Let them in." I instructed Eddie. "Then bring them through to my office."

He nodded. We'd discussed it earlier and decided that it was better if I saw Wood by myself. As far as he knew I was the only one who was aware of his secret sex life and it suited my purpose to let him keep thinking that I was prepared to use that knowledge for leverage.

I went through to the other office, which was about half the size of the outer one with a single large window. It overlooked a paved communal courtyard with a single, young oak at its centre and a scattering of wooden benches where the tenants could take their fag breaks and eat their lunchtime sandwiches al fresco. The office was furnished with a single, faux leather couch and a couple of matching armchairs arranged on three sides of a circular, knee height occasional table on which stood a tray containing a crystal carafe full of water and several glasses that I had placed there earlier. Next to the tray was an A4 pad notepad and the Mont Blanc fountain pen Clegg had gifted me right after we'd signed the office lease with it. It lent elegance and a touch of class to proceedings that all too often were born of motives that had little to do with either.

I had left the connecting door open and the sound of voices from without was followed shortly by Eddie's peremptory knock.

"Dastardly and Muttley to see you." he announced cheerfully.

See? Elegance and class.

Mr Glenn Wood looked younger in the flesh, every inch the modern metrosexual male in his slim fit Rock & Republic jeans and a lightweight, sky blue blazer worn over a plain white T. He sported a natural-looking tan and unnatural blonde hair, carefully gelled and shaped to give that tousled, just fallen out of bed look.

Dorian Wilde was the second man, dressed in white chinos and a tight-fitting Ralph Lauren polo shirt in canary yellow. Unlike the relaxed and seemingly unperturbed Wood, Dorian appeared ill at ease in the room and his own skin. His blue eyes were wary and watchful as I gestured them towards the armchairs.

"I take it that was your 'batman'?" Wood said in a voice that was consciously cool, sardonic and striving for disinterested. "He seems a little tetchy."

"Jadran and Bojan put him in a bad mood." I said. "I wouldn't let him throw them down the stairs."

"Ha! Sorry about that. I hope they were polite? Their remit was merely to ensure that our meeting space was sanitised. I really don't want the press getting wind of our – um – discussions."

"Because you're such a shy, retiring sort, after all." I said.

"I am when my contract is up for renewal." he said with a flash of honesty. "The network will shit if this gets out."

"But think of the possibilities it opens up for a new reality show on the porn channel." I pointed out. "You could reach a whole new demographic!"

It was meant as a joke, but I swear to God he got a look on his face that said maybe I might be onto something. He shook his head as if to rid himself of the fancy.

At Wood's side Dorian reached for the carafe of water and poured himself a glass. He offered the carafe to Wood, who eyed it dubiously.

"I don't suppose you have any Buxton Spring?" he said.

"This is better. Yorkshire Water. I keep it on tap."

He smiled and nodded at Dorian, who filled another glass and passed it to him. Wood set the glass down without taking a drink and looked at me speculatively.

"Let's hear it then." he said. "How much is it going to cost me to make you go away?"

"What? No cursing? No threats? No 'damn your eyes' defiance? That's not very Hellfire now, is it?"

"I'm a pragmatist, Webster. You know, or think you know, something that could cause me no little inconvenience. We're both aware that it doesn't actually matter if your suppositions are true. If they escape into the wild they'll take on substance irrespective of any empirical truth."

"That's surprisingly deep coming from the man who devised Yorkshire's Smartest Whippet." I admitted, my impression of him shifting slightly. Whatever else he might be he certainly wasn't stupid.

"I read a lot." he shrugged. "But let's be clear – I'm neither ashamed nor embarrassed about anything you think you know about my private life. It's not illegal and one hundred per cent consensual, though it is undoubtedly scandalous from the depressingly narrow viewpoint of society at large."

"Fair enough – and believe it or not I'm pretty broad minded about what consenting adults get up to in the bedroom – or any other room for that matter. I also have nothing but contempt for blackmailers, so you can get down from that high horse you rode in on. You can't buy me off, that's not what this is about, as I would have thought 'Dorian' here might have understood. My only concern is for the safety of Jennifer Jensen, his one-time girlfriend and, I suspect, a lay sister of your reborn Hellfire Club."

"Ha! Lay sister! I'll use that if I may?" Wood smirked. "And forgive me for jumping to unwarranted conclusions. You're right, Dorian did inform me of your interest in Jay Jay, but I confess that I suspected that to be merely a cover story for a more self-serving pay off. I'm afraid celebrity breeds a certain paranoia at times."

"Poor you." I said.

"The 'ups' outweigh the 'downs'" he said cheerfully. "But having cleared up our little misunderstanding I'm afraid I have to disappoint you. I believe Dorian made it clear that he hasn't had any contact with the lady since they ended their affair. I don't think I know anything else that might help you."

"Humour me. You might know something you don't know that you know. Tell me about the Hellfire Club – and how Jennifer came to be involved."

He regarded me thoughtfully, flicking a quick glance at Danny and, steeling himself, took a quick sip from his glass of water. He survived.

"Okay – I'll play." he said. "Where to start? The Club. Well, I started it myself, two, maybe three years ago. Things were just starting to take off for me and I was meeting a lot of well-connected people, getting tons of invites here, there and everywhere and over indulging in all the usual shit: booze, drugs, cheap sex."

"Ah, the sweet smell of excess." I said

"Don't knock it until you've tried it!" he grinned. "Though I admit it got old rather quickly. I was never quite at ease with that kind of open lifestyle. I prefer to indulge my vices a little more privately. As it turned out I wasn't the only one who felt that way. That's when I came up with the idea of reviving the Hellfire Club: a private gathering of like-minded individuals who choose to pursue their private pleasures with a degree of anonymity."

He went on to elaborate. The club was very select to begin with, boasting no more than half a dozen members, all of which were male. Female company was provided by working girls supplied by one of the founders, who by happy coincidence ran the city's foremost escort agency. Initially the group had met every six weeks or so and a hefty subscription fee was levied to pay for the 'entertainment'.

The club had no permanent base, meeting to begin with in various small venues well outside the city that were discreetly hired on line. Although the early members were all friends of Wood's to some degree or other they did not necessarily know each other, and it was agreed that masks would be born at all meetings to preserve their anonymity and prevent any of the 'Nuns' turning to blackmail to supplement their normal fees.

Over time several of the original members had lost interest or moved away and the nature of the club changed accordingly. It had been decided from the start that new members would be allowed to join but only on condition that they were sponsored by an existing member who was prepared to vouch for their discretion and good (?) character. That meant that only the sponsor knew the real identity of a new member and vice versa. This meant that Wood could no longer put a name to all his acolytes apart from a couple or so die-hards who had been with him from the beginning.

Not every member attended every meeting, but the venues had necessarily increased in size as the club grew. The female element still consisted of a few 'escorts' but there were now some adventurous non-professional 'Nuns'. Jennifer Jensen had briefly been included in their ranks and Wood was quick to credit Dorian for the part he played in 'developing the membership'. It seemed his wild good looks and easy charm made him the perfect 'head-hunter'.

"He has a knack for sniffing out the bad girls." Wood smirked lewdly, much to Dorian's obvious discomfort. "Our very own Captain Plume no less."

Wood was a creep without doubt but clearly a well-read one, as he had hinted earlier. Deep versed in books and shallow in himself, as Milton said.

"I don't think you should use that word. There's nothing 'bad' about liking sex." Dorian huffed defensively. "It makes it sound as if we're doing something wrong.

Wood squeezed Dorian's shoulder placatingly.

"Of course not." He smirked at me again. "Dori is such a sensitive soul. It's no wonder all the ladies love him so much!"

Dorian tensed again and looked for a moment as if he might punch Wood. When he didn't, I thought that perhaps I might – but I curbed the urge and pressed on.

"So, Jennifer was one of your 'recruits'?!" I said to Dorian.

"Yes. I first saw her in a bar one lunchtime with a few of that clicked with me. That's the way it works usually. Don't

118

ask me how. I just get a sense of, you know? I mean, when someone's – "

"Gagging for it?" Wood interposed crudely, and Dorian clenched his fists reflexively.

"Whatever." he mumbled. "It's just something I've always had where women are concerned. I've always been able to tell who's likely to be interested and who isn't."

He wasn't the first person I'd heard claim such a useful sixth sense. Eddie, of course, had it. It was a kind of sexual radar that all great seducers seem to possess; saves them a lot of wasted time and rejection,

"So, Jennifer got your spider sense tingling, did she?"

His lips twitched into a humourless smile.

"We just got talking, flirted a bit. When she told me where she worked I came on like I was interested in buying one of their alarm systems and fixed up an appointment to see her in her office a couple of days later. It was a breeze from there on. Our 'meeting' continued in the nearest bar and finished at her place in West Bretton the following morning."

He smiled, a touch wistfully at the memory.

"To tell you the truth, though. I'm not really sure if I really seduced her or it was the other way around."

It was a feeling I could relate to all too well.

12.

"So, what then?" I pressed "You did the dirty deed, smoked a cigarette and casually asked her if she fancied making up the numbers at your next orgy?"

"It wasn't – I'm not that crude." Dorian said defensively."

"He has a 'shtick' he uses on all the ladies." Wood interrupted with a smirk. "I love it. Tell him Dori."

"Yes, do tell me, Dori." I said.

He aimed a scowl at Wood, with a little bit left over me but after a moment's hesitation he went on:

"I show them the film." he sighed. "Okay? Once we've connected on a personal level I play that old film I told you about. The Hellfire Club. We watch it over a few beers, some take out -"

"A line or two of coke?" I suggested.

He shrugged, while Wood did that smirking thing again.

"Whatever they want." Dorian said.

"Do what thou wilt." Wood interjected. "That's the whole point of the exercise."

"I watch how they react to the film." Dorian continued as if Wood hadn't spoken. "Then I talk to them about it and about the whole idea of the Hellfire Club. You'd be surprised how many people don't know that it really existed."

"And how do they react?"

"Mostly they're very broad minded, even if they don't necessarily want to get involved. The ones who are really interested are easy enough to identify."

"Spider sense again?"

"It rarely lets me down." he said with another shrug.

"So, you felt that Jennifer was Hellfire material?"

He nodded.

"Yes – but I had to work a little harder in her case than some. After that first night she just blew me off when I asked to see her again. Said it had been great fun and thank you very much, but she wasn't into long term relationships and don't let the door hit you in the arse as you leave."

That echoed my own experience, though it seemed Dorian had taken a less pragmatic view than myself. He wasn't used to being rebuffed and he admitted that Jennifer had got under his skin. As she had subsequently broken her own rule and relented about seeing him again she must also have felt something more than the insistent pull of basic sexual need. Unless her untypical concession to his persistence had just been a caprice on her part?

Dorian had no doubts, it seemed.

"I thought we had something." he insisted. "More than just sex, I mean."

He sounded regretful, though I couldn't tell if that was because he had been right or because he had been wrong. Either way their one-night stand had becoming something rather more than that. I suspect he wanted to call it 'love'. Maybe my idea of what love should be is out of the sync with the times but it was hard to equate that emotion with the fact that he had still embroiled her in the sexual capers of the Hellfire crowd.

When I raised this, Dorian came over all defensive.

"I hoped she'd say she wasn't interested." he claimed. "But she thought the Club was a great idea. Anonymous sex with no responsibility? She said she wished she'd thought of it herself. Her attitude shook me a little to be honest with you."

"Why? She wasn't the first woman you recruited."

"No – no, that's true. It's just with Jen – well, I was never really convinced by her throwaway attitude to sex and relationships. There was always something a bit 'off' about it – as if it was a pose rather than a serious life choice."

Up until then Wood had largely just looked on condescendingly, taking occasional grudging sips of his water. He was clearly above the messy complications of genuine human feelings, except in situations where they could be exploited digitally and translated into pots of money. He couldn't help speaking up at this point, though.

"Dorian's an unreconstructed romantic." he interposed. "I think he hoped to save her soul."

"Oh, for God's sake Glenn! You don't know her. She's lost – a deeply unhappy woman who uses sex like some people use drink or drugs: to numb the pain."

He was probably right, I recognised but it smacked of 20/20 hindsight. Despite his alleged finer feelings for Jennifer he had clearly been complicit in her self-loathing behaviour. Then again, so had I - albeit unwittingly.

"Oh dear!" Wood scoffed. "Can't somebody just like sex for sex sake? Why does sexual appetite always have to be about something other than the simple pleasures of fucking? The woman joined in willingly and, I may say, with no little enthusiasm on those occasions that she shared our revels."

"How do you know?" I asked sharply. "I thought you said everyone wore masks and were anonymous to everyone but their sponsor?"

"Well, yes, that's true. I never knew her name or saw her face, but new members don't go unnoticed and we don't encourage voyeurs."

"Put out or get out?" I suggested. Hmm, there's another catchy motto for you. Maybe you should could get T-shirts done – I know a guy!"

"All I'm saying is that Sister Kamala was no wallflower."

"Kamala?"

"Her Hellfire name." Wood explained. "All new members take one at their induction."

He put an emphasis on the last word that hinted at a subtext that would probably only magnify the urge to punch his head off. I decided not to pursue it.

"She picked it herself." Dorian chimed in. "It's from a book, I think."

"It's from Siddhartha by Herman Hesse." I supplied. "Kamala is a courtesan who seduces the title character away from his chosen path only to lose him when he grows tired of their unsatisfying lifestyle."

Given her history it was easy to see why Jennifer had chosen that particular character as her avatar. If I remembered Hesse's masterpiece correctly there was a deep sexual irony embedded in Kamala's ultimate fate, which was to die from the bite of a venomous snake. I flicked a glance at Wood but it seemed that was one book he hadn't read. He looked back at me impassively.

"And yet you called her Jennifer when you first came in." I pointed out to him, hoping to dint his self-satisfied façade.

"Blame Dorian for that, I'm afraid. When she dumped him and dropped out of the Club he needed a shoulder to cry on. I was that shoulder!" he declared with an ironic smile. Not that he listened to anything I said on the subject. I think you'll find that he's still smitten."

"It's not a crime to care about the people you sleep with, is it?" Dorian demanded. "Maybe I do still have those feelings. I'm certainly not happy about the way things ended."

I pressed him to elaborate.

"It was all a bit sudden." he admitted. "Thinking back, I suppose I noticed she seemed a bit distracted about a couple of weeks before last Christmas. That's probably because she was working herself to up to dump me, but I honestly didn't see it coming, even when she cried off the Yuletide Revel." he went on, explaining: "It's the biggest event in the Club calendar."

"I saw her invite." I recalled. "Tasteful."

"It was quite the evening." Wood reminisced, unasked. "But then they do say 'Christmas is coming', don't they?"

"I can't think why she'd want to miss it." I said.

"She had a migraine." Dorian answered, apparently missing the sarcasm. "She gets them occasionally, so, like I say I didn't think too much about it. She said she was going to have an early night, wished me a Merry Christmas and hung up. I couldn't believe it when I got her email the next day."

"An electronic 'Dear John'!" Wood crowed. "How 21st century of her, don't you think?"

I didn't entirely share his cynicism. Like the letter Janet Lazenby had received, an email was all too easy to fake by anyone wanting to give the impression that Jennifer was alive and well when there was every chance that she might not be. Belatedly it now seemed to cross Dorian's mind as well.

"I did think it was a bit cold." he admitted. "I would have hoped she'd at least have the courage to look me in the eye when she ended us."

"Any chance that you still have the email?"

Without a word he reached into a side pocket of his short leather jacket and produced a creased and apparently much read printout. He passed it to me without further comment.

Hi Dorian,

Hope you are okay. Sorry I've not been answering your calls these last few days, but I've been away for a few days to catch my breath. Christmas hasn't been the greatest of times for me over the last few years but I think things may be looking up! Don't want to say too much and jinx it but for the first time in ages I've started to look in the mirror on a morning without despising the face that looks back at me. Fact is, this good time girl has finally realised that just maybe she's not been having such a good time after all.

I need to change - and you can take a lot of credit for that! You got past my defences but, then, I suppose you know that. What started out in the bedroom got into my headroom and, yes, into that tightly locked inner space where I've been keeping my feelings since Callum and I went our separate ways. I'm not going to use the L word, that's not where this is going I'm afraid, but you have awoken something in me that I thought was dead: the need for emotional sustenance that goes beyond the merely physical; the yearning to connect with a human being on every possible level. I realise that I have denied myself that possibility for too many years and my recent lifestyle has been merely an expression of self-denial, ironic as that must sound! I've known it for some time actually but somehow lacked the impetus to pull myself out of the nose dive that had become the flight plan of my life. I suppose I would have just continued on in that same, destructive spiral indefinitely but something rather unexpected and rather wonderful has happened, which after all is what Christmas is all about, isn't it? The time when wishes come true and all sins are forgiven!

I'm drunk by the way, can you tell? Drunk on so many levels and yet my head and heart have never felt so clear of doubt and sadness. And so, no more! I renounce the Devil and all his works! Joke! Well, his silly masks and feverish revels, at least. It was fun for a while but then it just became funny and, if I'm honest, more than a little sad and embarrassing. So - no more of your Hellfire antics, for me, love and, sadly, no more you either.

There, I've said it. Please don't be angry - or sad. We both knew this thing we had was just for a season and though our eternal Summer shall not fade, Winter brings with it the frosty sting of reality. A fresh start and a clean break are needed. Clichés, I know, but true for all that. I need to get away from here. Not just for a few days at the coast but far away, as far as possible, where the stain of recent follies can be washed away by healing rain under alien skies.

I feel so excited about the future, like a prisoner on the eve of their release - or escape! It is a wonderful feeling, Dori, how I hope that one day you will also experience it and that the real you will take flight from the shallow ambition and destructive relationships that have so mesmerised you. I wish that for you with all my heart and send that wish as a parting gift to you with all the love that I can spare. Think of me fondly, my beautiful boy, and may all your dreams come to you at last.

Yours

JJ xxx

I read it silently, mentally comparing it to the letter that Jennifer had allegedly sent to Janet Lazenby. Although the tone was more intimate, as you would expect between two people who had been lovers, the sense was essentially the same: a seemingly heartfelt piece of prose that was both affecting and affected at the same time. A stylistic signature or the studied artifice of an unknown hand?

"Did she write this?" I asked Dorian, who looked bemused by the question. "I mean: does it 'sound' like her?"

"I -? It's her email address." He said lamely. "Why wouldn't it be from her?"

The question was a dumb as his original response. I let it roll over me.

"Does – it – sound – like – her?" I annunciated. "Is it her 'voice'?"

"Oh!" He looked confused, then thoughtful, then shamefaced. "I wouldn't really know about that. We usually just texted."

"That does make textual analysis difficult." I agreed. "But you spent a lot of time with her, you must have talked on more than just a superficial level."

"Of course!" he bristled.

"Right then – from what you know of her from all those deep meaningful conversations – does this strike you as being an authentic glimpse into the heart and mind of the woman you say you loved?"

"I – I never questioned that she wrote it." was the best he could offer. It was an honest response, but it didn't really get me anywhere. Taken on its own it was susceptible to the same doubts that arose from the Lazenby letter but accumulatively it was another tick in the left-hand column of the white board.

"You think somebody might have faked it?" Wood said, showing he was sharper than Dorian. Alpha dog.

"I hope not – but until I find Jennifer I'm taking nothing for granted."

"Fair comment but as far as Dorian goes I can assure you he took that email at face value. He was every bit as sad and angry as she predicts."

"It hurt. It still does, if I'm honest." Dorian admitted." Nobody likes to be dumped."

"Did you send a reply?"

He nodded. "I did. I wanted to see her, wanted her to look me in the eye and tell me that it was over. I wanted that much, at least. She never replied though. I tried ringing her, same result. I rocked up at both her houses, but they were both shut up and when I tried to contact her through her work they told me she'd resigned. That's when I started to get the idea that she was serious."

I read through the email again, only half listening to his dejected reminiscence.

"Does she like Shakespeare?" I asked.

"What? How is that relevant -?"

I pointed to the email.

"This bit here: *eternal summer shall not fade*? It's a quote, from Sonnet 18. It's one of his most famous, the one that begins: *Shall I compare thee to a summer's day...?*"

"*Thou art more lovely and more temperate.*" It was Wood who completed the line. Dorian merely continued to look perplexed.

I thought back to my search of Moorside. I didn't recall seeing any copy of the Sonnets or the Complete Works amongst Jennifer's eclectic book collection.

"She studied Drama and English at University." Dorian said, final seeming to catch up "She did some acting too. She showed me her scrapbook once. She played Ophelia, I think. And the Duchess of Malfi – though that's – oh – Webster, isn't it?"

"Let's hope it doesn't turn out to be dramatic foreshadowing." I said.

I realised that I hadn't seen anything that looked like a scrapbook at the house. Like the absent wedding album, it was a nagging dissonance.

"Her reviews were very good." Dorian said, a little wistfully, I thought. "Only college productions but still..."

"If her performances at the revels was anything to go by she certainly knows how to throw herself into a performance." Wood interjected with a snort of laughter.

"Fuck off Glenn." Dorian instructed him half-heartedly.

I wondered what was really going on with the two of them. It was obvious that Dorian deferred to the older man, but I doubted that anything resembling admiration lay at the root of their relationship. Perhaps it was just Dorian's ambition rubbing itself raw against Wood's coarse aura of success.

"Is that it then?" Wood said, ignoring Dorian's directive. "Poor Dorian has bared his soul here. I don't think there's anything more he can add."

"That would be easier to believe if he had been more honest when I spoke to him yesterday."

"I was scared, okay?" Dorian admitted. "I didn't want any trouble."

"From who?"

"Don't look at me!" Wood laughed. "I'm not the one with blood on my hands, after all. Not that anybody holds that against you, of course. Well, anybody still breathing, eh?"

I was caught off balance and for once struggled for words.

"You shoot one psychopath!" I managed.

"Which is one more than the rest of us." Dorian observed. "I knew who you were straight away. Your face was all over the news for weeks after what happened and – well –you're a hard man. You took down a whole gang of lunatics who hurt women, for God's sake! Of course, I was scared."

"You'd only need to worry if you'd actually hurt Jennifer." I said tightly.

"Rationally, yes, but you caught me off guard and said something pretty intimidating things. I thought you were just looking for an excuse to get physical, okay? Sorry if you're offended but you were quite menacing.

"Only 'quite'? Now you've really hurt my feelings." I said.

I didn't know whether to laugh or cry. I might have done my best to put the White Devil behind me, but he was still dogging my footsteps it seemed. Did killing a monster make me a little bit of a monster too?

"When you gaze too long into the abyss, the abyss gazes into you'." Wood said, shocking me with his prescience, reminding me again that there was a clever, insightful brain behind the cool, metrosexual façade and professional cynicism.

"Everybody eventually finds their Nietzsche in life." I said. "You can leave whenever you like. For what it's worth the media won't hear anything about your 'revels' from me or my colleagues. I will have to tell my client though and if I'm not satisfied that Jennifer is safe and well by the time he

128

returns all missing person report will be filed with the police."

"And there is no inducement I can offer to avert that scenario?" Wood asked, more in hope than expectation.

"Help me find her. Ask your Monks and Nuns if they know anything. I take it you do talk to each other in between orgasms?"

"It's not our main purpose." he smiled. "But verbal intercourse also occurs, yes. It doesn't seem likely that any of our group will know anything about Sister Kamala's current status, but Dorian and I will put the word out."

I nodded my thanks and gave him one of my business cards and he studied it momentarily before taking out a slim calfskin wallet. He slid my card into one of its pockets and handed me one of his own in return. It was as over the top as you might expect with his name embossed in gold foil above the legend: Woodpecker Productions -Putting the 'real' in reality. I laid it on the desk in front of me, thinking that he didn't have a clue just how unpleasantly real 'reality' could get.

The meeting broke up and I walked them out through the front door and saw them off the premises. They wished me luck in finding Jennifer and they both sounded sincere enough, though for different reasons, I suspected.

Eddie had left for his lunchbreak, but Clegg had returned from whatever piece of accounting business had taken him away from the office. He was sitting at his desk reading The Racing Post and munching a chicken bake from the bakery around the corner.

"G'morrow, Hal." he greeted me through a mouthful of pastry.

"Back at ya' Cyril." I said.

I wandered over to the whiteboard to add what new information I'd gleaned from my recent meeting. The phone call and email that Dorian had received were the main entries in the right-hand column. Of course, I only had his word for the telephone call and anyone, could have sent the email. In both cases it worried me that Jennifer hadn't ended their relationship face to face. A termination letter to the

housekeeper or the gardener was one thing but her
relationship with Dorian was of a different nature. Ending an
intimate relationship by email didn't fit with my lasting
impression of the forthright and up-front woman I had so
fleetingly known.

"It does seem a touch craven." Clegg agreed. "It's hardly
conclusive of anything sinister, though. Perhaps she wasn't
one hundred per cent certain she was doing the right thing
and was simply afraid that she might weaken if she had to
look him in the eye."

I conceded the point, frustrated that firm conclusions were
proving so elusive. I sat down heavily at my desk and Clegg
eyed me shrewdly.

"You seem distempered, lad – and not necessarily about
m'lady Jennifer. What did the notorious Dashwood say that's
upset you so much?"

I hesitated, wondering if I was making too much of it but at
length I told him how the topic of the White Devil had arisen
and how it had prompted Wood to jab me with that sharp bit
of Nietzsche.

Clegg listened patiently, absently brushing crumbs of pasty
off his shirt front but never taking his eyes off me.

"And are you upset because you think he's wrong – or
because you fear that he's right?"

"Do I think that killing a monster makes me one too? No. I
might wish that I wasn't the one who did it, but it needed
doing."

"I wouldn't argue with that – but you've crossed a line most
of us have never had to. It's hard for outsiders to avoid the
thought that it must have changed you in some way, made
you less like the rest of us. 'Dangerous' as Dorian said."

"To myself and others." I said, half to myself. "Is that why
Eddie bought the baseball bat to work today?"

Clegg frowned. "I can't say that with certainty – but I can
possibly understand why he might do something like that.
Your experiences over the last couple of years have surely
left you in no doubt of how appallingly people with
unrestrained egos can act when they feel challenged or
threatened?"

In his usual erudite way, he made a fair point.

"You have a habit of rubbing up against people like that." Clegg continued gently. "Not only Rocky Van Dorn. What about Old Tony Allardyce? Paul Clayton? Even Jack Grey." He chuckled unexpectedly. "You have a talent for bringing out the worst in such people – not that the 'worst' doesn't lie very close to the surface in the case of most of them. You're like fly paper for the egocentric and morally challenged and your recent visitor is at least one of those things in Edward's eyes. You might do well to remember that Mr Wood's motto is, after all, 'Do what thou wilt'."

13.

Clegg had a point. It had indeed been an 'interesting' couple
of years and 'hazards of the job' seemed like a very pale
description of some of the situations I'd blundered into. I
didn't go looking for trouble, but it had an unerring GPS it
seemed and could always track me down. All the same,
considering the assorted head cases I'd encountered in that
period I doubt if a Louisville Slugger would have been much
help. Surely Eddie was over-reacting, wasn't he?

I chewed all the goodness out of that thought on my way to
a quick lunch at a nearby diner called the Butch Oven. It was
run by Angie and June, a pleasant married couple with a
sense of humour as delicious as their leek and potato soup
and home baked crusty rolls.

I got coffee to go and drank it in my car, while I smoked a
cigar and considered my next move. I wasn't really relying
on Wood getting any useful information out of his Hellfire
crowd, but I had at least one other obvious avenue to explore.
I finished my lunch break and headed back to *Moorside*.

The big house was still mired in the silence of
abandonment, enhanced by the motes of dust that swirled in
the pale beams of sunlight that poked through its many
windows. There was a handful of fresh mail lying on the mat
when I stepped in through the front door, suggesting that no
one had been there since my last visit. That thought recalled
the corrupted face of the gardener, Louis Sifer. Judging from
the pile of mail he obviously didn't see the custodial duty
laid on him to be a daily obligation. I glanced through the
half dozen or so envelopes, most of which were junk apart
from a quarterly statement from her gas and electric provider
informing her that she was £350 in credit for the period. I

shuffled the envelopes together and dropped them into the drawer with all the rest.

Despite the bright sunshine outside the house felt chilly and stand offish, making me feel more than ever like an intruder disturbing the deepening stillness of neglect. I felt the need to get out of there as quickly as possible and made my way quickly to the office. I went straight to the top left-hand drawer of her desk and retrieved the key fob I had seen there on my initial visit. The two keys attached to it would, I hoped, fit the locks on Jennifer's second property, the cosy bungalow where she took her pleasure in the arms of passing strangers like myself.

West Bretton was across the river, a large village that had evolved from a small settlement clustered around the ruins of a Carmelite monastery that had been well and truly dissolved during the Reformation. The oldest surviving houses dated back to the 17th century, a clutch of picturesque Quaker cottages built of stone from the now defunct limestone quarry at nearby Healey Gorge. The rest of the village was an eclectic mix; estates of solid 1930s builds rubbing shoulders with the less substantial spawn of the post-war building boom decades.

No 8, Old Willow Lane was a medium sized bungalow, in the middle of a row of six on a short, tree shaded street that ran down to the river off the village's main road. I knew at once that this was the place Jennifer Jensen had brought me, my hazy memory of that night's peripheral details stirred by the sight of The Old Willow Tree Inn on the opposite side of the road.

The day was warm again and a couple of old guys were enjoying the sunshine at one of the scattering of wooden tables outside the inn's front door. As I climbed out of my car they glanced across in my direction briefly, but they didn't see anything to engage them and quickly turned back to their beer and fags and their conversation. Maybe one day that would be Eddie and me, I thought, a notion that brought with it a curious pang; an odd kind of nostalgia for something that had not yet happened.

The bungalow sat at the top of a short drive running parallel between two strips of grass in urgent need of some urgent TLC. I followed the drive round to the side of the bungalow, which was screened from its neighbour by a tall, thick hedge of privet on one side and a tall, trellised fence on the other. . Like the grass at the front, the hedge was in bad need of a trim. It looked as if whatever arrangement Jennifer Jensen had with Louis Sifer it did not encompass Willow Lane.

The front door looked down towards the river, whose earthy smell drifted up on the warm air, bringing with it a memory of other days walking the bankside of another river hand in hand with my parents. I let myself into the house and stepped into a short hallway carpeted in shades of russet and gold, like a bright fall of autumn leaves in the stillness of a forest clearing. I walked a little way down the hall and turned into the first room I came to. It was a large living area that seemed even bigger because of the total lack of any furniture. Only the memory of it remained in the tell-tale imprints that lingered in the beige carpeted spaces where it had once stood.

Not exactly a home from home, I thought, and tried to remember if I'd seen the room when it was furnished. It didn't seem familiar and I figured we must have stumbled straight through to the bedroom in our drunken passion. I backed out and went through the door across the hall to find myself in the kitchen. Sluggish synapses stirred, and I recalled the grey Getacore breakfast bar where I'd drunk a hasty cup of coffee and swallowed a couple of slices of toast in the surly light of the morning after. Jennifer had offered me a lift back to the city, I remembered but I'd shrugged it off. I'd needed space to process what I was feeling, not sure if it was guilty pleasure or mild disappointment; if I was the used or the user. Mostly I was relieved to escape from any exchange of stilted morning after platitudes and wander off in search of the nearest bus stop.

The worktop was still there but not much else. The high stools and tall, silver-grey fridge-freezer were gone and the small utility room off the kitchen was no longer home to any washing machine or tumbler dryer. It was a story that repeated itself throughout the rest of the bungalow, which consisted of a bathroom-toilet and two bedrooms. Apart from the carpets the house had been emptied of all furniture and personal belongings, except for the fitted wardrobe in the larger of the two bedrooms.

I thought that the smaller bedroom was the one where Jennifer and I had crash landed through a thick haze of alcohol and lust. I'd been far more concentrated on the urgent collision of our slick bodies than on the furniture and fittings, but the position of the window fit with what I could remember of the physical space we occupied. I also seemed to recall a standalone wardrobe opposite the bed, a chest of drawers against the wall farthest from the window and a small bedside table on which stood the solitary lamp by which we made love. The faint imprints in the carpet seemed to support this memory. More lucidly I recalled that there had also been a small bookcase full of paperbacks on the other side of the bed under the window.

"I like a good book." she'd said.

Well, it sounded like that's what she said.

I thought about the DVDs of Jennifer's adventures in this room. From the camera angle they'd been shot from a camera that must have been placed directly opposite the foot of the bed. That probably meant it had been placed on top of the wardrobe, angling down. There was no evidence of any drilling in any of the walls and no adjacent sockets where the cameras could have been unobtrusively plugged in. That meant wireless, linked to a laptop that could have been situated anywhere in the house, probably the other bedroom I guessed.

I turned to leave the room, feeling oddly uncomfortable to be there, like a wandering ghost of myself. Before I left I checked the walk-in wardrobe. Given how thoroughly the rest of the house had been stripped, I didn't really expect to find anything in there and, indeed, it was mostly empty. However, on the single shelf at the back of the wardrobe I found a couple of books, one lying half on top of the other as if they had toppled over together.

The larger of the two was a thick A4 sized volume bound in maroon leather. An album of some kind with age-faded gilt

lettering on the cover spelling out the simple title:
MEMORIES. The second volume was less personal, a cheap
and well-read paperback with an unsettling cover
photograph. It depicted a demonic, horned figure astride a
coal-black, flying steed below the title: *The Devil Rides Out*.
I rifled its pages, but no hidden messages were secreted
there, unless you counted the few lines of verse that had been
lettered in an ornate script on the reverse of the title page.

> **To be weak is miserable**
> **Doing or suffering: but of this be sure**
> **To do aught good never**
> **Will be our task**
> **But ever to do ill our**
> **Sole delight**

Milton, I recognised. An extract from Satan's speech of
defiance at the beginning of Paradise Lost; the spiteful boast
of a sore loser standing in the ruins of his dream of power. It
had always rung with empty bravado to me, until that very
moment when the words pierced my chest with a sudden, icy
chill.

I took the paperback and Jennifer's scrapbook with me and
left. It was late afternoon by now and I had the office to
myself when I got back. I set down the books on the corner
of my desk, made coffee and booted up my PC. I spent a few
minutes bringing my notes up to date then lit a cigar and
thought about my trip to West Bretton. The obvious
conclusion to be drawn from the empty bungalow was that
Jennifer had cleared the place out because she intended to
sell or rent the property. Either of these options made sense if
she really intended to leave the country for an extended
period. On the other hand, there was no For Sale or For Rent
sign on the property, seeming to suggest that she had not
carried through with the plan for some reason.

Of course, signs go missing and the nearby river was surely
a temptation for any passing halfwit who might think it was
funny to uproot the estate agents board. With that in mind,
even though I didn't really believe it for a minute, I spent the

next hour checking the websites of every estate agent and property company in the city to assure myself that none of them had any listing for Jennifer's Willow Drive love nest.

I sat back, staring at the screen but not really seeing it. I had to admit that I was running out of options. I mailed an update to my client, along with a reminder to send me that list of friends and acquaintances he'd promised. Then, lacking any other ideas, I reached for Jennifer's scrapbook. Perhaps there was some scrap of reminiscence caught between its pages that might suggest a new line of enquiry.

The first thing that struck me was the hand-written inscription on the fly leaf, written in a neat, feminine hand that I recognised belonged to Jennifer herself. The black ink was fading slightly with age, in keeping with the well-stressed spine and dog-eared pages that suggested that it had been opened many times over the years. The words of the epigraph were as familiar to me, though far more benign in nature, than the Milton quote in the paperback novel.

Memory
Turn your face to the moonlight
Let your memory lead you
Open up, enter in
If you find there
The memory of what happiness is
Then a new life will begin

If not happiness itself then perhaps the lingering shadows of it lay within those pages, which on closer inspection was clearly a record of her experiences with the university drama society. It was soon apparent that it had played a big part in her life. The pattern seemed to amount to one major production per term plus various one-off entertainments for high days and holidays. Each production had its own page heading and the content included cast lists, production notes and photographs, reviews and programs. These were interspersed with personal photographs and brief biographies of individual cast members.

The first entry covered a one-off musical evening celebrating the work of Andrew Lloyd-Webber and pride of place went to a photograph of Jennifer as Grizabella, probably crooning the very song from which she had taken the epigraph. She must have been good to get such a major role as a freshman, I guessed, though the voice I remembered, husky with drink and sex, hadn't offered any clue to her vocal talents.

I felt myself growing a little warm at the memory and flipped the pages hurriedly. They told the story of a steady rise in status as Jennifer progressed through her college amateur theatrical career. In that first year, apart from Grizabella, it was mainly bit parts – Edna in An Inspector Calls, Cherry in The Beau Stratagem, Helen of Troy in Dr Faustus. In in her second and final years, however, she took on a succession of significant female roles. Dorian had mentioned her playing Ophelia and the lead in The Duchess of Malfi. In addition, she had taken on Cordelia in Lear, Nora in A Doll's House, Natasha in The Three Sisters, Andromache in The Trojan Women and Lilli Vanessi in Kiss Me Kate.

The accompanying reviews showed that she had been marked down from the start as an actress of genuine talent and a stage presence that shone through even the drabbest on-stage persona. It appeared that she had possessed that elusive thing called 'star quality', at least within the admittedly restricted sphere of the university drama set. More than one reviewer suggested that she might one day transcend that limited setting to shine on a larger stage.

That had never happened. Instead she had married Jensen and thereby apparently surrendered any personal dreams she might have harboured to help him pursue and fulfil his ambitions. She must have really loved him, poor fashion judgement and all, though it was trade off she might have eventually come to regret, I supposed.

I closed the book, feeling the treacherous undertow of nostalgia dragging at my spirits, a literal, if ill-defined aching in the soul compounded of my own failures and unrealised aspirations. *Wither is it fled that visionary gleam. Where is it now, the glory and the dream?*

I turned back to the front of the book and began to go through it again. I took care to read the content on every page, making notes of any names I came across as I went. It was slow, painstaking work made more laborious by the unshakeable feeling that I was simple going through the motions It didn't help that a quick Internet check revealed that currently the Durham Student Theatre had over 700 members. It was probably less than that in Jennifer's time, but membership was still substantial even then and the reviews and cast lists in Jennifer's scrapbook mentioned only the names of the actors and directors of each production. That left an anonymous array of back stage talent, stage hands lighting engineers and the like who might have been close friends with the talented young student actress.

I didn't hold out much hope that I was going to glean much from the exercise but then, three or four pages into the task I came across a name I recognised. That section of the scrapbook was dedicated to the final production of Jennifer's first year: a much-praised version of Marlowe's Dr Faustus. (It's magic! declared the headline from the Durham Times, who had apparently hired the late Paul Daniels as a reviewer for that night) Jennifer, as I had noted earlier, took the part of Helen of Troy – a famous but very minor non-speaking role that acknowledged both her beauty and her status within the company.

The scene in which Mephistopheles conjures Helen is probably the most well-known of the play, if only because of Faustus's memorable line about 'the face that launched a thousand ships'. It was not surprising that the photographs chosen to accompany the review featured this memorable theatrical moment, with Jennifer front and centre. In a bold directorial move, she was dressed not as some compliant, sexual trophy wife but in a breast plate and leather skirt that re-invented her character as a capable but still sexy warrior-princess: Xena of Troy.

By contrast Faustus looked effete, if not downright effeminate, in a silk dressing gown that looked like a leftover from *The Trials of Oscar Wilde*, as he stood with open arms to receive the anticipated embrace of mythology's most beautiful woman. Tellingly, Helen stood with her arms down, the fingers of one hand resting inside the waistband of her skirt, while the other toyed with the ornate handle of the short sword she wore at her left side. Her face was beautiful but her expression ambiguous, caught somewhere between sadness and an almost-tenderness that could have been regret. Whether for her own fate or that of Faustus yet-to-come.

It was an iconic moment in the play and one that clearly enthralled the reviewer, who praised "the unexpected depth that Jennifer Lawson brought to the role, taking it beyond the stock portrayal of a beautiful, vacuous puppet to project the living, breathing, liberated woman trapped within."

If all that was true she really must have been a hell of an actress but at that moment it was Faustus who really demanded my attention, or rather the actor who played the doomed scholar "with a manic, entrepreneurial vigour."

His name was Ellis Thatcher, once briefly my boss in his role as founder and CEO of Delphic Security, which also happened to be the parent company of Stentor Alarms. I'd wondered all along how Jennifer had happened to end up working there. Being an old college friend of the boss might possibly have had something to do with it. Or maybe it was more than friendship? Maybe there was a DVD back at *Moorside* with tight close ups of his plunging buttocks on it, though I hoped not. I had plenty of reason to dislike Thatcher and the thought of him with Jennifer did nothing to mellow my attitude to him. It was a possibility I had to recognise and follow up, much as the idea repelled me.

Despite my personal animosity towards Thatcher finding a new lead to follow energised me. I worked through the rest of the scrapbook with renewed purpose. At the end of the exercise I had a list of almost fifty names to work through, though none of them leapt out at me with the same impact as Thatcher did. They would be checked out anyway, though that was a job for the morning, when Clegg and Eddie were around to help.

I didn't intend to wait that long before fronting Ellis Thatcher, though. He wasn't on my Christmas card list, but my old friend Ben Cross remained on reasonable terms with him after Thatcher bought out Ben's company. They even played golf together occasionally. I knew Ben would put the two of us together if I asked him and I dug my mobile out of my pocket.

In the end I didn't make the call, though. I saw at once that I had received a message from Glenn Wood. It was timed about fifteen minutes earlier and though it didn't say much it certainly got my attention.

Need to see you. Now!

It was short and to the point, but its very terseness transmitted a sense of urgency. My first thought was that Wood had discovered something about Jennifer's disappearance but, if that was the case, why did he want a face to face meeting? I certainly didn't have any great desire to see him again and I would have been surprised if he felt any differently. If he had information to pass on the simplest option would surely have been to call me. Just in case I'd somehow missed such a call I checked my phone log but there was nothing.

I dialled his mobile number, only for the call to go through to voicemail. I disconnected without leaving a message, wondering why he wasn't answering the phone he'd so recently messaged me from. There were probably any number of reasonable explanations, but that rationalisation did nothing to allay the sense of uneasiness that had been growing steadily since I began the search for Jennifer Jensen. Something was wrong about the whole business and I couldn't shake the feeling that the unexpected, cryptic text from Wood was just another part of that 'wrongness.' That didn't mean I wasn't going to respond to it, of course, but the thought gave me pause and I considered calling Eddie and his Louisville Slugger just as a precaution.

In the end, I decided against it. Whether I was being stubborn or stupid only time would tell.

14.

Before I left the office, I sent a short text to say I was on my way. When I arrived half an hour later the electronic gates to Glenn Wood's demesne stood open, suggesting, at least, that my message had been received.

Beyond the entrance a long, sweeping, tree-lined driveway opened out into an expansive, paved parking area illuminated by spotlights mounted on a double garage to the left of the house. This was a three storey, early 20th century build that had undergone some essential re-modelling, adding the security and economy of modern double glazing to its original period opulence. It sat amongst extensive lawns, hemmed with ash and birch trees, the outliers of extensive woodland stretching off into the darkness at the rear of the house.

The doors of the garage were closed but a black Volvo XC60 stood on the forecourt. Apart from the exterior lighting there were lights on in the ground floor part of the house, but no obvious signs of life were visible through any of the windows as I walked round to the front door. From some distance away, I could see that this stood slightly ajar and light spilled out from within onto the front terrace. Through the partially open door I could see a small portion of polished, hardwood floor and hear the faint sound of music from deeper in the house. I took out my phone and speed dialled Wood's number. I let it ring without answer for a few seconds then lowered it to my side, straining my ears to catch any sound of it ringing within the house. I heard nothing and put the phone back to my ear, let it ring until it went to voice mail then killed the call. I moved a little closer to the open door.

"Wood? Are you there?" I called out tentatively. There was no response. No response. "It's Webster. You messaged me? Hello?" Still nothing other than the faint strains of music, a classical tune I vaguely recognised but couldn't put a name to. I called out again:

"Wood? Are you okay? "

"Hello? Is somebody there?"

The reply startled me, a querulous voice, perhaps even a little afraid, but not the voice of Glenn Wood.

"Yes." I answered. "My name's Webster. I'm a private investigator. Here to see Mr Wood?"

There was a pause, the sound of hurried footsteps on the wooden floor, then the half open door was drawn all the way back. I found myself face to face with a man of medium height and indeterminate age. A stranger to me and yet vaguely familiar, like that tune.

He had a neatly trimmed black beard in which a few strands of grey were beginning to show. The brown eyes that looked at me uncertainly did so from behind a pair of spectacles with heavy, black frames. He was wearing a long dark navy overcoat that, together with the grey trilby that sat firmly on his head, gave the impression that he was either just leaving or had just arrived.

"An investigator – a private detective?" he queried. "To see Glenn, you say?"

"Yes - and yes." I said. "Is he not here? I had a text from him about an hour ago asking me to meet with him. I haven't been able to contact him since. He doesn't seem to be answering his phone."

He frowned, pushing back his glasses with the index finger of his right hand.

"That doesn't sound like Glenn. He never strays far without his phone. But are you sure he meant to see you tonight? He never mentioned that anyone else was going to be here."

"I think it was a spur of the moment invitation." I said. "Mr - ?"

"What? Oh – sorry, how impolite of me." he held out a pale, well-manicured hand and I shook it. His palm was dry and cold in mine. "Black. Donald Black. I'm Glenn's agent –

but where are my manners! Please come in. It smells rather chilly out there. I don't think Glenn would mind if we had something to warm us up while we wait."

Without waiting for an answer Black turned away and I stepped after him, closing the door behind me. I found myself in a wide entrance hall with timber panelling and flooring. Directly opposite the front door a wide staircase curved up to the second floor. There were rooms immediately to the left and right as you came through the door and on either side of the staircase.

Black walked confidently across the entrance hall and towards the room to the right of the stairs, from which subdued lighting spilled out through the open door. The music came from there too, growing louder as we approached. A lively Baroque tune that the real Sir Francis Dashwood might have hummed in his bath.

I followed Black into a big, high ceilinged space with windows along one side and fitted walnut bookshelves running the length of another. An impressive wet bar took up most of a third side of the room, whose central space was filled with comfortable leather furniture. A few small tables were placed around the room to show off various items: photographs, lamps and other small antiques and, on one, a striking Staunton chess set with gold and silver-plated figures replacing the traditional black and white. At least, I assumed they were just plated.

The fourth wall was dominated by a large plasma screen, the centre piece of a wall length unit that also housed a DVR, satellite box, a Bang & Olufsen CD and media player and several shelves packed tight with DVDs and compact discs.

Black seemed quite at home there. He shed his overcoat, revealing the impeccably tailored black suit beneath it. He draped the top coat over the back of a brown leather sofa, placing his hat on top of it. Then, waving me graciously towards a second couch set at right angles to its twin, he strolled over to the wet bar.

"Now, how about that drink?" he said, as he scanned the well-stocked shelves.

On the area of wall to the left of the bar there were more framed memorabilia and photographs. I wandered over to check them out. There were stills from Wood's various hit reality shows mingled with the usual vanity shots: Wood playing golf with Lee Westwood, sweaty and grinning as he plodded round the London Marathon, looking thoughtful in a tuxedo at some awards dinner, unbearably smug by the side of a tidy looking blonde actress from Emmerdale, sharing a blokey pint with Jeremy Clarkson at the Smug Bastard of the Year Awards. (I made that up.) Of the wife that Eddie may or may not have slept with there was no sign. She was literally and figuratively not in the picture, having divorced Wood a couple of years earlier on the grounds of mental cruelty, according to Eddie. Probably made her watch endless re-runs of his trashy programmes, I thought.

Black finally arrived at a decision and reached down a bottle.

"How would this suit you?" he enquired, passing it over to me. It was a 17-year-old double wood Balvennie; a single malt that sold for around £80 a 70-centilitre bottle. Not the stuff you usually gave out to Wassailers, carol singers or strange private investigators you've only just met. Still, I suppose we can all afford to be generous with someone else's whisky.

"It'll do in a pinch." I said, and he brought over a couple of nosing glasses from the bar, holding them out to me in his gloved hands.

"You can be mother." he said and watched appreciatively as I twisted off the top and poured us each a generous dram.

I carried mine, along with the bottle, over to the sofa he had indicated and sat down, savouring a mouthful of the malt's spicy, honeyed tones. I set the bottle down on the small coffee table that sat by the side of the sofa. There was already a glass sitting there; a heavyweight tumbler with a couple of inches of something a shade or two darker than the Balvennie still left in it. Unable to resist, I picked it up and sniffed the contents, getting a hit of the unmistakeable smokiness of a Lagavulin. A bit too peaty for my preference but, still, not a drink that a real whisky drinker would willingly leave unfinished. I wondered what might have induced Wood to do so.

I set the glass down again and glanced across at Black, who had settled himself comfortably at one end of the other couch. He seemed to have been watching me intently and met my look with a brief, embarrassed smile as he pulled off his gloves and set them on the arm of his seat.

"Sorry – I've never seen a real life private detective before. Let alone one as celebrated as yourself. You are that Harry Webster, aren't you?"

"Original and best." I said. "Accept no substitutes."

"I thought the name was familiar – but I didn't recognise you at first, the light wasn't so good at the front door."

"Believe me, I don't mind people not recognising me."

"Your modesty does you credit but I imagine it happens quite a lot."

"Not as much as you might think." I said. "My 'brief hour' was over a long time ago."

"You need a good agent." he joked.

"What I really need is to see Glenn Wood." I said, anxious to get off the topic of my lingering celebrity. "You say you're supposed to meet him here? At what time?"

"Oh..." he looked at his watch. "Well, now-ish, I suppose. We didn't fix a specific time, Glenn just asked me to drop by in the early evening."

"And what time did you get here?"

"Hmm..." He wagged a finger at me. "You know, if I didn't know better I'd think I was being interrogated."

"Force of habit." I smiled.

"Well, to answer the question I arrived perhaps ten minutes before you did. I was a little surprised to find he wasn't around, I'll admit. Enough to carry out a quick check to make sure he hadn't had a heart attack in the bath or something like that. Thankfully not. The thought of seeing Glenn naked was not a prospect I relished."

"Or dead?" I suggested.

"Or dead, indeed! Very good." He frowned. "But, seriously, should one be concerned by Glenn's absence?"

146

Was I concerned? I considered Black's question. The answer was: perhaps a little. The peremptory text, the unanswered phone calls, the half-full whisky glass, the open front door, the CD left playing. They were little things on their own but add them together and they added up to – what?

I laid out these points for Black and he nodded along in apparent sympathy.

"My goodness! What a true detective's mind you have! To see all these connections so clearly. The little oddities and discrepancies that mean nothing in isolation. Yet, put them together and they do sound a vaguely dissonant note. I do think I can put your mind at rest on one point at least, I'm afraid the open front door is my fault. I keep a set of Glenn's keys in case of emergency. When he didn't answer the door, I let myself in and I clearly failed to close it properly behind me. The Queen of Sheba's down to me as well."

That threw me for a second but then it clicked.

"The music."

"Indeed, I do like my Handel. I was about to pour myself a stiff one and bathe in his splendour when I heard you call out."

"There you go then. There's probably a reasonable explanation for the other dissonances too." I said, trying to convince myself as much as reassure Black. Not that he seemed much in need of reassurance.

"You say you were surprised not to find him at home?" I asked.

Black stroked his goatee thoughtfully, took a swallow of his drink. Taking his time, as if weighing up the value of every word. Perhaps they taught them that at Agent School.

"A little nonplussed, yes." he confirmed at length. "Though you must understand that Glenn is unconventional and impulsive. He always tends to act entirely in his own self-interest. If he took it in his head do something off schedule, then he's quite likely to just do it and disregard any previous arrangements."

"Any idea what that something might be?"

Black smiled thinly.

147

"Oh – well… How to put it? Glenn has certain appetites."

"You think he slipped out for a Big Mac?" I suggested.

"I think you know exactly what I mean, Mr Webster."

"Club business?" I hazarded but if he knew what I was getting at he didn't show it. "A woman?"

"As I said – appetites." Black repeated with a knowing smirk that seemed disconcertingly familiar for some reason.

I thought about what he was saying. I had no problem believing that Wood liked sex to the point of addiction but all the same…

I took my phone out of my pocket and checked the message again. It was timed at 18:15. It was now just after half past seven, which meant that Black had got there about a quarter past.

"You got here about an hour after Wood messaged me. Are you're thinking that in that brief window something -?"

"Arose?" Black completed with nimble irony.

"Came up, that is occurred -" I amended, not wanting to get sucked into a duel of double entendres. "- that caused him to rush out of the house without finishing his glass of very expensive whisky or making any attempt to contact either of us to put us off?"

Black swirled his own glass of very expensive whisky and took another drink before answering.

"Needs must." I suppose. "Though I do agree that the timing seems a little curious. His well-known lack of consideration for others – not so much. What was it Dostoevsky said: 'let the world go to hell but I should always have my tea.'?"

Which seemed a fair enough assessment of Wood's character from what I'd gleaned on my own brief acquaintance with him. Maybe I was just over-reacting. I knew little enough about Wood after all. He was separated from his wife, I knew, but there could be other people he would always place above the rest if they reached out to him. After all, most of us have at least one person in our lives that command our unconditional loyalty. He could just have been called away by a family emergency, or perhaps an unexpected phone call from a troubled friend, as he sat drinking his premium whisky and killing time while Black and I arrived.

As I thought about that possibility my eyes fell again on the unfinished glass of spirit and the remote unit on the table beside it. I picked it up absently. It was one of those expensive all-in-one remotes that operated all the devices. It had a bewildering array of buttons in addition to a small touch screen that gave instant access to the most important functions. According to the information in the window the last operation performed involved the sleek, black DVD recorder that was hooked up to the plasma TV.

Curiosity got the better of me and I turned the remote towards the TV and pressed the standby button. The red light at the bottom corner of the set turned to blue and after a few seconds the set came to life and a brief message appeared at the top of an otherwise blank screen, identifying the input on that channel as the DVR.

I tapped the 'Play' command on the touch screen. After a view seconds of nothing obvious happening the low murmur of many intercut voices came from the speakers, though the screen remained blank. The volume of the babble gradually increased but it was not possible to pick out any distinct voices or identify any coherent sentences. The screen gradually brightened, and a picture finally crystallised of a gathering of maybe thirty people, standing at rapt attention in the body of a medium sized hall. Every one of them was stark naked but for the variety of garish masks that covered their features!

.

15.

Some were simple domino masks covering only the top half of the face, whilst others were more elaborate: fantastic, winged, leather constructions or flamboyant ball masks stylised to evoke the look of birds or animals. Cats were the most popular, but I noted a couple of peacocks, a wolf here, a fox there, even an elephant, as well as several Venetian style jester masks and character masks from the commedia del arte. Scarammucia, with the long proboscis seemed to be particularly popular amongst the men. After all, you know what they say about men with big noses.

The focus of this strange congregation was a couple standing side by side before a tall, black pulpit. It was designed in the form of a bird, wings outstretched, beak wide open, fierce eyed. A raven or a crow perhaps, some bird of ill-omen anyway, carved in exquisite mockery of the screaming eagles favoured in Christian churches around the world. From their respective rear views, it looked like the duo were a man and a woman, also masked and otherwise naked. Their head were tilted slightly upwards to focus on the figure behind the lectern.

Music was playing, something antique and unfamiliar, but this dwindled into an expectant kind of silence that was abruptly shattered by the sound of a gong being struck once, twice, then a third time. As its reverberations died away and silence fell with a rush on the room a single figure emerged from out of shot and took up position behind the strange pulpit. This was another male judging by his smooth, flat chest. His features were obscured by a gold-coloured mask depicting the lascivious, god Bacchus, the eerily blank face capped by golden grapes and golden leaves in lieu of hair. While one hand held the edge of the pulpit, the other reached

out towards the two figures standing before him. With the
middle two fingers tucked beneath the thumb, he extended
the index and little fingers to form the sign of the 'horned
hand' familiarly associated with ageing rock stars and
Aleister Crowley wannabes all over the world.

"In Nomine Dei Nostri Satanas Luciferi Excelsi! In the
name of Satan, I call upon the powers of Darkness and the
infernal power within! Consecrate this place with the power,
love and light of the Lord of Hellfire. Join with us to
welcome Sister Kamala into our brazen ranks through her
union with our honoured master Brother Eleutherios, binding
her in word and flesh to the Fellowship of the Friars and
Sisters of St Francis Redux."

"In the names of Venus and Bacchus welcome her into our
embrace and bless our Sister in the name of the infernal gods:
Amon, Astaroth, Ishtar, Bast, Lilith, Pan, Asmodeus, Thoth
and in the name of He who is Lord of All, the Bringer of
Light"

At this point he paused to take up a single red candle from
the pulpit, raising it towards the camera.

"I call upon the element of fire to bless us, for we are Satan.
We ask that you rouse the passion of Sister Kamala that she
may know the all-consuming ardor of unfettered lust."

Now he turned to the East and raised the candle in that
direction.

"I call upon the element of the air to bless us, for we are
Lucifer! Awake in Sister Kamala the wisdom and unified
vision of our fellowship."

Next, he swung to the North, turning his back to the
congregation. The camera angle changed to give a brief, full
frontal view of Bacchus before zooming in for a close-up of
the figures before the altar. Jennifer – Sister Kamala – was
wearing a half face mask of purple velvet, decorated with a
single, purple bloom amidst a spray of black feathers above
the right eye. The male figure standing to her right, in the
traditional groom's position, was presumably Glenn Wood in
his Brother Eleutherios guise. His mask was that of a horned
and leering Satan. While the camera lingered on the happy
couple, the presiding figure's voice continued with the

151

John Seeley

invocation

"We call upon the element of the earth to come serve us, for we are Belial! We ask that you fill our Sister with your boundless love and lust for life."

The screen split now to show Bacchus alongside the happy couple, turning with his candle to the west.

"We call upon the element of water to serve us, for we are Baphomet, the leaping goat. We ask you to free our Sister from the chains of pale morality that ensnare her and lead her boldly into the blessed light of liberty."

He turned to face the couple again, setting the candle back on the pulpit before him. He picked something else up and, coming from behind the great black bird he stepped down off the makeshift stage. He was now holding a piece of black ribbon that he held out before him in both hands.

"Sister Kamala with this cord I bind you to our master, Brother Eleutherios and to the sinful order of St Francis"

As he spoke he used the cord to bind together the man's left hand and Jennifer's right.

"Hereby the energy of Babalon, the Great Mother; boundless, dark, intuitive, and soft, blends with the energy of Satan; expansive, bright, logical and hard. By this symbolic union you are welcomed to the infernal ranks of the Fellowship. Repeat after me the sacred vow that guides us all. Do what thou wilt shall be the whole of the law. Love is the law. Love under will."

Jennifer response was word perfect, her voice clear and strong, leaving no room for doubt.

"Do you swear to live by this rule and by the will of the Fellowship to do no harm to Brother or Sister in the pursuit of that goal?"

"I swear in the name of Ishtar and Tammuz and by the names of all the sacred lovers since time began."

"So mote it be. In their name and in the name of the Anointed Covering Cherub. We make you welcome to the circle of Hellfire that it may burn away all doubt and inhibition in the pursuit of earthly pleasure. Ou'est ce tu voudra!

His voice rose on the last phrase and it was picked up as

one by the whole gathering. It was repeated in ever rising tones as it rolled around the room for long seconds until Bacchus raised his arms and the chant died instantly on everybody's lips. The figure in the golden mask laid his hands upon the bride and groom. Solemnly untying the cord, he held it up before the gathering and spoke again.

"The work of joy is done and yet begun! Let the revels begin!"

What that implied I decided was best left to the imagination. Watching the mock wedding ceremony was an experience that was uncomfortable and yet oddly compelling, in the way even the most self-conscious rituals can seem to the observer. For myself I'd seen enough of the inner workings of the Hellfire Club or The New Order of St Francis of Whippem or whatever they called themselves. I stopped the DVD, switched off the TV and tossed the remote aside.

"Is that what Glenn asked you here to see?"

The sound of Donald Black's voice startled me. In the intensity of the last few minutes I'd completely forgotten he was there. I glanced across at him. He was raising his glass to drink but it didn't quite mask the sardonic smile that accompanied his words.

It could have been. I doubted that it was just a coincidence that a DVD of what was clearly Jennifer's initiation into the Hellfire Club should be in the DVR. Maybe there was something on the video that had triggered a useful memory or suggested a possible a clue to Jennifer's whereabouts?

"It's not my kind of thing." I said. "Did you see anyone you recognised?"

The question seemed to amuse him.

"How do you imagine I could tell? I don't know Glenn or any of my clients that well!"

"You're not in the Club then?"

"I'm sure I don't know what you're talking about."

"Fair enough." I said and took an appreciative sip of my drink, studying him closely. He met my gaze frankly.

"Best spit it out, wouldn't want you to choke on it." he said.

"Sorry?"

"Your antennae seem to be quivering as if I've made some misstep. Enlighten me."

"Your own antennae are pretty acute too." I acknowledged. "It's just a small thing but when I asked about the Club somebody who was really ignorant about it would have asked 'What club?'."

"Ah! Yes, you've got me. You're quite right, I am aware of the sad, tawdry little coven that Glen calls his Hellfire Club. Being aware and being involved are not interchangeable terms, however."

"Not invited?"

"Not interested." he bridled. "Group sex is so 1960s, don't you think?"

"You prefer solitary pursuits?"

"My preferences are not for you to know." he said primly.

"Killjoy was here!" I said, trying to decide if I believed him when he said he wasn't one of Dash's group. With his portly frame and thick glasses he certainly didn't look like a sexual athlete – or indeed an athlete of any kind – and his disapproval seemed genuine enough.

"So – you really have no idea where Wood might have gone?" I said, changing the subject.

"Perhaps a last-minute orgy came up." he said facetiously.
I smiled obligingly.

"If you don't mind me saying so: you don't seem to like your client very much, Mr Black."

"Believe me, in my business it's not obligatory to like the people you represent. It can even be a handicap."

"Wood does strike me as being hard to like."

"He's a born showman. He's venal, shallow and insincere – but he has his faults too."

He smiled at me. I smiled back. Drank more whisky.

"For what's worth I don't imagine he intends to be gone long."

"Because -?"

"If he was going to be out for any length of time he would have set the alarm. It didn't trigger when I let myself in."

"Quite the detective yourself, it seems." I said.

He raised his glass towards me in an ironic toast. I returned it, took another generous sip. It was nectar on my tongue, almost worth the trip out here just for that. Almost. I considered my glass and thought briefly about asking for a top up, decided against it. I wasn't inclined to hang around too much longer waiting for Wood to show up. His absence and my inability to contact him worried me more than a little but worrying was something I could do anywhere. I decided that if he had not returned by the time I'd finished my drink I'd leave – but I didn't intend to go empty handed.

I reached for the remote again, located and pressed the 'Eject' command. The DVD tray opened with a mechanical whirr and I walked across the room to remove the disc, casting around for a case to put it in.

"Should you really be taking that?" Black wondered sternly.

"Well, if he misses it, tell him he can always report the theft to the police."

"Ha! I might just do that, if only to see the look on his face!" Black smiled. "Do you really think it's evidence of anything other than a fatuous sense of theatre?"

"There may be something on it that will help with the matter I'm looking into, yes." I said,

That wasn't my real motive for taking it, though. The fact is I just didn't like the thought of Wood being able to sit there leering at his mock marriage to Jennifer and its inevitable aftermath whenever he felt like it. Taking the DVD was probably a futile gesture – for all I knew it could just be a copy and the original could be stored on his computer hard drive or drifting somewhere in the Cloud. There was also the possibility that Jennifer had enjoyed every minute of the experience but, nonetheless, it was a gesture it seemed right to make.

I spotted a plain black disc case on one of the shelves of the media centre and picked it up. It felt light enough to be empty but when I prised it open, something slid out and drifted to the carpet. It landed about an arm's length from Black's left foot and he leaned over and picked it up. It was a rectangular piece of thin cardboard and I could see there was a distinctive blue pattern on the side that faced upwards, like what you might see on the reverse of a playing card. From the look on Black's face, however, the obverse was clearly less innocuous.

"What is it?" I asked.

"You tell me." he said, holding it out to me as distastefully as if it were a dead rat.

I took it from him and flipped it. The dominant image on the card was that of a bearded figure with pointed ears and curved goat's horns sprouting from his head. From the waist up the figure had the naked torso of a man, with bat-wings spread behind him. Below the waist his lower limbs were those of a goat, except that his feet were not hooves but talons. In the figure's left hand was clutched a burning torch, the flame pointing downwards. The right hand was empty, palm facing outwards, right elbow resting on a hairy thigh. The figure crouched on a black cube with a single silver ring set into it, anchored to which by chains were two other figures, one male, one female, both human but for the horns that they too were crowned with. At the top of the card was the Roman numeral XV and, at the bottom, writ large and somewhat superfluously were the words: The Devil. I recognised it immediately for what it was.

"It's from a tarot deck." I said.

"Ah, that is a relief. I thought it might be a mock-up of Glenn's new business card!"

It was an amusing thing to say but I didn't much feel like laughing. The image on the card was quite crudely done but powerful and disturbingly evocative of the events we'd just seen on the screen. Perhaps that was why it had been in the DVD case in the first place; a shorthand reminder of the disc's contents. Then again, maybe it signified something else entirely. It was the second time in just a few hours that I'd encountered not so subtle images of the Devil – three if you counted Wood in his Satan mask. I found the coincidence – if that's what it was - more than a little unsettling

"Glenn's a fool to mess with such things." Black said with a degree of contempt in his voice. "Surely, nothing good can come of such dabbling?"

"I suppose that's the whole point." I said.

Black frowned at that and suddenly came over all concerned.

"Do you think -?"

"What?"

"Well – I mean – the people on that video – who knows what kind of psychopaths might be hiding behind those masks? Do you think Glenn might have -? Could one of them -? Should we inform the police, do you think?"

"And tell them what? That Glenn Wood's been away from home for all of an hour and insulted a glass of Lagavulin by leaving it unfinished when he left?"

"Ah, quite. Sorry, over-reaction. Tell you the truth I found that bloody video more than a little unsettling."

I sympathised. It was certainly more creepy than salacious – and he had a point about the masks. Faces weren't all they could hide.

"Well, at least you won't be tempted to look at it again." I said, slipping the DVD case into my jacket pocket.

"I'd burn it first!" he said, with a vehemence that startled me. Then, realising that perhaps he'd shown me more of himself than he would have liked he had a quick sip of his drink and glanced at the chunky watch on his left hand. Taking it as a cue I finished my own drink and stood up to go.

"You off? I'll hang on a bit longer." he said. "If he's not here by eight o'clock he can go hang."

"I'm sure you won't get lonely while the Balvennie holds out." I said, nodding at the bottle. "If Wood does get back remind him that the clock's ticking. He'll know what that means."

Black toasted me again with his now almost empty glass.

"Got it." he assured me. "He shall be told: time runs, the clock will strike!"

I thanked him with a brief nod and headed for the door. His parting words played in my head all the way back to the car and halfway to the city before it finally sank in that Black had quoted part of Dr Faustus's final, terrified soliloquy from Marlowe's famous play. If I recalled correctly, the complete line read: *the stars run still, time runs, the clock will strike, the Devil will come, and Faustus must be damned.*

16.

The darkness is almost palpable, thick and clinging and seemingly endless. I move through it as if through deep water, half-swimming against an implacable tide. I hear a drumbeat in my ears, rapid and persistent, pounding out a rhythm that is like a vibration of pure terror; the sound of my heartbeat sending the blood roaring through my veins in a black torrent that threatens to overwhelm me.

I feel as if I'm literally drowning in fear of some nameless horror. It pursues me with a fiercely relentless tread; a devil at my back reaching out to clutch me with fingers that are knives of bone slashing at the darkness. I feel the hot breath of its undying hatred on the back of my neck. I hear his voice rasping through bony lips that struggle to articulate all the thwarted fury that died with him. The words bubble like acid, scarring the enveloping darkness as I stumble and fall, twisting onto my back to look up at that so familiar skeletal figure, the bleached phantom of my deepest nightmares, as it screams: "If the devil did ever take good shape behold his picture!"

I woke with a sudden gasp, like a drowning man lunging from the depths of a murky river with his last breath. My hair and torso were soaked with sweat, and my heart was a mad engine running out of control. The pain in my left shoulder was back; the knife of memory twisting in a phantom wound. For a few seconds I remained confused and disoriented; the ragged fog of the dream clouding coherent thought. Unsure of where I was, I looked around me, trying to pin down some familiar landmark to which I could anchor my shaky consciousness.

The first thing I recognised was the Neal Adams Batman

print that hung on the wall opposite. I realised then that I was at home in my own bed, which looked like I'd spent the night wrestling with an unvanquishable foe. I seemed to have survived, though, and as that thought sank in I collapsed back gratefully onto the pillows. I regretted it immediately as even that mild impact sent ripples of pain through my shoulder. I lay there for a few seconds, gently massaging it, while the last vestiges of my latest nightmare dissolved in the pale light of morning that seeped around the edges of the curtains.

I roused and dragged myself to the bathroom. Ten minutes in a shower as hot as I could stand it seemed to ease the ache in my shoulder and I felt barely a twinge as I dressed. Nonetheless I swallowed a couple of ibuprofen to smooth out any remaining discomfort. By the time I'd drunk two cups of coffee and eaten a three-egg omelette with two slices of toast I was more or less awake, alert and focused on the day ahead.

As I left the house the sun was beginning to burn through the lingering early morning mist that lurked between the houses. It was not yet half past seven and there was a fresh, unopened feeling about the quiet streets. The morning gridlock was still a good half an hour from tightening its grip fully on the city and I reached the office in less than twenty minutes without having to swear once.

Despite the earliness of the hour I was the last one in. Clegg and Eddie were both already at their desks looking busy. We exchanged cheerful 'Good mornings' and I left them to get on with it while I made a coffee and settled at my terminal to check my emails. There was still nothing from Callum Jensen, though. I reached for the phone and called him again but just got the automated brush off. I left another clipped message and hung up, reasoning that perhaps his phone could be switched off because he was sitting on some panel at the conference. All the same, his lack of response to my previous efforts to contact him was starting to seriously niggle me. Just how seriously was he really taking the disappearance of his soon-to-be-ex-wife?

The hitch in communications with the client also served to remind me that Glenn Wood was being annoyingly elusive. I picked up the phone again and dialled his home number and his cell with no better luck than I'd enjoyed last night.

"Everything okay, H?" Eddie queried, looking up sharply from his terminal.

"What?"

"I thought you said something."

"Did I?" Swearing under my breath probably, I thought. "Just thinking out loud."

"About this Jennifer Jensen business?" Clegg ventured. "Sorry – couldn't help overhearing your rather strained message to our client's voice mail. There's been no progress, I take it?"

"There is something." I admitted and filled them in about the text from Glenn Wood and my subsequent visit to his home. They reacted visibly, sharing a look that telegraphed a shared concern.

"You went to Wood's place on your own?" Eddie said. "After all we talked about yesterday? That wasn't very smart, H. What if that text was just bait to get you out there? Bojangles and his mate could've been standing by to give you a good kicking!"

"Bojan." I corrected automatically.

"Huh?"

"The bug hunter from yesterday? His name is Bojan not Bojangles."

"Yeah? Well, I bet he's tap danced on a few faces all the same."

I allowed this was a strong possibility but if Wood was after payback for outing his little sex club I doubted that he would have designated his home as the venue – or anywhere else so obviously connected to him. This drew grudging agreement, but Eddie and Clegg remained convinced I wasn't fit to be let out on my own.

"You should've called me, anyway." Eddie grumbled.

"I concur." Clegg agreed. "You should have notified Edward or myself, if only so someone knew where you were going in case -"

He didn't elaborate. We all knew what he meant. Going it alone had nearly got me killed more than once in the last few years. I didn't have to anymore, but the cycle of stubborn, self-dependence was hard to break.

"Well, clearly in this case there was no cause for concern." Clegg said diplomatically. "What did the fatuous Friar Dashwood have to say?"

"Wasn't there – and I haven't been able to contact him since." I admitted.

Clegg pursed his lips thoughtfully. When he spoke, his words were like an echo of something Donald Black had said.

"Hmm – in my experience people in Wood's line of business never stray too far from their mobile phones. They are virtually an extension of the individual's personality. Am I alone in thinking his continued silence a little ominous?"

"Could be he's been partying all night with his Hellfire buddies." Eddie pointed out. "They'd turn their phones off, wouldn't they? Wouldn't want to risk having the mood spoilt on the vinegar stroke or risk their GPS app giving the location away."

"You'd obviously given serious thought on hosting the perfect orgy." I congratulated him. "You could be right – then again maybe he just got cold feet after he sent the text and decided he didn't want to speak to me after all about whatever it was."

"The contents of that disk that's sitting on your desk, perhaps?" Clegg said shrewdly.

"Possibly." I agreed, describing briefly what it contained. "It's just badly shot soft porn. The mock wedding ceremony is a bit creepy, but Jennifer seems to be a willing enough party to it all – including the after-match debauch.

"I'll take a look if you like." Eddie said nonchalantly. "A fresh pair of eyes and all that. I might see something you missed."

"Or miss something you see." I said. "Trust me. After the Satanic vows are exchanged its nothing but a lot of sweaty people in masks exchanging bodily fluids. If Wood saw anything in it that's important the chances are it's something that only means something to him. It's just as likely that he was watching it for self-gratification."

"Do you think he's had every woman who joins the club?"

Eddie wondered, his tone half-curious, half-wistful.

"I would imagine that is how he seals the Satanic wedding contract." Clegg said. "Though it begs the question: who initiates the new male members? If you see what I mean"

It was not a problem I was inclined to waste too much time considering. Not so Eddie.

"Maybe he swings both ways." he suggested. "Like Woody Allen said: 'it doubles your chances of a date on Saturday night'".

"I don't care if he swings upside down from the chandelier." I said testily. "Wood's a game player. The text message, the DVD, the tarot card...they could all just be him trying to wind me up."

"Tarot card?" Clegg and Eddie spoke up almost simultaneously.

I explained about the card that had been inside the DVD case. I retrieved it from the top drawer of my desk and held it up for them to see. Eddie squinted across the room for a few seconds then hauled himself to his feet and walked over to take it from me. He regarded it solemnly for a few seconds then, shaking his head dismissively, he passed it over to Clegg.

"Our Bronson can draw better than that." he said. "And he's only five!"

That made Clegg smile, until he took hold of the card and got a good look at it. The smile slid off his face then, replaced by a look that was both thoughtful and distant.

"Le Diable." he said, almost to himself. His smile re-appeared, fleeting as a shooting star, as if some fond memory had glided momentarily across his cortex.

"That's French!" Eddie said. He made it sound like an accusation.

"Indeed – that is the card's designation in the Marseilles deck. Probably not the oldest of tarot designs but almost certainly the most influential and historically significant. Most subsequent decks tend to be modelled after the images in the Tarot de Marseilles – including this one."

He tapped the card in his hand for emphasis.

"I believe this is from a set known as the Rider-Waite deck, or sometimes the Rider-Waite-Smith. It's comparatively recent in conception – the first decade of the 20th century – but it is also one of the most popular."

"How do you know that shit?" Eddie asked, clearly impressed. "One of your old clients work the fairgrounds?"

"I am a child of the 60s, Edward." Clegg said. "There was a period in my student days when an interest in and a knowledge of 'that shit' opened certain – ahem – doors."

"Sweet." Eddie approved.

"It was love, Edward." Clegg said gravely. "It makes us all a little mad. *We that are true lovers run into strange capers.*"

"So – what does it mean?" Eddie asked.

"Love?"

"The card, Cleggy, the card. It tells a story, I guess."

"A part of one, certainly." Clegg agreed. "The journey from folly to wisdom – so some would say. A full tarot deck consists of 78 cards. 56 are broken into four traditional suits that are the precursors of the modern diamond, clubs, hearts and spades. In this deck the suits are cups, swords, pentacles and wands and these cards are known collectively as the Minor Arcana.

"The remaining 24 cards in the deck make up the Major Arcana, which aren't aligned to any of the suits. They are all picture cards showing complex images that, in a general sense, represent certain eternal principles, concepts and ideas. In an actual reading they are interpreted as specific people or forces that surround the subject.

"The Major Arcana are numbered from zero, which is the Fool to 21, the World. Each card represents a step along the road from ignorance to knowledge as the Fool evolves spiritually by meeting and overcoming various external and internal limitations. The Devil is the 15th step along that road. It signifies the persistent ignorance and hopelessness that anchors us to the material world. It represents a formidable obstacle on the way to enlightenment and breaking free of its influence is often a painful process of self-revelation initiated by a sudden crisis or great personal upheaval. Beat the Devil and it is largely downhill from there to achieving the successful re-integration of the disparate aspects of the initiates personality into a coherent, healthy and happy whole."

"That's cool!" Eddie said.

"No fool like a whole fool." I agreed. "But that card you're holding wasn't part of a spread. What does it mean on its own, Clegg?"

He frowned, turning the card over in his hands then laying it down on the desk top in front of him.

"It could just mean that Wood's not playing with a full deck." Eddie quipped.

"Indeed." Clegg smiled, then he continued: "You're right, Harry – there are certain key themes associated with this card. None very positive, though their impact can be softened, or indeed exacerbated, by the cards that fall around them in a reading. In isolation it signifies anger, jealousy and resentment, selfishness, violence and self-delusion. Most cards in the Major Arcana are about seeking balance and restraint – but not this one. It's all about revelling in extremity and excess. At its worst it can represent addiction or an unhealthy pre-occupation with something – or someone. It could refer to an addict, or a stalker, or someone who has surrendered completely to the impulse for excessive self-gratification and self-indulgence."

"Bad mojo." Eddie agreed. "That sort of sounds like Wood, though, doesn't it?"

I allowed that it did.

"Then perhaps it represents no more than a personal affectation." Clegg said. "A touch of vanity for a self-professed Devil. The image on the card does evoke something of the flavour of the video you describe, after all."

"Yes, that thought did occur to me. But then there's this…"

I held up the copy of *The Devil Rides Out* and explained how I'd found it in the bedroom at the bungalow in West Bretton.

"A coincidence?" Clegg said.

"Or a deliberate motif?" I suggested. "It was the only book in the place – and not typical of Jennifer's tastes in fiction judging from the shelves at her home. The dedication's a bit off too."

I opened the book and read out the inscription.

To be weak is miserable
Doing or suffering: but of this be sure
To do aught good never
Will be our task
But ever to do ill our
Sole delight

"Sounds like the introduction to the latest Tory manifesto." Eddie said.

"There's nothing warm and cuddly about it, certainly." Clegg agreed. "But is it evidence of anything more than juvenile poor taste? Didn't you say that her toy boy Dorian gave her a signed copy of a book about the original Hellfire Club? Couldn't this be just another relic of his recruitment drive?"

"I'm pretty sure the handwriting is different. I don't think Dorian wrote this – or Jennifer."

"Wood himself then? His idea of a mock wedding gift, perhaps? He is the leader of the new Hellfire Club, after all. It's surely not a stretch to believe that he might have something of an obsession with the Devil and all his works? You do know that the tarot deck is often referred to as the Devil's Picture Book? "

I did – and I didn't feel any less edgy for knowing it.

"I would have said that the only thing Wood is obsessed with is himself – but I take your point."

"Yeah, he's probably just trying to mess with your head." Eddie said.

Clegg looked as if he wanted to say something else, but he seemed to think better of it, dismissing the thought with a quick shake of the head.

"Is it any good?" Eddie asked. He had retrieved the book from my desk and was flicking through it idly.

"It scared the pants off me when I was 16." Clegg admitted wistfully.

"So – maybe Wood gives a copy to every woman he meets!" Eddie grinned.

We were interrupted by my mobile. I picked it up off the desk top and glanced at the screen. The caller ID said it was Glenn Wood.

"Speak of the devil." I said and accepted the call. "Webster speaking."

"Fucking hell!" was the response, uttered in a loud, proud and uncomfortably familiar Geordie accent. "I might have fucking known!"

17.

I hadn't had the pleasure of seeing Chief Inspector George
'Gloria' Swanson for over a year – which had been a
welcome respite for both of us, I suspect. The interval didn't
seem to have improved his notoriously short temper and his
favoured expression still lingered somewhere in the long
grass between a sneer and a glare.

Even without his trademark death glance he was an
intimidating figure' just a couple of inches short of six feet
with the build of a prop forward grown slightly flabby from
too many pints and pub pies. I guess he had probably been
good looking as a younger man, but the chiselled lineaments
of his youth had been scuffed and coarsened by hard times
and hard crimes. His once black hair was now more salt than
pepper, razored close to his skull and giving off a
disconcerting Abel Magwitch vibe. Somehow, I doubted that
he had summoned me here to Rain Hill nick to tell me he
was going to pay to put me through elocution classes,
though.

I was glad that I was accompanied by my own version of
the kindly lawyer Jagger in the shape of my friend and
sometime employer, Raphael Gainsborough. We were sitting
in Interview Suite 3, which was a claustrophobic hutch with
generic grey walls and a pale blue carpet. A single, well-used
table stood against one wall and Rafe and I sat on one side of
it facing Swanson and his sergeant, McKinley Ames, who
was busy unwrapping new tape cassettes and slotting them
into the twin-drive recorder that was set against the wall.
Swanson, meanwhile, sat looking at his phone and studiously
resisting any urge to exchange pleasantries.

"Sudoku?" I enquired.

He looked up irritably.

"You and your mouth." he said.

"Never leave home without it." I said.

He shook his head dismissively and went back to peering at his smart phone. Mac finished loading the tape decks and sat down. Swanson continued to fiddle with his mobile for a few seconds longer, just to let us know who was in charge, then turned it off and slapped it down on top of the buff-coloured folder that lay in front of him on the table top.

"Howay, Macca lad. Let the games begin."

An official police interview typically has three stages – four if you count the more or less polite invitation to "drop in for a little chat". (Translated from the Swansonese: "Get your fucking arse down here yesterday!")

Once they get you on the premises the first phase proper is Disclosure. This is when they tell you exactly what the subject of the 'little chat' is going to be, though of course, most people have probably worked that part out for themselves long before this stage of the process. In my case Swanson was keen to know why my cell phone was the last number dialled by a popular local TV celebrity who had been found hanging naked from a tree in Brindlethorpe Woods early that morning!

The seconds stage of the interview is a private consultation between the interviewee and their legal representative, during which they discuss the matter in question and how much or how little the principal is prepared to divulge to the police regarding his knowledge of, or involvement in, the crime in question or the circumstances leading up to it.

As far as my knowledge of the crime went it was a very short discussion. The first I knew of it was when Swanson dropped the news on me during our original phone conversation. Almost an aside in a very one-sided conversation that mostly consisted of a familiar tirade about "fucking private dickheads who seem to have made it their life's work to turn up when and where they are least fucking wanted."

I told Swanson I'd missed him too, but my heart wasn't really in it. I didn't like Wood or trust him, but I didn't wish him dead and the news of his murder only validated my concern for the well-being of Jennifer Jensen. If her disappearance did somehow play into her involvement with Wood and his reborn Hellfire Club, then it was also possible that his murder might be linked to her fate in some way.

When I had briefed Rafe he had listened attentively, occasionally asking questions and making notes with his Mont Blanc Meisterstuck on the yellow legal pad he produced from his Aspinal of London attaché case. I'm glad I got the friends and family discount. I would never have been able to afford him otherwise. When I'd brought him up to speed he doled out the usual sound advice that a solicitor gives his client on such occasions.

"Just answer the questions put to you and don't volunteer information unless it's relevant in a non-incriminating way. Such as, for instance, it establishes that you were at least twenty miles away from the scene of the crime at the time it took place. Just give them facts, Harry, not speculation. Be co-operative - in so far as it's in your nature - and whatever you do don't get defensive. Remember that you're a helpful witness, not a suspect."

"Do you want to tell Swanson, or shall I?" I said.

Which brought us to where we were now. With the tapes rolling Swanson gave a summary of the purpose of the interview and the date and time. We were all then invited to identify ourselves for the benefit of the machine before Swanson started the questioning.

"Mr Webster can you tell us how you come to know Glenn Wood and the extent of your relationship?"

"I contacted him professionally in the belief that he might have information relating to a job I'm working on. Our 'relationship', if you can call it that, consists of a half hour interview in my office and the brief exchange of text messages that you retrieved from his phone."

"So – tell me about this job?" Swanson said. "What does it involve and was Wood connected?"

"Missing person." I said, "and possibly."

They naturally wanted a bit more detail, so I told them about Jennifer Jensen and how my search for her had led to Dorian Wilde, Glenn Wood and his latter-day Hellfire Club.

"Dirty bastards!" was Swanson's response. He was probably the most foul-mouthed Puritan I'd ever met.

"And did Wood know anything about your missing lassie?"

"He admitted knowing her- "

"I bet he did."

"- but claimed he had no knowledge of her present whereabouts."

"Did you believe him?"

I shrugged.

"Could you put your answer into words for the tape, please?" Mac said, as always, the reasonable voice in the partnership.

"I've got an open mind on that question. I didn't see any obvious signs that he was lying but he isn't – sorry – wasn't someone you would instinctively trust to tell the truth."

"Unlike your average private investigator." Swanson snorted.

"That kind of remark is uncalled for, Chief Inspector." Rafe advised him sternly. "I would remind you that my client is here voluntarily to assist your enquiry."

"Oh, right… sorry if I've bruised your delicate feelings, Harry." Swanson retorted sarcastically.

"Now you, on the other hand, are a terrible liar." I said.

"Tell us about your client." Mac said hastily. "How did he react when you told him about his wife's – er – relationship with Mr Wood? You say that the couple are estranged but might he not have still felt some anger towards Wood."

"He doesn't know about him." I said. "I told Wood I'd keep it to myself until my client got back to the city. It was an incentive for him to ask around amongst the Hellfire set to see if any of them could shed any light on Mrs Jensen's whereabouts."

Swanson's perpetual scowl deepened. A jealous husband is every copper's dream suspect and he wasn't happy that I'd probably just torpedoed his best chance for a quick arrest.

"When is Jensen due back?"

"He's at a Gamers' Conference in Cork. I'm expecting him back after the weekend."

"Gamers." Swanson repeated, as he might have said

'Rapists'. "Overgrown kids blowing imaginary shit up because they're too scared to deal with the real world."

"You'd rather they blew up 'real' shit?" I wondered.

"It's not something a grown man should be wasting his time with." he said obstinately.

"Well, it's made him a millionaire." I pointed out. "Though I expect he's really embarrassed about it."

Swanson glowered at me briefly then glanced down at his notebook, which lay open on the table in front of him.

"So, when was the last time you actually saw Mr Jensen?" Mac asked.

"Monday. The night before he flew to Ireland."

"Four days ago?"

"Wow, I'm impressed! You didn't even have to use your fingers!"

"Have you been in contact since?" Mac hurriedly intervened once again, earning himself an irritated glance from his boss.

"I've been sending him daily email reports, as he asked. I did have a brief telephone conversation with him on Tuesday evening, but we've not spoken since." I admitted.

"Doesn't sound to me as if he's all that concerned about his missing wife." Swanson observed.

I couldn't really argue with that.

"He only wants to find her so that he can get her to sign their divorce papers."

"Sounds like a real charmer." Swanson sneered.

"They say it takes one to know one." I said

"Huh. Well, let's forget about your client for now and get back to you." Swanson continued. "This meeting with Wood took place when exactly?"

"Yesterday morning between about eleven o'clock and half past. We met in my office and he was accompanied by a friend of his called Dorian Wilde."

"A 'friend'?" Swanson repeated heavily. "By which you mean…?"

"A boon companion, a familiar spirit, a confrere…"

"Are they gay!" Swanson snapped, and Raphael caught my eye as if to say, 'Stop it'.

"Well, they weren't wearing scarf-ties." I elaborated. "So, they're probably straight."

"Just seeking clarification."

"So – another convenient motive shot down in flames then." I said.

"And is Mr Wilde a member of this Hellfire Club? Mac asked patiently.

"A founder member I'd guess. He's their 'talent scout'. I'm sure his number is also in Wood's phone."

"We're aware of Mr Wilde – and we will be speaking to him and everyone else in the deceased's contact list." Swanson said brusquely. "Are you personally acquainted with any other members of Wood's nookie club?"

I know somebody who would like to be, I thought. Out loud I said:

"No. From what Wood told me they guard their identities very carefully. They all wear masks and most of them only know the name of the person who nominated them for membership. That said, I expect that Dorian knows the names of most if not all of the women members since he recruited them."

"No doubt." Swanson agreed. "But - go on, tell us about your day after Wood and Wilde left your office."

"Any particular time of day you're interested in?" I asked innocently, fishing for some clue as to when Wood had been killed.

Swanson wasn't falling for it, though.

"Just talk us through it all and I'll tell you if any of it interests me."

"You're not obliged to tell the Chief Inspector about any aspect of your work that doesn't impinge on his investigation." Rafe pointed out, with a stern look at Swanson, whose habitually rosy jowls grew a shade redder, as if he was allergic to lawyerly words like 'impinge'.

"There's no concrete evidence that any of it touches on what happened to Wood." I pointed out "I've got nothing to hide, though."

"Then have at it, lad!" Swanson invited. "We've got lots of tape left."

I didn't see any reason not to, so I told them about my visit to the house at West Bretton on Thursday afternoon. I didn't mention the items I'd taken from Jennifer's closet, nor the fact that it wasn't my first visit to the place. Until events proved otherwise neither those things were any of Swanson's business. In fact, neither Swanson or Mac seemed that interested, though they grew more attentive when I moved on to the events of the early evening. When I reached the point when I got Wood's text, Swanson interrupted.

"What time would you say that you received the text?"

"I'm sure you know from Wood's phone that he sent it at a quarter past six. I didn't notice it until about twenty minutes later."

"That's quite a lapse." Mac offered. "Does your phone not alert you when you receive a text?"

"It was on vibrate and I wasn't wearing my jacket. I checked the phone when I put my coat on to head off home."

Mac nodded and subsided again. Swanson glanced down at his notebook, flicked over a page and read from it.

"Need to see you. Now. Is that what it said?"

Rafe interrupted testily,

"Since you're obviously in possession of the man's phone I'm sure you know very well what the text message said."

"It's okay, Rafe." I assured. "I think the Chief Inspector's just having a problem deciphering his handwriting."

Swanson skewered me with his eyes but refrained from biting back.

"Need -to -see-you - now.'" he re-iterated, emphasising each word with a little pause. "What did you think he meant, by that?"

"That he wanted to see me. Now"

"For fu -! Why did you think he wanted to see you – and where?"

"I presumed he meant me to come to his home since I wouldn't have any idea where else he might be. As to why? My first thought was that he had something to tell me that might help me find my client's missing wife."

"If that was a case why send a text asking for a face to face? He could just as easily have called you and told you over the phone."

"Which was my second thought." I agreed. "My third thought was that if I wanted to know the answer to that then I ought to ask him. I'm sure you know that I rang his mobile immediately after reading his text and again several times last night and this morning. When he didn't answer the first time I tried his landline with the same result. I thought it was a bit odd that he didn't pick up either phone since the text had been sent so recently. At that point I decided that it might be a good idea to just do what the text said."

"You went to Wood's home."

"On wings of wind came flying." I said.

"At what time?" Swanson said, irritable.

"About a quarter to seven; got to Wood's house about half an hour later."

"And you were there how long?"

"Maybe three quarters of an hour."

"And was Wood there?"

"No."

"So – what? You sat in your car waiting for him to come home?"

"That's what I would have done – but I didn't have to."

I told them about finding the front door open and being invited in by Donald Black. The two detectives exchanged a look, then Mac's eyes went down to the file in front of him. If I'd had to guess, I would have said he was scouring the list of contacts they'd lifted from Wood's mobile. After a few seconds he looked up at Swanson and gave a brief shake of the head. Interesting.

"Did you ask him what he was doing in Wood's house?" Swanson said, his interest really quickening now.

"He said he was there for a meeting with Wood. Black is his agent-"

"No, that's not so." Mac said, checking the list again. "Max Hazel. That's the agent. We've already spoken to him. He identified Wood's body."

"Maybe Wood had two agents?" I said. "One for every day and one for best."

"What did he look like?" Swanson demanded testily

I gave a brief description of Black. Once again that looked passed between the two men.

"That sounds like Max Hazel." Mac said, puzzled.

"Maybe he's having a crisis of identity." I said.

"It can't have been Hazel." Swanson reminded Mac. "He was at a party for one of his other clients over in Manchester. He was there when we contacted him about Wood's death."

"It's less than an hour over the tops to Hotpot land." I pointed out, feeling I was clutching at straws.

"That's true." Swanson conceded. "But if it was Hazel why would he tell you he was Wood's agent then give a false name?"

It was a good question and one I couldn't readily think of an answer to.

"All I can tell you is that he seemed at home and comfortable in Wood's house – and he knows good scotch."

"You had a drink with him?"

"It would have been rude not to."

"So, you stayed for a while."

"I've said. About three quarters of an hour, maybe slightly less."

"And talked about what?"

"Our absent host, chiefly. Black – or whoever he was – didn't seem to like him on a personal level but I sensed a degree of respect for Wood's unapologetic superficiality."

"Hmm – and did he venture an opinion as to why Wood wasn't home to keep his appointments with the pair of you?"

"He implied that Wood was impulsive by nature; prone to act on sudden whims without due consideration for the convenience of others. Black speculated that he might have received a phone call from somebody whose company he found more congenial than ours. He did seem to have left in a hurry."

I told them about the alarm not being set and the half empty glass of Lagavulin but left out the part about the DVD he'd apparently been watching.

"If anyone called him it wasn't on his mobile." Swanson said, "The only incoming calls after the time he sent the text to you are unanswered calls from you."

"Landline? Email?"

"Will be checked." Swanson bristled. "This isn't our first hootenanny."

"Rodeo." I corrected automatically

"What?" he glared.

"Nothing. Forget I spoke."

"Do you have any contact details for this Mr Black?" Mac pressed on.

"He didn't offer – and I didn't ask." I admitted. He'd seemed innocuous and irrelevant to my purpose.

"Well, can you tell us anything about him – beyond his physical description?"

"He's intelligent, eloquent in a smug, self-satisfied sort of way. Prudish, perhaps even puritanical by nature but not without a studied, decidedly theatrical sense of irony."

Like a man playing a part, I thought with a sudden clarity that brought with it a wave of uneasiness. I pushed the feeling away and focused my head on getting through the rest of the interview. It was running down now. There was little else to tell them. After leaving Wood's place I'd driven straight home, had a light snack and a Miller Lite then headed to bed, where I was accompanied only by my recurring nightmare. When I'd finished the last bit of my narrative Swanson asked a few more desultory questions then brought things to a close.

"That's about it for now." he announced. "Do you have any more questions, sergeant?"

They exchanged another look that clearly telegraphed the fact that Swanson knew very well that Mac had been primed to deliver a sting in the tail of the interview.

"Oh – well – just one last thing." Mac said, doing the Colombo bit with complete lack of spontaneity.

From the file folder on the table he took out a clear, plastic evidence bag containing a single sheet of paper. He looked at me almost apologetically as he spoke for the tape.

"I wonder if you are familiar with the following, Mr Webster." He paused, cleared his throat and began to read the words typed on the sheet of paper. *"I would have you give o'er these chargeable revels. A visor and a mask are whispering rooms that were never built for goodness – fare ye well."*

He lay the envelop down on the table top and checked for my reaction. I didn't look at Swanson, but I could feel his gaze on me, doing the same. A sudden tension had entered the room and Rafe was quick to sense it.

"You don't have to respond to the sergeant's question, Harry. Unless he or the inspector are prepared to speak to its relevance to the subject of this interview?"

Mac looked to Swanson for guidance.

"Boss?"

Swanson switched his glare from me to Rafe.

"It's relevant." he said reluctantly. "I can't say more than that at this stage of our enquiries."

"It's okay, Rafe." I assured him. "I think we can assume that the piece of paper that the sergeant has just read from was found on or near Glenn Wood's body."

Swanson switched his scowling gaze back to me again.

"What? It doesn't take a genius to work that out." I said, unable to resist adding: "It's not my first barn dance, either."

"Well? Do you know anything about it?" Swanson demanded. "Are you familiar with the passage that Sergeant Ames has just read to you?"

"It rings a vague bell." I admitted. "If you're asking me why somebody would leave this on Wood's body I have no idea. Have you identified its source?"

"We're working on it." Swanson said

He held my gaze for a long moment, trying to make his mind up whether I was being straight with him. Distrust being his usual default position, I suspected not. After another couple of beats, he looked away and nodded to Mac to wind things up.

"That's it for now, then. Thank you for your co-operation Mr Webster. Interview terminated at 11.57."

"It's more than possible we may need to speak to you again, like." Swanson warned. "You can bugger off now but don't be taking any out of town job offers, Harry."

"Always a pleasure to help point you in the right direction when things get a bit sticky." I assured him.

"Ye cheeky -! Get gone the pair of ye's before I spoil my manners."

"I'm not sure how that would be possible, Chief Inspector." Rafe said sweetly,

It was as good an exit line as anything I could come up with, so we left on it.

Rafe was thoughtful as we made our way out of the building, but only when we reached the car park and were about to go our separate ways did he finally speak his thoughts aloud.

"You recognised it, didn't you?" he said.

"Sorry?"

"Harry, I'm your lawyer and – I hope – your friend, you can tell me anything. That note the sergeant read out? It meant something to you, didn't it?"

"What makes you say that?"

"Oh, don't worry, you're a reasonably accomplished dissembler."

"Thanks for not calling me a liar." I said. "I did say it rang a bell."

"More than that, I think. Like yourself, long experience has made me sensitive to a client's veracity. A trait, I'm sure, that DCI Swanson has also acquired over his long career."

"Undoubtedly – but he always thinks I'm holding things back even when I'm not."

"But this time you are." he persisted.

"You're right." I admitted. "I did recognise the words in the note. It's a quotation from a play. The Duchess of Malfi?"

"Ah! Then why didn't you say so?"

"I didn't like to show off." I said evasively.

"Wait a minute – The Duchess of Malfi? Isn't that by -?"

"Webster, yes."

"That seems like too much of a coincidence to be any such thing. I'm assuming, as you suggest, that it was left by Wood's killer? That business about 'masks' and 'visors' seems like an obvious reference to this Hellfire Club nonsense. The killer is obviously sending a message."

"Oh yes. The question is who is he sending it to?"

18.

We shook hands and parted.

"Call me anytime." Rafe said as he climbed into his black, E-class Mercedes. "Maybe you should put me on speed dial?"

I'm not sure he was joking, either.

I watched him drive away then turned and slid into my own car. Before I moved off I turned my phone back on to check if there were any calls, texts or emails from my client. There was just one missed call but not from any number I recognised. I checked my voice mail and found myself listening to a pleasant, female voice:

"Oh – hi – it's Molly? Remember me? From Stentor Alarms. Sorry to bother you, it's probably nothing, but you did say to give you call if I had any thoughts that might help you locate Jen. Not sure about that but – um – call me back? 'Bye."

That sounded like the best suggestion I'd heard all day, so I did what she asked. A few seconds later that same, bright voice was speaking to me in real time, though our conversation was a short one as I'd caught her on her way to the weekly staff meeting.

"Sorry." she apologised. "Shall I call you back when the bitchings done? It should be finished by five o'clock. Nobody likes to stay behind after school."

"I've got a better idea." I said on an impulse. "Why don't I meet you from work and you can tell me your news over a drink – or maybe a bite to eat?"

There was a pause, that momentary hiatus that seems to stretch on forever in the space between acceptance and rejection. Then she said:

"That would be lovely. Got to go now."

The line went dead, and I glanced at myself in the driving mirror. I appeared to be smiling.

Back at the office I found Clegg enjoying a solitary tea break, his chin resting on his steepled fingers as he stared into a Krispy Kreme box.

"Penny for them." I said.

His eyes shifted focus and he regarded me seriously.

"I am in something of a quandary, young Hal." He said. "To wit: Cookie Crunch or Chocolate Custard?"

"A question for the ages." I agreed. "Eat both?"

"Ha! *Out of the mouths of babes and sucklings thou hast ordained strength!* A verdict of Solomonic elegance – and one which I heartily endorse."

He beamed at me again and turned his attention to applying my suggested solution to his dilemma. I left him to it and made myself a coffee to go with the plain chocolate doughnut he had thoughtfully set aside on my desk. We munched companionably for a few minutes until Clegg had hoovered up the last crumb of Cookie Crunch. At this point he cleansed his palate with a mouthful of coffee, wiped his lips on a spotless, white handkerchief and sat back contentedly in his chair.

"*Hunger is insolent and will be fed.*" he said. "Homer."

"*Donuts. Is there anything they can't do?*" I riposted. "Homer Simpson."

Between further mouthfuls of doughnut and coffee, Clegg filled me in on what had been happening in my absence. This consisted of not much at all, other than the fact that the new computers that we were waiting for had been delivered in my absence and were currently stacked in my office awaiting installation. Left to the three of us that was likely to be sometime after the 12th of Never but Eddie – of course – knew somebody who could do the job at a very generous price. The fact that the 'somebody' just happened to be his niece was purely coincidental, I expect. I wasn't entirely sure it was a good idea, but Clegg had let Eddie persuade him to the contrary and had gone off to fetch her.

"The lass is keen." Clegg told me. "When Edward rang her, she volunteered to come in and sort everything tonight so the system is up and running for the morning."

"And we're sure she's related to Eddie?"

"She might be from Maureen's side of the family." Clegg pointed out.

I was surprised that any of Maureen's relatives were still talking to Eddie, but I don't suppose I should have been. Roguish though he could be, especially with the opposite sex, he had unfathomed depths of charm that few people were immune to.

"Oh well, let's just hope she's not their Ronnie's kid or we'll be lucky if we've still got desks in the morning never mind computers."

Clegg chuckled, and the conversation moved on to more serious matters. In particular, the continued lack of any communication from Callum Jensen. While I was out Clegg had done his best to track down our elusive client at the Cork hotel he was supposedly staying at but had succeeded only in confirming that he no one of that name had been resident during the previous seven days. Furthermore, he had learned that the only computer gaming convention taking place in Ireland the previous weekend - Leprecon, if you can believe it – was not taking place in that city but at Trinity College, Dublin. A call to the organisers also gave the lie to our client's claim that he was one of the guest speakers.

"The chap I spoke to knew Jensen's name, naturally enough, and he has been a guest at a previous convention. He definitely wasn't on the programme for this year, though. Perhaps he just attended as an ordinary fan?"

"It's possible – but then why lie about being one of the speakers and the venue - if he was just geeking out as a fanboy?"

"True." Clegg acknowledged. "Though claiming to be fulfilling a professional engagement would give him a more acceptable excuse for leaving town instead of sticking around waiting for news of his wife's whereabouts."

"Which begs the question: why he didn't want to stick around?"

"Afraid of learning the worst? Or because he already knew it?"

"If that was the case then why hire me? Unless…?"

Clegg paused on the brink of swallowing the last portion of his Chocolate Custard and frowned across at me.

"Unless…?"

"Unless this whole business is somehow about me as much as it is about Jennifer Jensen."

Clegg laid aside the past piece of his doughnut and pursed his lips around that thought.

"Are you still thinking about that book and the tarot card? Surely, it's more likely that they relate to Glenn Wood and his Hellfire Club charade? If indeed they have any significance at all beyond a random synchronicity."

"I might agree – especially as someone obviously hated him enough to string him up in the woods – if it wasn't for the note they left at the scene."

I told Clegg about the fragment of blank verse the police had found with Wood's body and the original context of the passage. Clegg's fingers reached absently for his unfinished snack and retrieved it.

"A gobbet of Webster! That does seem an unlikely coincidence – though why not hammer the point home and choose something from the White Devil?"

"That's where Wood's murder intersects with Jennifer. In her university days she was a star of the drama club. According to the reviews in her scrapbook The Duchess of Malfi was one of her signature roles."

"Which means – what? Wood's killer is someone who knows Jennifer from way back? Someone who feels aggrieved that Wood ensnared her in his grubby sex games?"

"Not sure what it means." I admitted. "I just have this feeling that Wood's death and Jennifer's disappearance are linked in some way."

"You don't think she's on holiday, do you?" Clegg said.

I hoped she was, but he was right. I didn't think there was going to be a happy ending to this drama. Just like the Duchess of Malfi,

It was only just turned five o'clock when I pulled into the car park of Stentor Alarms but already several spaces had opened up as staff headed home. It seemed Molly Grayson wasn't joking when she said nobody liked staying after school. The reception desk was already closed and as I crossed to the elevator the doors opened to spill out a clump of chattering escapees, clearly buoyed by that end of the shift feeling of release. None of them was Molly or gave me more than a cursory glance as they headed for the exit.

On the second floor there were still a few bodies at their desks and I spotted Molly cradling a mug of tea or coffee as she chatted to Gareth, the pony-tailed gopher in corduroys who I'd briefly encountered on my earlier visit. Sensing my approach Molly broke off eye contact with Gareth and glanced up at me with a questioning look that segued quickly into one of recognition, accompanied by a warm smile.

"Mr Webster." she acknowledged.

"Ms Grayson." I replied.

"I'll leave then, shall I?" Gareth said with an archness that somehow didn't jibe with his bland expression. "You know where the key to the store room is?"

"Gareth – stop it!" Molly chided with a laugh.

He grinned at her conspiratorially and with a friendly nod in my direction he drifted off towards a desk across the room by the window. He paused there long enough to snatch up a black rucksack before heading out of the office with a lazy wave in our direction.

Molly was not quite ready to leave and busied herself shutting down her computer and sifting loose papers into a pile, which she then dropped into her 'Out' tray. Although it was the end of a long day she looked as cool and unruffled as if it was just starting in a steel blue silk blouse and black Karen Millen jeans. She topped it off with a black, quilted fleece jacket that she scooped off the back of her chair and the look was completed by a plain black, cross body handbag from Paul's Boutique. With her lustrous chestnut hair and sparkling green eyes the effect came off like some feisty, kick-ass FBI agent from a US TV show and brought my hot flush out in a hot flush.

We made small talk as we walked to the elevator, but the subject of Glenn Wood's murder didn't arise. I hadn't mentioned his name to Molly when we'd spoken earlier so it was more than likely that she wasn't aware of his connection to Jennifer. Come to that, I had no idea how much coverage Wood's murder had received so far, so maybe she didn't even know about it. I decided I wasn't going to be the one to broach it.

On the way down to the car park I learned that Molly owned a house in Easewood, which was little more than a mile down the road from Stentor alarms. On fine days she walked to work and on the other three hundred and odd she caught the bus. That simplified the logistics of the evening.

Coming out of the building onto the car park the driver of a bright yellow Lotus Elise sounded his horn as he went past with a raised hand and a glimpse of a ponytail.

I looked at Molly.

"Was that...?"

"Gareth?" she finished. "Yes. You sound surprised."

It was a fair comment but a sporty job like the Elise didn't really seem to go with the Gareth I had encountered, admittedly only briefly. I'd pegged him as some kind of office gopher, but I couldn't have been more wrong it seemed.

"He's the IT Manager." Moly explained, unable to disguise her amusement at my misconception. "And Sandra's number two, incidentally. I can see why you might mistake him for the caretaker or something, like that, though. He certainly doesn't dress to impress but he's a real sweetie – and there's nothing he doesn't know on the tech side of things."

"Still, that model doesn't come cheap." I observed. "Maybe I should apply for a job with Stentor."

"Maybe you should." she said, giving me a look that I felt all the way down to my Earthkeepers. "But the money isn't all that, believe me. Gareth used to run an old 94' Volvo until a few months ago. His mother passed away just before Christmas and he came into a bit of money. The car's part of his makeover."

"And what's the rest?" I wondered.

"Well, I think he bought a new hair band too." Molly said.

I figured Molly and I were going to get along just fine.

Gareth turned out of the car park and shot off in the

direction of the city Reflecting on what Molly had just told me I couldn't help but think about what chaos Eddie and his niece might be creating back at the office setting up the new computer system. In the circumstances knowing where to find a friendly IT guru could be a distinct advantage.

I told myself I was being unreasonably pessimistic and pushed such thoughts out of my head as I swung out into traffic and headed towards Doranstown. I was headed for The Holly Bush, a gastro-pub where I occasionally met up with Raphael and his wife Grace. On the way I chatted easily with Molly and it felt like our acquaintance rested on much more than our two brief encounters had so far encompassed. I reminded myself that tonight was primarily just about my interest in finding Jennifer Jensen, but I would have been fooling myself if I'd tried to deny that a part of me hoped things between us might develop beyond the merely professional.

It was enough in the moment to be sitting alongside Molly listening to her chat wittily about her life and the people in it. She had been at Stentor for almost five years and was ready for a change. After leaving school at eighteen with a wall full of qualifications she had opted to take a gap year and go back-packing around America with her then fiancée, Jesse. The engagement failed to survive the trip and he had disappeared from her life in LA, where he took up with a cocktail waitress and would-be actress called Loretta.

It sounded like a scenario from a bad country and western song that could only end in tears. On the contrary, Molly had re-connected with Jesse through social media and discovered that he and Loretta were happily married with three children and that she had given up acting to become a soccer mom. Molly sounded pleased for them both – and just a little wistful.

At the time the break-up had shaken her confidence badly, as such betrayal will. It had robbed her of more than just her innocence. Ambition was listed among the missing when she returned to England. University fell off the radar altogether and she had drifted into a series of temporary clerical jobs and even more temporary relationships until fetching up at

186

Stentor. Despite the length of time she'd worked there, this too she saw as a temporary arrangement and just lately she had taken steps to jump the tracks of the life she had fallen into. She was doing a Foundation course in Humanities at Mid-Yorkshire University and, if all went well, she wanted to progress to that degree course that she had put on hold a decade or so ago. She had not yet decided on what subject to pursue, however.

"Psychology, maybe." she said. "I'd make a good psychologist."

"Most women think that." I teased, earning a playful punch on the arm for my trouble.

"It's because men offer such a rich and bottomless source for study." she assured me.

All too soon, it seemed, I was pulling into the car park at The Holly Bush, an L-shaped stone pub that had started life as a pair of barns on a long defunct farm. It had been scheduled for demolition until a consortium of wealthier residents had stepped in to re-purpose the site as an independent village local. Over the years it had achieved a reputation for selling good beers and excellent food at surprisingly reasonable prices, which had attracted the attention of more than one of the country's homogenous pub chains. So far, its co-owners had resisted all offers. The day they caved in and sold out would be the day the pub saw the back of me, too, but until then it remained on my – very short – list of the city's hidden treasures.

Although it was only late afternoon the place was well subscribed but I'd taken the precaution of booking in advance. A pretty, blonde haired teenager, with a manner as crisply laundered as her uniform of black trousers and monogrammed polo shirt, showed us to a table for two and handed us a couple of menus she scooped up on the way.

I ordered drinks – white wine for Molly, a lime soda for me – and by the time they were delivered we were ready to order. Molly had a healthy appetite and ordered seared scallops with mustard stuffed chicken to follow. I went for the parsnip soup and a slice of the game pie that was the house speciality, The food was excellent and the conversation remained light and mildly flirtatious right through to the sticky toffee pudding we both chose for dessert. It was only over coffee that Molly finally turned her attention to the real, or at least, alleged, purpose for this assignation.

"That was lovely." she said, setting aside her cutlery at length. "Thank you for this, Harry. I'd almost forgotten how nice it is to eat out in good company."

"No reason why business shouldn't sometimes be a pleasure." I assured her.

"Thank you. For me too – but still, I haven't forgotten that I was the one who contacted you – or why, I take it that you've had no success in finding Jen?"

"That would be a fair assessment." I admitted. "Why? Did you think of something that might help?"

"I suppose you'll have to be the judge of that. It's second hand information but – well – I thought I should pass it on."

"I'm listening." I assured her.

"Right – okay. This is it. I told you Jen and I first met at the gym, yes? Well, she dropped out when her social life started to get – er – interesting, if you know what I mean."

"Sex is more fun than cross-training, I can see that."

"I suppose it depends on who the sex is with, but you get the idea. My social life isn't that crowded, so I've kept up with the gym. I have – or rather, had a very good trainer – Stacey. Jen knew her too and the three of us became quite good friends. Well, Stacey broke her leg last November playing for the Doncaster Belles and she hasn't returned to work yet. She's back on her feet, though, and she's started dropping by the gym to get her fitness back. I saw her there yesterday and, as you can imagine we had a lot of catching up to do. Naturally, she asked about Jen and I brought her up to speed with the situation. I told her about Jen leaving Stentor and how you were trying to get hold of her. I hope that was okay?"

"Sure. Just getting the word out to a wider circle people is often all it takes to find somebody when those closest to them can't help."

"Well, Stacey didn't know where Jen is, I'm afraid, but she

did tell me that she saw her a few days before last Christmas at some Italian place in Blackmere?"

I knew the place, an upmarket commuter village a couple of miles west of *Moorside*.

"Jen was with a man." Molly continued, adding a little ruefully. "Not unusual these last couple of years, of course."

"But…?" I prompted, sensing a punchline that I wouldn't necessarily like to hear.

"Well, neither Stacey or I ever met Callum – he was out of the picture before Jen and I became friends – but she used to carry a photograph of him in her purse so we're both familiar with what he looks like. The thing is, Stacey is sure that the man who was with Jen at the restaurant was her husband."

"That's -"

I was about to say unlikely given that Jensen had told me he hadn't seen his wife since he walked out to return to America two and a half years ago. Then I reminded myself that he had also told me he was going to Cork but had never showed up there.

"– interesting." I finished lamely. "And Stacey was sure it was Callum?"

"That's what she said. She never got a chance to speak to Jen. Stacey and her partner had a table by the window and she only saw Jen and the guy as they were leaving, holding hands like a proper couple. I suppose it could just have been someone who resembled Callum? People do tend to fall for the same kind of look – though Jen never seemed that fixated on a particular type."

We were interrupted by the waitress bringing our coffees. I stirred mine thoughtfully and waited for her to wander off again while I processed what Molly had just told me.

"Harry?" she prodded, tentatively.

"Sorry – just thinking."

"Good thoughts?" She grimaced. "It's not much, I know. I hope you don't feel I've got you here under false pretences."

"I wouldn't mind a bit if you had." I assured her. "But, no, I wasn't thinking anything like that. I was thinking that if your friend is right then Callum Jensen lied to me in a big way when he hired me."

I explained to Molly what Jensen had told me about how things stood between him and Jennifer. It didn't include holding hands and dining out in classy Italian restaurants five minutes down the road from the house he once called home. A house that he claimed not to have revisited for two years prior to the day before our meeting at the Tanglewood Inn.

"Stacey swears it was Callum." Molly responded. "I know how important it might be, so I really pressed her on that point. From what she told me the car park is extremely well lit and Jen and the man passed right by the window where Stacey and her fiancée were sitting."

It wasn't the kind of evidence you'd take to court, maybe, but if it was true what did it mean, other than the fact that I had a client who lied to me? Well, that had never happened to me before. Not this week anyway.

"You're not convinced, are you?" Molly said, with a hint of disappointment.

"I didn't say that. I'm just not quite sure what to make of it if Stacey really did see the Jensens together."

"You don't think -?" Molly hesitated, then shook her head as if to clear it of some inconvenient or unpalatable thought.

"Go on – don't be shy." I urged her. "It's not in your nature, I suspect."

"Ha! You – detective, you." she laughed. "No – I mean – you don't think Callum could have done something to Jen? Hurt her in some way?"

Killed Jen, she meant. It was a thought that had occurred to me too. It was easy enough to imagine a scenario where A kills B then hires C, the eternal gooseberry, in some convoluted attempt to avert suspicion from himself. Did people really do that kind of thing in real life, though? I didn't see it myself but sometimes you have to think a thing out loud to see just how improbable it really is. Improbable – but not completely impossible.

"It's an uncomfortable thought, I agree, but I wouldn't leap to any conclusions just yet. Hopefully my client will turn up soon and straighten out the kinks in his story."

Even as I said it, I knew it wasn't going to happen but, whatever the significance of what Molly's friend had

190

witnessed now wasn't the time to ponder it. I thanked Molly
for passing it on and then steered the conversation away from
work. I tried to get us back to the relaxed, easy-going place
we'd been in just a few minutes before, a place where mutual
liking might easily progress to something more. Maybe it
still could, but not tonight I soon recognised. We chatted
amiably enough for a few more minutes but the impetus had
gone out of the evening. When Molly stole a quick look at
her watch I decided to admit defeat gracefully.

"I'll get the bill." I said, showing that I could take a hint.

"What? Oh God, I'm so rude!" Molly flustered. "It's not
you, honestly. This has been lovely – well – mostly – it's just
that I've got an unfinished essay that's got to be Dropboxed
by eleven o'clock."

"Your course? You should have said. We could've done
this over the phone."

"Oh, bugger that! Pardon my French. I know you were only
being polite, but I was never going to turn down an invitation
to dinner. You never know when the next one's going to
come along!"

"I find that hard to believe. You must get plenty of
invitations."

"Not so many as you might think. Not that I'd care to
accept, anyway."

"Then consider me flattered. Maybe I'll invite you again."

"Then maybe I'll accept." she smiled. "You'll let me know,
though? About Jen, I mean."

"It might not be anything good." I cautioned her.

"Let me know anyway." she said.

I settled the bill and we left. It was still early, not yet seven
thirty and Molly had plenty of time to finish her essay if that
was really what she had planned. I hoped that was the case
and not just a convenient excuse for cutting short the
evening. I decided that I liked Molly Grayson a lot. She was
an intelligent, funny, gorgeous redhead. What was not to
like?

When we got back to town she gave me succinct directions
to her house amidst an otherwise unbroken stream of bright
chatter. The words seemed to come effortlessly to her and put

you so readily at ease that you might have known her for
years rather than days. When we finally pulled up outside a
neat, semi-detached house behind Green Park the chatter
stalled at last and we sat quietly for a moment or two, each
waiting for the other to say something. Then we both started
talking at the same time, our words dissolving into shared
laughter. When the hilarity petered out we each said our
piece.

"Thanks for the call, Molly, and the information. Please
don't hesitate to pass on anything else you might hear."

"I won't – and thanks again for dinner. It really was
lovely."

So are you, I thought, but it was probably too soon to be
saying things like that out loud, so I just said:

"It was more pleasure than business, believe me."

She smiled at me then and somewhere and angel cried. No,
not really, but it was a very nice smile. So was the kiss that
she leaned across and planted on my cheek.

"Call me." she said and then she was gone.

So was a little part of me.

19.

When I got home I took a long shower, reflecting on how pleasant it would be to be sharing it with a certain redhead. The evening in her company only confirmed my first impressions that Molly was intelligent, funny and way over-qualified for the position she currently occupied in life. Despite her light-hearted reminiscences it seemed to me that the emotional fallout from her fiancée's abandonment had knocked her world seriously out of kilter and that the loss had cut more deeply and lastingly than she cared to admit. I knew all about that. I had scars of my own, not least from the failed marriage that I still hated to talk about. Within six months of it ending I'd also walked away from a job I'd seriously believed would also be for a lifetime.

I no longer missed either but for a time I had been seriously adrift without an anchor. I dealt with it by becoming a would-be novelist, churlish drunk and emotional anarchist for a couple of years. I finished more bottles of Macallan and relationships than novels, but I came out of it more or less whole and emotionally intact. I still liked a drink and still flirted with the written word and the occasional unsuitable woman, but I no longer pursued any of these things to excess. Looking back from a safe distance to those days I saw it as a kind of derangement; the predictable blowback that always comes when love self-destructs. Everybody deals with it in their own way, I guess.

This brilliant philosophical insight somehow steered my thoughts back to Jennifer Jensen. Her chosen method of self-flagellation seemed to be a headlong plunge into promiscuity. It was an emotional analgesic, both self-aware and self-mocking. The absolute antithesis of the deep emotional and sexual bond that she had with her husband and which had been shattered by his abandonment of her. It seemed to me that sex just became a way for her to feel something other than pain.

I dried off and pulled on a pair of faded 501s and my Arkham Asylum T-shirt. Wandering through to the kitchen I pulled an ice-cold Miller from the cooler and carried it through to the living room, where I settled back with the beer and Tom Holland's history of the first Caesars. Any one of them would have fit nicely on my client list, I thought. I was up to Caligula's manic reign, but I found it difficult to pick up the threads, unable to lose myself as readily in the past as I usually could. My thoughts kept on skipping back to the present and how the information Molly had passed on that evening factored into my so far unsuccessful efforts to locate Jennifer Jensen.

The immediate question concerned the validity of the supposed sighting of Jennifer and Callum Jensen. I didn't know Molly's friend – let's face it, I hardly knew Molly – so I couldn't speak to her reliability. I also knew from past experience how unreliable eye witness testimony can be. On the plus side, Stacey knew Jennifer well and had socialised with her for many months. That made it less likely that the restaurant sighting was just a case of mistaken identity, though they say everybody has a doppelgänger, so it couldn't be entirely ruled out. On the other hand, she had also claimed that the man with Jennifer was Callum. It would have been one hell of a coincidence if a double of Jennifer had been walking out with someone who also happened to be the double of her estranged husband. If I accepted that the sighting was genuine then it clearly cast doubt on Jensen's claim that he had not seen his estranged wife or returned to England since their break up. So why would he lie? There were two possible explanations as far as I could see, neither of which was particularly comforting

In the first scenario Jensen kept quiet about his pre-Christmas visit because something had occurred then that he didn't want me to know about. Something, perhaps, that might cast him or his motive for wanting to contact Jennifer in an unfavourable light. It certainly wouldn't be the first time a client was economical with the truth, I reflected. Indeed, I believe many of them saw it as a sort of contractual obligation to tell me half-truths or downright lies if it made me more sympathetic to their cause. If that was the case with Jensen, then I wondered what could have occurred last December that made him feel it was necessary to airbrush it from his personal history when he hired me? Might it be that his motive for wanting Jennifer traced was a good deal less innocent than a desire to speed up their impending divorce?

I'd fallen for that kind of deception all too recently – and had the aching scar to prove it. I found myself absently massaging the wound site again as that memory stirred. It brought with it an unwelcome image of that duplicitous client's bloodied corpse twisting in the wind that howled through the shattered window of a blazing warehouse. I'm sure that was an outcome Corinne Winfield had never expected when she hired me to locate her supposedly missing lover but at least there was something left of her to bury. They had never found Bryce Mansell's body and, though I didn't kill him myself, I would always know that I was the one who bought death to his door.

I pushed the memories aside and refocused. It was a waste of time and energy to theorise ahead of the facts – of which there were regrettably few of a concrete nature. I grabbed a notebook and a pen from the coffee table drawer and itemised them chronologically.

Mid-December
Jennifer (?) seen with man (Jensen?)
Jennifer sends a 'Dear Dorian' email
December 31st Stentor receive Jennifer's resignation letter
Early January
(A Tuesday, possibly 3rd rather than the 10th?) Mrs Lazenby receives letter of termination and cheque
On a Wednesday (January 4th?) Jennifer tells Louis Sifer that she's going away and asks him to keep on top of the garden.

If this was a true timeline, then the gardener was the last person to see Jennifer in the flesh as far as I'd been able to establish. His story about her going away seemed to be backed up by both the email to Dorian and the letter to Mrs Lazenby, though there seemed to me to be a marked difference in the tone of the email and the letter. The latter was more prosaic, downbeat almost, compared to the message she sent to Dorian, which was filled with an excitement that bordered on the euphoric. Not the words of someone striking out blindly in the hope of finding a better tomorrow but of a woman almost bursting with the certainty of it.

When Dorian had first shown me the email it struck me, as it must have struck him, that she was dumping him because there was someone new in her life. Someone, moreover, in whom she had an emotional investment that had brought about an epiphany. Maybe not a new man coming into her life, after all, but an old one returning to it? Given that the email had been sent only days after the alleged restaurant sighting, was it possible that the hope that shone through her words was for a reconciliation with her husband? Could it be that he had flown over at Christmas not to finally end their relationship but to repair it? After their cosy reunion dinner did the two of them go away together for a few days to seal the deal, returning just long enough for Jennifer to tie up a few loose ends before they planned to fly off to together for a fresh start?

It made sense up to a point but the fact that the note of optimism in the email hadn't apparently carried over into her letter not so many days later to Mrs Lazenby. There was no hint in that of any romantic impetus for her planned departure. It seemed as if hope had given way to something altogether more tentative and wistful that, nonetheless, demanded the same outcome: the abandonment of her home and her job to fly to the other side of the world?

Things must have turned sour very quickly and traumatically to provoke such an extreme reaction, though to be honest I had never been completely convinced of the provenance of the Lazenby letter. Or indeed of the Dorian email, though that had now gained a little more context that made me more willing to accept that it had indeed come from

Jennifer. After all, if both were written by someone else then it was logical to expect that the letter would reflect the same mood as the former. Either both had indeed been written by Jennifer and reflected a genuine emotional downturn or else the letter had been written by someone else who was unaware of the email she had sent to Dorian.

Something had changed in the time between the two communications. If Jennifer was responsible for both then it could mean that any planned reconciliation had been derailed, leaving her disappointed enough to walk away from her unsatisfying lifestyle altogether rather than slip back into it. If that was the case, though, why hadn't Jensen mentioned his pre-Christmas visit? A couple of possibilities suggested themselves.

1. He was embarrassed by the failure of his attempt to mend their relationship and his ego was so fragile that he couldn't bring himself to admit to a stranger that he had been rebuffed.

   Or, a more sinister possibility,

2. He had reacted badly, perhaps even violently, to her rejection and wanted to keep it quiet in case I didn't take him on as a client.

   That lead me to consider an alternative scenario, which was that in the period between the mail and the letter being written, something had happened to Jennifer and another party, unaware of her upbeat message to Dorian, had composed the letter to explain her disappearance. If that was the case the author of the letter probably knew very well what had become of Jennifer, which probably ruled out Jensen. If he already knew her fate, why would he hire me for that purpose?

   Not that he was a trustworthy client in any way. He had also lied about going to Cork – and if he didn't go there, where did he go? And why, apart from his brief email and our short conversation on Tuesday, had he not contacted me since our meeting at the Tanglewood Inn? He had not even re-sent the corrupted Word document containing Jennifer's list of friends.

The murder of Glenn Wood added an extra dimension and urgency. Given Jennifer's involvement with the Hellfire Club and the fragment of verse found on his body, there was little doubt in my mind that Wood's death and Jennifer's disappearance were linked in some way. It was also clear to me that my connection to both would be noted by the police. Swanson had seemed to accept my explanation for getting in Wood's face but whilst Jensen remained in the wind there was no way to confirm exactly what had passed between us. That left the way open for other interpretations and I knew too well that if you gave Swanson too much rope he would inevitably try to hang you with it.

That thought brought me back to Wood's murder and I lay back and reviewed my interview with Swanson that afternoon. I had been honest with him in a Jesuitical kind of way. I hadn't actually told him any lies and though I had certainly omitted a few details I had no qualms about the interview. In fact, set alongside some of my previous, more volcanic encounters with the Chief Inspector it had been positively tame. I had to admit, though, that my complacency had been shaken more than a little when he challenged my account of my encounter with Donald Black, Wood's supposed agent.

Except he wasn't. That was someone called Max Hazel, apparently, who had been a good 40 miles away in Manchester by all accounts whilst I was drinking Wood's best whisky and verbally sparring with Black – whoever he was. I reached for my tablet and Googled the name. The search came back with over 100,000 hits so I refined it with the term 'agent'. That brought the total down to only 40,000 or so but the only Donald Blacks who were any kind of agent seemed to be American realtors.

I typed in Max Hazel, which produced just a single page of results, prominent amongst which was: Max Hazel Associates. I clicked through to their website, which confirmed that they were a Leeds based theatrical agency fronted by the man himself. There was a photograph of him on the website, a well-fed, middle-aged man who, at first glance, looked exactly like the man I knew as Donald Black!

I was also now pretty sure that I was looking at the face of the man who Eddie and I had both seen from a distance at The Kestrel a few nights before Wood's murder. But was that Max Hazel or Donald Black? I remembered that he had had driven away from the pub in a Lexus, whereas the car in Wood's drive, which I presumed was Black's ride, had been a Volvo. So, it was probably the real agent, Max Callum, at the Kestrel, but who was the look alike who called himself Black? More to the point why, if he had gone to the trouble to make himself resemble Wood's agent so closely physically, had he not also used Hazel's name during our encounter? There didn't seem any obvious reason for it. As it happened I had not known the name of Wood's agent at that time, but he couldn't have been sure of that, so he was clearly taking a gamble by giving me a fake name that could have instantly given his deception away. Why would he do that? He was clearly a risk taker, but it seemed a rather pointless risk to take unless -?

I turned back to Google and searched for 'Donald Black' again, spent a fruitless five minutes scrolling through the list of results, scanning for anything that might give me a clue as to why he chose that name above all others. Nothing jumped out at me until I spotted a headline that read "Black Donald Trump Is Back On The Daily Show'. It was obviously nothing of any significance to my purpose, but it gave me pause. After a moment's hesitation I cleared the search box and typed in 'Black Donald'.

The very first search result jumped off the screen at me. A Wikipedia entry that was short and to the point:

Black Donald is a highland colloquialism for the Devil in Scottish mythology

There was a further reference further down the list from a general site about mythology. It was also short on detail but added the information than that he could take many any shapes, including that of a man in a black suit! Just the outfit Donald Black had been wearing.

What was going on here? First the cheap paperback, then the DVD and the tarot card and now an unknown stranger bearing a name that played on an old folk euphemism for Satan? Whatever it all meant, if anything other than a strange run of coincidences, the Devil was everywhere it seemed just now.

Grimacing at the thought, I glanced at the time at the top of my tablet screen and noticed it was almost ten o'clock. I switched on the TV and tuned to Northwards FM for the late-night news. Predictably, they led with the discovery of Wood's body, though there was precious little flesh on the story's bones at this early stage, dress it up as they might.

"Mystery surrounds the death of city TV personality Glenn Wood after the innovative host of Extreme Bouncers and other popular reality shows was found dead early this morning. This report from our crime correspondent Lucy Blaze outside Rain Hill police station a few hours ago."

The segment cut smoothly to a confident female voice clearly relishing the moment.

"In a brief statement at five o'clock this afternoon police confirmed the identity of the body found in Brindlethorpe Woods as that of Glenn Wood. Details are scanty at this time, but Detective Chief Superintendent Ray Kendrew of the Serious Crimes Unit stated that the death of this popular and well-liked local figure is being treated as suspicious,

"The exact circumstances surrounding Wood's death have not been released, though it's understood that the body was discovered by an early morning walker. The identity of this witness has not been revealed at this time, nor have any arrests been made.

A full press conference has been scheduled for 11.00 a.m. tomorrow when it's expected that a fuller picture of this tragedy will emerge."

"That was Lucy Blaze, reporting from Rain Hill. The news of Glenn Wood's death has shocked his many friends in the world of broadcasting, as well as the legions of fans of his often controversial and self-mocking reality shows. Our TV critic, Meg Faraday now with a brief tribute to the man who, in his own words, "stretched reality to its breaking point.""

I switched off and thought about getting another beer, settled instead for cognac and a cigar, though I treated neither with the respect they deserved. I couldn't get Glenn Wood out of my thoughts. I didn't like the man but nothing I knew about him led me to believe that he deserved the fate that had been visited on him. Who had hated him enough to kill him? The mysterious Donald Black, perhaps? If so, he was a cool customer indeed to stand in Wood's living room and make small talk with me about the man he had just killed or was about to kill.

And where did Jennifer Jensen figure in all this? The fragment of verse the killer had left at the scene was surely proof that she did. It seemed to refer very specifically to both the masked antics of the Hellfire Club and Jennifer's association with The Duchess of Malfi. The name of the playwright may just have been an accidental correspondence, but it somehow felt as if the killer's message was clearly aimed at me in some way. A personal jibe or a challenge perhaps but disturbing either way. It was an artifice that smacked somehow of an obsessive and unstable intelligence, craving attention and who knew what else?

I washed the thought away with the last of the cognac. I thought about going to bed but dismissed the idea. I was too wound up to sleep. I picked up my book again and read a couple of paragraphs before I realised I hadn't taken in one single word and put it aside. For a moment I thought about ringing Raphael. The police were obviously keeping their cards close on this, but information has a way of leaking round the edges of the tightest official seals. I knew Rafe had an in with somebody senior at Rain Hill but in the end, I decided it was too late to bother him. It could wait until morning.

John Seeley

I turned back to the internet instead, though I soon discovered that cyber space wasn't exactly overflowing with stories about Wood's death. I found a handful of tweets, mostly innocuous expressions of dismay or surprise, with the usual smattering of gratuitous nastiness from the basement dwellers.

The report on the News pages of the Northwards FM website was pretty much just a rehash of the bulletin I'd listened to, though the Mid-Yorkshire Chronicle had filled up a few column inches, leading with the headline:

CITY ROCKED BY REALITY MAESTRO'S MYSTERIOUS DEMISE

The story beneath was for the most part a re-iteration of the sparse information included in the news bulletin, though it was fleshed out without a little more detail concerning the spot where Wood had been found.

The body was discovered at or near to Hob's Tump (pictured) a small mound within the bounds of Brindlethorpe Wood five miles east of the city. No details have been released regarding the cause of death, though police are treating it as suspicious

As we await further details to emerge, however, it seems appropriate to note that this local landmark is no stranger to tales of violent death. As recently as 1927 human remains were discovered in the vicinity, claimed by some to be the bones of Jack Stark, a local sheep stealer who supposedly met with rough justice at the nearby, ominously named Hangman's Stone sometime in the late 17th century. According to the folklore of the surrounding rural communities Stark's ghost still haunts the area around the Tump.

This is just one of many picturesque legends that surround this curious lump in the earth, which some insist derives its name from an old English nickname for the very Devil himself!

202

20.

Perhaps the beer and brandy helped but I enjoyed a
dreamless night's sleep and woke about seven to a clear but
blustery late March morning. After a shower and a quick
breakfast, I headed to the office, where Eddie and Clegg
where already in residence, drinking coffee and getting to
grips with the new computer system.

I was relieved to see that the changeover seemed to have
passed off without any visible signs of trauma to the rest of
the fixtures and fittings. The clunky, old Acers with their
CRT monitors were history, replaced by sleek, streamlined
Hewlett-Packards with razor sharp, HD monitors, networked
to an all-in-one printer/scanner and connected to a ProLiant
microserver and 20 Terabyte NASA with automatic cloud
back-up. So, Eddie informed with a note of pride in his voice
that couldn't entirely disguise the fact that he was reading it
all off his PC screen and probably understood less than half
of it.

"Sounds great." I agreed. "But can it make a good cup of
tea?"

"It's state of the art, H!" Eddie chastised me. "Well, for a
bijou private detective agency run by a smartarse and two
Luddites." he amended with a grin.

"Bijou?" I repeated.

"Indeed." Clegg concurred. "Small but elegantly formed."

"Fashionable and sought after." Eddie added, nodding
sagely.

I looked from one to the other, wondering affectionately at
what point these two totally different individuals had
morphed into a double act.

"Well, best keep it on the down low. I don't want them
putting the rent up." I said, pouring hot water onto a

Yorkshire Tea bag in my favourite Batman mug. I added
milk and sugar and carried it over to my desk.

I sat down and switched on my shiny new computer. While
it booted up, I squeezed the last drop of goodness out of the
tea bag and dropped it into my waste bin. Yesterday I could
have knocked off a full English breakfast waiting for
Windows to load but the new machine booted in less than
half a minute.

"Okay, now I am officially impressed." I said.

"They boot from SSDs." Eddie was starting to show off
now. "Much faster than conventional hard drives. I told you,
Alex is really switched on about this IT stuff. Always was a
smart kid. She's our Sylv's youngest"

"Adopted, right?"

"What are you tryin' to say?" Eddie grinned. "Oh, and by
the way, I said Alex could have the old gear. That's okay
isn't it?"

"Ah ha! Planning to clean it up and flog it down the next
car boot?

"Planning to clean it up and donate it to the Homeless
Centre in Duke's Row."

"So, definitely adopted then."

Eddie cheerfully shot me the finger.

"You've not seen the invoice yet." he smirked.

"Worth every penny, I'm sure." Clegg interjected gently.
"But the best computer system in the world won't – as yet –
do the work by itself. Shall we check our diaries, gentlemen?
Edward?"

"Got some stuff to do for Rafa this morning but I should
have it sorted by lunchtime. You got something for me,
Cleggy?"

Clegg consulted his notepad.

"Background check on Widow Lawrence's toy boy, couple
of debt defaulters to chase down, possible matrimonial in
Snaresbrook -. Do stop me if I happen to mention anything
that appeals, dear boy."

"Widow Lawrence?"

"Sixty but could pass for fifty-nine in poor light."

"Ah, cougar!" Eddie said.

"More of a sabretooth tiger I'd say." Clegg muttered. "Her new paramour is a thirty-year-old stonemason called Toby Rawlins. They met when she was ordering a gravestone for her late husband, apparently."

"That's what I call after sales service!" Eddie said admiringly.

"Yes, but she is a very wealthy woman and wants to assure herself that he's not just some cheap chiseller." Clegg said with an impressively straight-face.

"I'll take it." Eddie said, reaching across for the thin, blue file that Clegg passed him.

"And you, Hal?" Clegg asked, turning to me. "Anything you might like to turn your hand to? Do your bit to keep the old family firm afloat?"

"I need to try and get hold of Callum Jensen. I'll stay here and do the skip traces, then take look at the matrimonial, work out a surveillance schedule. Anything else?"

"Odds and sods, nothing too taxing or time consuming. I'll split the jobs between you both and email you the details."

He busied himself doing just that, while I stared at my sparsely populated PC desktop and finished my tea.

Eddie finished whatever he was typing with a vicious flourish and stood up, shrugging himself into the fake Burberry trenchcoat that was draped over the back of his chair. He completed the effect by slotting a brown fedora atop his madly curling mop of hair.

"Hmm, the Inch-High Private Eye look." I said. "I like it."

"It's called style, son. I'm sure you must have read about it sometime." he scoffed, carefully knotting the belt of his coat just so.

"Yeah? You got your dinner money? And don't be taking sweets off any strange men – or women."

"Bollocks – listen, though – about this Jensen business? Don't you think it's a bit dodgy that you haven't heard anything from him or been able to contact him? I mean, don't you think it's a bit off that he should go off the grid just when the bloke who was shagging his ex-bird gets himself topped?"

"Wood wasn't the only one." I reminded him, not without a small twinge of conscience. "But, yes, it does look a bit shady."

"There's also the fact that Wood was killed within twenty-four hours of you outing him as 'Dash'." Clegg pointed out. "That can't just be coincidence, can it?"

Well, of course, it could but I doubted it.

"In a way it kind of exonerates Jensen. I gave Wood a few days grace to come up with something that might help locate Jennifer. I never even mentioned him to Jensen in any of my reports to."

"Yeah, but we don't really know where Jensen's been these last few days." Eddie pointed out. "If he didn't go to Cork, maybe he never left town at all. Maybe he just set you on the trail and then followed you around until you led him to Wood, just like…"

Eddie caught a look from Clegg and left the sentence hanging but it was easy enough to fill in the gaps."

"Just like the Crusaders let me lead them to Bryce Mansell?"

"No! Well, yes." Eddie admitted. "Sorry."

"It's okay. You're not as sorry as me."

It was true, but I had to admit that Eddie had a point. I had taken Jensen on trust just as I had taken Corinne Winfield on trust. The thought that I might have been played the same way again was not a comfortable one.

"But why target Wood in particular?" Clegg said. "I mean, as you say, he was not her only swain. Why him above any of her other – um – conquests? I mean, why not what's his name? Dorian. Isn't he a more regular beneficiary of her amorous impulses?"

"Don't he talk lovely?" Eddie said with a grin. "Who's to say that the killer is going to stop with Wood, Cleggy? Maybe he's working through a list – and from what H has found out, it will probably be a bloody long one!"

I bit back a retort that would have been sharper than it needed to be. I felt defensive of Jennifer Jensen's honour, I had to admit, though the pile of DVDs I'd found in her home made it difficult to disagree with Eddie's jibe.

"It would be quite a project." I agreed. "But I don't think that's the agenda the killer's working to. I'm more inclined to think that Wood wasn't killed because he was one of Jennifer's lovers but because of what he represents."

Clegg looked thoughtful.

"The lamentable descent of popular entertainment into the cess pit of mediocrity?" he suggested. "You think Wood was killed in protest at the relentless dumbing down of the nation?"

"A nice idea but, again, Wood wouldn't be top of that particular list, either. No – I'm thinking more of him in his role as the head of his reconstituted Hellfire Club."

Clegg and Eddie exchanged a look of wary comprehension. It said all too plainly that they knew in which direction I was heading and thought that I'd got the map upside down.

"You're back to the tarot card and that trashy paperback again." Clegg said in a tone that teetered very close to the edge of the accusative.

"Hear me out." I said. "It's not just the card and the book anymore. There are other correspondences. Do you know where Wood's body was found?"

"Up in Brindlethorpe Woods, wasn't it?" Eddie said promptly. "I once had a bird there."

And in other news..., I thought.

"Well, that 'somewhere' is not Snow's Hump but Hob's Tump." I said, "And Hob just happens to be an old country nickname for – well – guess who?"

"I'll venture out onto a limb here and say, 'the Devil'?" Clegg said. "Would I be correct?"

"Well, that's the last time I touch a Hob Nob." Eddie murmured.

"There's more." I continued." Wood's agent – the man I met at his cottage? The man who isn't Wood's agent after all? Donald Black? Or should I say 'Black Donald' which is, I discovered-"

"Another pseudonym of the Devil?" Clegg supplied.

Cue Eddie's off-key rendition of the X-Files theme. Clegg looked more concerned, not to say pained, than amused.

"Yes, as it happens and that's not all. As I was leaving that night I asked Black to pass on a message to Wood reminding him that time was running out if he wanted to stop me exposing the Hellfire Club. Black said he would pass on the message. If I remember, his exact words were: He shall be told: *time runs, the clock will strike!*"

"*The devil will come, and Faustus must be damned.*" Clegg finished.

"Exactly! Whichever way you look at it the Devil in some form or other keeps cropping up. First in regard to Jennifer and now to Wood."

"Which means -?" Eddie spread his arms wide to invite an answer.

"If I'm right, it means somebody is playing mind games with us, well, with me specifically. Quite probably the very same somebody who killed Glenn Wood and – maybe Jennifer Jensen too."

"That would indeed be tragic." Clegg agreed "But we shouldn't get ahead of ourselves here. Have you actually found any concrete evidence that the lady has come to harm?"

"Not as such." I admitted.

"And, sinister as this possible satanic motif may be, do you really think the redoubtable DCI Swanson would give it credence?"

He steepled his fingers, regarding me, not unkindly, over his glasses. It was a look I imagine Mr Chips might have worn when pointing out his favourite pupil's grave misreading of Hamlet.

"I think you should be very cautious here, young Hal. The correspondences you have noted may indeed represent a pattern, but I am mindful of what Jung has to say about synchronicity."

"Not as good as *Zenyata Mondata* in my opinion." I said.

"Which he would recognise as a blatant example of 'deflection'." Clegg said with a tolerant smile. "But that's a different concept. I'm sure you're fully aware of what I'm referring to. I believe the exact quote is 'Synchronicity is the coming together of inner and outer events in a way that cannot be explained by cause and effect and that is meaningful to the observer'. That last part is the crux. Coincidences do occur and though they may very well have meaning for a particular individual it's more likely to originate from within that individual's personal experience rather than exemplify some supernatural or deliberately engineered causation."

"Jackie Lennon." Eddie said. "I get it Cleggy!"

"Well, that makes one of us."

"Jackie Lennon?" he repeated. "You must remember her. She was the first love of my life."

"I thought that was Jessica Rabbit?" I said.

"Well, all right, the first non-animated love of my life. We went out for ages."

"Ah, the blonde who dumped you after three dates? I remember now.

Eddie bared his teeth at me.

"The thing is, after she dumped me, I always seemed to be seeing blonde birds in 'Bite Me' t-shirts for weeks after."

"It sounds a little more Freud than Jung." Clegg chuckled. "But it's a reasonable layman's example, Edward. Oh dear, that was perhaps a poor choice of words, but to elaborate the point I am trying to make: any significance in the coincidence of Satanic references may originate in personal experience. It isn't so long ago, after all, that you vanquished a very personal devil of your own. Given the traumatic fallout from your ordeal it would be quite understandable if you were to see evidence of his presence in otherwise mundane events."

"Your very own Jackie Lennon." Eddie approved with a nod.

Clegg could tell I wasn't seeing the funny side, however.

"Hal, please believe that I speak only out of concern for a friend. Think of me as – oh –um – a devil's advocate, if you will, offering an alternative interpretation of this pattern you believe you are observing. I just think that you need to be very sure of the evidence before rushing to a hypothesis."

"So – not questioning my judgement, then?"

"Your perspective, rather. I just wonder if your experience of last year has truly been resolved at the psychic level. You went through a truly horrific ordeal and yet, to the best of my knowledge you have never spoken to a mental health professional about what you went through beyond a couple of brief sessions with Dr Prakash during your stay in Stonecross?"

"I was offered trauma counselling." I said shortly. "I didn't think it was necessary."

"And I thought at the time you were wrong." Clegg reminded me gently.

"I do recall that but at the time I felt I was handling it. Yes, I had a very bad experience that could have been even worse, but I survived it and I didn't feel any guilt or remorse just an all-consuming sense of relief that I was alive, and that bastard Rocky van Dorn was dead. Any pain I was feeling was physical not psychic in nature. I just wanted to get out of hospital as soon as possible and put the whole nightmare behind me. I didn't see how rehashing everything that happened to a complete stranger was going to contribute to that outcome.

"An understandable reaction and a common one, I'm sure." Clegg agreed. "And perhaps you were right. You were okay then and you're okay now. All I would say is that the fallout from traumatic events can creep up on a person gradually. Post-Traumatic Stress doesn't always manifest in the immediate aftermath of a crisis or tragedy. It can take months, years even, before it kicks in – and the smallest thing can trigger it: a car backfiring, a photograph in a book, a snatch of conversation. Almost anything could be the madeleine that bites back."

"Who's this Madelaine then?" Eddie said. "You've kept her quiet!"

Which effectively put an end to the conversation. By the time Clegg had stopped hiccoughing with laughter and I had explained to Eddie why he was wetting himself the moment for further discussion of my mental state was passed. I didn't doubt that it would only be a brief respite. It was clear from the passion with which Clegg had spoken that he had just given voice to something that had been giving him concern for some time. That both touched and annoyed me in roughly equal measures. I thought it was misplaced, though the point he had made about the insidious nature of PTSD did give me pause, I admit. I hadn't told either of my friends about the dreams I'd been having lately and, now, I was glad I hadn't handed Clegg any more ammunition for questioning my grip on reality.

After Proust had left the room Eddie shrugged philosophically and again prepared to leave, scooping up a file folder from his desk.

"Well, it's a shame, she's just a cake." Eddie said. "You need to get laid, H. There's nothing a good shag can't put right."

"Like your marriage?"

"That wasn't because of the shagging." he grinned sheepishly. "That was about Maureen finding out about the shagging! Anyway, I'm off now about Master Raphael's business. These papers won't serve themselves. You two play nicely while I'm gone."

With a cheeky grin he touched the brim of his hat to both of us and was gone. As always, the room seemed to shrink the moment he left it.

21.

After Eddie had left Clegg and I busied ourselves with our allotted tasks and worked in silence. Over the following minutes the last vestiges of my irritation ebbed away. Try as I might, though, my thoughts refused to engage with the mundane task of skip tracing and wandered back to the Jennifer Jensen/Glenn Wood conundrum. Despite any suspicions I might have had, Clegg was right about one thing: there wasn't much I could do about it. It simply wasn't my job to find Wood's killer and, it was even debatable whether I was still being employed to find Callum Jensen's missing wife given his continued failure to contact me or respond to my own calls and mails.

Nothing happened over the next three hours to clarify the situation. Several more phone calls and an email had failed to elicit any response and by the time Eddie returned I was fully resigned to the idea that there wasn't going to be any. I also doubted that there was cheque in the post for the effort I'd already made to find Jennifer. It looked like Jensen was just one more name to add to the debtors list I was working through. It was just then that the phone rang, and I snatched up my extension before either of the others could react.

"Webster." I said.

The voice on the other and was instantly familiar but did not, unfortunately, belong to Callum Jensen.

"DCI Swanson." came the familiar growl.

"Ah, how I love you, how I love you, my dear old Swanee!" I said.

Sounds of heavy breathing on the other end, as of somebody wrestling with a powerful emotion.

"I haven't got time for yers nonsense today, Harry." As if he ever did. "Dorian Wilde – know where he is?"

My stomach lurched. Dorian on the missing list now?

"He's not at home...?"

"Oh, well, why didn't we think of that? No, he's not at home and according to the neighbours he hasn't been there since the day before yesterday."

"You think he's got something to do with Wood's murder?"

"It's none of your fucking business what I think."

"I'll take that as a yes, then. Can't help you though. I only have the one address for him. I presume you got his mobile number from Wood's phone?"

"Not answering." he said shortly. "Phone's turned off."

"Maybe he's working out of town. You know what actors are like."

"Poofters?" Swanson suggested

"The political correctness training didn't take then? I meant, that if he's off rehearsing, say, he might have his phone off to avoid being disturbed."

"Hmm, well, we're looking into that side of his life, but I thought I might as well check with the fount of all knowledge in case you could save us some time."

"Well, sorry to disappoint you. Why exactly did you think I might know where Dorian is?"

"Oh, didn't I say? Naturally we've been over his place top to bottom and imagine our surprise when we found a smashed-up, little, electronic spy in his waste bin. It just occurred to us that whoever left that might also have thought to put a GPS tracker on his car?"

"Isn't that kind of thing illegal?" I asked innocently.

"You know damn well fuckin' fine it is!" he stormed. 'And if we lift one of your prints off the little bug we found you know what will happen!"

"The folks back home will see me no more?" I ventured.

Swanson, not bothering to retort, just slammed down the phone with his usually brio and all was silence.

Eddie and Clegg looked at me expectantly.

"Wrong number." I said.

"Ho, ho." Eddie said. "So, Gloria can't find Dorian, eh? Doesn't surprise me, he couldn't find his arse in the dark with both hands. You think Dorian's a suspect?"

"Not necessarily but he was probably as close as anybody
to Wood. It stands to reason they'd want a word."

"S'pose – but it's bloody funny him going missing. And
Jensen as well! Mark my words, something's rotting in the
Straits of Denmark."

"Just because Dorian can't currently be found, doesn't
actually mean he's lost." Clegg pointed out, looking at me
over the top of his glasses. "In any case finding him is a job
for the police, yes?"

"Nobody's paying us to find him." I agreed

"And when did that ever stop you?" Eddie wondered.

I shrugged. It was fair comment and I had to admit that I
was curious about Dorian's sudden unavailability. I didn't
see him as a killer, somehow, but it wasn't difficult to think
of him as another potential victim. Could it really be possible
that a would-be serial killer was out there working his way
through Jennifer's video library? I shrugged the thought
away. I was starting to go a little stir-crazy, I decided. I
needed to get out of the office for a while and take an early
lunch. I shut down my computer and took off.

Down in the car park I turned on the car radio and caught
the midday news bulletin. The lead story was the Glenn
Wood murder and that morning's press conference which,
given that it only started at eleven, must have been short and
sweet to make the lunchtime news. The official statement
confirmed that cause of death was strangulation by person or
persons unknown. The police appealed for any possible
witnesses to come forward and expressed an interest in
speaking to Mr Dorian Wilde. He was described as a close
friend of the deceased who they hoped might be able to
provide vital information concerning the victim. They didn't
say he was a suspect, but it was a fair bet that the press
would spin it that way until he turned up – if he did.

The story finished with details of the Tip Line number and
a promise of further updates throughout the day and on the
station's website, Northward Ho. I turned off the radio and
thought about the poor sods who would be manning the
phone lines that would soon be buzzing with the voices of
the lost, lonely and plain demented of this great city of ours.

I decided I was in serious need of cheering up, so I took out my phone and speed dialled Molly. She picked up almost at once.

"Hi Harry, what took you so long?" she said.

When I pulled up outside Stentor ten minutes later she was sitting on the low wall at the street end of the car park. She was wearing high-waisted black jeans with a pale blue hoodie and Oakley sunglasses with polished chrome frames and blue lenses. Her red hair was slightly tousled by the wind as she slid into the car and I caught the now familiar citrus rush of her perfume as she brushed a kiss against my left cheek.

I pulled away and drove about half a mile back towards the city to a little coffee shop called *The Last Drop*. It sat in the middle of a line of other businesses that consisted of two charity shops, a bookmaker and a Payday loan shop; a smear of lipstick on the cracked and defeated face of a typical 21st century suburban high street.

A handful of metal tables, scattered outside the coffee shop front door, added a faux air of Parisian je ne sais quoi to the scene. Despite the occasional chilly jabs of wind there were a few hardy punters in place, sipping their favourite strange brew in the intermittent Spring sunshine. We both agreed it was not the weather for al fresco dining and stepped inside. The place was about half full and we found a table by the window with a perfect view of the Mr Hand Job car wash across the street.

We had hardly settled before a waitress with an Audrey Hepburn hairstyle (circa Breakfast at Tiffany's) was at our side, inviting our order with a bright smile and an accent that was a real chip off the old Eastern bloc. Molly ordered prawn salad and a bottle of sparkling water. I settled for a brie and bacon ciabatta and a diet coke. A man of eclectic tastes, that's me.

The waitress wandered off and Molly sat back with a contented little sigh. Taking off her sunglasses she folded them carefully and set them down on top of her shoulder bag on the chair next to her,

215

"I – am – so – glad you called." she said, flashing me that smile which was rapidly becoming one of my favourite things. "The place has been like a madhouse this morning."

I raised an eyebrow at that.

"You having a fire alarm sale?" I wondered.

"Ha! Actually, it's not unusual for the market to go a little crazy the first few days after a major crime hits the city headlines."

"People panic buy security alarms? To safeguard their stockpiles of bread and bottled water?"

"You'd be surprised. Crime is definitely good for business in some areas. Do you know that gun sales in America rocket every time some lunatic goes on a shooting rampage? It's the same principal at work. A sensational murder really sets the alarm bells ringing – no pun intended."

"You're talking about Glenn Wood?"

Molly nodded.

"Yes. Isn't it horrible? I mean, I would rather stick pins in my eyes than watch any of his shows, but I suppose he was a big deal as far as local celebrities go."

"He certainly thought so." I agreed, and her expression faltered somewhere between amusement and a reflex kind of disapproval.

"You weren't a fan, either?" she deduced, going for the smile.

"No – but that doesn't mean he deserved what happened to him. Well, not just for being a giant arsehole."

"You're so right. I mean, where would it end?"

We were interrupted by the arrival of our food and we indulged our mutual hunger in silence for the space of several mouthfuls. Molly ate with relish. I had noticed the night before that she genuinely seemed to enjoy eating. Food wasn't just fuel for her, it was a kind of communion

"Did Jennifer ever talk about him?" I asked eventually, picking up the thread of our conversation,

"Jen? Wood? I don't – you don't mean? Ew! Really?"

"I'm afraid so."

"I shouldn't be shocked, I suppose." she sighed. "Probably just another celebrity notch on her headboard. Sorry – I didn't mean…"

"It's okay. I don't feel used."

"I shouldn't judge her, I know, but – Glenn Wood?"

I thought about explaining the Hellfire Club to her, but I didn't think telling her that sleeping with Wood was just club rules would make it any more palatable. Especially as there was no way of knowing if that represented the sum of their sexual encounters.

"Is that why you called?" Molly asked, looking down at her fast diminishing salad. "To ask about Jen and Wood?"

"Not at all." I assured her. "I wouldn't have mentioned Wood's name if it hadn't come up in conversation. It just reminded me that he and Jennifer had crossed paths. To tell you the truth, I rang you because I've spent all morning worrying at that connection and I really needed to get out of the office and out of my head for a while. Lunch in pleasant company seemed the best antidote – and your company is as pleasant as it gets."

"Flattery will get you everywhere." she laughed. "But, since we're one the subject, do you think Jen's disappearance could have something to do with what happened to Wood?"

"It could have but that's a matter for the police now. I've told them about Wood and Jennifer's – ah – relationship. It remains to be seen if it casts any light on Wood's murder."

"But what about you? Aren't you still looking for Jen?"

"At the moment that's up in the air. Callum Jensen seems to have gone dark and he deliberately misled me about where he was supposed to be during the last week. He said he'd be back in town next Monday, so I'll wait and see if he turns up. If he continues to be a no show, then there's no client to pay the bill and I'll have to drop the matter. Reluctantly, I'll admit, but we're a small operation with a growing client list I can't afford to neglect on a personal whim."

She nodded understandingly but I thought I saw a shadow of disappointment in those beautiful hazel eyes.

"You have to be realistic, I get that." she acknowledged. "It's just that since you came along looking for her I've realised just how much I miss Jen – and how guilty I feel for letting our friendship cool."

"Sometimes you've got to accept that, no matter how hard you work at them, some relationships are just toxic and back away to save yourself."

Which was easier to say than put into practice as I knew from bitter experience. The look Molly gave me said that she knew it too but was grateful that I'd said it all the same.

"It isn't easy for you to just let go, is it?" she said perceptively. "Especially after all the energy you put into looking for her – and all for nothing in the end."

I answered her sympathetic smile by impulsively reaching across and laying my left hand on top of hers. The look she returned was quizzical but by no means alarmed.

"Who said it was for nothing?" I said.

22.

At first glance Len Gilligan was nobody's idea of the cheating husband. He stood barely five feet seven in his Under Armour tactical boots, a squat figure with a Magwitch haircut and more fat than muscle crammed into an olive green 'I'd rather be shooting' t-shirt and camo trousers. He had a doughy face, with a big nose and slightly crazed eyes that gave him the look of the improbable love child of Kim Jong Un and Katie Hopkins. He looked, indeed, as if he'd been born under an ugly bush and never ventured out of the neighbourhood.

Despite his natural disadvantages Lenny's wife Angela, a slim blonde with a severe but attractive face and a slaughter-man's eyes, was convinced that he was playing away and cheerfully paid a week up front for confirmation. Well, that's a slight exaggeration. Angela didn't seem to have much of a handle on 'cheerful', a deficiency that owed much perhaps to the surly bundle of fun that was Len.

After a couple of days discreetly watching him in shifts with Eddie, he had done nothing so far to justify his wife's suspicions. He had left home every morning at eight o'clock and returned home at six, where he had remained all night until the couple turned in about eleven. The time in between he had spent in First Flush, the gun shop he owned in the Redbrook area of the city, except for his daily hour-long lunch break. This he took in the pub across the way, The Canal Tavern, a name I had found vaguely puzzling as, by my reckoning it was at least three miles from any body of water, let alone the canal. According to Eddie though, the name seemed a little more comprehensible after a taste of their best bitter.

On the third morning, however, it looked like there might be a significant variation to Len's usual routine. He left the house at the usual time in his casual, shooting-bum outfit but this morning he brought along a suit carrier, which he hung with great care in the back seat of his red Jeep Cherokee before shooting off for town.

I didn't let myself get too excited. Maybe he was just going to drop something off at the dry cleaners, or perhaps it wasn't a suit in the bag at all but some item or items of stock for the shop. Nothing to do but wait and see if its contents had any less innocent purpose.

Once Len was safely inside his shop, I settled down in my usual vantage point at the rear of the public car park at the top of the narrow cul de sac where the shop was situated. For company I had a flask of coffee, a couple of energy drinks, three donuts, a slab of chocolate and a spoken word version of Bill Bryson's Mother Tongue. None of these things, or any speculations about Len and his suit bag, could stop my thoughts drifting back to graver matters. So, I ate a donut, drank some coffee and thought about Jennifer Jensen and Glenn Wood.

The weekend had come and gone, so had the following Monday and there was still no word from the client. I doubted that there would be by this stage. Maybe he was nursing a craft beer somewhere and laughing hard over whatever little game he had played with me. Or perhaps he was in some lonely, haunted spot swinging from a tree like Wood and waiting for somebody to stumble across his body. Then again, perhaps he'd tripped and hit his head on a railway buffet sandwich and was wandering around with concussion and amnesia.

The possibilities were endless, but the bottom line was the same. That is, there was no bottom line and since I wasn't operating a charity I had to forget about the Jensens and move on. That, as I had assured Eddie and Clegg, was what I intended to do, except of course, it wasn't that easy. It might just have been the fact that I had, however fleeting, a personal connection to Jennifer, but she had never strayed far from my thoughts over the last few days.

The same was true of Glenn Wood, whose murderer remained at large despite the efforts of Swanson and his team to unearth a viable suspect. That didn't stop the local media filling their pages and the airwaves with the usual mix of rumour and speculation. Much of this concerned various local dignitaries and celebrities who had, allegedly, been questioned about their relationship with Wood. Speculation also touched briefly on some of the more notable oddballs who had been famous for five minutes for making twats of themselves on one or other of his reality shows.

There were mutterings aplenty that Wood's death might be linked to a promiscuous lifestyle, though only in the very general sense that he was famous-ish and therefore certain to be getting laid a lot. No hint of the Hellfire Club's existence had so far surfaced. A testimony, perhaps, to how well its members adhered to the protocols Wood had laid down for preserving the group's anonymity. Still, I was a little surprised that word hadn't leaked out of Rain Hill by now; probably a tribute to Swanson's fiercesome reputation and his iron grip on his team's loyalty/balls.

Then there was Dorian Wilde, who continued to be elusive. With Wood dead and Jennifer also missing that meant the only real proof of the Club's existence rested on my word and the shaky DVD of Jennifer's initiation that could easily be written off as nothing more than the tacky introduction to a one off masked orgy.

And where was Dorian, anyway? Could he really have snapped and killed Wood? Was he now on the run? He seemed to have genuine feelings for Jennifer and had certainly shown a flash of genuine antipathy to Wood when he had appeared to disrespect her. It was quite a leap from there to murder though. Dorian may have had a slightly dodgy moral compass, but I couldn't see him as a killer.

That is, I couldn't envisage him expending the amount of effort that Wood's killer had employed in getting the job done. Anybody might lash out in a moment of anger and injure or kill the object of that anger but there was nothing spontaneous or accidental about the way Wood had died. That had the hallmark of a crime meticulously planned and executed by someone with a deranged agenda of which I was convinced, despite Clegg's reservations, the chosen location was an essential part.

I dug out my smartphone, opened the Facebook app and brought up Dorian's profile. I'd been checking his page regularly since I'd learned that he was missing. There was no change to his status since the previous time I'd looked. He'd last posted on the previous Monday evening with the simple, capitalised phrase GOT IT! and a big smiley face icon. This was the follow up to an earlier post: Up for Algy in 'Ernest' with Galligaskins! I had taken this to mean that he had auditioned for the part of Algernon Moncrieff in a production of The Importance of Being Ernest. A little research revealed that the Galligaskins Theatre Company was a small but respected touring company based in Leeds. Their web page had confirmed that Dorian Wilde would join them for their forthcoming production of the other Mr Wilde's classic comedy, due to go into rehearsal at the beginning of the next month. It seemed like a real opportunity for him to progress his career and I would have expected him to make more of it on his social media accounts. Apart from his short triumphant outburst on getting the part, however, he had not commented on that or anything else, or responded to any of the, mostly, congratulatory comments his success had provoked.

I killed a few more minutes scrolling down the gallery of Dorian's friends. There were a lot of them and by far the majority were female. Very attractively so in many cases. It would be a tedious process of elimination for one of Swanson's team to work their way down the list trying to pick up a lead on Dorian's whereabouts and it certainly wasn't one I was inclined to attempt. It was enough to be able to confirm that Molly Grayson was not of the company.

I was about to close the app and put my phone away when I had a sudden notion. I cleared the Search box and typed in another name: Danny Walczak. It was a rare name, but I got a couple of hits. One was a teenager from Illinois, the other was Dorian, though if you didn't know that was his real name you probably wouldn't have made the connection. The photograph was clearly from an earlier time. Dorian looked as if he was still in his teens and the wild Irish gypsy look was somewhere several years in the future. His hair was cut short and he wore a blue and white hooped rugby shirt that I recognised as the colours of The Mendicants Academy, formerly my own old school, the City Grammar. Or Hogfarts, as Eddie insisted on calling it.

Danny's page was a lot quieter than that of his alter ego and his friends list a lot shorter. Judging by the names a lot of them were related to him to some degree and most of the remainder seemed to be locally based, probably old friends from school or university. His feed was full of the usual inconsequential mix of gossip, nostalgia, YouTube music videos of deep personal or satirical meaning, reports of local rugby and soccer games and the usual trite, philosophical sound bites in the name of Buddha and the spirit of Hallmark. For all that I found it encouraging that the heart of Danny Walczak still beat somewhere within the studly breast of Dorian Wilde; an oddly reassuring sign that his new persona hadn't completely absorbed the boy from Heronshaws.

What was even more encouraging was that there was more recent activity on this account than on the other, albeit still a couple of days ago.

Going dark for a few days. I think I'm having a Damascus moment and need space to think in. No one remains quite what he was when he recognises himself.

There were a few comments, mostly sympathetic and supportive – Hear you, bro/Hope you find the answer Waz/Just promise me you won't start a new religion! – though somebody called Brett Lane seemed to have had the last word: Fucking Drama Queen! A trio of laughing emoticons stripped the sentiment of any malice but, like most jokes, there might have been a kernel of cynicism at its core.

If nothing else Dorian/Danny's cryptic message suggested that perhaps his sudden absence from the city might not be so sinister after all. It had been posted late in the evening of the same day I had met with Dorian and Wood in my office. I couldn't help wondering whether that meeting had any bearing on whatever inner conflict he found himself wrestling with. guess.

I shut down the app and put away my phone, suppressing a momentary impulse to let Swanson know about Dorian's second Facebook account. Chances were they'd already discovered it, in which case Swanson would be pissed off at me for implying his team were incompetent. If they hadn't then he would be pissed off at me for proving it. In either case there was nothing about the post to indicate Dorian's whereabouts, so it didn't really help beyond providing a slight lessening of anxiety for his safety. I settled for that and brought my mind back to the job in hand. Time for another donut.

The morning wore on and the promised rain came and went in brief spurts punctuated by bursts of warm sunshine. At eleven o'clock a familiar, gangly figure in a black field jacket ambled along the street and went into the gun shop. Len's part-time assistant turning up for his shift. A few customers drifted in and out, including a couple of women, though neither of them looked like they'd just dropped by to put their hand down the front of the owner's pants.

At half past the hour the pub across the street opened and traffic down the street increased as the daytime drinkers started to appear like forlorn extras in a zombie flick. I died inside at the prospect of spending another lunchtime in the glum and gloomy interior of The Canal Tavern when, as was his habit, Len emerged from his shop almost on the stroke of midday. The moment passed with the realisation that perhaps the usual pint and a pie weren't on today's menu. Gone were the camo pants and corny T-shirt. Len Gilligan was transformed. Suited and booted like a gentleman. A gentleman who, if the undeniable spring in his step was an indication, was definitely up to no good.

After that the day developed in a predictable enough way as I followed Len's SUV out of town and into the Pennine foothills skirting the border with Derbyshire. After about half an hour he pulled into the car park of an out of the way pub called The Drovers Arms poised above the Derwent Valley. I followed him inside, where I ordered a lime and soda and watched discreetly from a seat at the bar as he nursed half a pint in the restaurant area, gazing out from time to time through the big windows with a kind of nervous longing.

After about ten minutes, he finally saw whatever it was he had been looking for and launched himself towards the bar, where he collided happily with a slender ash blonde in a faux leopard-skin coat. Her sharply attractive features seemed disconcertingly familiar as she leaned down to brush Len's beaming cheeks with a quick kiss. Only when she straightened and turned her face more fully towards the room did I realise why she seemed so recognisable. She was an almost dead ringer for Len's suspicious wife, Angela, though with kinder eyes and a few less miles on the clock. It was possible that he just had a type, of course, but it looked to me that if Len really was cheating on his wife he was keeping it in the family!

Slipping his arm around the woman, Len steered her towards the table he'd reserved in the restaurant and I managed to take a few photographs of the pair as they studied their menus. Leaving them to their lunch I finished off my drink and wandered back to the car to wait them out.

An hour or so later they emerged, and both climbed into Len's SUV for a fifteen-minute run down into the Derbyshire Dales, where they spent the next couple of hours in a luxury log cabin style holiday lodge on the Brookside holiday park. What they did there I couldn't say for definite, but I doubted they were playing cribbage. Strip poker, maybe.

From a safe distance at the edge of nearby woodland beyond the park's boundary fence, I took a few photographs of the SUV parked outside and later a few more shots of them leaving, including a long, lingering kiss they shared before climbing back into the car and shooting off back to The Drovers. He dropped her at the car park entrance, after another long exchange of spit, and she skipped out of the car and waved him off on his way back to the city.

I drove past them into the car park while they were still snorkelling and parked up. I made like an ordinary punter, fiddling with my phone and checking for emails while I waited for the blonde to get into her car and leave. There was nothing from Jensen, but I noticed a couple of missed calls from Eddie, followed up by a sharp text: Is your phone on mute again or are you effing deaf? Call me.

I thought about a few things to call him but that would have to wait as Len's guilty secret was by now pulling away in a very nice silver Audi A5 Cabriolet. I tossed my phone aside and followed on her winding way home. This proved to be The Rowans, a newish, detached house in the Hope Valley with a double garage and a tall Leylandii hedge poised to take over the world. Once I had the address it was easy enough to confirm that the property was occupied by a Mr and Mrs Dettinger, Mike and Alice. It was back to Facebook then and sure enough the lovely Alice had a lively presence there and a gallery of friends that included Len and Angela Gilligan – who her profile confirmed were indeed her sister and brother-in-law.

It gave me no satisfaction to be proved right. The fact is I always had an ambiguous attitude when it came to the 'domestic' side of my business. On the one hand it was a core service for an operation my size and, on a personal level, I always had visceral sympathy for the client who was being cheated on. This was mainly because I'd been on that end of a relationship myself – more than once – and it hurt like hell to be deceived. On the other hand, I could never entirely shake the feeling that the 'marital' side of the operation was tawdry and shoddy and reflected badly on all parties – me included. One day I hoped that I, the firm, would be in a position where we didn't need the business – but today was not that day.

I still had the phone in my hand when it began to buzz urgently, reminding me that it was still switched to vibrate. I flicked the ringer back on and took the call. It was from Eddie – and I could tell he wasn't happy. The conversation was short and sharp.

'Something's come up, H. You need to get back here sharpish."

I'd tried to pry more out of him, but he wouldn't be drawn, just muttered:

"It's not something we should talk about over the phone".

Which in itself was worrying, coming as it did from someone to whom 'Delicacy' and 'Sensitivity' were just double-digit Scrabble scores.

He hung up on me then, which also seemed off but by the time I'd driven back from Derbyshire I'd just about convinced myself that it was just tiredness making me paranoid. That changed when I got back to the office. Eddie and Clegg were at their desks, but they weren't alone. Sitting at the desk I usually occupied was a young woman wearing a black T-shirt and a look of serious disapproval that seemed entirely focused on me.

"This is Alex. My cousin?" Eddie explained.

"She doesn't look happy? Did our cheque bounce?"

I didn't expect anybody to fall about but the lack of any reaction at all was as bad as a slow handclap. Now I wasn't so sure. The vibes the three of them were giving off were definitely resonating at the frosty end of the spectrum. I looked from Eddie to Clegg, to Alex and back to Eddie, waiting for one of them to tell me why they all looked as if somebody had died and started to smell.

"H-"

"Hal -"

Eddie and Clegg started and stopped speaking almost simultaneously and looked at each other for a second or two before Clegg gestured that Eddie should be the nominated spokesman. He didn't look like it was a contest he was happy to win but he ploughed on.

"Thing is H – well, you know Alex has been cleaning up the old office PCs for the Homeless Centre?"

"I do recall it, yes"

"Yeah, well – oh, bugger it – she found something on one of the machines."

"Found? Was it lost then?"

"More like hidden." Alex said brusquely.

"A virus?"

"No – but something nasty." she said cryptically.

227

"It's a document, Hal." Clegg said. "A very troubling one –
but perhaps you ought to see it for yourself before we get
into any discussion about it. Young lady -?"

Alex looked annoyed, perhaps at being addressed in that
way, or maybe it was just her default setting.

"Here." she said to me, pushing a green document binder
across my desk towards me with just the tips of her fingers,
as if merely the act of touching it might leave an unpleasant
deposit.

I frowned at the binder and then at Clegg.

"Aren't you going to give me any clues?"

"Just read it, Hal, please. Unless you already know what it
is?"

I didn't like the sound of that. It wasn't an accusation
exactly, but it wasn't an entirely friendly question. I looked
at their faces again and saw only concern – except for Alex,
who was now looking at me in much the same way she had
looked at the binder on the desk. Whatever it contained, there
was no doubt it was the cause of the odd atmosphere I'd
walked into. With a brief nod of acquiescence, I scooped up
the binder and gestured with it towards my office.

"I'll read it through there, if you don't mind? Being stared
at like the only man at the party in fancy dress makes it hard
to concentrate." I said, which seemed to cause an unexpected
amount of consternation all round.

Swallowing my rising irritation, I strode into the other
office without another word and banged the door shut behind
me with the same degree of satisfaction acting like a five-
year-old always brings with it. Settling myself at the table
where I had sat with Glenn Wood and Dorian only a few
short days ago, I reached for a bottle of water from the tray
that still stood in the centre of the conference table.
Wrenching the top off, I took a long swallow before turning
my attention to the enigmatic blue folder. Opening the cover,
I turned to the first page and began to read.

PART TWO

23.

10/06/2017

I have seen the Devil. Looked him in the eye, watched him die. Not black but fair, his hair white as bone or the relentless snow that drifted about us. I battled him by the black, asphaltic waters of an urban Styx, bloated and gloating with sin, wreathed in the coppery stink of slaughter, revelling in his wickedness. I faced him, and I fought him, watched him fall into those dark waters with all his crimson dreams in ruins about him.

They say I slew a Devil but, in doing so, did I become one myself?

This is the question I have asked myself many times in this last year, searching my soul for some glimmer of remorse. I have found nothing except the savage joy of being alive, which shoots through me from time to time like an unexpected bolt of lightning. At these moments I am filled with sudden optimism and a deep conviction that there is nothing I cannot accomplish.

This rush of confident certainty is all too brief, and I am soon dragged back to earth by the clutching, tacky grip of reality. How weary, stale, flat and unprofitable seem to me all the uses of this world! I am tired of the daily drudge; the furtive sniffing at the piled-up dirty laundry of this mediocre city; the unseemly pawing through the debris of broken marriages and petty frauds; the endless sifting of lies and deceit in search of truths that bring no comfort with the knowing. I needed to break this monotony. Write the novel that has been scrabbling for so long to escape from its cage, perhaps? Or get laid.

I wonder sometimes, though, if anything will ever make me feel as alive as I did when I challenged Death and dared him face to face.

24/06/2017

It was the end of long evening spent cruising the better class of pick up bars, swimming through thick shoals of available women without any of them registering on my sonar. It shouldn't have been so hard. I wasn't looking for a soul mate, after all, just a roll in the hay. This may have been the root of my problem, to be honest. I am not the casual sort who is given to hasty friendships and the pursuit of shallow pleasures. It cuts against the grain of my romantic nature.

I had effectively written the evening off and only went into the *Barracuda* because I couldn't face the thought of going home alone again without a last, stiff drink inside me. Isn't it always the case though? The minute you stop actively looking for something, it finds you.

Her name is Jennifer, from Guinevere, which itself derives from the Celtic Gwenhwyfar - the Fair One, the White Shadow whose otherworldly beauty captivates the heart of kings. She certainly captivated mine, though I must confess that it was not in my chest where I felt the first pangs of longing. I did say it had been a long time.

Not to descend to crudity but it was no meeting of minds that brought us together last night. It was just a collision of bodies, each reeking of their own kind of desperation. We both walked away from the wreckage this morning and now I sit alone here in the darkness. As I smoke my last Romeo y Julieta (how apt!) and sip a fine cognac, I realise that one of us left something behind in the cold dawn. A deep longing rises up in me with a sudden, choking urgency. I need to see her again if only to recover what she has ripped from me. My heart and soul?

27/06/2017

A wasted day. Hardly got a thing done for thinking about Jennifer, my White Ghost, and in the end I gave in and left the office early and drove straight to the Barracuda. I stayed there all evening, nursing my drinks and watching the doors, my hopes rising every time someone came through them, only to plummet the moment I realised the newcomer was not her. I have not felt this way since forever. *She stains the time past, lights the time to come.*

28/06/2017

Slept badly, left the office early to haunt her doorstep. Another fruitless evening, drinking warm beer in the chintzy pub across the street. She never came home, and the house remained in darkness. Only when I fell into conversation with a garrulous, ale-drenched local did I discover that no one is currently living there! The owner died these twelve months past - Jennifer's mother I suspect – though her daughter visits from time to time to air the sheets! Nudge, nudge, wink, wink. Know what I mean? He looked into my eyes and didn't like what he saw. He drank his beer and scuttled off into the night like a cockroach in a pork pie hat. If I hadn't drunk so much, I would have stepped on him.

15/07/2017

These last two weeks have been a salutary experience, blunting any optimism my encounter with Jennifer may have nurtured. She is a troubled soul, lost in a shallow lifestyle of cheap sexual gratification that places little or no emotional demands upon her. Revelatory as our shared experience had been for me, I now realise it meant as little to her as the need to scratch an itch, so armoured is she against the potential disappointment that lies dormant in any human relationship that might demand more than just an easy commitment to physical pleasure.

I see now I have become a part of that depressing pattern that I took such offence to when the stranger in the pork pie hat so pruriently hinted at it. I have myself witnessed her trawling the singles bars of the city for sexual partners, shamefacedly tracking her and her latest conquest back to the quaint bungalow where she took me to bed and beyond. Each time is a kind of betrayal, but I cannot find it in me to hate her for it. Rather, the anger that at times threatens to overwhelm me, is not centred on Jennifer but on the men, who so knowingly use her. For though I know that she is also using them – as indeed she used me – I see that she is broken and emotionally adrift. She needs to be saved – from herself and from those who prey on her without even the pretence of tenderness and understanding.

The question is: am I equal to the task? She is deep inside me now, gnawing at me, paring me down to the emotional bone. I am wasting away like a convict abandoned in the dungeon of my feelings. How can I save her if I cannot save myself?

Must stop drinking late at night. It makes me maudlin and pathetic.

16/07/2017

There does not appear to be any discernible pattern to how Jennifer selects her sexual partners. They seem to come in all shapes, sizes and condition. Subject to the inexplicable whim of the moment, perhaps? Or chosen against some unfathomable criteria unrelated to their physicality? Because they make her laugh or remind her in subtle ways of former friends or lovers? Maybe it is simply that mysterious human chemistry at work, which so often confounds our expectations of who should be attracted to who.

One thing that they – we – have in common, is the transient nature of the experience we share with Jennifer. Her sexual radar is so finely tuned that she can readily discern potential partners who share her apparent disdain for any commitment that stretches beyond the few torrid hours shared between her sheets.

21/07/2016

After several days following Jennifer around the city centre pick up bars the time finally seemed right to reintroduce myself to her. With that in mind, I followed her this lunchtime to The Delta, a public house about half a mile from her office. It's a quiet but pleasant little place by the river side with a reputation for decent pub food and craft beers from half a dozen micro-breweries in and around the city. It represented a noticeable break in her lunchtime routine, which generally entailed a quick trip to a nearby sandwich shop or coffee shop, usually with at least one of her colleagues for company. It was unusual enough for her to be on her own that it seemed likely she was meeting someone, I realised. With that thought in mind, I sat indecisively in the car as I watched her walk into the pub and for several minutes afterwards as I debated how to proceed. Just as I had decided to follow her into the bar, silently rehearsing the pantomime of pleased surprise that I would go through when we 'noticed' each other, she re-emerged into the autumn sunshine.

She made her way into the beer garden, which consisted of half a dozen or so bench tables occupying a well-trimmed, gently sloping lawn, enclosed by a wooden fence. She took a seat at one of the empty tables and sat nursing a glass of her favoured chilled Chardonnay. As she gazed over the fence at the river beyond, flowing murkily towards the city, she seemed lost in her thoughts.

Is it wishful thinking to suppose that they were not particularly happy? I would like to believe she is dissatisfied with her current lifestyle and is secretly yearning to break the dangerous cycle of promiscuity she seems locked into. I would also like to think I might be the one to fill the role of saviour if she could be persuaded to offer me that role.

Catching her alone like this seemed like an invitation to audition. I would buy a drink at the bar, wander out into the beer garden and, looking around insouciantly, I would catch her eye and look pleasantly startled. She would take a moment to recognise me then she would smile, perhaps raise a hand in tentative acknowledgement, which I would seize on as an invitation to join her and...

I was roused from this reverie with heart-sinking suddenness when I realised that, while I had been sitting blocking out my moves, someone else had upstaged me!

As I feared, Jennifer was not there to enjoy a solitary lunch after all. She had been joined by a good looking, dark-haired man, carrying a glass of beer in one hand and a wooden spoon in the other; a table identifier for the benefit of the waitresses serving lunchtime diners, I supposed. Whoever he was, the newcomer must have already been inside the bar when she arrived and lingered within to order their food before joining Jennifer for an al fresco lunch.

After the initial sense of frustration, I admit to being intrigued. This was after all a complete deviation from the normal social routines I had observed over the last few weeks. The quiet setting, the relaxed way they chatted to each other, the way one of her hands would casually touch his from time to time, suggested a comfortable acquaintance and familiarity with each other. It spoke to an intimacy beyond the merely physical and recognition of this brought on a pang of jealousy far sharper than anything I had previously suffered when observing her interactions with other men. On these occasions only, the threat or promise of sex bound them together and though that same tension was there between Jennifer and this man, some subtext of the scene they were playing piqued my interest. I had no doubt that they were lovers but not, I thought, of the casual, easily disposable type. He was no throwaway stud but someone for who she seemed to have a genuine affection.

This is clearly a problem as I have no intention of sharing Jennifer with anyone!

I studied my unexpected rival through the binoculars I always keep to hand. He was younger than Jennifer or myself, I estimated. Somewhere in his twenties or else remarkably well-preserved. His thick, curly black hair lent him that roguish Irish-Gypsy look so many women seem to swoon over. Heathcliff in tight fitting black jeans and a matching leather-look faux shearling jacket, which he wore over a white roll-neck sweater. He probably thought he looked good enough to eat. She probably thought so too, which made my hands tighten involuntarily around the binoculars.

After a few minutes a waitress in a maroon tabard came out of the bar carrying two plates of food, pausing at the beer garden gate to shout out the relevant table number. At the sound of her voice Heathcliff turned and waved the wooden spoon languidly in response. She wended her way over to their table and set down the food and cutlery, exchanging smiles and a few brief words with Jennifer's companion before returning to the bar with, so it seemed to me, considerably less alacrity than she had left it and an almost wistful expression on her pretty, commonplace face. Heathcliff it seemed had made another conquest without even knowing it. Or, if he did, he gave no indication of it, as he was already deep in conversation with Jennifer once more.

While they were so absorbed I got out of the car and entered the cool interior of the bar. Their choice of whiskies wasn't extensive, but they had Laphroaig, which will always do at a pinch, so I bought myself a shot and sat down on one of the bar stools with a good view down the room through the double doors that opened onto the beer garden.

There wasn't a lot to see, other than Jennifer and Heathcliff talking and laughing between mouthfuls of food or drink. The only interesting thing that happened was when their conversation was briefly interrupted while Heathcliff consulted his mobile. He studied the screen, as if reading a text, which was not in itself remarkable. However, within a couple of seconds Jennifer was delving into her shoulder bag to consult her own phone. A simple coincidence, perhaps, though I couldn't help wondering what the odds were on them both receiving unrelated texts at the same time.

They both read their messages quickly and did not reply, putting away their phones and slipping back into whatever stream of banalities flowed so easily between them. This continued unabated until the lunch hour ended, and Jennifer's body language suggested he was on the verge of leaving to return to work. This she did with a smile and a quick peck on the lips, hoisting her bag onto her right shoulder and striding off without looking back.

There seemed little point in following her back to Stentor, nor did I have any appetite for pursuing my tedious business, so I stayed where I was. I was intrigued to have discovered Jennifer's relationship with Heathcliff and finding out who he was and just how serious a role he played in her life seemed worthy of my attention.

He didn't linger long, downing the last couple of inches of the half a lager he had been nursing and rising to leave. I sank the last of my whisky and headed back to my car. Heathcliff did not emerge for several more minutes and I was just beginning to think he was merely replenishing his drink when he finally appeared and climbed into a black Porsche Boxster with ten-year-old plates.

This caused me some concern as I doubted I would be able to keep up with him if he cut loose. However, he proved not to be in any hurry and it was a simple enough task to keep him well in sight for the twenty minutes or, so it took to drive to Miller's Goit and onto the gated forecourt of an upmarket warehouse conversion called the Loxley Apartments. I hung around long enough to watch him use his keys on the front door of the apartment building, then left. Duty called, stale, flat, if not entirely unprofitable, as it seems to me these days.

09/08/217

Can't sleep. Thoughts are buzzing around my head like glutted carrion flies frenziedly seeking escape. It is some time since I was last moved to make an addition to this sordid record of my obsession. This is not because it has become quiescent but merely that its routines have become banal through repetition.

Also, if I am being honest, the dull recording of Jennifer's continued decline into promiscuity is a chore not worth pursuing. It merely becomes commentary on an ongoing tragedy and my own inability to forestall the minacious currents that swirl around her. Yet, I am more convinced than ever that her lifestyle puts her in genuine, perhaps mortal danger. I have stood face to face with a genuine evil that claimed the lives of women far more nuanced in the twisted ways of men than Jennifer seems to be. She believes, I am sure, that she is control, confident in her ability to pick up and use any man on a whim, then crumple him up and toss him away with no more regret than he might dispose of a used condom.

Such is the contract she strikes with her lovers, a transaction that has so far been satisfactory to both parties. What she does not see is that, with each encounter that ends in a quiet, post-coital glow of mutual satisfaction, the odds decrease on the next reaching an entirely different, perhaps even cataclysmic conclusion. What I failed to see, in my turn, is that the greatest danger might emanate not from any random stranger but from a source much closer to home. I should not be so surprised, I suppose, since experience has taught me that people we know and trust may harbour a darkness in their heart as deep as that which fuels any of the sexual psychopaths who range the night. Indeed, they may very well be that sexual psychopath. After all, how many times have we heard the bewildered wife, friend or mother of a serial rapist or murderer proclaiming their horrified ignorance of his vicious nature? What it comes down to is this: are any of us truly as innocent as we seem?

11/08/2017

I have just re-read last night's ramblings, which were fuelled by one too many glasses of Lagavulin taken as a panacea to dull the memory of the scenes I had observed earlier in the evening and which I could not bring myself to describe at the time. The emotional cost of concretizing the shabby tableau I had witnessed was too daunting. I returned home filled with a smouldering anger that needed just a spark to flare into full-blown, perhaps homicidal rage. More whisky and the typing of platitudes soothed me and now, sober and fuelled only by copious cups of coffee and the occasional cigar, I am in calm, reflective mood. Now I feel able to set down a record of last night's dismal events, which if nothing else have given fresh impetus to the cause of saving Jenny Jensen's soul.

Where to begin? You have met Dorian. The boy with gypsy black hair and a roguish smile. I thought from the first he would be trouble. I was right. After I followed him back to Miller's Goit that day I spent an hour or so learning a little more about him. His name, improbably: Dorian Wilde, though it suits him no less well than Heathcliff, I suppose. Age: 25 years and 4 months. Occupation: Catalogue model, Would-be-actor and, as I discovered over the next couple of days, Jennifer's boy toy.

I followed him the next evening to Jennifer's home, Moorside, and he was still inside at midnight, when the lights went out. Before I called it a night myself I slipped over the front gate and worked my way around to the side of the house where his Porsche was stabled in one half of the double garage. I admit I had the childish urge to slash is tyres or key the paintwork, but my aim was covert surveillance not emotionally stunted vandalism. I suppressed the urge and lingered only long enough to slip a magnetic GPS tracker out of my pocket and fix it beneath the rear end of his vehicle. I had placed a similar device on Jennifer's Evoque a couple of weeks earlier. Linked to an app on my cell phone the devices are accurate to within three feet and eliminate any risk of losing track of whoever I happen to be following at the time. After returning to my own vehicle I briefly checked that both trackers were functioning and headed back to the city.

When I checked this morning, Dorian's car had not moved and remained static until almost midday, when he returned briefly to his apartment. He stayed, long enough for a shower and a change of clothes, perhaps, before he drove to Leeds, where his Porsche remained stationery for the next three hours at a multi-storey car park near the city centre.

Jennifer, in the meantime, had remained at home. Or, at least, her vehicle had. It was one of her non-working days and I wondered for a while if she had accompanied her toy boy on his jaunt into wild West Yorkshire. A brief trip to Waitrose mid-afternoon dispelled this scenario, and by four o'clock, she was back at Moorside, where she remained for the next couple of hours before she was on the move again. This piqued my interest a little since it was, on past evidence, too early for her to begin her established troll of the singles bars. Besides which, it soon become obvious that, wherever her ultimate destination was, it did not lie within the city limits. Indeed, her current trajectory was firmly in the opposite direction towards the M1.

This fleetingly suggested the possibility that she might also be heading to Leeds to meet up with Dorian but when I checked the signal from his tracker he too was on the move, heading out of Leeds but for the M62 rather than the M1, which would have brought him home by the quickest route.

I was by this time in my own car and following Jennifer, who was by now perhaps ten miles ahead of me. This gap remained more or less constant until she left the motorway just south of Barnsley for the A628 and from there onto the A629 and then the A635, the Holmfirth Road. In this small, picturesque town, at a residential inn called The Huntsman, she eventually stopped.

By this time, it was almost seven o'clock. I arrived there myself about ten minutes later and easily spotted her Evoque in the spacious but sparsely populated car park. There was no sign of Jennifer but there was nowhere else she could be except the pub. I settled down to wait for Dorian to arrive. The location of the tracker on his car showed that he was now on the A616 out of Huddersfield just half a dozen miles down the road. I no longer doubted that they were meeting up, but the chosen location and the fact that they had travelled separately gave me something to reflect on.

I was still pondering this when Dorian's Porsche pulled onto the car park about ten minutes later. The overnight bag he was carrying as he sauntered towards the pub entrance a few seconds later made the picture a lot clearer, though I remained puzzled as to why they would choose to spend a night away together in a place so relatively close to home. A quick internet search told me that the inn had a good reputation for food and hospitality but there were more Michelin starred restaurants in Yorkshire than any other county and this place was not amongst them. Nor did it advertise any pending events or special gatherings unless you counted one of those bloody annoying pub quizzes. That seemed to rule out gastronomy or a social motive for their trip out of town, at least. There was always sex, of course, and it was possible, I supposed, that the place held tacky, romantic memories for them.

Such speculation aside I debated what course of action to follow. If they were, indeed, staying the night simply for a change of bedroom wallpaper I might as well return to the city. On the other hand, I could not shake the feeling that something other than a simple carnal away day was playing out here. Sound instinct or fortuitous paranoia? Either way, I decided to bide my time. It was a decision vindicated within the hour when Dorian and Jennifer emerged together, laughing and joking as they quick-stepped to her car.

I let them get a good start before pulling out after them. The signal from the tracker on Jennifer's SUV was strong and I kept well back. She followed the main road for a couple of miles before diving off onto a narrow network of country byways; a fine skein running between dry stone walls that delineated a landscape of fields broken only occasionally by a lone cottage or farm.

After three or four miles of this they took a right turn onto a narrower road that barely deserved the name. In truth it was more like a rustic cart track, which may once, in the distant past, have been crudely surfaced but had now shed most of its top layer. It was now more a loosely connected set of pot holes than a viable by-road. Not so much unadopted as ruthlessly cast out to fend for itself.

It was obvious by now why they had chosen to take the Evoque and I began to fear for my suspension. It was a relief when, a couple of minutes later, the signal on my phone display stopped moving and settled into the steady pulse, indicating that they had apparently reached their destination.

I slowed to a stop and turned off my lights while I studied the GPS signal and Google maps. They were parked in front of the very last building on this abominable stretch of road. It ended about a hundred yards further on, where it dwindled into little more than a dusty track. Though, ironically, it appeared to offer much smoother passage than the road up to that point afforded, the track ended abruptly with only empty fields stretching on beyond it.

With a better idea of how the land lie, I started the car again. I left the lights off and edged slowly forward until the dark shape of the building came into view. Light streamed from several windows and bled out onto the track as I drove by. It also illuminated a paved courtyard where several cars were parked. I could only hope that no one was around to wonder why I had just driven past on a road leading only into the middle of nowhere.

Just past the boundary of the property the track dipped sharply downwards and a glance at the map on my phone indicated that, about a quarter of a mile beyond the house, it split at right angles. With my headlights on low beam I bumped along to the junction where I reversed to face back towards the 'main' road before parking up and switching off my engine.

I spent another five minutes on my phone checking out the building on street view. It was a two-storey barn conversion with a small garden at the rear and the courtyard at the front, edged by two or three out buildings within a low, stone perimeter wall. It stood the top of a slope and I was parked at the bottom where the arm of the branching road I had taken was little more than a narrow, sunken lane whose steep banks were crowned by dry stone walling. It meant I couldn't physically see the house or be seen by anyone in it, which was a useful if entirely fortuitous circumstance.

I got out of the car and went to the trunk where I kept a bag containing certain items I had assembled for covert, night-time surveillance: a black crew neck sweater, balaclava, gloves and a pair of night vision, lunar optic binoculars. Suitably prepared, I locked the car and walked the few yards back to the branch in the track, from where I could survey the terrain between the sunken road and the rear wall of the property, which backed onto a small wood that ended halfway down the slope at the verge of an uncultivated field.

A few minutes later, I had reached the edge of the trees, through which I could see the glow from its lights, if not the house itself. I drew nearer, working my way towards that glow until I was close enough for a close inspection of the house through the night vision binoculars.

Whatever had brought Jennifer and her Heathcliff to this place they were not alone. I counted at least twenty, neatly parked cars in the courtyard and even as I finished the mental count another vehicle turned in through the tall double gate that opened off the weathered track I had so recently driven along.

The vehicle stopped just inside the open gates, its engine still running, and after a few seconds a figure climbed out of the right rear door. Their back was towards me as they stood for a moment looking at the house before them and from the figure's general shape and height, which was around six feet, I assumed it was a man. He wore a dark hooded sweatshirt and was carrying what looked like a large sports bag over his right shoulder.

The newcomer stepped clear of the car and, reversing quickly out of the gate, it took off back the way it had come. The hooded figure walked unhurriedly to the gates and closed them. Whatever the purpose of the gathering within the house it seemed he was to be the last arrival. Once the gates were secured, he turned and walked at the same, leisurely pace towards a door set about halfway along the side of the building. It was unlocked and opened smoothly inward, allowing a further splash of light to escape from inside. As he was about to step through the door, he paused briefly and turned to survey the crowded courtyard. With my binoculars now firmly fixed on him, I willed the figure to push back the hoodie and give me a look at his face.

Who was it said: "Be careful what you wish for"?

He turned to scan the car park one last time, thrusting back the hood. My mind reeled at what that gesture revealed. It was not the face of a man that starcd out across the dimly lit courtyard but a smirking Satan with eyes as deep and black as the pits of hell!

The moment passed and, as quickly as it had seemed to rise into my throat, my heart settled back in my chest, as I realised that I was looking at a mask. Or was the mask somehow looking at me, peering through the darkness directly into my soul? In the shadow of the trees I smiled nervously at the conceit and the uneasy feeling passed as the masked figure turned and entered the building. He closed the door, but I could see him through its glass panel for a few more seconds as he turned to lock it behind him.

I realised that I had been holding my breath and released it in a long exhale, chiding myself again for my fancies as I considered the probable truth that Jennifer and the boy had driven all this way simply to attend a cheesy costume party.

And yet… that hooded figure in the devilish mask had unnerved me, if only for a rapidly accelerated heartbeat, and I could not shake off a sudden feeling of foreboding. This grew stronger the longer I stood there replaying that eerie moment when the pitch-black eyes of that Satanic vizard had seemed to pierce the very darkness and freeze my soul.

Almost without realising it, I was moving forward cautiously. Ghosting through the last few trees I stooped low to cross the wide strip of open ground between the edge of the wood and the boundary wall, crouching to peer cautiously over the latter before vaulting over it and working my way around the inside, keeping to the deep shadows, where the lights of the house did not penetrate, until I reached full cover in rear of the trio of brick outbuildings that faced the main house's western exposure, one of the long sides of a half-brick, half-siding rectangular structure with a high, sloping roof.

There was a wide, glass panelled door situated at the midpoint of the exterior wall and another, smaller entrance at the far end. There were windows to the left and right of the large door. There was another to the right of smaller and two more evenly spaced. between the doors. All of the windows were hung with slatted blinds. These were not completely closed judging by the thin strips of light cast onto the courtyard, though from my vantage point, standing back in deep shadow I could see nothing through the narrow slats but an occasional, indistinct flash of movement.

I needed to get closer but crossing the courtyard directly risked being seen by someone glancing out of one of the windows. To minimise this risk, I retreated to the boundary wall and followed it round to the bottom end of the property. This was marked by a high wooden fence about a hundred feet from the rear of the building. The intervening space was a well-kept lawn edged with flower beds. Dim light spilled onto the front end of this garden area from whatever doors or windows occupied the rear of the building but did not extend to the fence where I again found friendly shadows from which to contemplate my next move.

After studying the rear of the building for a few moments – another panelled door flanked by a couple of windows - I detected no movement behind the ubiquitous blinds and scurried - yes, that is the word - across the lawn to flatten myself against the wall between the door and the right-hand window. A quick glance confirmed the room beyond to be a kitchen area that was currently unoccupied. Emboldened by this discovery, I groped for the handle of the door and turned it stealthily. It proved to be locked, which was probably as well, I chided myself. Sneaking around outside was reckless enough, sneaking around inside would surely be to invite discovery and embarrassment, at the very least.

I withdrew my hand and edged around to the side of the building, cautiously easing along, my back to the wall, towards the first of the windows along its length, crouching beneath the level of the window ledge as I reached it. I squatted there for long seconds, drawing deep, slow, calming breaths, straining my ears to pick up any noise that might herald my discovery. Heard nothing but my own breathing and the faint sound of music from beyond the glass above my head, an old song from half a century ago that reverberated in my chest with a deep and troubling urgency and recalled the figure I had lately seen slipping through the back door in that hollow eyed, smirking mask.

I am the god of Hellfire and I bring you
Fire, I'll take you to burn...

As the fierce anthem raged on, I slowly raised myself to peer through the window between the half-opened slats of the blinds on a bizarre, Bacchanalian scene of male and female revellers sprawled on couches or amidst piles of luxurious cushions, or simply standing in little, chattering clusters, drinking from elegant goblets, smoking or nibbling from the lavish buffet that was laid out against one wall of what seemed to be a single long room with a polished wood floor. It was a prosaic enough party scene, had it not been for the fact that all the revellers were naked from the neck down. Only their faces were covered, obscured behind a fantastical assortment of masks that ranged from plain, black dominos and eerie white masks to elaborate, zoomorphic creations.

It was a scene both unexpected and vaguely disturbing. I am not one to be affronted or intimated by nakedness but the contrast of bare flesh and garish vizards created an effect that was at once both tawdry and sinister. It produced in me a mixture of amused disdain, vague embarrassment and a sudden, gnawing anxiety. A presentiment, if you will, of the impending catastrophe that was to be enacted over the next few minutes. This was heralded by the sudden cessation of the frenetic rhythm of that Satanic old pop song that filled the room.

A more sedate piece followed, though it was not without an unsettling undercurrent. It was a classical composition I guessed though not one that fell within the limited catalogue of works I am familiar with. Its sombre tones seemed to act as a rallying call to the naked throng as the loungers scrambled to their feet and the knots of standing gossipers broke apart. The attention of everyone present swivelled towards the rear of the room, which lay beyond my field vision. A few seconds later, however, the objects of their sudden scrutiny appeared, a man and a woman, walked side by side through the now silent crowd. They were masked and naked like their peers, the woman in a royal purple ball mask, decked with plumes and flowers, knowing and yet mysterious. The man was instantly recognisable in his distinctive, garish guise as the devil-visaged figure I had recently seen in the courtyard. With slow, measured strides they advanced towards the bottom end of the room and came to a halt before what I can only compare to a church lectern, though from what dark and twisted church it may have inhabited I could not say, for it was in the form of a shrieking carrion bird carved from ebony or some other black wood.

The music played for a few seconds longer then faded out slowly. The ensuing silence was suddenly shattered by the sound of a gong being loudly beaten: once, twice, three times.

Since they had first appeared in my view I had been focusing on the Devil and his companion, who I believed, with growing certainty, to be Jennifer. How could I be sure? Her hair for one thing, its colour and styling were giveaways to anyone who knew her well, or at least, saw her often. The small tattoo of a rose in the small of her back was probably less well known. It was not, of course, an uncommon choice of design or location but the odds of their being two such women with that same tattoo amongst so small a gathering seemed statistically improbable. Did I also, perhaps, recognise at a subconscious level the sight of that body of which I had enjoyed such intimate knowledge, and which had seemed to mesh so perfectly with mine?

Such whimsical speculation was far from my mind at that moment. I could not tear my gaze away as the lubricious pageant continued to unfold beyond the glass. Another figure now appeared in the developing drama, taking his place behind the grotesque, birdlike ambo. His features hidden by a golden, grinning visage framed by a tangle of leaves and dangling grapes, he faced the two supplicants and the watching crowd like a Dionysian regisseur, his left hand extended to form the familiar sign of the 'manu cornuto'. The devil's horns.

He began to speak though the glass was too thick for his words to carry as clearly as the lyrics of a rock song or the clangour of a ceremonial gong. All I could really make out was its incantatory tone, or should that be 'drone', which was interspersed with dramatic ritual gestures and culminated, several minutes later, in a final, shouted but still unintelligible phrase. This was taken up by the whole unholy congregation into a fervent chant that, at this magnified volume, was, at last, audible to me.

Ou'est ce tu voudra. Ou'est ce tu voudra. Ou'est ce tu voudra.

It rolled ecstatically around the room for long seconds before the Dionysian cheer leader raised his arms to silence it, ending whatever charade of a ritual I had just witnessed. However, it rapidly became clear that it had merely been the overture to the serious business of the evening as more frenetic rock music boomed out into the room and the orderly ranks of respectful guests that had observed the twisted ceremony dissolved in a matter of minutes into a raucous assembly of pleasure seekers. Copious amounts of drink and food were consumed, joints were lit, pills popped, and any remaining inhibitions cast off as the anonymous revellers gave vent to their wilder natures.

I found myself both fascinated and appalled by what followed, commencing as it did, with the woman in the purple mask kneeling shamelessly before the altar as her devilish partner thrust into her from behind to the cacophonous chorus of "Bat out of Hell". It was a performance greeted with riotous approval by the other revellers, who circled the rutting couple and urged them on with raucous hoots and cat calls until the man climaxed with a great cry of release that threw their audience into a frenzy of mutual sexual activity, splitting off into pairs, threes and even a foursome to slake their own appetites.

I will not elaborate further, other than to say that over the ensuing minutes I bore witness to a display of unfettered lust and debauchery that might have been choreographed and directed by Russell or Fellini. I watched until I could stand no more and reeled off across the courtyard, no longer caring if I was discovered. I was drunk with an emotion that was part-rage and part-despair as I contemplated the new depths to which Jennifer had sunk or, rather, to which she had been dragged.

The drive back to the city was a blur, a task accomplished on automatic pilot whilst my mind was elsewhere, struggling to process the events of the evening and to calm the seething anger that they had awoken. Now, hours later, that anger has not abated but has resolved itself into a sudden clarity of purpose. Every time I close my eyes I see nothing but the smirking face of the unknown Devil who peered into my soul across an ill-lit courtyard. That same Devil who so feverishly possessed Jennifer in the orgiastic climax of the blasphemous ceremony that I had seen enacted. I am no stranger to the Devil. I have seen the Great Corrupter's works before but could not save those unfortunates who fell before his knife. This time it will be different.

This time I will not fail.

PART THREE

24.

When I emerged half an hour later Alex was still sitting at my desk, engrossed in something on her tablet. Eddie and Clegg sat in a semi-huddle around the latter's desk, drinking coffee and talking in low voices. Probably about me and the contents of the blue binder in my hand, which I slapped down on my desk loud enough to get everybody's attention.

"I did not write that!" I said emphatically.

Everyone stopped what they were doing and looked at me with a variety of expressions, none of which seemed to speak of unconditional trust in anything I said.

"Hal- "Clegg began.

I cut him off with a sharp hand gesture.

"You don't believe me?

"Nobody's saying that."

"Well, let's just admit that it's an idea that's in the air, shall we?"

"I believe you." Eddie said, more loyal than truthful. I suspected.

"Hal, we just need to talk about this." Clegg said. "The document in that binder doesn't reflect well on its author – and this young lady is clear that she recovered it from the machine that was until yesterday your own personal office computer."

'This young lady' again looked annoyed to be addressed as such, laying down her tablet with great emphasis.

"It's Alex, if you don't mind." she said. Alexandra if you want to use my Sunday name and don't mind a knee in the coin purse. Lexi, when you know me better."

She flicked her eyes in my direction.

"I'd say I was pleased to meet you but the jury's still out on that."

"Looks like they're all here to me." I said, which sparked more murmurs of embarrassed protest.

"We're your friends, Hal." Clegg insisted. "No one is making any accusations, but you surely see that this has to be addressed?"

He was right of course, I knew that well enough. I hated what I'd just read. It had chilled me to the bone, not least because some parts of it seemed like an uncanny echo of my own thoughts about Jennifer Jensen and her dangerous lifestyle. So much so that there was a part of me that even doubted myself given the discussion I'd had had with Clegg earlier that day about the possible manifestations PTSD might take. I wasn't about to admit that, but I was shaken by the possibility, however remote I believed it to be.

"Then let's talk." I said, helping myself to a cup of coffee to lubricate the process, and sitting at Eddie's desk in the absence of a free chair. "You first, Alex. Tell me where you found the document. You say it was hidden? Where?"

"In the Programs directory, tucked into a Windows Games folder."

"And you just happened to come across it – how?"

"Hey – hold on. Are you trying to say I put it there? That is such bullshit – "

"Hey, yourself. I'm not suggesting anything, just asking what made you look in that particular folder. I thought the idea was just that you'd just reformat the discs before passing the machines on to the homeless centre?"

"Well – okay, yeah, that's what I told Eddie and that's what I usually do – just scrub the data storage disc and reset to factory settings. No big deal. Only in this case, given that Eddie spent so much time last night banging on about not leaving any confidential material on any of the machines, I thought I ought to take a bit more trouble. Eddie told me you store work files in the cloud and back them up on USB but he's a bit of a numpty when it comes to tech and I didn't want him getting into any trouble 'cos he left something irreplaceable on his hard drive by mistake."

"Oy, cheeky mare!"

"Love you too, Snowdrop." she shot back, which would've cracked me up any other time. The last person to call him Snowdrop ended up eating their lunch through a straw for a month.

"Anyway, as I was saying before I was so crudely interrupted, you use Word for your reports and stuff, yeah? All I did was just run a quick search on all the machines to make sure there weren't any stray documents lurking on any of them. They were all clear in that respect, except – well – except for that." She nodded at the binder on the desk in front of her. "It caught my eye because it was sitting in folder where you wouldn't usually expect to find a Word document."

"At which point you opened the file and read it because...?"

So far, I'd only seen her look bored, disdainful and irritated. Now she looked briefly nonplussed, her cheeks reddening with what might have started out as embarrassment but quickly segued into anger.

"It was the name." she said tightly.

"And what was that?" I pressed. I felt more than a little annoyed myself, which was a defence mechanism that was really no defence at all.

"Killdevil." Alex said. "It was called 'Killdevil'".

There was a sharp intake of breath and for a moment I couldn't work out who it came from. Then I realised it was me.

"That would certainly catch your attention." I agreed.

"She thought it was going to be something about you and that Van Dorn nutcase." Eddie offered. "You're a bit of a hero to her."

"Eddie!" Alex said, blushing even more. She glanced at me. Whatever was in that look, it wasn't hero worship. "Yeah, well, we all make mistakes."

"Soon as she saw what it really was she called me and emailed us a copy." Eddie went on hastily.

"Eddie and I read it and that's when he started calling you." Clegg concurred. "You weren't picking up so – "

"You decided to form a lynch party?" I said, only half-joking.

"That's not what this is." Clegg intervened. "Check your phone again. I've called you several times too, as has DCI Swanson and Raphael, who eventually gave up and called me. The police want you in again. It's obvious that you're very much on their radar for Wood's murder and I think you can see that the contents of this 'Killdevil' document could have disturbing implications for you – whatever it's actual provenance."

I swallowed a mouthful of coffee and considered his words. He was right, of course. If I could recognise something of myself in the journal, then so could everybody who knew me – and not everybody who knew me was sympathetically inclined as two out of the three people in the room with me now.

"You're right." I admitted eventually. "I shouldn't jump to conclusions. None of us should."

"Agreed." Clegg said, to accompanying murmurs of assent. "So, to sum up, the situation is that this extremely troubling document has been discovered hidden away on a PC that until yesterday was in regular use in this office. Primarily by yourself, though Edward and I have used it occasionally when you have been out of the office, as it was less sluggish than our own machines."

If Raphael had been there I'm sure that fact would have gone straight down in his notes as something he could use if he ever needed to build a legal defence for me. For my part I would sooner believe I'd written the Killdevil journal myself than accept that either of my friends had any hand in it.

"Alex, what can you tell us about the document from an IT perspective?" I asked.

"Well, it's a Word document or, to be precise a document in the WordX format, which has been the standard file type since the 2007 release of the software. According to the file's metadata it was created on the 11th June 2017 and updated several occasions through to January 2017." She passed to consult her tablet. "The 12th, to be exact, and it was authored by H. Webster, at least that's the name attached to it."

"The metadata can be edited though, can't it?" I said.

She nodded. "Some of it, yes. It's straightforward to delete or change the author's name. You can't physically alter the editing record but all that really tells you is the dates on which the document was updated. It doesn't necessarily mean that it was updated on the same machine that it's currently sitting on. Same with the location data to be fair. You can't change it manually but once the document is saved to another drive the location on that copy will change accordingly. If you were really devious, as well, you could change the date/time data on whatever PC you were using to write the document, so you could make it seem the document was written months ago when it was really only composed last week."

"Right, so that we clear then: you're saying it's possible that the document was written on another machine at any time and in any location and then transferred onto Harry's PC where, to all intents and purposes, it would appear to have originated in the first place?"

Clegg was going full on lawyer now and it was comforting to think he was on my side, even if the jury in this case was a sympathetic one.

"It was planted then?" Eddie, clearly relieved at the thought. "It's obvious."

"There's a case to be made for it, certainly." Clegg agreed cautiously, which wasn't quite the ringing endorsement of my character I would have liked to hear.

"What's the alternative? You think I wrote it in my sleep? Or in some PTSD-induced fugue state?"

I was looking at Clegg as I said this, but he wasn't about to laugh off the notion.

"I realise that you're being facetious, Hal, but my concern for you is genuine. The idea might seem preposterous, but the fact is that whoever the author of that – thing is, they seem to know an awful lot about you."

"Most of which they could have found out from the back files of last year's newspapers." I pointed out.

"Indeed." Clegg agreed. "But it's interesting that you say, 'most of'. Does that imply that there may be something of you in that disturbing document that was not common knowledge in the gutter press? If so, then surely that might provide some clue as to who 'Killdevil' might otherwise be? Is there something in those pages that is true but wasn't ever in the media?"

I thought about denying it, but I was never comfortable with telling outright lies and there wasn't much room to skate around the one glaring truth in Killdevil's journal.

"I may have slept with Jennifer Jensen. That is, I did sleep with her. That much is true."

"You dog!" Eddie said. "I mean – you never let on."

"I was saving it for my memoirs." I said defensively. "Do you tell me everybody who you – oh, well, never mind."

"I meant that you never mentioned it when you took the job." Eddie went on equably. "You never told us that you'd been to bed with the woman you were hired to find."

"Well, I didn't actually think she would still be there." I blustered facetiously.

"Hal, you know that Eddie makes a valid point." Clegg said sternly. "Didn't you think that might represent a conflict of interest?"

"I'm not a police officer or a lawyer." I said. "I don't have to be bound by such considerations. It was a bit of shock when Jensen showed me her photograph, but I was hardly going to tell him I recognised her – or why. As far as taking the job goes, I didn't think twice. It was a one-night stand, it was months ago, and I didn't even know her real name until last week."

As I spoke I couldn't help glancing at Alex. She looked as if Tinker Bell had just died and I felt an unexpected pang of guilt. Clegg was more sanguine in his reaction.

"Now there's an obvious discrepancy with what the writer of the journal implies. He clearly knows from the first that her name is Jennifer. Remember how he rhapsodises about 'sweet Guinevere' when he's recalling the night they spent together?"

"Wasn't she a bit of an old slapper too?" Alex muttered.

"The timing's wrong too." I said. "I didn't stalk her all through summer – I didn't even know her then. I know exactly when we met. It was the 1st of September, the night before my birthday, and I haven't seen her since."

"So, you say." Alex said quietly, though not quietly enough.

"Alex!" Eddie cautioned her.

"No, it's okay." I said. "She's right. You've only got my word for any of this."

"That's good enough for me." Eddie avowed. "It should be good enough for anybody who knows you." he added pointedly.

"Those aren't the people that should concern us." Clegg said patiently. "Let's not lose sight of the fact that, whatever else it may be, the document under discussion provides a clear motive for Glenn Wood's murder. For which let's not forget, Harry seems to be very much a person of interest."

"Which is the whole point of the journal, surely?" I pointed out. "To point the finger in my direction by making it look as if I was obsessed with Jennifer and saw Wood as a convenient personification of every man who played a role in corrupting the 'perfect woman' of my deranged imagination."

"Wood was the leader of the Hellfire Club, after all." Clegg mused. "Hence the conceit of the mask, of course: the face of the Corrupter-in-Chief himself. And you do have a history when it comes to killing devil's in human form."

"I didn't kill this one." I insisted. "Though someone obviously wants people to think I did."

"But that doesn't make sense." Alex piped up in a stubborn, adversarial tone. "It was hidden away on your personal PC. How is that meant to be a frame up? I only came across it by chance."

"Yes, that was a stroke of luck. Thank you."

"She's right, though. Isn't she?" Eddie said, querulously.

"It was hidden, yes, but not to conceal it so much as in anticipation of it being found – only not by Alex or anyone else in this room."

"Then – who?"

"The police." Clegg intuited. "Of course! If they really see you as a viable suspect for Wood's murder they'll act on that suspicion at some point. That means search warrants to pick your home and this office apart, including every computer you have access to!"

"Exactly. A nasty little surprise that would really have put me in the spotlight – only whoever is responsible didn't anticipate that we'd have an IT upgrade that would bring his handiwork to light prematurely."

"Even if you're right – and it sounds a very reasonable scenario - it doesn't really get us any closer to identifying the mysterious diarist." Clegg pointed out. "Or, for that matter, how the journal ended up on your computer."

"That wouldn't be as difficult as you might think." Alex observed thoughtfully. "The obvious way would be for somebody to have downloaded it onto your machine from a memory stick and then altered the metadata in Word. They'd need direct access to your PC for that, though."

"Someone posing as a cleaner perhaps?" Alex suggested. "Or a caretaker? Somebody with a key to your office."

"There's a cleaning service and a building manager." Clegg offered. "But they wouldn't be able to access any of the computers in the office. We operate a two-factor authentication system. Each of us has his own Yubikey, which an outsider would need in addition to the normal log in password, which is not written down anywhere in the office, by the way."

"So, we can rule that method out." Alex said. "Unless you're in the habit of leaving the computers logged on when you all happen to be out pf the office?"

"Absolutely not." Clegg said, firmly squashing the idea. "We don't take chances with a clients' personal information. We take Data Protection very seriously."

"Good to know."

"So – any other ideas, Alex?" Eddie prompted.

"A remote access Trojan would be my best guess." Alex said.

"I think we may all have a rough idea what that is." Clegg said. "But please elaborate, Alex."

257

"Basically, it's just a simple piece of software embedded in a link or attachment in some harmless looking email. Only when you click on the link or open the attachment it uploads a program that gives the sender complete access to your computer to mess with it as they like."

"Such as copying a document onto it without the owner's knowledge?" I said.

"Sure – it might also contain a key logger, so they see everything you type and enable them to take control of your machine's web cam and microphone, so they can see and hear everything that's going on."

"Wouldn't our security software have picked something like that up?" I wondered.

Alex gave me a pitying look.

"Your software's not bad but it's not really top end – and there are literally thousands of these RATs out there. A Trojan called GlassRAT went undetected for three years before anyone identified it. Who's to say how many others there are that haven't been detected yet?"

I might have been wrong, but she sounded almost cheerful at the prospect.

"That must be it then." Eddie exclaimed. "That's the answer."

"It's certainly preferable to the alternative explanation." Clegg agreed. "If Alex is right, you've dodged a bullet here, Harry."

"For the moment." I agreed.

"The question is what else has this Killdevil character hidden in the woodwork? And what are you going to do about the document? Would it be politic to turn it over to Chief Inspector Swanson?"

"I think the main priority is to get everybody's home and work computers thoroughly checked out." I said.

"I can take care of that." Alex volunteered. "At a competitive price, of course."

I smiled at her and then at Eddie.

"You must be so proud." I said.

"The labour is worthy of their hire, Hal." Clegg noted.

"Of course. Do it, Alex, asap. Maybe you could look at beefing up our security while you're at it?"

"Sound. I'll get straight on it. I'll need your computer keys and passwords, of course."

I nodded my agreement,

"That's settled then. As to the police – I'd rather not get them involved at this point. Even if they accept that it's not my handwork it will still give them the excuse to sequester our computers – which we certainly don't want to happen until Alex has made sure there are no more unpleasant surprise hidden away. If you both agree I suggest that Alex should remove the original hard drive. If you'd write out a full report on how you found the document, Alex I'll lodge that, along with the drive and the printout, in Raphael's care. I don't want any of it lying around the office."

I thought for a moment that Clegg was going to object but eventually he gave a slow nod.

"That seems like an acceptable short-term solution." he agreed. "As long as you accept that sooner or later it needs to be handed over to the police. One way or another it's evidence of a very disturbed personality in play."

Which didn't sound ambiguous at all.

25.

Not a lot had changed in Interview Suite 3, where Raphael and I dutifully presented ourselves the following morning. Swanson was his usual, blustery self – imagine the world's most unsociable bus driver forever teetering on the edge of road rage – whilst the faithful Mac was, as ever, a stoic Gromit without the cheese. As for Raphael, he had swapped his dark blue Hugo Boss suit for a heavier wool blend in black to reflect the cooling change in the weather. The only addition to the generic fixtures and fittings was the laptop computer in front of Mac, with which he fiddled briefly before he sat back with a brief nod to his boss.

"So – are we all sittin' comfortably? Then start the tape Macca and let the pantomime commence."

Mac complied and, after the usual preamble and introductions, began the interview proper.

"Mr Webster, we've asked you here again because of some concerns that have arisen regarding your previous statement." he said.

"Aye, concerns that most of what you told us was a bigger fairy story than Pinocchio." Swanson added, looking at me as if he half expected my nose to grow before his eyes.

"A colourful metaphor but evidence of nothing other than a lack of professional restraint." Raphael said languidly. "Perhaps you'd better elaborate, Chief Inspector."

Swanson glared at him across the table and then at me for good measure.

"Ah, I love the smell of fresh testosterone in the morning!" I said.

Swanson's habitual glower ratcheted up a couple of points, but he held his tongue.

"Sergeant -?" he said through gritted teeth. "Elaborate away."

"Yes, well, there are several points of difference between your previous statement and the facts as we have subsequently ascertained them. Firstly, regarding the explanation you gave concerning how you came to cross paths with Mr Glenn Wood. You stated that you were hired by a Mr Callum Jensen, is that correct?"

I agreed that it was.

"You also stated that Mr Jensen had recently arrived from the United States and was anxious to trace his estranged wife and finalise their divorce?"

"That's what he told me, yes."

"Well, we have been trying to get hold of Mr Jensen to verify your version of events." Swanson said, taking over. "That's proved difficult since, according to your statement he was supposedly flying to Ireland the day after your meeting to attend a –" He squinted at his notes. "– computer gaming conference?"

"That's what he said. Apart from a brief telephone conversation and an exchange of emails the day after he hired me, I haven't had any further contact with him, despite several efforts to reach him. He was supposed to return yesterday but, if that's the case, he hasn't been in touch. I've since discovered that there was no such event in Cork last week. Is that what you were about to tell me?"

Swanson scowled, clearly unhappy to be pre-empted but he recovered quickly, nodding to Mac to continue.

"Yes, that corresponds to what we've learned concerning Mr Jensen's supposed plans but there's also a problem concerning his earlier timetable and his stated motive for wanting to hire a private detective. You say that he was in the country to finalise his divorce so that he could marry his current girlfriend?"

"That's what he said, yes."

"The trouble with that story is that none of Jensen's friends and associates in Boston know anything about this supposed fiancée." Swanson said. "He's not known to have been seeing anybody for a year or more and the general consensus

261

is that he was still hankering after his wife and not interested in any new relationships. We've also been unable to find any record of him entering the country at any time during the last month."

Mac looked a little worn around the edges. He was smartly dressed, as always, in a fresh, pale blue shirt and a plain navy tie, and freshly shaven, with a hint of Joop for Men. If you looked closely, though, you could see that the razor had missed a bit near his right ear and his eyes were bruised by the late nights and lack of sleep that a murder enquiry always engendered. Swanson, on the other hand, looked much as he always looked: like a badly dressed bear waking up in mid-December with the worst case of piles ever.

"That makes sense." I said. "Despite what he told me about only being in the country for a couple of days I now believe that he actually arrived just before last Christmas."

"What makes you think that?" Mac said.

I explained about the supposed sighting of the Jensens at the Italian restaurant before Christmas and my speculation that a reconciliation might have been in the air

"If that was his intention, he never mentioned it to any of his friends, though we do now know that he did indeed fly into Manchester airport a week or so before Christmas. We also know that none of his friends in Boston have seen or heard anything of him since then." Mac admitted.

"Which means that as far as we've been able to determine you're the only person who seems to have seen hide or hair of him since he landed last back end." Swanson rumbled.

"In fact, my client has just informed you of at least two other people who seem to have seen him, including his wife."

"An unconfirmed sighting by a lassie who may well have had a glass too many Prosecos with her supper?"

"Is that kind of narrow-minded assumption what passes for police work these days?" Raphael wondered.

"Whatever." Swanson said, who was half-duck, half-rhinoceros when challenged on points of political correctness. "It doesn't really matter who did or didn't see him last Christmas. What concerns this enquiry is Mr Webster's recent, alleged encounter with Mr Jensen. Mac?"

"Hmm, yes, you said in your statement that you met Mr Jensen at the instigation of Mr Don Charles, a solicitor acting for Jensen. You agreed to meet with Jensen and this meeting then took place later that day at the Tanglewood Inn. Is that correct?"

"It's what happened." I said, not much liking the quiet smirk that seemed to creep onto Swanson's face while Mac spoke.

"Aye, well Mr Charles tells a different story. "Swanson said, unable to contain himself. "In fact, he denies all knowledge of Mr Jensen and, though he has certainly heard of you, he is equally adamant that he has never spoken to you about Jensen or any other matter and he expressed in fairly strong terms that he expected this state of affairs to continue until hell becomes a skating rink. Not his exact words, but it was the general gist. Wrong school tie, I expect, or maybe your oppo Eddie Snow deflowered his daughter?"

"Envy is not attractive in a police officer." I said without any great energy. I felt like I'd been punched in the guts and there was worse to come. Though Swanson saw it differently.

"It gets even better, bonny lad," he went on. "See, we also spoke to the barman at the Tanglewood and it's true that he remembers you meeting someone on that night because they were apparently unimpressed by the cuisine on offer. Trouble is, according to the barman, and the hotel's records confirm it, the man you met was not a guest at the hotel, nor was anyone called Callum Jensen registered there on that day."

I felt that sickening impact in my stomach again but did my best not to let my confusion show. Before I could respond, however, Raphael smoothly intervened.

"I'm sorry, Chief Inspector, but I'm not sure quite what point you're trying to make? It's seems obvious that Mr Webster has been the victim of a calculated deception by his client. The information your enquiries have uncovered surely confirms this but since my client was unaware of the fact when he made his original statement I fail to see how this impugns his version of events? The worst inference that can be drawn is that perhaps Mr Webster suffered a slight lapse of professional judgement in not confirming the validity of Don's supposed phone call, but I doubt many people would have thought to do so. As for the rest of Jensen's deception, well, my own experience has taught me that clients often lie in matters both trivial and significant."

Swanson nodded slowly, just to make us think he was actually listening, I suspect. Then he looked pointedly at me.

"Harry?"

"What he said." I replied.

"Fair enough." Swanson conceded. "Not quite the all-seeing private eye then, eh Harry?"

"I'm not a copper anymore. I don't have to automatically distrust everybody I have dealings with."

Though maybe I should start, I was thinking.

"Well, for what it's worth, we did show the barman a picture of Jensen that we managed to get hold of and he did acknowledge that it looked a lot like the man you met with." Swanson continued. "Though, of course, he couldn't positively confirm they were the same. Perhaps it was just someone who resembled Jensen enough to be mistaken for him if, oh I don't know, if for instance somebody wanted for some reason to make it seem like they had met with the real Callum at the Tanglewood?"

"And why would anyone go to those lengths?" Raphael wondered, though I suspect he knew as well as I did where Swanson was going with this.

"Well, I don't know, let's think. Oh yes, perhaps because they wanted to make it appear that Jensen hired them to look for his missing wife to cover up the real reason they were interested in Mrs Jensen and provide a supposedly legitimate reason for looking for her?"

"That 'person' being me, I suppose?" I scoffed. "Well, go on enlighten me."

"Yes, please do." Raphael said sternly. "And I sincerely hope you have more than mere fanciful speculation to offer, or my client and I will be walking out of here in-" He ostentatiously checked his TAG Heuer Formula 1. "Shall we say three minutes?"

"Now, don't be so hasty Mr Gainsborough. I have something to show you both that might take a little longer than that – and I'm sure you won't want to miss the big finish."

With a knowing smirk, he nodded to Mac who obediently began to fiddle with the laptop again. He adjusted it so that all four of us had a good view of the screen, on which in a few seconds a video began to play There wasn't much to see at first, just a blank, dark screen, which suddenly burst to life to show a full-on view of a double bed with a rose patterned duvet that seemed uncomfortably familiar. It wasn't until a few seconds later, when two figures joined at the mouth tumbled into picture and onto the bed, that I realised why. We were looking at one of Jennifer Jensen's private video collection. The couple rolled about, kissing enthusiastically, for the next few minutes, punctuated only by the occasional throaty laugh from the woman and a medley of the usual sounds of mouth to mouth combat. At no point during this time was it possible to really see either of their faces clearly but the woman's distinctive, erotically tangled, ash blonde hair made it obvious enough that I was watching Jennifer grappling with one of her passing fancies. As to who that fancy might be, the biggest clue was the black chambray Boss Orange shirt that I had bought myself last July on Amazon. I really liked that shirt, but it did not come out of that evening's gymnastics in the best of condition as several of the buttons went flying as Jennifer virtually ripped it off my back!

Even as I recalled it, the scene began to play out again on the screen of the laptop before us, prelude to a mutual frenzy of drunken undressing that ended with both figures on the screen virtually naked. It was only when I sat up to pull off my socks – classy as ever – that the camera finally caught me full face and it was all I could do to stop myself groaning in embarrassment and burying my head in my hands. As it was I kept my eyes glued to the screen and my all too familiar face, flushed and slack jawed with drink and lust, until Jennifer's eager hands reached around to drag me back into another steamy embrace.

At this point, Raphael, who seemed to have been equally as shocked as I was, raised his voice in protest.

"All right, Chief Inspector, I think that will be enough of that. Did you bring my client down here simply to embarrass him? Or is there a point you'd like to make."

Swanson smirked unapologetically but signalled Mac to stop the playback, which he seemed more than happy to do. Still smirking, Swanson turned to me.

"Believe me, you ain't seen nothing yet!" he said. "But I had a big breakfast, so I think we'll stop it there. As to the point, well, given Mrs Jensen's connection to Glenn Wood, as reported by your client, we naturally needed to explore that angle. That lassie has got quite a library of films like that, ye nar? And some poor bugger had to watch 'em all! Imagine their surprise when our favourite, nebby private eye turns oot to have a starring role in one of 'em! Especially, as he never indicated that he had actually met the lady in question."

"And, why would he? As far as Mr Webster knew you were only investigating Wood's murder. It was only through his professional interest in Mrs Jensen that my client came across Wood's connection to her, which he told you all about. The events on that film were and are irrelevant to the case you're investigating."

"Well, that would be a matter of opinion." Swanson said. "Some might say that it's evidence of an intimate relationship with a woman who may also have been sexually involved with our victim. It wouldn't be the first time that sex led to murder. Mrs Jensen is clearly a very attractive lady; the kind men have been known to kill over perhaps?"

"The kind who, as I understand it, had quite a few lovers other than my client and Mr Wood – as I believed you just mentioned. I suppose you'll also be hurling unsubstantiated accusations at all of them too?" Raphael responded scornfully.

Swanson's eyes narrowed but he didn't bite back.

"Just tossing out a thought, that's all. You're right, of course, and if we need to we will speak to every one of her co-stars. About which, I don't suppose you've heard anything from Dorian Wilde since our last conversation, Harry?"

"No, but I wouldn't expect to. I'm sure he'll surface soon." I said, though my mind was still half on the video. I was particularly wondering how, it had come into their hands. From what Swanson said it sounded like they'd come across it with all the other discs in Jennifer's collection. That struck me as odd, since I was sure it wasn't there when I myself had looked through them.

"Aye, probably, if he's able." Swanson said. "But, howay, shall wi proceed, sergeant?"

Mac bobbed his head subserviently and checked a sheet of paper in his file, on which I suspect were written all the questions they wanted answers for.

"Yes, going back to your previous statement, you mention that while looking for Mrs Jensen you eventually uncovered her connection to Glenn Wood through Dorian Wilde, who you described as 'procurer in chief' for Wood and his Hellfire Club."

"A dirty job but somebody had to do it."

"And you are sure that you had no knowledge of Wood or his relationship with Mrs Jensen prior to being hired by the man claiming to be her husband?"

"Absolutely sure. I didn't even know that Jennifer was someone I'd slept with until Jensen showed me her photograph. She used a false name the night I spent with her. As for Wood, I may have vaguely heard of him because of his alleged celebrity but that's the extent of it."

"So, it was good, solid detective work that led you to Wilde and then to Wood." Swanson sneered.

"Nice of you to say so." I said. "I'm sure you could have done it just as well."

"You -!" Swanson controlled himself with an effort, remembering that all this was going down on tape.

"I've given you chapter and verse on how I came to rain on Wood's parade." I pointed out. "Where I went, who I interviewed. You can check."

"Thanks, we would never have thought of that." Swanson scowled. "But, see, we've had a bit of trouble confirming some of what you said. Wilde is in the wind, as you know, but we've also had trouble tracking down this other gadgie – what's his name, Macca?"

"Err – Sifer. Louis Sifer."

For a second, I couldn't place who they we were talking about but then it clicked.

"The gardener?"

"Well, that's according to you." Swanson amended. "Only no one else seems to have ever heard of him. Isn't that right, sergeant?"

Mac once again made a big show of checking information in his file.

"Er – well the housekeeper Mrs Lazenby certainly hasn't." Mac said, and Swanson looked annoyed at his hyperbole being shrunk down to size. Mac soldiered on anyway. "According to her Mrs Jensen's gardener is a Mr Humphries…"

"A seventy-year-old ex-steelworker whose been in the job for the last five years." Swanson continued. "And he's never heard of anybody called Louis Sifer – or Harry Webster for that matter. What do you say to that?"

I could think of several things to say, not one of which would have helped cover my confusion at this unexpected revelation. Saying nothing didn't seem like an option, though.

"He said he was the gardener and the man I spoke to was no pensioner. He was in his forties I'd say, though his face was so badly scarred I wouldn't like to put money on that."

"Ah, the face! Nice touch that. Fallujah, you said?"

"That's what he claimed. I wasn't going to call him a liar."

"Except that we checked and there's no record of anybody of that name ever having served in the armed forces, let alone left half his face in Iraq."

"He didn't say he was in the army." I said, though I wasn't sure one way or another. "He could have been a private contractor. There were a lot of them."

"Which doesn't alter the fact that he was not Mrs Jensen's gardener. That much we do know for sure. In fact, we only have your word that this man exists at all, which is starting to become a worrying theme of our little chats. We still don't seem to have had any luck tracking down Donald Black, the man you claim you met at Glenn Wood's house on the night of Wood's murder."

I didn't much care for the way Swanson was eyeing me just then, which was less predatory than pitying and, not for the first time that day, caused a pang of self-doubt. I didn't care to look at Raphael in case I saw the same expression on his face. Was it possible? Was I delusional? No. I wouldn't accept that. There had to be another explanation, didn't there?

"I met a man called Louis Sifer and another called Donald Black. I spoke to them both at length. I even shared a drink with Black."

"Hmm, so you said." Swanson recognised. "Did we find any evidence of that at Wood's house, sergeant? In the form of empty whisky glasses or a bottle with Mr Webster's fingerprints on it?"

"Yes, we did find an empty glass and a half full bottle of whisky – both of which had Ha – Mr Webster's prints on them."

"Thank you, sergeant. A half-full bottle, eh? Now, I would have said 'a half-empty' bottle. That shows the difference between a bright young copper with some optimism still left in the tank and a cynical bugger like me running on empty. More importantly, it shows that you did indeed partake of Mr Wood's finest malt but that you apparently did so alone."

"So? I poured drinks for both of us, which is why only my prints are on the bottle." In fact, I remembered that he had passed it to me from behind the bar, at which point he was still wearing his driving gloves! "As for the glass, he must have washed his own and put it away but left mine. Some people are so self-centred."

"Or, perhaps he just wanted to make it seem that my client was the only one present." Raphael suggested "This man declared himself to be Glenn Wood's agent – a lie you've already disproved – so he was obviously on Wood's property under false pretences. He may even be the killer you're looking for – or should be instead of harassing my client."

Swanson glowered at Raphael, then turned to me.

"Are you harassed, Harry? "

"Me? No, sir. Got to maintain an even strain. You should try it."

Swanson looked like the only thing he was likely to strain was a blood vessel. In truth, I was anything but calm myself, but I certainly wasn't going to let it show.

"Not so easy when you've got a high-profile murder to solve." Swanson observed. "But, rest assured Mr Gainsborough, we are very keen to speak to Mr Black. The problem is, as with the aforementioned Mr Sifer, we have only your client's word that he even exists."

"Which begs the question, why would Mr Webster freely inform you of his meetings with these people? What possible reason could he have for inventing them?"

"Well now, that is the question, isn't it? Not one I'm best qualified to answer, perhaps. "

"Meaning?" I said, though I already knew.

"Meaning, the way I see it, you're way too smart to tell an outright lie that could be so easily disapproved so perhaps you really do believe that you met Donald Black and Louis Sifer. That still doesn't mean they're real. The mind plays funny tricks on people sometimes, especially if they've got – issues, unresolved issues, that might cause – ah – psychiatric fallout of some kind, shall wi say?"

Raphael stirred as if he was about to say something but didn't speak.

"I'm not sure what you're suggesting." I lied. "But I'm sure I'll like it. Your theories are almost as entertaining as 'Ancient Aliens'."

"What I'm suggesting," Swanson said carefully. "Is that maybe all the time you've supposedly been looking for Jennifer Jensen you weren't looking for her at all? Maybe that was just a clever way to obscure the identity of the person you were really trying to find?"

"And who might that be? Raphael asked. "Lord Lucan?"

Swanson's jaw tightened but he didn't bite, his teeth too deeply buried in the marrow of his conjectural scenario.

"Bear with me, I'll get to that. Let's just supposed to start with that your client, during his normal working activities happens to learn about the existence of a private little sex club where the wealthy and privileged of this fair city are free to indulge their every debauched whim. Let's call it the Hellfire Club, just for, well, just for the hell of it, eh?"

"Go ahead. It's your fantasy, sorry, theory." I said.

"Well, it's not illegal, just an excuse for a bit of rumpy pumpy between consenting adults, nothing to get too bent out of shape about, you'd think. Not unless, of course, you were to discover that someone yous maybe really cared aboot had been sucked in and been, what's the word I'm looking for, Macca? Oh, aye, defiled. What if someone you cared about had been defiled by the sleazy merchant who was running the show?"

"Sounds a bit Victorian." I said. "But go on."

"The only trouble being that you don't actually know who this – "

"Besmircher of innocents?" I suggested

"- who this toe rag is. A problem for a lot of folk, perhaps, but not for Harry Webster, the tabloid's favourite detective, maybe? Surely, the man who stopped the White Devil wouldn't have any trouble sniffing out some sex mad gadgie and his sad little gang? And, let's face it, you did, didn't you?"

"My client explained that much during his previous interview." Raphael said in a bored tone. "Make your point chief inspector."

"My point is that Mr Webster claims to have identified Glenn Wood as the moving spirit behind the Hellfire Club as a by-product of his search for Jennifer Jensen. I'm suggesting that this is the opposite of what happened, that Mr Webster set out from the start to find out who was behind the club and used the pretext of searching for Mrs Jensen to allow him to unobtrusively pursue the true purpose of his enquiries: to identify, expose and punish the man he saw as a corrupt, exploiter of women and, in particular, one particular woman that Webster himself knew intimately. I mean, be honest, Harry, you see yourself as a bit of a white knight, don't you?

271

Always ready to provide a strong arm in defence of a lady's honour. Even if she's not exactly a lady."

"That is Byzantine nonsense even by your standards Chief Inspector." Raphael scoffed, and I was thankful he wasn't yet aware of the fake journal Alex had found on my old computer and how uncomfortably it meshed with Swanson's imagined scenario.

My heart was genuinely in my mouth for a few seconds, half-expecting Swanson to produce a copy of the Killdevil document from his folder with a suitably brash flourish. The moment passed, and my world settled back, uneasily on its axis. I realised all eyes were on me, awaiting my own response.

"Is it nonsense, Harry?" Swanson said, giving me what he thought of as his soul-penetrating stare.

"I suppose that depends if your definition of unobtrusive includes inventing witnesses, leaving an intimate DVD of myself and Mrs Jensen lying around for the police to find and then openly murdering Glenn Wood only a few hours after at least five witnesses can place the two of us together in my office."

"Not exactly a masterplan for getting away with murder, is it?" Raphael chimed in.

"Nobody will be getting away with murder." Swanson blustered. "You can rest assured on that point. We're following several lines of enquiry and one of them just happens to lead towards your client. The pair of yers have to recognise that the discrepancies in his previous statement, his personal involvement with Jennifer Jensen and the confrontational nature of his known acquaintance with Wood demand close scrutiny."

"As you say." Raphael conceded. "And you must recognise that it is a very thin line between justifiable scrutiny and harassment. I will be vigilant in ensuring that you don't step over that line with regard to my client. I don't expect him to be called in again unless it is to be interviewed under caution in the light of genuine evidence rather than a hotch potch of pop psychology and speculation."

Swanson gave the pair of us that look which scares pit bulls.

"Be careful what you wish for, bonny lad." he growled, checking his watch and giving Mac the nod to turn off the tape. "Interviewed terminated at 11:45, Thursday April 3rd 2018."

26.

At Raphael's suggestion I followed him to *The Redoubt,* an upmarket bar about ten minutes' drive from Snow Hill. It wasn't quite midday and a little early for real drinking but if ever there was a day to break a rule today was that day. Raphael obviously agreed and, without deferring to me, ordered two *Taliskers.* Not my first choice, maybe, but up there in the top ten. After a session with Swanson I would have just as happily swallowed a blended.

"Are you okay?" Raphael asked, once we were settled in a quiet corner with our drinks.

"I'm fine, I think. It's not my first time in the Mastermind chair with Swanson."

"Indeed, though some of your responses seemed, ah, more circumspect than I've grown accustomed to."

"I never like seeing myself on the telly." I said.

"Ah, yes, that must have been embarrassing for you. You handled it pretty well, though the Chief Inspector's correct to suggest it might hint at a motive for Wood's murder. I take it you were unaware that Mrs Jensen had filmed you –"

"Fucking?"

"Your carnal exuberance, I was going to say. "Raphael grinned.

"No. At least, I knew she was in the habit of taping some of her – encounters. That pile of DVDs Swanson referred to? I went through them all when I came across them – and today's feature wasn't amongst them."

Raphael's interest perked up. "Are you sure about that? I mean, could you have just missed it?"

"Despite what Swanson said, there weren't that many discs - only about half a dozen." I said, shaking my head. "The one

Swanson found so amusing wasn't amongst them. It must have been put there after I'd been through the house."

"Planted?" Raphael mused.

Like the Killdevil journal, I thought.

"It was probably an original part of her collection, removed from the pile before I got there and put back when I left so the police could eventually find it and uncover our relationship."

"If that's so then we're talking about someone with convenient access to the house." Raphael said thoughtfully.

"That's probably not a long list. The cleaner, she had a key, though she told me she gave it back when she was let go. Apart from her, I'd just be guessing. Dorian, maybe, but until he shows up I can't confirm that. And Jensen, of course. He gave me the set I used but he could have kept a set for himself. It is his house after all. Then there's the gardener – the real one, I mean. He may have a set."

"What about the fake gardener? Since nobody seems to know who he is or why he should be pretending to be Mrs Jensen's gardener, he would seem like the most obvious candidate." Raphael pointed out. "Though there's someone else you're overlooking, I'd suggest."

That caught me off guard momentarily. Who was I missing? Did he mean 'Donald Black'? He clearly had gained access to Glenn Wood's house, so it wasn't as if locked properties were a deterrent to him. I didn't think Raphael was thinking about Donald Black, though.

Then it struck me.

"You mean Jennifer herself?"

Raphael nodded and took a swallow of his whisky. His sharp, blue eyes regarded me shrewdly, watching me process the idea. My first thought was just to reject it out of hand, but Raphael's mind was as sharp as his tailoring and I had to give him credit for thinking out of the box.

"You see it, don't you?" Raphael said. "If there's any truth in Swanson's theory that Wood was killed because of his sexual exploitation of Jennifer, then who would have more motive than the woman herself?"

I thought about it some more. Was it really feasible? How would it work?

"Except she wasn't exploited – at least not according to Dorian. She knew what she was getting into when he told her about the Hellfire Club. Nobody twisted her arm."

"Maybe not in the first place, I see that, but you don't know what might have happened down the line, do you? Maybe she liked the idea that Wilde sold to her, but the reality turned out to be against her expectations? A bit rougher, a bit wilder than she bargained for? Things getting out of hand in the heat of the moment? Suddenly it's not fun anymore, she's been physically hurt, perhaps or treated like a victim rather than a willing participant. She feels humiliated, betrayed even, and decides she's not going to stand for it. She wants redress…"

He sat back, took another drink and watched me thinking about it.

"That could have happened, I suppose."

"Indeed. Regret is often sex's toxic best friend."

"Regret doesn't usually live on the same street as murder." I said. "And why involve me?"

"Well, to take the blame of course, but also because, if I understand you correctly, Wood kept his identity secret, as did all the members of the group?"

"Mostly, each member's real identity is generally known only to the person who introduces them to the group. Dorian knows all the women he personally recruited – and vice versa. He also knows that Wood was the leader of the gang. I'm pretty sure Jennifer could have persuaded him to give that bit of information up without having to go to the lengths of tricking a private detective into finding it out."

"That may be so but by hiring you on a seemingly unrelated matter she distances herself from Wood and gets a ready-made suspect when Wood turns up dead."

"So – she stages her own disappearance and then – what – gets her newly re-surfaced husband to hire me, knowing that I'll identify Wood for them?

"Indeed. If what you surmise is correct, and they intended to reconcile, then I'm sure he could have been easily

persuaded to go along with the plan. He may not even have
realised what her endgame was, though it would make more
sense if was fully engaged with the plan. Two people
working together could handle Wood's murder and the body
drop much easier than a lone woman. It would also explain
why Jensen himself has now also dropped off the map."

"No. That would just draw attention to him and make him
look guilty."

"Except that you're forgetting one important fact. You are
the only person who seems to have met Jensen. Likewise, the
bogus gardener and this Donald Black, neither of whom the
police have been able to trace and don't seem to exist outside
the narrative you gave Swanson. Face it, Harry, he half
believes you either hallucinated them or, more likely,
invented them to pad out that narrative, and those kinds of
doubts apply just as much to your meeting with Jensen. You
heard what Swanson said, there's no record of Jensen staying
at the inn where you say you met him, and the lawyer you
claim recommended you to Jensen denies having any
knowledge of either one of you. The Jensen you say hired
you is as much of a chimera as Donald Black and the
gardener."

He was right, of course, at least about Jensen. The fake
phone call, the meeting outside office hours in the back of
beyond, his subsequent failure to show up at the office where
Clegg or Eddie would meet him and verify his existence.
Add them all together and it seemed blindingly obvious that
Jensen had gone to great lengths to ensure that nobody else
could confirm that we had ever met, let alone hired me to
find his wife! Whatever set up was in play Jensen clearly had
to be a part of it, I could see that now, but I had a hard time
accepting that Jennifer was also a knowing part of it and I
said as much to Raphael.

He smiled ruefully.

"Swanson is right in what he says about you, isn't he?" he
said

"You'll have to be more specific. Over the years he's said
enough things about me to fill the Domesday Book, I should

think. He's bound to have got something right along the way."

"I'm talking about the "White Knight" remark. Despite ample contradictory evidence from your own experience, you maintain a stubborn reverence for the female of the species that disinclines you to think badly of them. It has proved your downfall in the past, I think."

"And probably will in the future, I expect." I smiled ruefully. "Still, I stand by what I said about Jennifer Jensen. Whatever part she really plays in all this I don't think it will turn out to be Lady Macbeth."

"I hope you're right but, irrespective of that, you still find yourself in a very vulnerable position. Swanson doesn't have enough to arrest you yet and if jealousy really was the motive for Wood's murder then Jennifer's husband and Dorian Wilde would both seem to have more cause than yourself to commit murder. Until their whereabouts and their alibis, or lack of, are established Swanson will probably not move to bring a formal charge against you. Unless, of course, something was to force his hand."

Such as the Killdevil document, which as yet Raphael had no knowledge of. I debated telling him about it there and then but decided to wait until I had the disc to hand over to him. As far as it's actual author knew it was still sitting on my office PC like a ticking time bomb, waiting for the police to find it. There was always a chance that he would get tired of waiting for them to do so and find another way of getting it to Swanson. Just another reason for finding out his identity as soon as possible.

"I'm not going to sit around and wait for Swanson or anyone else to make the next move." Whoever pulled that trick with the DVD is almost certainly the one who really killed Wood. They're obviously trying to point the finger at me and I could use your help in finding them."

"Well, I'm lawyer and a friend so it goes without saying – unless you were going to ask me to do something ethically unsound?"

"That would be your judgement to make." I admitted. "I need information, as detailed as possible, on the circumstances of Wood's murder. A look at the actual case file would be ideal, though I accept that's wishful thinking. All the same, I know from working with you on Tom's case that you have 'sources', shall we say, that might be able to fill in some of the gaps in the official press release?"

He regarded me steadily but said nothing until, finally, he downed the last mouthful of his whisky and put the glass down firmly between us. He seemed to be weighing something up – our friendship versus the possibility that he might overtax whatever arrangement he had with his police source.

"I'll see what I can do." he agreed eventually. "Just don't let Swanson find out you're getting involved in his investigation."

"I'm already involved." I pointed out.

We shook hands and Raphael left. I lingered to finish my drink and consider my next move. Despite anything Swanson (or Clegg) might try to infer I did not believe that I was the victim of some psychotic delusion. Nor was I working some complicated scam to make it seem as if I was. The phoney telephone call, disappearing client, non-existent witnesses and deranged secret diary were not products of my damaged psyche but the pieces of a devious plan by a clever killer to expose Glenn Wood's sleazy alter-ego and to punish him for his perceived exploitation of Jennifer.

Despite the case that Raphael had made, I did not see Jennifer herself in the role of Killdevil. Callum Jensen, on the other hand, seemed a much better fit. He had obviously lied to me at our meeting and his subsequent failure to re-appear only reinforced my suspicion that he was the orchestrator of recent events.

I drained the last of my whisky, but I wasn't ready to go back to the office quite yet to face an interrogation about my interrogation. After a brief detour to the car to pick up my tablet, I returned to the bar and ordered myself a coffee. The place was still quiet, though as lunch time approached a few more people had started to drift in and I guessed it would soon get busy. I carried my coffee to a quiet booth at the back if the bar and settled down to refresh my memory about the few facts I had gleaned about my erstwhile client before our encounter at the *Tanglewood Inn.*

According to his admittedly sparse Wikipedia entry Callum Luther Jensen (yes, really) was born in 1972 in Castleford, West Yorkshire. He was educated at Castleford Academy and Durham University, where he obtained a first in Computer Science. After leaving the North-East he completed an MSc in Software Engineering at New College, Oxford, while working for *Brainsalad Software*, as a games designer. In 1995 he married his long-term fiancée, Jennifer Beneventi, who he had met, as I knew, during their time at university.

Two years later the Jensens moved to his native Yorkshire, where he launched his own games company, *Dragon's Tail.* Over the next few years the company issued a string of successful role-playing games, culminating in 2002 with its most successful and lucrative release: *Dungeons of Spite.* The game won a fistful of awards and, according to the man himself, was the final realisation of an idea that had first gestated in his university days. On the back of its success, Jensen was induced to sell *Dragon's Tail* to the American games juggernaut *Harbinger.* As part of the deal Jensen became lead designer for *Harbinger,* a role which had necessitated a move to the United States, where he had remained for eight years before cashing in his shares and returning to England to enjoy his money and his two favourite pastimes: fine dining and watching Castleford Tigers rugby league team. His retirement had lasted just as long as it took for his marriage to drift into rough waters, causing him to jump ship and return stateside alone in 2014.

That was as far as the entry took Jensen's life story. There was little else about him on the Internet other than a few mentions on tech and gaming sites that dated back to the time when his reputation was at its zenith. Whatever he had been doing since he had returned to America it did not appear to have caused any great ripples in cyber space.

There was a photograph to accompany the Wikipedia article, showing a smiling, slightly self-satisfied man in a virulent red and yellow Hawaiian shirt and aviator sunglasses. He was posing nonchalantly in front of the tall glass doors of an office building, his thumbs resting lightly in the waistband of his stonewashed jeans. There was something about the photograph that nagged at me, but I couldn't quite put my finger on what it was. I studied it carefully, but the glasses made it difficult to say with any certainty that this was the man I'd shared a drink with at the *Tanglewood*. Other than that, there was something odd, something out of place, but I couldn't quite put my finger on it.

Am image search turned up a few more uncluttered pictures of Jensen and after scrutinising them I was as sure as I could be that they were of the same man who had hired me to find Jennifer Jensen. I also reminded myself that the barman in the pub had recognised a photograph of Callum Jensen as the man he had seen me speaking with. Still, it remained a generic sort of face, a little handsome, a little time worn, a face that fitted a middle-aged entrepreneur living on past glories. Could it also really be the face of a Machiavellian killer?

There is no art to find the mind's construction in the face, I reminded myself.

I remembered my coffee and took a drink. It was lukewarm, and I'd forgotten to put sugar in. I pushed the cup away and turned back to my tablet. If Jensen was Killdevil, he hadn't acted alone. I believed there were at least two other people working with him: Donald Black and the bogus gardener, Louis Sifer.

The Tanglewood barman could prove that I had met Jensen but there was no third party to confirm the existence of the other two. Swanson had made it very clear that he had doubts that either of them were real. Given the absence of a second whisky glass at Wood's place, I might have even doubted myself but there was fairly compelling evidence that Black, whoever he really was, had been at the house. He may not have been Wood's agent, as he had claimed, but my subsequent efforts to track him down showed that, fake name apart, he did bear a striking likeness to Wood's real representative, Max Hazel. Since I had certainly never met

Hazel previously, how likely was it that I would suffer a hallucination that bore such a startling resemblance to a real person who was previously unknown to me?

No, Black, like Jensen was a real, flesh and blood person and so, was the third man – Louis Sifer. It was an unusual name and I wasn't sure how to spell it but Google picked up several alternative spellings. The entries included a Toronto based brewery – the Louis Cifer Brew Works, Louis Chypre, a film character, and the Facebook page of a French man called Louis Sifer. The latter was clearly of no relevance and, though the brew works sounded like the kind of place I'd like to visit, it also didn't help. It was only when, for the want of something better to do, I clicked on the De Niro link that the penny dropped. It took me to a page on a site dedicated to horror movies, which revealed that Louis Cyphre was a character played by Robert De Niro in a 1987 film *Angel Heart,* a wealthy and manipulative businessman who was eventually revealed to be the ultimate fallen angel. Louis Cyphre was Lu -Cifer – the Devil himself!

27.

If there had been any lingering doubts in my mind that someone was deliberately trying to mess with my head, they disappeared in that moment. I drove back across the city feeling both vindicated and disturbed. I seemed to be in the cross-hairs of an obsessive and highly dangerous personality who either had a genuinely fixation with the Devil or, at the least, had gone to great trouble to create the impression of such a deluded persona.

Clegg was alone in the office, engrossed in the minutiae of a forensic audit for a troubled, local, not-for-profit organisation. Eddie was out with Alex. She had spent all morning running advanced security checks on our new system and installing top end software to ward off any further attempted cyber-attacks. He was now driving her over to my flat to run her checks on my home PC.

As expected Clegg was eager to hear all about my latest go round with Swanson. He listened sympathetically and agreed that everything I'd learned from the interview supported the conclusion that I had been deliberately targeted to take the fall for Glenn Wood's murder.

"Which, if the Killdevil document is to be taken at face value, implies that sexual jealousy was one of the drivers behind that event. That certainly seems to support the view that our elusive client is the perpetrator."

"I'd say so. I think he came back here last Christmas with every intention of patching things up with Jennifer and, judging from the way she dropped Dorian and the Hellfire Club at the same time, I'd say she was all for making a fresh go of it too."

"So, what went wrong?" Clegg wondered.

"Best guess? Jensen found out that Jennifer hadn't reacted to their separation by simply shrugging her shoulders and joining a Pilates class."

"The lady's film collection?"

"That would explain why he decided to make me a part of his intricate little revenge drama but that probably came later. I think the real impetus behind his actions must have been his discovery that she was mixed up with the Hellfire Club crowd. I don't believe he can have witnessed Jennifer's initiation into the Club, that took place months before he arrived back in England. I think he must HAVE cobbled that part of the document together from the DVD I found at Wood's place. On the other hand, I don't think the journal is entirely fictitious. Not when it comes to the intense rage Killdevil expresses over what he sees as Jennifer's corruption by the man in the Devil mask. That felt real to me."

"Indeed". Clegg said soberly. "The rage of the document's author is almost palpable at that point but also impotent, as he has no idea who the man behind the mask may be – which is why he embroiled you in his scheme, of course. Using your professional skills to identify the man in the mask, so he could kill him and make you a prime suspect! There's a kind of genius at work here, Hal, albeit it a very dark and disturbed kind. If you're right about Jensen it must have occurred to you that, yourself and Wood apart, there might be a third victim of his rage?"

"You mean Jennifer? I've been concerned for her safety from the start. Nothing that's happened since has changed my mind about that."

"*Fell jealousy that troubles oft the bed of blessed marriage.*" Clegg murmured softly. "Are the police even looking for Jensen?"

"If they are, they're not looking very hard. Apart from myself, the only other person who saw him at *The Tanglewood Inn*, is the barman. He identified him from a photograph as someone he saw me speaking to – but he couldn't confirm the man's name as it turns out Jensen wasn't even a resident there. In one of Swanson's scenarios, the man I spoke to was just somebody with a passing resemblance to Jensen who I employed as part of some clever smoke screen to legitimise my search for 'Dash'

"Which in a way is not that far from the truth." Clegg observed. "Only you're not the one who created the smokescreen. For all his bluster, Swanson is sharp. He'll get at the truth."

"Maybe, but I don't intend to sit around waiting for that eventuality. I'll find Jensen myself."

Clegg smiled wryly.

"And, of course, if experience has taught you anything it's that there's no way that smoking out a psychopath can wrong. "he said.

I let him have that one and he went back to picking apart the accounts he was working on. I decided I probably ought to turn over a shovel myself and I spent the next hour typing up a less than comforting report for Angela Gilligan informing her that her gun-mad husband Vince was shooting a low bird, so to speak. Very bad form, I understand. Just how bad I expect he would find out roughly thirty seconds after he walked through his front door tonight.

When I had finished the report, I printed off two copies and then uploaded the photographs I'd taken and printed copies of those. I put one copy of the report into a plastic document file and the photographs into a clear plastic wallet. Report and photographs then went into a large manila envelope that I dropped into my out tray. I emailed another copy of the report to Clegg, along with a meagre list of expenses, so he could put an invoice together for the client.

At some point he had left the office to go for his lunch and with the Gilligan case closed my thoughts immediately swung back to what, I guess, we were now calling the Killdevil case. It was never a comfortable feeling being a suspect, though, if not for Alex, things might have got infinitely worse somewhere down the line. Still, the prospect of Swanson turning up with a search warrant, like Alaric at the gates of Rome, was not a beguiling one. The immediate threat of the Killdevil journal had been neutralised but the inevitable inconvenience of a police search would hinder the day to day business in general and my efforts to locate Callum Jensen in particular.

With that in mind I decided to take steps to safeguard what information I had already gathered. I retrieved Jennifer's scrapbook and the inscribed paperback from the bottom drawer of my desk, along with the Devil tarot card and the DVD of Jennifer's 'initiation' into the Hellfire Club. I scanned the scrapbook, the inscription from the book and the tarot card onto my PC. I added the files to the case folder that already held copies of all my reports to Jensen and any information I'd gathered over the past week or so. I then copied the folder onto a flash memory stick I carried with me in my wallet. It was cleverly designed to look like a credit card and I'd seen it on Amazon a couple of months previously while I was looking for something else entirely. I don't even remember exactly what, but I thought the credit card drive was cool, so I bought it.

That just left the DVD, which I had no intention of having around the office in any form to become another stick to beat me with if Swanson and his team ever did descend on us. I slipped the DVD into one of my jacket pockets and the flash drive back into my wallet. The two books I put into a brand-new box file and returned to my desk drawer.

That done I turned back to the immediate business in hand and rang Angela Gilligan to bring her up to speed on her errant husband. She took the news of his infidelity calmly enough at first, as if she had already reconciled herself to that reality. When I told her who Vince was sleeping with, however, the stoic front crumbled spectacularly, and she met the news of her sibling's betrayal with an impressive outburst of foul language, tears, and blood curdling threats involving her best pair of hairdresser's scissors and her husband's wedding tackle. When she had thoroughly vented I arranged to drop off a full report and a set of photographs at her salon later that afternoon. She thanked me through clogged sinuses and we hung up.

When Clegg returned from his lunch a few minutes later I set out to keep my word to Angela but detoured first to *Cache 22, a* self-storage company on the Crossway Industrial

Estate, west of town. I paid a month's deposit in cash for
their cheapest and smallest locker in which I stowed the
Hellfire Club DVD out of harm's way. That accomplished, I
had coffee and a hot dog at a nearby food van before heading
to *Planet Waves,* Angela Gilligan's hair salon. storage. Given
the name, I wondered idly if she was a Bob Dylan fan, but I
never got the chance to make small talk as she had locked
herself in her office with a bottle of vodka and a fresh packet
of *Silk Cut* to drowned or choke her sorrows. She opened the
door just long enough to give me a glimpse of what rage and
wet mascara can do for a woman. She snatched the envelope
out of my hands and told me "Thanks very much – now piss
off!"

True gratitude takes many forms.

Instead of going back to the office straight away I drove to
the main library and booked an hour on one of the public
computers to review everything from the Jennifer Jensen file
and try to fit what I knew into a workable scenario,
beginning the previous September when Jennifer and I met
and spent the night together. As I subsequently learned I was
just the latest in a series of casual relationships that Jennifer
had pursued since her husband Callum had walked out on
her. Amongst her other lovers was Dorian Wilde, with whom
she had developed a deeper involvement than most.
Irrespective of any finer feelings between them Dorian had
fulfilled his role as the Hellfire Club's chief 'whipper in' by
introducing Jennifer to its promiscuous delights. She seemed
to have needed little persuading to sign up for their revels,
which represented just another way to numb the lingering
pain of her marital break-up through conscienceless acts of
sexual excess.

In December Callum Jensen had apparently re-entered
Jennifer's life, full of regret for ever leaving her, and eager to
heal the breach between them. The indications were that
Jennifer had responded positively to his embassy, ending her
involvement with both Dorian Wilde and the Hellfire Club,
leaving her job at Stentor Alarms and making plans to make
a fresh start somewhere beyond these shores. Best guess: to
return with her husband to America, where they had

previously enjoyed the best years of their marriage.
However, the indications were that the rapprochement
between the couple had not quite materialised as hoped.
Quite possibly because Jensen had learned the extent of his
wife's sexual adventures during their separation and reacted
badly to the discovery.

Sometime between Christmas and the present Jennifer had
disappeared but not apparently with her husband, whose
whereabouts in that period were also unknown. He had not
returned to America, that much I knew from my interview
with Swanson. So where had Jensen been and what had he
been doing in the three months or so that elapsed between his
Christmas reunion dinner with Jennifer and our meeting at
the *Tanglewood Inn*?

It was just possible, I supposed, that after their
reconciliation had floundered Jennifer had decided to deal
with it by seeking the fresh start she had written of without
Jensen. The image of her lazing on that distant beach had
always been a hazy one, however. I no longer invested any
hope in it, or indeed in any possible outcome that was
favourable for Jennifer. Wherever she might be lying now, I
doubted it was anywhere that the sun could reach.

Had Jensen killed his wife in a jealous rage and spent the
ensuing months shaping the current twisted scenario from his
sense of betrayal? It was obvious from the Killdevil
document that the leader of the Hellfire Club had earned for
himself the author's murderous enmity. The document also
made it clear that the author knew nothing of that figure's
real identity. The target of his hate and rage was just a
mysterious, figure in a grotesque mask. Before he could
exact revenge, he needed to learn that figure's real identity.
This was the point where I had entered his calculations.

Jensen had been in America when the White Devil business
blew up in my face, but he knew all about it. It was why he
had chosen to hire me, he'd said. When he recognised me in
the DVD of my one-night stand with Jennifer he must have
realised he'd found the perfect catspaw to uncover the
identity of the Hellfire Club's leader. Clearly, at some point,
he had also realised that I would make a perfect scapegoat for

the murder that would complete his revenge. It would be a suitably ironic climax to a scheme that was distinctly theatrical in its planning and execution, leaning heavily on the Devil theme that had a mocking relevance to both my life and that of Glenn Wood.

The paperback book and the message written on the fly leaf, the Tarot card, the two 'devilish' witnesses that I had encountered, were part of a deliberate design to taunt me and, perhaps to make myself – and others - question my sense of reality. The Killdevil journal was meant to be the final proof that I was in the grip of some dissociative mental disorder that conflated the trauma of my brush with the White Devil with a desperate obsession with Jennifer Jensen. The obvious conclusion being that it had driven me to once again to confront a devil – in the shape of Glenn Wood – who preyed on women.

It was an unfolding drama that was the work of an impressive creative imagination, albeit malevolent in nature. Drama being the keyword. Jensen and Jennifer had originally met through the university drama society. He claimed to have been no more than a humble spear carrier himself, though he may have been deliberately self-deprecating about his acting talents. It was also possible that he had maintained contact into later life with some of the other students from the society. Old friends who had, perhaps, filled the roles of Louis Sifer and Donald Black in Jensen's malicious production?

What was the alternative? That he paid professional actors to play those parts? He had the money, certainly, but logistically it would be a problem. He would have to find people he was sure could carry off the roles he wanted them to play. That implied copious research, auditions and inevitable wrangling with agents. Not to mention the need for a convincing cover story to explain the purpose of the charade he was recruiting them for.

No, I was sure he would not have gone down that route. Too many things that could have gone wrong, too many unknown egos in play. There was also the obvious drawback that he would be dealing with strangers who had no built-in

loyalty to ensure they kept quiet about the odd little cameos
he had asked them to play. Surely, it was much more likely
that he would turn to people he knew and could trust to go
along with the deception he had choreographed? Individuals
who possessed the necessary skills (and lack of scruples?) to
convincingly play the roles he had devised for them

I turned back to the computer and opened the list I had
compiled of the students who had shared the spotlight with
Jensen and Jennifer twenty-odd years ago. I was reminded
again of the one familiar name amongst them who might be
able to shine some light on his contemporaries. It was time
for that long overdue reunion with Ellis Thatcher.

I rang my old boss, Ben Cross and, after a brief catch up, I
raised Thatcher's name. As I hoped, Ben still saw Thatcher
from time to time at the golf club where they were both
members. Knowing my history with Thatcher, Ben was
surprised by, and suspicious of, my request but he agreed to
lean on their acquaintance to get me a meeting with Thatcher.

"On one condition. Don't punch him this time." Ben
sighed.

I promised to do my best and we hung up. He called me
back in half an hour as I sat drinking a coffee in the library
cafeteria and idly scanning the list of former drama students
that I'd just printed off.

"He'll see you – as long as you agree to keep your hands in
your pockets at all time."

I think he was joking but I couldn't be sure. Thatcher was,
after all, a notorious control freak and all-round shit, which
was how I came to punch him in the first place.

"He'll be at *Vespers* from six o'clock until eight, tomorrow
night. That's your window. He'll leave your name at the
door."

Vespers was a private club, part of *The Heritage,* a five-star
hotel that occupied the old National Provincial bank, an
impressive building of biscuit-coloured stone that was
designed by Edward Lutyens in the 1930s. Admission to
Vespers was a perk for all residents but, otherwise entry was
restricted to fee paying members and their guests. It didn't
surprise me that Thatcher would chose to meet me there. It

was just the kind of act of self-conceit he was unable to resist.

"And if you want a drink, I'd take your credit card." Ben continued with a chuckle. "I don't think you should rely on the warmth of his hospitality."

We said our goodbyes and ended the call. I finished the dregs of my coffee and headed back to the office.

28.

Eddie had returned in my absence, during which time Alex had checked out my home PC and found no unpleasant surprises lurking in it. She was now back at her workshop checking the logs on the original, compromised hard drive for any lingering traces of Killdevil's intrusion. When that was complete she would switch out the hard drive and bring it to me to give into Raphael's care.

"So, what's next?" Eddie asked.

I told Eddie and Clegg about my planned meeting with Ellis Thatcher.

"You really think Jensen's behind all this?" Eddie wondered. "If that's true, surely he'll be well away by now."

"Not necessarily. If I'm right killing Wood is only part of his plan. He wants to see me take the fall for it. If that's the case, he'll hang around see how that pans out."

"It's also not clear that he intends to stop with Wood." Clegg pointed out. "He may have other targets in mind. There's still no news of young Mr Wilde, I take it?"

"Not that I'm aware of."

"It seems rather coincidental that he should go missing at the same time as Jensen – and he is actor, isn't he? Could he be one of Jensen's accomplices?"

It was something I'd considered but that didn't fit with the verifiable facts about Louis Sifer and Donald Black.

"Dorian is easily six feet tall, about the same as me. Black and Sifer were both considerably shorter. They looked older too – though make up and prosthetics could account for that, I suppose."

"What about this Thatcher guy, then?" Eddie asked. "If they were mates at university maybe he's one of the people helping Jensen? You could be asking the wrong person and walking into trouble. Perhaps me and the Bambino should go with you." he suggested, jerking a thumb towards the corner where his Louisville Slugger rested.

"The Bambino? You gave the bat a name?"

"Yeah. Cool right? King Arthur had Excalibur, Davy Crocket had Old Betsy-"

"I get the picture." I sighed. "Why the Bambino, though?"

"It was one of Babe Ruth's nicknames, wasn't it? Seemed appropriate. What do you think?"

"Wikipedia, I hate you." I said.

When the pair of them had gone I hung around catching up on some office routine. I felt wired and a bit jittery, as if I'd drunk too much coffee. I needed some down time, I decided, a good meal, a couple of beers and pleasant company. I knew just who to call.

Molly sounded as pleased to hear my voice as I was to hear hers and said 'Yes' to the drinks, though she just sitting down to eat at home as she had a lecture at the university starting at seven.

"I'll be done by half nine, if that's not too late for you?" she said diffidently.

"I find it's never too late for a beer." I said, then wished I hadn't. I didn't want her thinking I was alcoholic. I needn't have worried.

"Same here – though in my case it would be a nice, chilled rosé."

"Then let's all take hands till that conquering wine hath steeped our sense in soft and delicate Lethe." I said

"Oh, Harry, I love it when you talk dirty!" she said with a mischievous laugh. "See you in *The Admiral Rodney* about half nine? 'Byee."

Then she was gone, leaving my thoughts a little lighter for our brief exchange.

A thin, persistent drizzle had set in, deepening the murk of an already overcast afternoon. I was wondering how best to kill the next few hours before I met Molly when that problem was taken out of my hands by the ringing of my cell phone. Number unknown, though the urgent voice I heard when I accepted the call was familiar and unexpected.

"Webster? Is that you?"

"Dorian?"

"Yes, it's me. What the hell's been going on? I just heard about Glen. Is he really -? I mean – fuck."

He sounded freaked out, panicky. Maybe even a little afraid.

"Where have you been? The police are looking for you."

"I know – I know – I – look, can we meet? I'm just heading back to town. I heard about Glen on the radio news. Fuck."

"Okay, calm down. How long before you get back? I'll come over to your flat."

"No! I'm not going back there! I'll come to you – but make it somewhere public, okay? No offence, but I'm jumping out of my skin just now. Not even sure why I called you, of all people-"

"Fine, don't worry about it." I said, cutting him off. "How about *The Admiral Rodney?*"

There were a couple of pubs within walking distance of the office but since I'd already arranged to meet Molly at the *Rodney* it seemed like the logical choice.

"I know it." Dorian said. "By the university, isn't it? I'll be there in about twenty minutes."

The Admiral Rodney was a cosy, traditional pub in West Ridge, which housed the main campus of the oldest of the city's two universities. It was in an older part of the district and had so far escaped being swallowed up by developers. In the same way the pub itself had managed to stay out of the grasp of any of the big chains. It had few frills, but a lot of hand pulled beers that made it a magnet for the Real Ale crowd. It was also a handy off-campus hangout for students and a refuge for an older core clientele lapping up the pale ghost of the real Barnsley Bitter they remembered from their youth.

You didn't go to the *Rodney* for food, which was limited to three flavours of crisps and pies that were no longer so pukka. Nor to meet girls, though there was a healthy smattering of female students among the early evening crowd, unselfconsciously knocking back pints and probably considerably raising the average IQ of the place.

It must have been at least five years since I'd last stepped through the pub's doors, but it still felt reassuringly familiar in the way of an old, well-smoked pipe or your favourite, faded jeans. I ordered a Talisker to chase the cold and damp from my bones as I sat at a corner of the bar where I would be easily visible to Dorian when he arrived.

He arrived about fifteen minutes later, rocking the rain swept 'Heathcliff Look', with a side of *Sherlock;* his dark mane even more than usually tousled; swaddled in a Belstaff trench-coat. He drew more than a few appreciative glances from the distaff side of the clientele – and even from some of the men. It must have been a chore to be so irresistible, but he appeared to bear the burden lightly. He hardly seemed aware of the minor stir he created, or perhaps he was just so used to it that it hardly registered anymore.

Dorian scanned the room quickly and half raised a hand in acknowledgement as he veered towards me. Although he was the one who had asked to meet he seemed wary; a residue of our previous encounters, perhaps. Or maybe he had belatedly realised that he could be entering the company of a murderer.

I offered him my hand in a conciliatory greeting and asked him what he was drinking.

"Whatever that is." he said, nodding at my glass.

I thought about telling him it might be a bit too grown-up for him but decided to play nice and held my tongue. When I'd been served I led the way to one of the pub's little side rooms. It was empty, except for a middle-aged guy with a bushy beard and an Arran sweater, who looked as if he was waiting for the next great Folk revival to hit town. He didn't seem very happy with life. Perhaps his Bonny lay over the ocean.

Dorian and I took seats in the opposite corner and he sipped his whisky appreciatively.

"Damn, I needed that! This is a fucking nightmare!"

I assumed he didn't mean the whisky or the pub. He clarified the point in a hushed voice.

"Who would do that to Glenn?"

The look that accompanied the question was, if not accusatory, certainly speculative.

"A discerning TV critic?" I suggested. "It wasn't me, if that's what you're worried about."

"No – well, course not. I wouldn't be here if I thought that. It's just a shock, is all."

"It's okay. You won't hurt my feelings. The police certainly think I make a good suspect – and I have killed someone before. I can promise you it hasn't proved habit forming, though. You do realise that you're a suspect as well, don't you?"

"Me?" He looked alarmed. The thought clearly hadn't occurred to him. "Why on earth would I want to kill Glenn?"

"I don't know. Why would you leave town on the same day he was murdered?"

He looked hunted for a moment, his face pale, and he seemed much younger than his twenty-five years. He took another drink to try and steady his nerves, but I don't think it helped.

"I didn't know he was going to be murdered!" he almost yelped, glancing nervously across at Arran Sweater, who sat stoically in his corner stating into his half-drunk pint of Guinness. He gave no indication that he heard or cared about anything we were saying.

"You don't need to worry about him." I assured Dorian. "Unless he sticks his finger in his ear – then I think we should run for it."

"How can you be so flippant and relaxed about being suspected of murder?" Dorian wondered.

"*Make believe you're brave and the trick will take you far.*" I said. "So why did you leave town – and where have you been?"

"I was on retreat." he said, which on the list of explanations I might have expected him to offer came somewhere below 'Rounding Cape Horn in a leaky bathtub'.

"Where? In a nunnery?"

"That's not funny." he huffed. "The Avaloka Buddhist Centre. It's up in Northumberland, middle of nowhere. I go there once a year. It helps me re-energise and balance my chakras. What are you smiling at?"

In fact, I was reflecting for a moment on how Swanson would react when Dorian laid that one on him. I didn't tell him that though.

"Sorry, just a little surprised that's all. I take it they don't have cable?"

"No TV or radio. No mobiles, laptops or tablets, not even a newspaper – and everyone observes Noble Silence throughout."

"Which means what exactly?"

"It's a technique that demands complete, calming silence. It helps us see things more clearly and achieve deeper contact with ourselves and those around us. It's part of the Eightfold Path and issues from Buddha himself as his response to the fourteen unanswerable questions."

"Ah, the Silence of the Lamas!" I said.

"Mock if you must. What it means is that nobody speaks for the entirety of the retreat. It's dedicated to quiet meditation remote from the world and everything in it outside the gates of the centre. It's an incredibly peaceful and spiritual experience. Some people actually become permanently changed by it and never go back to the outside world."

He sounded a little wistful at that thought. Who could blame him for hankering, just a little, for a way to escape a world wobbling ever more precariously on its moral axis?

"Silence can't come easy to an actor, surely?" I said. "And, don't take it to heart, but Buddhism doesn't seem that good a fit for someone with your – er – particular lifestyle?"

"I suppose you're thinking about the 3rd Precept." he said earnestly.

"I suppose I must be." I said.

"Fair comment - though it is all a bit vague as to what actually constitutes sexual misconduct – at least for a lay Buddhist like myself."

He said that without any trace of irony, too.

"It's generally supposed to be a proscription against non-consensual or exploitative sex. You might not approve of my lifestyle, but I have never coerced any woman into doing something she didn't want to. Yes, I've recruited women for the Hellfire Club but every one of them knew what they were getting into."

He sighed and took another small sip of his scotch.

"That's what I've always told myself, anyway. I'm right aren't I?"

The question took me by surprise or, at least, the fact that he had asked it of me.

"I guess you are. I've no problem with consenting adults doing their thing, whatever that might be, but it sounds as if you're the one who's not so sure anymore."

He smiled wryly and ran a hand through his dark locks. It came away damp and he wiped it absently on his coat.

"Well, as I said, I've had plenty of time to think about my life choices over the last week or so and not just at the retreat. You getting in my face like you did about Jen was the catalyst, I think. I may have been following Glenn's agenda when we first met but even then, I felt something more than just sex between us. She meant - means - a lot to me. I wish I'd realised just how much before I sucked her into Glenn's orbit. Do you think – is there a connection between her disappearance and his murder?"

"What makes you think that?"

"Oh, let's see! I've known Glenn Wood for the last three years and he's always been a bit of a shit. It's just that nobody ever killed him until you came around asking about Jen."

"Could just have been an oversight." I said, not unimpressed all the same that he had put it together for himself. "You're right, though. I do think there's a connection.

I told him that I suspected Callum Jensen had killed Wood – and why I thought so.

"Then it's my fault, isn't it? If I hadn't brought Jen into the Hellfire Club…"

"And if I hadn't obligingly found out that Glenn Wood was its guiding light There's enough guilt to go around but most of it belongs to Jensen – and if it's any comfort to you, if you hadn't introduced him to Jennifer then you might have been the one they found swinging in the woods. Jensen knows all about Jennifer's relationship with you – and others besides. He's seen all her home movies, Dorian. If he hadn't had Wood to fixate on you might just as easily have become his target."

"I've been thinking about that, as well." Dorian said. "I don't believe that Jen would have made recordings of herself with her lovers."

"Sorry to disillusion you but I've seen the results. As I told you when we first spoke. That's how I got the picture of you."

"I'm not doubting what you've seen or told me previously." he said, shaking his head slowly. " It just doesn't seem like something Jen would do. Oh, I know I wasn't the only guy she took back to her mum's old place for sex, but none of them meant anything to her. It was her way of sticking two fingers up to her husband after he walked out on her. She likes sex and was never coy about it but, believe me, most of the time she couldn't even recall the names of her one-night stands. I always thought she was happy to join the Hellfire Club because there's no pretense about what it offers. It treats sex as just an anonymous, emotionless, physical transaction. Jen wasn't looking for love because she was still in love with him, with Callum. I think I always knew that, which is why I was always surprised that she let me at least a little way inside her defences. Behind the cynical outer shell, she was kind, funny and intelligent. A real sweetheart. There's just no way the woman I know would make secret recordings of events that meant nothing to her. No way. That's more the kind of sleazy thing a man would do."

Maybe he had a point, I thought, though there was no way he could be certain that the hidden camera wasn't put there by Jennifer. No matter how well we think we know someone, can any of us really be sure that we have peered into every dark place in their soul? That said, he did know Jennifer a whole lot better than I did, so if he was right who else could have installed the camera that had so mercilessly recorded her hectic one-night stands?

"Jensen?" Dorian suggested when I posed the question out loud. "Planting a hidden camera is something a jealous husband would do, isn't it?"

"That's true enough – but the recordings were made over a period of months, starting long before Jensen's known to have been in the country."

"He could have hired somebody to spy on Jen for him." Dorian persisted. "You're not the only private detective in town. She could have had her under surveillance from the moment he walked out on her."

"Why though? Why would he bother when he was the one who chose to walk away from their marriage? It also looks very much as if Jensen came back to England last December hoping for a reconciliation. Not what you'd expect if he already knew all about her busy sex life."

Dorian looked a little deflated but recognised the logic of what I said.

"It doesn't seem likely, does it?" he agreed. "If Jensen wasn't the one having her spied on I don't know – unless?"

"Go on."

"No. "He shook his head in denial. "I mean – I thought she was just being paranoid. She got that way from time to time. I mean, you've seen her photograph, you know how stunning she is?"

I'd seen a lot more than her photograph, of course, but I didn't think it was the right moment to mention it. I wasn't sure there could be a right moment. I just nodded.

"She turns heads." Dorian went on. "Always did, I expect, so she was used to guys giving her the eye or hitting on her, even if she didn't reciprocate. Didn't mind most of the time but just now again somebody would get under her skin – stare at her a little too long or seem to be turning up all the time in the bars we went to. There were a couple of occasions when she got pretty freaked out that somebody was watching her. I mean, not just looking, but watching."

"A stalker, you mean?"

"Well – I couldn't say that, really. It only happened the twice and it wasn't the same guy."

"Tell me." I insisted.

300

"O-okay. First time would be last summer. We took a drive
out of the city and stopped for beers at this pub on Top
Edge? It was a really hot day, everybody was sitting outside,
and place was absolutely mobbed. There was this one guy, a
wannabe biker dude with a big beard, sleeveless denim jacket
and this tatty old T shirt with the cover of an old Rolling
Stones album on the front. Sympathy for the Devil, naturally!
He would've looked the part, I suppose, if it wasn't for the
fact that he had on a real retro pair of glasses. Michael Caine
style - with the big black frames? He looked a bit of a dick to
be honest, but Jen was convinced he kept staring at her. I
could never catch him at it, myself. Whenever I looked over
he would be looking the other way or fiddling with his
phone. Jen got pretty freaked out about it, though, so in the
end we just moved on. She was on edge for the rest of the
night, which definitely wasn't like her."

"Did you ever see this guy again? Or did Jennifer ever
mention seeing him?"

"No on both counts." Dorian admitted.

"So, what about the other incident?"

"At the races." he recalled. "The St Leger meeting last
September? This one guy seemed to be everywhere we were
that afternoon. In the bar, down by the paddock and the
unsaddling enclosure, in the betting ring. To be honest, I
didn't think anything of it myself. I mean, people always
wander around at the races, don't they? I know I do. There
was just something about this guy that set Jen off, though.
Maybe it was just the glasses."

"Another Michael Caine fan was he?"

"What? Oh no, these were sunglasses, those wrap around
ones with the blue tinted lenses. Oakleys, maybe. I think
they're cool myself – except it wasn't really sunglasses
weather. It was overcast most of the afternoon and hurling it
down by the last race. I wondered if maybe he had something
wrong with his eyes, you know, but he could just have been a
poseur. Whatever it was about him, he seemed to get under
Jen's skin. Said he gave her goose bumps."

"Did he speak to her?"

No - at least – I went to the bar a few times and the loo, so I suppose he could have approached her then, but she would have said, I'm sure. He just always seemed to be around in the general area where we were. Mind you, he was hard to miss. Apart from the glasses he had on this bright blue, padded ski jacket and a baseball cap. Yeah, I remember thinking he must be a Manchester United fan because it had their logo on the front? You know – the red devil holding a pitchfork or whatever?"

"Trident." I said absently.

"Huh?"

"I think it's meant to be a trident. That's a pitchfork with ideas above its station."

"I know what a trident is!" he said, affronted. "Does it really matter?"

"Not of itself." I agreed. "Though the devil is in the detail, they do say – and that could definitely be significant."

"You've lost me." Dorian grumbled.

"The t-shirt, the baseball cap? What do they have in common?"

"I don't – oh – the Devil! I never thought of that – but it's just a coincidence, surely?"

I didn't answer him. A week ago, I would probably have accepted that conclusion without question but, knowing what I knew now, I didn't believe it for one second.

"Well, I'm not sure if any of what I've just told you is of any use." Dorian said at length. "Maybe I'm just clutching at straws because I don't want to believe that Jen could have made those films – but if she was paranoid for a reason and somebody was genuinely stalking her, couldn't they be the ones who planted the camera?"

He was right, it did sound as if he was in denial, except maybe Jennifer really did have a stalker. I thought about the Killdevil diary. I'd been assuming that the document was just a clever fiction born out of Jensen's twisted imagination to point the finger at me. Certainly, there were parts of it deliberately framed to identify me as the author. What about the rest of the document, though? Could it be that it wasn't fiction at all but a true record of how Killdevil had stalked

Jennifer? What if someone had indeed followed Jennifer for weeks, shadowing her to work, to the bars she prowled in search of men and, ultimately, to the gathering where Glenn Wood had initiated her into the 'mysteries' of his Hellfire Club?

It spoke of just the kind of obsessive personality that might plant a hidden camera in the West Bretton bungalow.

I knew from experience how difficult it could be to follow someone without being spotted unless you had backup, or some means of changing your appearance. If Killdevil was real, then it was understandable that he would have affected means of disguising himself. It might also be the case that, on occasion he might have studied her too ardently and made her, if only subliminally, aware of his unhealthy interest in her. That would explain why she had been spooked by the hairy biker and the man in the blue sunglasses. Characters who were not, in fact, two different, socially inept individuals, but the same man, heavily disguised, yet subtly badged. The man who, for want of a better name, I called Killdevil. It was a label I was now beginning to doubt could be hung with any degree of certainty on Callum Jenson.

Dorian sighed, nudging me out of my reverie. He drained the last of his drink and smiled at me wanly.

"Anyway, I'd better go. Thanks for agreeing to meet me. I know you don't think much of me because of all the Hellfire Club stuff – and I don't blame you. To tell you the truth, I don't think much of myself right now and dealing with that is what's been occupying most of my time while I've been away. With Glenn dead I expect it will all just fizzle out now, but I'd already made up my mind I was done with it before I heard about his murder. Don't get me wrong, it was kind of fun and nobody did anything they didn't want to, but I suppose the masks and the secrecy made it all seem a bit unreal. It was like: if you can't see somebody's face nobody's getting hurt. Well, that's what I'm telling myself – and what's done is done. I can't change any of that, but I can change myself or at least try to."

He offered me his hand this time. I shook it happily, feeling a certain grudging respect for him.

"If I were you I'd report to the police as soon as possible. Your alibi should get you off their list of suspects but they're going to ask you about Wood and the Hellfire Club and if you can think of anybody who might have hated him enough to kill him. I don't think anybody in the club killed him, but you'll probably have to give up the names of any of the members you know. I'm guessing that will just be the women you recruited? You might like to give them a head's up before you do talk to the police."

He grimaced at the thought but nodded his agreement.

"And I'd continue to stay away from your apartment for a while." I said. "Just to be on the safe side."

"Don't worry! I'm booking into a hotel for the next few nights. I start rehearsing in Leeds at the beginning of next week and I'll be staying with a friend across there from Monday."

"Well, break a leg." I said.

29.

I still had a couple of hours to wait before Molly got out of
her lecture, so I finished my whiskey and wandered back
through to the main bar. I'd already decided that I'd leave the
car and get a taxi to take us home, so I resumed my former
spot by the bar and killed the time drinking pints of Cinco
Estrellas and people watching.

Molly walked in a little after half past nine with a group of
about half a dozen people who I guessed must be some of the
other students from her course. The place had filled up
considerably and they hovered just inside the door for a few
seconds, scoping out where they might find enough seats.
One of the group spotted a free table and they moved towards
it en masse, apart from Molly and another, older woman,
who lingered to finish what seemed to be an animated but
friendly conversation. It ended with a brief hug, then the
woman joined the rest of the group. Left alone Molly
scanned the room nonchalantly and I raised my hand to catch
her attention. When she spotted me, her face lit up with a
smile that took my breath away.

She joined me at the bar, planting a swift, unselfconscious
kiss on my right cheek. She was dressed for the weather in a
navy spotted Windermere jacket that she wore over a plain
white, cashmere sweater and high waisted 501s. A black
canvas messenger bag was hung over her left shoulder, from
the top of which protruded a file folder that I assumed must
contain her course work.

I ordered drinks, another Cinco Estrellas for me, a glass of
Mirabeau Cotes de Provence for Molly, and we moved away
from the bar to one of the few remaining free tables. As we
sat, she shook her hair back in a free, unfettered gesture that
somehow thrilled me to the core. I realised then, that

although I had known her for only a short time, Molly Grayson was already someone I needed to be in my life.

The next hour or so passed quickly as we chatted about everything and nothing: her university course, the latest gossip from work, the films and books we loved, the friends and family we cherished and those who drove us up the wall. Not once did either of us mention Jennifer Jensen or Glenn Wood and I think, for a short time at least, they slipped from my mind altogether as Molly and I negotiated the pleasant shallows of our new relationship and edged towards enticing deeper waters.

In the end the spell was broken by the college friends who she had arrived with. The woman Molly had been speaking to when they entered approached us diffidently to wish her good night, offering me a shy smile in passing. The woman and Molly hugged and bussed each other's cheeks and promised to meet for lunch sometime the following week. With another smile at me she re-joined the rest of the crowd, who were busy pulling on coats and preparing to leave. One of the group in particular caught my eye, a tall man in a duster coat and an Indiana Jones hat, who seemed somehow apart from the easy, jovial banter of his companions. I noticed him because he seemed to be making no attempt to hide the fact that he was staring over in our direction with a fixed, unashamed earnestness. Molly seemed to notice too and mouthed 'Good night' to him, sketching a brief wave of her right hand that seemed to magic a smile onto his previously taciturn face.

I raised an eyebrow at Molly.

"Do I have a rival, Miss Grayson? "

"Are you jealous, Mr Webster?" she bantered back.

"Insanely." I said, and she laughed, reaching for my hand.

"I should hope so." she said, leaning in and kissing me on the lips to my surprise and pleasure.

I couldn't help but glance across the room again to see how the man in the Indy hat reacted, but he and the rest of Molly's friends were straggling towards the door and he was no longer watching.

"Seriously, though." I said. "Indy seems a little intense."

"Indy! He'd love that. That's only Jake. He's our English Lit tutor. I'm supposed to fall in love with him, I think but I'm managing to avoid it so far. It's surprisingly easy actually. Do you know you're scowling, by the way? I rather like it."

"You think I have a cute scowl?"

"Don't let it go to your head, now." she teased. "You don't have to worry about Jake, honestly. He flirts like mad with all the women, only he's not that good at it, really. "

"So, he's not been inappropriate in any way?"

"Other than wearing the coat and that hat, you mean? No, not really. He's just your average English lecher – er - I mean lecturer."

She started giggling infectiously and I couldn't stop myself joining in. When the laughter ended, however, so did my brief vacation from the day job.

"Well, if he ever gets out of hand, let me know. I'll challenge him to a quote off."

"My hero!" she said, gifting me another guess. "But I'm sensing there might be more behind this conversation than simple concern for my virtue.

"Ouch, that smarts." I said. "You're right though. Seeing the way that guy was checking you out touched a nerve. It reminded me of something Jennifer's toy boy Dorian said to me. Can I ask you, did she ever mention that she thought someone might be following her?"

"What? Following? You mean like -?"

"A stalker." I suppled bluntly.

"N-no, I don't believe so."

"You sound unsure. Just think about it. Maybe she didn't make a big thing off it, just an off the cuff remark that somebody made her uneasy or was showing too much interest in her?"

"A lot of men showed interest." Molly admitted. "She was used to it, ignored it really, unless she felt some interest in them. Sorry."

"It's okay. Just a thought." I told her about the incidents that Dorian had described.

Molly looked concerned but shook her head.

"She never mentioned anything like that to me. It's funny you should mention it though."

"In what way?"

"Well, another friend of mine had all sorts of problems with his ex-girlfriend. She made his life miserable for months after they split up with phone calls, emails, sending him little gifts. Turning up unexpectedly in places where he hung out. You know the kind of thing I mean, I'm sure. In the end Zack, that's my friend, had to get a restraining order against her. Things improved then, and she eventually met somebody else to obsess about."

"They do say there's a lid for every crackpot." I said.

She punched my arm playfully.

"I haven't finished. You asked if Jen ever mentioned that she feared she was being stalked. Well, no, she didn't – but she was very sympathetic towards Zack when she heard his story. Said she knew exactly what it felt like because she had the same kind of trouble herself. Not recently, though. We're talking way back to her time at university up in Durham? Does that count?"

It was a long time ago, true, but, from what I'd learned about stalking behaviour during my days on the force there was no fixed limit to it. Research suggested that the average length of time it persisted was from between 6 months to two years but there were many extreme examples, I knew.. A woman called Margaret Mary Ray had stalked the American talk show host David Letterman for ten years, frequently breaking into his home, camping out on his tennis court and even stealing his Porsche before she eventually committed suicide at the age of 46. And that was nowhere near the unofficial world record for stalking which was believed to be forty-three years! So, who knew?

"Did she go into detail?" I asked.

"Just that it was one of her fellow students. Not a classmate, though. They were in some club or society together…"

"The Drama Society?" I suggested.

"Yes, yes that's right. How did you know that?"

"Just an educated guess." I told her about finding Jennifer's scrapbook.

"Yes, well this guy was a friend of Callum, she said. One of the mainstays of the society. Very talented but a bit out there, is how she described him. They had a drunken one nighter after some college party and he took it all a bit to heart. Declared his undying love and made a nuisance of himself from then on"

"Did she tell you his name?" I asked as casually as I could.

"No." She shook her head for emphasis. "It wasn't something she dwelt on. She only mentioned it to show support for Zack, I think. It went on for about two years, she said, then he suddenly dropped out."

"I don't suppose you can recall anything else she may have said about this guy?"

"Sorry, n- oh, well, there was the creepy tattoo!"

"Tattoo?"

"Yes, on his back. All over his back! Jen said it really freaked her out."

"What was it?"

"Good question, it was something weird, she said. Some kind of occult, woo-woo, dark arts kinds of thing. He was into all that stuff apparently. I remember now, it was one of those five-pointed star things. Pentacles?"

"Pentagram, I think. That doesn't sound especially freaky..."

"Well, it gets better, believe me! It wasn't the pentagram thing that freaked her out – it was the goat's head in the middle staring at her!"

Molly laughed and gave a little shudder at the thought.

"Please tell me you don't have any bizarre body art, Harry?"

"Does the Bat Signal on my chest count?"

"You're joking!" she laughed. "Aren't you?"

I smiled enigmatically and drank the last of my beer. The place had emptied but they were still serving and I was debating asking Molly if she wanted another drink when delicately stifled a sudden yawn with the back of a hand.

"Sorry. It's not the company, honest! It's been a long day with work and college and though the last couple of hours have been the best bit by far, I think it's time for bed – I mean! Oh my God, I didn't – "

She dissolved into a tipsy giggling fit and hid her embarrassment behind her glass, blushing a nice complementary shade to its contents.

"I know what you mean." I assured her with a smile, reaching into my pocket for my phone. "You just want to see my tattoo."

30.

After dropping off a slightly merry and very affectionate Molly at her house the taxi took me home to what proved to be the best night's sleep I'd had in weeks. The next day dawned brighter but with the threat of more rain later in the day. I ate breakfast and rang for a taxi to take me back to the *Rodney* to pick up my car. I was in the office by nine o'clock,

I spent most of the day on my own. Eddie was out on a job that kept him busy in Wakefield all day, whilst Clegg had booked one of the occasional midweek days off he took throughout the year to catch a production of the *RSC* in Stratford in the company of a nice widow lady called, aptly enough Miranda It was *Anthony & Cleopatra* this year. *Finish good lady; the bright day is done, and we are for the dark.*

Oh yes, bring it on, Jake!

I spent the morning finishing of a Home Security Plan for a client in Crowfield, the nearest thing to a garden suburb that the city could boast. It was the place you chose to live until you could afford to move to Ravencliffe or Ebdon, or one of the other up market commuter villages that ringed the urban sprawl.

I'd finished by lunch, which was a BLT and three cups of coffee, and spent the rest of the afternoon answering the phones and working my way down the list of names I'd copied from Jennifer Jensen's scrapbook. Even with access to the people finding database and other online sources we subscribed to it was slow and often frustrating work. At least half of them were women, all of who could have married and changed their names during the last quarter of a century, whilst there were a lot of common name combinations –

David Walker, Ian Thomson, for example - that were hard to pin down without additional context.

By five o'clock I had managed to track down and speak to only about five people, two of whom were false positives. Of the other three, none admitted to more than a nodding acquaintance with Callum Jensen during their time at university – and all of them claimed not to have seen him since. Of course, if they really were his accomplices they would say that, wouldn't they?

I suppose at the end of the day it was always a futile exercise, though it at least created the illusion that I was doing something to try and get to the bottom of what was going on. At half five I gave up and, after a quick visit to my executive washroom, shut the office and set off for my meeting with Ellis Thatcher. As I was leaving I'll admit to casting a brief glance towards the corner behind Eddie's desk where his Louisville Slugger now seemed to live permanently. Part of me couldn't help picturing Thatcher's face if I walked in with it slung nonchalantly over my shoulder, but sanity prevailed, and I left El Bambino where it was.

In accordance with the instructions Ben Cross had passed on I gave my name at the reception desk of the hotel. They relayed it to the *Vespers* club and I was invited to take a seat and wait for someone to collect me. I half-expected Thatcher to keep me waiting just because he could but in less than five minutes a familiar, broad shouldered figure stepped out of one of the lifts and cast his gaze around the hotel reception area. When his eyes lighted on me he flashed a huge, cheerful grin and lumbered across the lobby to greet me.

"Harry Webster. We meet once mores! It is, I, Jadran Stojanovic."

"So, it is." I said, accepting the large hand that he thrust towards me as I got to my feet. "The ubiquitous Jadran Stojanovic, indeed."

He pulled a face and rolled his mouth around the word as if it was a piece of sour gum.

"Ub-iqui-tous? What is meaning?"

"Seeming to be everywhere."

"Ah – like asshole Farage, yes? Good word. I like. Always I try to learn new words. Make powerful."

I agreed, unable to avoid returning his huge grin, which I was beginning to realise was infectious.

"So, what are you doing here? I wouldn't have expected *Vespers* to need bouncers."

"We prefer be called 'doorman'. More class, better suit but you are right. This place top shelf, no trouble mostly, but you have rep, yes? Tough guy. Mr Thatcher say Jadran must watch back. I tell him Harry is fun guy, no problem, but Thatcher say he have bill from dentist that say different so Jadran must be bodyguard, so you don't try break his face again, okay?

"No face breaking. Got it. I will resist all temptation."

"Good – though you ask me Thatcher is a *drkadzija[1].* "

"Bless you." I said.

"You are welcome. So, you come now Harry. I take you to the boss. He waits with tender hooks."

"You seem to have a lot of bosses." I said, walking alongside him to the lifts.

"Huh? Oh, you mean Mr Wood? We just do favour for him because boss Thatcher say so. They big buddy buddies. Was. He is dead Wood now, yes?"

"Yes."

"You did not kill him, did you Harry?"

"Not guilty." I assured him.

He looked on me approvingly.

"Jadran believes you but Mr Thatcher is big wuss.

He was also Jadran's actual boss, it seemed. His company, Oracle, supplied security for over half the pubs and clubs in the city and Thatcher often used Jadran or one of his colleagues as personal driver/protection. I was kind of flattered that Thatcher was wary enough of me to bring along a bodyguard – though I suppose it may just have been an affectation. Another way to show the world what a big, important man he was.

---

[1] Tosser

313

The club was on the top floor of the building, in company with the gym and sauna. It was a spacious room with a high ceiling and a large curved bar at the far end. In between there were acres of monogrammed carpet and heavy leather furniture that went perfectly with the dark wood panelling. There were a few bodies scattered around, lounging with their drinks and newspapers, or chatting in small groups at one or other of the low tables scattered amongst the chairs. As far as I could tell, Thatcher was not amongst them and Jadran strode across the room and through a pair of swing doors to the left of the bar that apparently lead to the Conference Suite and Smoking Rooms.

Thatcher was in the latter, sitting in one of the club's signature heavy, burgundy leather armchairs. He was noodling on a MacBook and smoking one of the Monte Cristo Edmundos that he favoured. The stocky, taciturn figure of Jadran's partner, Bojan stood watchfully behind Thatcher's chair. He nodded briefly to me and fired off a question to Jadran in their native tongue. It made Jadran smile but Thatcher looked up in annoyance.

"What is he saying? Tell him to speak fucking English!"

Jadran inclined his head apologetically.

"Bojan just ask: where is Shoeless Joe?"

Thatcher stared at him blankly. It was a look that fit comfortably on his face.

"Is private joke." Jadran shrugged.

"Well do the jokes on your own time." Thatcher instructed them petulantly. "Go sit over there while I speak to Sir Galahad here."

He gestured to an adjacent table and Jadran ambled over to it with Bojan in his wake. Thatcher watched them settle then turned his attention to the brandy snifter that stood next to his laptop. He took a leisurely sip and puffed on his cigar. He was in no hurry to look me in the eye or invite me to sit and it was comforting to realise that he was still a complete creep.

Not waiting to be asked I sat down in the chair across the table from him and took a long, slow look around the room.

"Well Ellis, isn't this nice? More Drones than Diogenes, I bet."

"Fuck you, Webster." he swore.

"Ah, yes, oh how I've missed your gay banter – but play nice. I didn't come here to open old wounds."

"**You** didn't have any." he said pointedly.

"What? Skinned knuckles don't count?"

"You're lucky I only fired you. I should have pressed charges."

"I resigned." I pointed out. "And you didn't press charges because you would have had to admit why I punched you."

He glared at me, but he knew it was the truth. Ellis Thatcher was not a big man, except in his head. He was five feet nine in his stocking feet but thought he was ten feet tall. The extra feet and inches were crammed into his ego. It made him both a control freak and an entitled bully who thought it was the boss's privilege to sexually harass every woman in the office – even a shy eighteen-year-old work experience kid.

When I told him to stop was the first occasion he ever said "Fuck you, Webster" to me. They were also the last coherent words he spoke for several weeks on account of the broken jaw I handed him in lieu of a resignation letter. I must admit that I'd fully expected him to call in the police, but he never did, probably because he didn't want his trophy wife to find out what a sleazy piece of work he really was.

"To mourn a mischief that is past and gone is the next way to draw new mischief on." I said. "For what it's worth, I told everybody you tripped and fell onto my fist."

"Spare me the poetic bullshit and just say what you came to say." he said stiffly. "I don't know what story you spun to Ben Cross, but he said it was important. Think yourself lucky that I hold Ben in such high regard. It's the only reason you're here."

"Fair enough. I'll get straight to the point then."

I reached into my jacket and took out the photograph of Jennifer Jensen that I'd brought with me. I handed it to him and he snatched it from me, tight-lipped and irritable. As he studied the photograph, however, his expression softened noticeably.

"Jennifer Juniper." he murmured. "Hair of golden flax."

"Jennifer Juniper. Longs for what she lacks." I said, completing the couplet. "Is that how you remember her?"

His mouth twisted into what might have been a smile or the onset of a stroke, but he didn't answer the question directly.

"What's your interest in Jen?" he asked, passing back the photograph. "And why do you think I'd help you?"

"She's missing, or rather, nobody seems to know where she is, which might not be the same thing at all. Her husband hired me to find her, except now he's gone missing as well."

"Callum? He's back in the picture?"

"Well, he was. Now he isn't and since he hasn't paid me yet I'm anxious to track him down and collect what's owed."

"I have people to do that kind of thing for me." Thatcher sneered.

"Well, Thatch, you better than most know that I'm a hands-on kind of guy myself."

He scowled but let it pass.

"I can't help you anyway. I haven't seen Callum for years."

"You were friends once upon a time though, right? Trod the boards together at university?"

"Done your homework, I see." he sneered. "I was more Jennifer's friend, as it happens. I tolerated Callum because of her, really."

"Ah, yes, that 'hair of golden flax'. Is that why you gave her the job at *Stentor*?"

"What of it? She reconnected with me when they first moved here. My wife and I made a foursome with them now and then. Right up until Callum buggered off back to America."

He scowled again, though whether at me or the thought of Jensen's desertion, I wasn't sure.

"She was in bits when he took off. Getting back to work was part of how she coped, and I was happy to help her out. Apart from when she reached out to me, I haven't seen much of her these last couple of years. Callum's marriage wasn't the only thing he broke when he walked out."

316

His voice held a note of genuine feeling at this point and I almost felt sorry for him. It didn't take any great leap of intuition to realise he had probably been in love – or at least, lust – with Jennifer at some point in their past. He stared into his glass for a moment now, as if it contained the last few, glowing embers of those feelings.

"What about other friends?" I asked, pulling him out of his moment. "Apart from yourself did Jensen or Jennifer ever mention any other old university friends they kept in touch with? Somebody who Jensen might be staying with?"

I took the list of names I'd brought with me from my pocket and passed it to him.

"Perhaps this might jog your memory? These are some of the people who were in the university drama club during their time there. It's a long shot, probably, but do you remember if any of the people on that list, apart from yourself, were particularly friendly with the Jensens – Callum especially."

"It's nearly twenty-five years ago!" he protested but he took the list and scrutinised it.

He took his time looking over it, frowning or half-smiling as the odd name clearly touched some memory of that time in his life. When he had finished he lay the list on the table and pushed it back towards me.

"I don't remember half of these people." he admitted. "But I'd bet Jen knew them all by their first names back then – and probably kept in touch with some of them over the years. Callum never did like sharing her, though, so I doubt he made any real friends amongst them. There was one guy though..."

He leaned over and tapped a finger on a name about halfway down the page.

"Marius Drommel? I read.

"I know, right? Weird name for a weird fucking guy. Him and Callum were tight though, for a while. They lived on the same corridor in halls and they were both computer geeks; did the same course I think. They were certainly friends before Callum joined the drama club. In fact, it was Drommel who first brought him along, I seem to remember.

It surprised me, really. Callum was always a bit strait-laced and unobtrusive, whereas Drommel was really out there. Always dressed in black, wore mascara, swanned around in a long black cloak and looked as if he had his hair done by Edward Scissorhands. Didn't much look like the next Olivier, let me tell you, but he certainly surprised a few of us there!"

"How's that?"

"Because it turned out he could act the pants off everybody else in the club. He may have looked more like Frank N. Furter than Hamlet but when he got on the stage he just killed it, whatever the role. I heard one of the Drama tutors say once that he had 'a flexible skin' and that about sums him up. He didn't have the looks or the swagger for leading roles but he could grow or shrink into any part he played. He seemed happy enough with secondary roles, even turned down the chance to play Faustus in our second year! Weirdo. Extraordinarily, annoyingly gifted but also kind of creepy and unsettling. When Callum started seeing Jen his relationship with Drommel cooled. I always figured that the freak had designs in that direction himself, but I don't think he ever stood a chance. Mind you nobody did once she hooked up with Callum – though I could never work out what she saw in him either to be honest."

Maybe just the fact that he wasn't Thatcher played a part in it, but I decided to keep that thought to myself. I had nothing against antagonising Thatcher but while he was talking freely I didn't want to knock him off his stride.

"Still, can't really blame either of them for falling for her." Thatcher continued with a disconcerting flash of honesty. "None of us were entirely immune to the golden girl back then, other than the bum boys and the straight females."

He gave an unpleasant bark of laughter, reminding me in timely fashion that he was still an insufferable jerk.

"Still – her and Callum, I never really got it."

"*The heart has its reasons which reason knows nothing off.*" I said.

"Fuck Shakespeare."

"It was Pascal, actually."

"Who cares? Whatever it took to get her attention, Callum must have had it in spades. They got engaged at the start of our third year – but Drommel was gone by then."

"Gone? As in - ?"

"Who knows? Turned into a bat and flew off to Transylvania maybe?" He gave that harsh laugh again, pleased with his stab at humour. "He never showed up at drama club that year and word was he just dropped out. Maybe somebody knew why but I couldn't care less so I never inquired. To be honest, until I saw his name on that list I don't think I'd given him a thought in all the years since. Not my kind of people."

"I would probably have liked him then." I said.

"Go screw yourself."

"Well, it's not Pascal but at least you're making an effort to expand your repertoire."

"This conversation is over. You've had your five minutes, now get out."

"So, no chance of a drink for old times' sake then?" I said. "One last question. Did Drommel have a tattoo on his back?"

"'Fuck do I know? Maybe – yes – some moody occult shit. Made him look like even more of a dick! And that's it. Time's up."

He waved his cigar dismissively in my direction and turned furiously towards Jadran and Bojan, who had produced a deck of cards from somewhere and were engrossed in what looked like gin rummy.

"You two! Schwarzenegger and De Vito, or whatever the hell your names are! Webster will be leaving now – and if he happens to fall down the stairs on the way out there'll be a bonus for both of you."

Jadran shrugged and with an apologetic smile invited me to leave with an outstretched palm. Bodran stood up, looking vaguely disgusted as he spat out another mouthful of his homespun wisdom. His tone was disappointed, but the words again drew a bark of laughter from Jadran. I looked at him questioningly.

"*Ain't gonna be no rematch.*" Jadran translated with a grin. I grinned back, touched my forelock briefly to Thatcher and headed for the door. Jadran walked alongside me.

"You think I look like Schwarzenegger, Harry?"

"I thought you were De Vito." I said.

Jadran laughed. "You are funny guy, Harry. Come. We take lift. Bojan have bad knee."

31.

Back on the street the temperature had fallen, and the threat of imminent rain carried on the blustery wind that had sprung up while I was in the hotel. I walked briskly back to the car and headed home. It had been a long day and I was cold, hungry and tired; in need of nothing at that moment more than a warming shower, a hot meal and a reviving beer.

With those basic needs satisfied, I had just cracked open a gratuitous second beer when my phone rang. It was Raphael. True to his word he had tapped his contact inside Rain Hill and was calling to pass on the results. First and foremost, the details of Glenn Wood's murder.

"No great mystery there." Raphael said. "Strangulation by ligature – though not the one he was strung up by apparently. It looks as if he was manually strangled and the body suspended from the lower branch of an old elm tree on Hob's Tump. His body was discovered there by some early morning jogger as you've no doubt read."

"Manual strangulation? That's a close-up and personal method for the killer to choose. Didn't Wood fight back?"

"The forensics say not. The police are still waiting for the full toxicology report but they're thinking he was 'roofied' to make him pliable. The Tump is a good three quarters of a mile from the nearest road and there was no sign of any type of vehicle being at the scene. It looks as if the killer walked Wood there, where he strangled him, stripped the body and hung him upside down to ruin the early bird jogger's day."

"Upside down?"

"Yes, not simply hung up by his feet, either. Deliberately posed. Suspended by his right ankle with his left leg bent at the knee and the foot secured to the opposite knee. Just like..."

"The Hanged Man tarot card." I finished.

"Indeed." Raphael asked. "Should I ask you how you know that?"

"*I am the whistler and I know many things.*" I said evasively. "Let's just say that it's not the first time a tarot image has cropped up these last few days. I'm a little surprised the police picked up on the significance of the body's positioning so quickly, though."

"Yes, well, that fragment of Jacobean verse Swanson mentioned wasn't the only thing found in Wood's hand. It was wrapped round an actual Hanged Man tarot card."

"It's all part of his game – whoever he is. He thinks he's the smartest person in the room. The tarot cards are his little private joke, his way of announcing his intentions or, rather, gloating about them after the event."

"That is doubly troubling in light of the latest development." Raphael said, drawing a meaningful breath.

"Which is?"

"Swanson's team has received an anonymous communication that may be from the killer. It's another tarot card."

"Which one?" I asked.

There was a brief silence on the other end of the line before he answered.

"Sorry, just needed to check my notes. The card is Judgement. Which has an ominous ring to it, I'm sure you'll agree." There was another pause, then: "What did you mean?"

"About what? The Whistler? It's just an old black and white movie from the forties."

"No – you said: Whoever he is.' I thought you were fairly certain Callum Jensen is Killdevil."

"He still might be but I'm not so sure now. It seems that Jennifer may have had a stalker."

I explained how my conversations with Dorian and Molly had raised the doubts I now had about Jensen's involvement. Raphael was cautious in his response.

"Mrs Jensen's experience at university was a very long time ago to have any relevance, surely? As for Mr Wilde - couldn't his comments just be emotional displacement on his part? He finds Jennifer's behaviour uncomfortable or unacceptable, so he creates an alternate narrative to deflect the blame elsewhere."

"Possible." I admitted. "But if he was making up a story on the spur of the moment why would he mention that the two men who Jennifer thought were watching her wore items of clothing that referenced the Devil? Whoever's behind Wood's death and the attempt to frame me obviously has some kind of satanic vibe going on. Lou Sifer. Donald Black. Hob's Tump. The Sympathy for the Devil t-shirt and the Red Devils baseball cap could well be part of that same preoccupation."

"I take your point." Raphael said. "Irrespective of how much credence you give Dorian Wilde on this matter his reappearance is problematic in another sense, though. You realise, of course, that if his alibi is substantiated that removes him from the suspect list and leaves just you or Jensen in pole position? If this stalker exists it would be very timely for your cause if you could find him."

"In that case I'd better get off the phone and start looking, I said.

I hung up and turned back to the computer. It took less than ten seconds to find what I was looking for.

Judgement. The 20th card in the Major Arcana. In the Rider-Waite deck that the killer seemed to favour the top half of the card is dominated by the looming figure of an angel with outspread wings sounding a horn from which flutters a white flag with a red cross. The lower portion of the card depicts a series of open coffins out of which arise several naked men, women and children. Their arms are raised in supplication to the cloud-wreathed figure, who is generally accepted to be the Archangel Gabriel summoning the dead to the Last Judgement. In isolation, it signifies absoluteness, finality, an irreversible change or decision.

That much I gleaned from a few minutes of further online research, none of which offered much comfort. It seemed to me that the previous cards had not been left as threats or predictions but as a symbolic acknowledgement of acts that had already been committed. The Devil card I found at his home signified the abduction of Wood and mocked his role as leader of the Hellfire Club. His ritualistic murder was then exactly mirrored by the Hanged Man card clutched in his dead hand.

What, then, did the latest card he had dealt reference? A judgement that had already been rendered? That would seem to be the obvious inference - but to who?

Apart from the dominant figure of Gabriel, the most prominent figures were in the foreground. A dark-haired man, a child and a woman with long, blonde hair. It was this last figure that appeared to be the focus of the archangel's gaze to the exclusion of all others, while she in turn looked up at him in awe or adoration. It was difficult to look at that image and not hear the 'voice' of Killdevil writing about "Gwenhwyfar, the Fair One, the White Shadow, whose otherworldly beauty captures the heart of kings". If the woman was indeed meant to represent Jennifer, it only confirmed her place at the very centre of the tangled scenario I'd been entrapped in. Did that mean that the man was another of her lovers? Dorian had dark hair – as did Callum Jensen, for that matter.

And, I thought queasily, how significant was it that they were standing in coffins?

I stared at the image on my computer screen for a long time, trying to peer into the mind of a killer. I considered Callum Jensen again. Could whatever was in play here really be just about the vengeance of a disillusioned husband? The killer was clearly obsessive, audacious and highly intelligent. Jensen certainly met the last of these criteria. He had also made a substantial living out of devising intricately plotted games, which was effectively what I found myself caught up in. All the same I couldn't really buy that his feelings for his estranged wife were based in obsession. He may have tried to reconcile with her but prior to that they had lived apart for two years on separate continents. There was no evidence that there had been any significant contact between them in that time. During that period the only person whose behaviour could be described as obsessive was Jennifer in her defiant and desperate search for sexual solace.

Jensen, on the other hand, seemed to have handled their break-up much less dramatically. Not surprising, perhaps, since he had instigated it in the first place. After walking out on her the way he did had he really spent the intervening period fixating on a woman who would most likely have welcomed him back in a heartbeat?

Having finally made the decision to try and reconcile with Jennifer, I could understand that Jensen may have been upset to learn of the sexually charged lifestyle his wife had pursued in his absence. The question I asked myself was: did I believe that he was so thrown off balance by that discovery that he had been driven to devise the elaborate, labyrinthine plot to murder Glenn Wood and frame me. Of course, it was difficult to predict how any specific individual might react in that situation, and particularly someone you didn't know. All I had to go on was a growing instinct that my original conclusion was wrong and that someone other than Callum Jensen was Killdevil.

I turned back to the computer and brought up the Wikipedia page about Jensen again. I re-read the article without gaining any further insight into the man then focused on the accompanying photograph. There was something nagging me about it from the first time I'd examined it but stare it as I might I still couldn't see what it was that niggled.

I saved the image as a jpeg file and loaded it into the editing software on my PC. Starting at the top I enlarged it in sections to see if anything emerged in close detail. The first thing I noticed was that the sunglasses he wore had the distinctive Rayban signature in the corner of the right-hand lens. I doubted if that detail was what had nudged my subconscious, though and the parts of his face unobscured by the sunglasses had no distinguishing marks or features that might have caught my eye.

Lower down, however, I noticed that he was wearing a pendant that, which on close scrutiny proved to be a dragon's head on a thin silver chain visible at the open neck of his gaudily patterned, short-sleeved shirt. I couldn't recall Jensen having such a pendant when I met him but then it was an old photograph and maybe he was no longer the kind of person who would wear something like that. He also hadn't been wearing a wedding ring, which the younger Jensen in the picture still did. In fact, the only item of jewellery he had displayed was that chunky Rolex he'd flashed when he shook hands. The same watch, or one very similar, that the man in the photograph was wearing on his left wrist.

His left wrist! That was it! That was the detail that registered on my subconscious when I had first looked at it! In the photograph Jensen wore his watch on his left wrist but at *The Tanglewood* he had been wearing it on his right! I remembered noticing as much when we shook hands! Was it significant, though? I wore my watch on my left wrist and always had. I pulled up the search engine and did a little research. It turned out that there is no hard and fast etiquette about which wrist a watch should be worn on, though the general rule was that people wore their watch on the opposite hand to that which they favoured. A right-handed person would therefore wear his watch on the left wrist and vice versa. As a left hander myself I was clearly in breach of that suggested protocol, but I was at least consistently out of step and consistency seemed to be the norm. Left or right, people generally picked one and stuck with it unless circumstances – such as the loss of an arm or hand - dictated a change. That did not apply to the man I knew as Callum Jensen, so either the change was just a matter of personal whim, or else…?

I'd wondered at the time whether the Rolex he wore might be a knock off but maybe it was not the watch but its wearer who was the fake? Was it possible that Callum Jensen, like Louis Sifer and Donald Black, was not who he claimed to be? That the man I had spoken with at the *Tanglewood Inn,* was not Jennifer Jensen's husband at all but the same man who had planted the camera in her mother's former bungalow, the unknown stalker Dorian had hinted at? An even more revelatory thought struck me. Could the same, audacious personality also have hidden behind the faces of the brutally scarred Louis Sifer and smug, bearded Donald Black? Was the creator of this whole mad drama also its sole enactor?

The more thought I gave it, the more sense it made, more so than the notion that the killer had recruited an accomplice for those roles. Stalkers were generally loners with no meaningful relationships outside the one they seek to establish. It was a goal they usually pursued with exactly the kind of reckless effrontery it would take for someone to insert themselves so blatantly in my investigation. It was also true to say that, though they themselves viewed their behaviour as perfectly normal, it would not seem so to other people. That didn't rule out the possibility that they might occasionally acquire a similarly psychologically damaged acolyte but their solitary, driven nature and the possessive character of their obsession would generally rule it out.

I picked up my cigars and lighter and wandered through to the kitchen. I grabbed another beer from the fridge and cracked the kitchen window. I stood there with the lights off, smoking, thinking and drinking with nothing but the faint hum of distant traffic and the steady patter of the rain for company. When I had finished my cigar and my beer I made coffee, black and sweet, and retreated back to my office. I thought for a moment then opened up a new Word document and begin to type in everything I thought I knew or could adduce about the theoretical stalker.

- Very intelligent and arrogant, probably thinks he's the smartest person in the room. Demonstrated by his ability to devise a complex plan to taunt and incriminate me and to plant the fake diary on my computer via a Trojan. The quality of the writing and language used in the stalker diary supports his intelligence and suggests he is both devious and manipulative.
- He's obsessed with Jennifer and it was possible that he also knows her on some level. He was able to gain access to her mother's bungalow to rig and remove the camera and plant the book and tarot card. He also had to have access to *Moorside* to plant the DVDs I had discovered there, masquerade as the gardener, and return to slip the missing DVD of Jennifer and I onto the shelf with the others.

- His obsession fuels a homicidal jealousy. He has no problem with killing and gloating about the fact. Probably a psychopathic personality.
- He had a knowledge of and/or fascination with the occult evidenced by the taunting use of the tarot cards and his apparent obsession with the Devil. May believe he is the Devil, which would make Wood an impostor in his eyes and provide another motive for wanting him dead. It could also explain why he has also drawn me- into his crazy scenario: his way of throwing down a deliberate challenge to the man who one tabloid had, embarrassingly, actually christened the Devil Slayer.
- Confident to the point of recklessness. If I was right, he had deliberately inserted himself into my investigation on three separate occasions – first when posing as Callum Jensen to set me running, then as Louis Sifer and Donald Black to further manipulate me and, ultimately, undermine my version of events.
- The ease with which he can assume alternate personalities again speaks to his arrogance and a reckless self-confidence. It also suggests an impressive talent for mimicry and dissembling, demonstrated by the varied accents and convincing alternate personas he employed. Probably also has considerable expertise in the use of prosthetics and other methods of altering one's appearance. In short, he seems to be able to employ all the skills and techniques of a very accomplished actor to flesh out the devious narrative he has constructed.
- Physical characteristics – medium height. Jensen, Sifer and Black were all shorter than my six feet two by several inches. Black was on the portly side but Sifer and Jensen were both quite trim. You can add physical proportion easily enough with padding but not take it off, which probably meant the stalker wasn't carrying any excess flesh either. All three – Jensen, Sifer and Black - had moved around easily, like men in the prime of life, and at the time I estimated each of them was in early middle age. Of course, if all three were the same

person in different guises, he could have been a younger man who had created deliberately older proxies.

I sat back and reread what I had written. Most of it, though probably an accurate reflection of the type of person who had killed Glenn Wood, was non-specific – his intelligence, his brazen self-confidence, his meticulous planning, etc. – and wasn't much help in identifying any possible suspects. On the other hand, the killer possessed two very distinct characteristics that in tandem formed a more unique identifier. Namely: his obvious theatrical flair and a fixation with the Devil that he seemed to have made his personal signature. In the last twenty-four hours, I had now twice encountered traces of a person in who those characteristics might intersect: Jennifer's old, disgruntled suitor with the creepy tattoo that Molly had spoken of.

From her brief, second-hand description, it sounded very much as if this was the same person Ellis Thatcher had identified as the star of the university drama club and reluctant second fiddle to Callum Jensen in their long-ago pursuit of Jennifer. The man Thatcher had named as Marius Drommel. It was the thinnest of leads, but it was the only one I had right now, and I couldn't just ignore the synchronicity.

I pulled up a search engine and typed his name into it. It was not a common name and the search yielded no results for an individual with that exact name. There were a few hits for the surname 'Drommel' alone, but they were mostly for a Dutch goalkeeper. A little more research indicated that the surname itself was, in fact, comparatively rare and most examples were recorded in the Netherlands. From the sources available to me I found just five currently extent examples of the name in the UK. None of them were Marius but maybe they were family members or other relatives.

I looked at my watch, surprised to see that it was by now getting on for midnight. Nobody was going to thank me for ringing them up at this time of night to ask questions about a theoretical relative, I recognised. That was something for another day. A wave of tiredness suddenly washed over me, and I began to shut down the computer. The last search window left open was the tarot card sent to the police by the killer. The image of the blonde-haired woman and the dark-haired man filled me with a sudden foreboding thought: if the Callum Jensen who hired me was a fake then what had become of the real one?

I went to the bathroom and brushed my teeth. It was still raining hard as I headed for bed. As I drew the curtains I watched some stoical dog owner bracing the downpour. He was dragging a reluctant spaniel along the pavement and I felt some sympathy for the dog. I knew all too well what it was like to be dragged out of your comfort zone into uncomfortable situations.

I stripped off my clothes and slid between the sheets. I fumbled off the light by my bed and let my head sink gratefully onto the pillow. I fell asleep almost at once to the staccato lullaby of the rain against my window.

I woke up sometime later, my pillows damp with sweat, my heart thundering in my chest. Somewhere in the darkness I heard a sound, faint at first but becoming louder, drawing nearer with a ponderous insistence that filled me with a sense of rising panic that I felt like the pressure of a powerful, irresistible hand on my chest. Or else the weight of some grinning, invisible incubus that squatted there.

I tried to move, to sit up, but could not. My whole body seemed to be gripped by a paralysis that flowed directly from the unseen force that oppressed me. Meanwhile, the sound was now recognisable as the drag of ungainly but remorseless feet across the floor of some dank, forgotten dungeon.

With a mounting sense of fear and helplessness I struggled to break free of the relentless pressure that pinned me to the bed but without success. I remained helplessly immobile and increasingly more terror-stricken as the remorseless footsteps came ever nearer until, as they reached my bedroom door, they ceased abruptly. I hung suspended in the long, dreadful silence that followed, immovably snared in a clinging web of darkness and dread.

After what seemed like an eternity as I continued to regain control of my body, the door of my bedroom began to creak slowly open, revealing a figure that seemed both familiar and yet subtly altered.

It was that same gaunt, skeletal presence that had so often tormented my dreams but this time what glared at me were not the dark, empty sockets of a skull but two eyes burning red with hate in the face of a horned and grinning devil.

Still unable to move so much as a finger, I could only lie there transfixed as the malevolent figure drew near the bed. Thrusting its hateful visage to within inches of my face, it spoke in a harsh, guttural whisper, demanding:

"Do you not know me?"

I tried to speak but no words came out, nor could I move my head one inch in denial. My silence served only to enrage the Satanic figure, who repeated his demand more urgently than before.

"Do you not know me?"

Once again, I tried to answer back but my jaw was locked, and my lips would not form the words.

"Do you not know me?"

The question was repeated a third time, louder, more insistent than ever and with a herculean effort I finally willed my lips to move and feebly croak an answer.

"The devil. You are the devil."

"No!" he answered, in a voice of triumph and as it spoke it raised a skeletal hand to its face and tore away the leering face, which was I realised a mere mask. As the figure tossed it aside I looked upon the face beneath the mask in disbelief. It was a face I knew well. A face I saw every time I looked in the mirror. The face beneath the mask was my own!

"No, you – you are the devil!" the doppelgänger crowed.

32.

I jerked awake, breaking out of the grip of sleep like an exhausted marathon runner lunging for the tape. I felt off kilter, unsure of what space I occupied and aware of little beyond the rapid thrumming of my heartbeat and my panicked breathing. I pushed myself upright, throwing the bedclothes aside and fumbling to switch on my bedside lamp. I was stuck in fright or flight mode and only when the familiar angles and artefacts of my bedroom settled into focus did the lingering residue of my recent nightmare fade. I fell back onto my pillows, which were so drenched in my sweat that I thought for a moment that the rain had someone blown in from outside to soak me while I slept.

Sitting up again, I glanced at the radio alarm. It was a little before half past six in the morning. Most days I would have simply rolled over and drifted back to sleep until my alarm sounded at a quarter to eight. That was out of the question this morning. Every nerve ending was still jumping as if I'd drunk a crate of Red Bull. I had as much chance of going back to sleep as I had of doing fifty-one-finger push ups in a suit of armour.

I kicked my way free of the sheets and headed for the bathroom. Half an hour later, after a long, hot shower, I got dressed and stripped the bed. Down in the kitchen I threw the sweat soaked bedding into the washing machine before sitting down to a breakfast of toast and strong coffee. This restored my equilibrium to a degree, though I was left with a lingering awareness of the sense of helplessness and terror that had filled the dream space. That, and the inevitable physical indicators: the sweats, the thumping heartbeat, the racing pulse and, sometimes, the icy sliver of pain from that phantom dagger drilling into my shoulder. For once that nagging ache had not materialised, though it was small comfort. Not for the first time during these last few days, I found myself wondering if Clegg could be right about post-traumatic stress. The dreams were occurring too often now to be simply written off, but I wasn't yet quite at the point of dealing with the problem head on. Leaving aside the nightmares I seemed free of any other notable signs of PTSD. I wasn't depressed, I ate well, my intellectual and reasoning faculties were as sharp as ever and I was not prone to violent outburst of anger or other irrational behaviour. Unless renewing my season ticket at Utd counted.

After checking off all the symptoms I didn't have I had reassured myself that I was fine. All the same, once the current problem had been dealt with, maybe I should seriously consider Clegg's suggestion about getting professional counselling.

I finished breakfast, brushed my teeth and headed out. The rain had stopped sometime in the night and the street outside seemed fresh and clean in the cold morning air. That sensation of freshness soon began to fade once I joined the embryonic rush hour crawl. It had dissipated altogether when I finally swung into the car park of our building thirty minutes later.

Clegg was already at his desk when I entered the office, looking cheerful and reinvigorated as always from "bathing in Shakespeare's pure spring of verse". While I was pouring myself a coffee, Eddie arrived and when we both had our drinks I convened the morning brief.

Once Eddie had reported back on the business in Wakefield it was down to me to run down the new jobs and enquiries that I had fielded the day before. I had booked appointments with a couple of prospective clients for that afternoon and arranged a security consult for after the weekend. I'd do that myself, but Eddie would come along to learn the ropes. He was almost ready to go solo in that area, but I wasn't going to cut him loose until he had his licence.

That took care of all the billable business and I was content to leave it that, except that both Clegg and Eddie were anxious to know how my meeting with Ellis Thatcher had gone. I briefed them on that and filled them in on the latest details that Raphael had passed on about Wood's murder, though I kept his name out of it. I was pretty sure he didn't want the existence of his source at Snow Hill to be common knowledge.

I finished off by explaining my tentative reasoning concerning the possible identity of Wood's killer. They both listened attentively, with no secret sidelong glances or eye rolling. That in itself was a surprise to me. I was fully aware how 'out there' it all sounded and I fully expected Clegg's natural pragmatic caution to shoot holes in it. Even more surprisingly, however, it was Eddie who expressed scepticism.

"Twenty-five years panting after the same lass?" he said incredulously, which to be fair is pretty much the reaction you would expect from someone whose own attention span in that area was closer to twenty-five minutes.

"Actually, the idea of an unknown stalker is certainly worth considering." Clegg said before I could respond. "Especially in light of that deeply unsettling journal that we have all read. Whilst it's obvious that the perspective has been deliberately managed to make it appear that Hal was its author, the general content may well be a true record of individual obsession. It is certainly disturbing enough."

"Exactly what I thought." I said.

"I think there's also a problem with apportioning blame to Callum Jensen. I think we can now assume that Hal was hired under false pretences in the belief that in his search for Mrs Jensen he might uncover the identity of the man behind the Hellfire Club. "

"I'm sure of it." I said.

"A not unfamiliar scenario, I'm sure we can agree." Clegg went on smoothly, though it was hard to miss the mild rebuke behind his word. "On reflection, what bothers me however is that if Callum Jensen had murder on his mind would he be so obvious about hiring a private investigator to be his cat's paw? Even if no one else were to witness your meeting it still entailed making himself known to the person he hired. The person, who we assume he intended all along to frame for the murder he himself planned to commit! If you think about it, by exposing himself to you in this way then Jensen would simply be making a case for your defence by, in effect, offering himself as an alternative suspect. To then disappear immediately after killing your target only serves to strengthen the theoretical case against him, wouldn't you say?"

"My head hurts." Eddie said cautiously.

"On the other hand, if you are not the real Callum Jensen but merely someone posing as him then there is no actual threat to yourself. Jensen may still be offered as a possible other suspect but the killer himself is in no danger."

"Yeah, I see that." Eddie said. "But doesn't that still get in the way of his plan to hang Wood's murder on H?"

"No, because nobody but me ever met the fake Jensen and even though the barman at the Tanglewood saw us together he knew the guy by another name." I explained for Eddie's benefit. "For all anybody knows it might just be some look alike I dragged along to support my story that I was working for Jensen when really I was hunting down Glenn Wood. It's a thought that's already occurred to Swanson."

"And as a theory it would gain even more traction once the police track down the real Jensen and he denies, quite truthfully, that he's never even met you, let alone hired you." Clegg finished.

"Did I mention my head hurts?" Eddie said.

"You have to admit that it all has a certain Byzantine elegance to it." Clegg said. "As the schemes of psychopathic, Satanic stalkers go, of course."

"Nobody's saying he isn't smart."

"Okay, stalking, I get." Eddie mused. "I mean, I don't 'get it' get it but I know it's a thing. But, I mean, twenty-five years?"

"It isn't unheard of Edward." Clegg volunteered, pre-empting me. "In 1322 Petrarch saw a beautiful young woman called Laura in church and it awoke in him a passion that burned in him until her death twenty-one years later. They never so much as kissed and it's by no means certain that they ever even spoke to each other."

Eddie was not convinced.

"Well, we've all had moments like that, I s'pose but did it turn whatsisname into a bunny boiler?"

"In a fashion." Clegg smiled. "Yes, you could say he stalked her. Over the years Petrarch wrote over three hundred sonnets in praise of her. She would probably have had grounds for a restraining order today."

"One way of exercising his right hand, I s'pose." Eddie chortled. "But, that's a good point, isn't it Cleggy? If somebody is that obsessed could they really go for so many years without being sussed? Stalkers don't usually go in for the 'worshipping from afar' approach, do they? They intrude in people's lives. They get noticed because they want to be."

"That's generally true, I think." Clegg agreed. "You would expect to discover that the Jensen's had some history over the intervening years with this character if he is indeed the same person who harassed her at university."

"They might have for all we know. I pointed out. "They're the only people who could tell us one way or the other if there's a persistent history of harassment. In any case, it doesn't necessarily follow. The Jensens lived in America for a long time, that could have forced the stalker to temper his obsession because he was unable able to follow or keep track of them there. Other factors might also have got in the way of his passion over the years. He might have suffered from some long-term illness, been in prison or living abroad himself because of his work. He might even have got married."

Any or all those things were plausible obstacles that might have absorbed his energies in the past. but had now been removed, allowing him to pick up the threads of his compulsion to pursue the golden-haired ghost that had haunted him since his youth.

"We just don't know." I said. "And maybe I'm wrong. Maybe Killdevil is someone entirely unknown. One of Jennifer's recent one-night stands who took it to mean more than it did. Or perhaps one of the Hellfire Club who developed too great an affinity for the mystery blonde Dorian brought into the circle. If that's the case we, I, don't have the resources or access to information to pursue those options. Hopefully, Swanson and his team do and will. In the meantime, this is the only lead I've got and there are enough similarities between what I know about Killdevil and what I know about Marius Drommel to make me believe it's worth following."

"Indeed." Clegg said. "And this, I think, may strengthen that belief."

While we had been speaking I had noticed that his fingers had been busy on his keyboard. He turned the monitor towards us so that Eddie and I could see the results. Filling the screen was the image of an inverted pentacle, inscribed within a circle and set against a black background. Superimposed upon the pentacle was a skeletal goat's head with a smaller pentacle set in its forehead, whilst other esoteric symbols filled the spaces between the points of the larger figure.

"That's – what **is** that, exactly?" Eddie queried.

"That is the Goat of Mendes." Clegg explained. "Or rather, one particular symbolic interpretation of it. From Hal's description this, or something very like it, could be the tattoo that Drommel has on his back."

"Bloody hell! Why didn't he just have 'Loony' tattooed on his forehead? It would have been cheaper and a lot less painful."

"A fine jest, Edward." Clegg acknowledged. "Though it's a fact that there has been extensive research into the psychological aspects of tattoos and tattooing that suggest there is indeed a positive correlation between body art and personality disorders. "

Not for the first time I found myself quietly impressed by the eclectic depth of Clegg's knowledge. I'd have him in my quiz team any day of the week.

"Leaving that aside, we are still talking about a very potent occult symbol and one which is firmly associated, at least in the popular imagination, with the dark magic of the so-called Left-Hand Path. In a slightly different form it has even been adopted as the official emblem of the Church of Satan and the image of the Devil tarot card that you found in Wood's home is also clearly influenced by the Goat of Mendes. I would say that choosing to have this symbol etched into your very flesh speaks, at the very least, to a serious intellectual obeisance or commitment to the familiar archetype."

Eddie looked at me.

"Idiot's Guide version, please."

"They think the Devil's cool." I said.

"It may be something rather more than that in the case of your Drommel chappie." Clegg added sombrely. "Bearing in mind your recent encounters with Messrs Sifer and Black I've been indulging in a little onomastic research as we've been speaking."

I glanced at Eddie.

"I'll look it up later." he said.

"Forgive me, Edward. Onomastics is the field of research concerned with the study of names. They can speak to us of many things: identity, history, psychology, a sense of belonging or an expression of individuality or isolation. A badge of honour that people have killed for. *Good name in man or woman...is the immediate jewel of their souls,* although perhaps to some a bad name might be similarly cherished."

"Drommel...?"

Clegg nodded. "It is Dutch in origin. It means Devil."

33.

If Clegg was sympathetic towards the case I made against Drommel he proved less supportiveof my decision not to share it with Swanson for the time being. It was, after all, just a theory and Swanson had a long history of not listening to my conjectures, even though they had proved correct on more than one occasion. It was also a fact that my suspicions rested heavily on two pieces of evidence that, for different reasons, I was not particularly keen on disclosing to the police.

The first of these was the Killdevil journal, which was very much a double-edged sword since it blatantly seemed to identify me as the stalker. The killer's habit of leaving tarot trumps as his calling card was also a prop in my argument, suggesting as it did that, like Drommel, he had a fascination with the occult and things Satanic. However, as the police had not released details of this foible to the public, inevitable questions would be asked about how I had come by that detail. That would be difficult to explain without letting on that I somehow had access to a source close to the investigation. This would certainly not go down well with Swanson and his team and might eventually prejudice Raphael's relationship with his unknown informant.

So, for the moment I'd decided keep the police out of it until, at least, I had gathered more information about Drommel. To that end the three of us spent the rest of the afternoon trying to flesh out a picture of Marius Drommel, with only limited success. We had managed to track down the few documented individuals who shared his unusual surname but none of them had a relative called Marius or knew anybody with that name. Not that they would admit to, at least.

The same was true of the people from the university drama club that we managed to track down. Most of them certainly remembered Drommel for his outlandish persona and his impressive stage presence but nobody recalled him as a friend or had ever been in contact with him since his departure from campus. He was remembered by various terms: loner, freak, gothhead, creep and a few even less complimentary. One or two people did recall that he had been close to Callum Jensen, at least for a while, and the one new piece of information I learned was that they had supposedly bonded over their mutual passion for computer gaming. A former course mate remembered that they had often talked about making a career in the games software industry and even boasted that they were working together on a game that would make their respective fortunes. It had been more than just a boast for Jensen, of course, and it was possible that after leaving university Drommel had also achieved success in that area. Though if that were the case, he had somehow done so without making any kind of splash on the internet. Not under his given name, at any rate.

In the end the only hint of a breakthrough came from an aside by a woman called Penny Sparks, who was now a lecturer in linguistics at York St Johns. Most people when asked where Drommel came from simply had no idea – an indicator perhaps of his own stand-offishness and the unease he seemed to rouse in others. Dr Sparks herself admitted that she had barely known Drommel. However, she claimed to have recognised his accent as typical of the Dark Peak area, a dialect she was familiar with from childhood summer holidays with an aunt in Hathersage.

It was little enough to go on, but it helped to narrow down a search on *Ancestry*, which revealed that a male child christened Marius Abel Drommel had been registered in Matlock on the 14th June 1972. The parents were Geert and Sarah Abra Drommel, nee Ruane, who were residents of the village of Felldyke, Derbyshire at the time. A deeper search also revealed that Geert had died in August 1992. There was no record of Sarah ever re-marrying and the absence of a death certificate suggested she was still alive. Both

Drommels were listed on the electoral roll up until 1992,
Marius would have been eligible to vote from 1989 onwards
but his name did not appear on the Felldyke roll. He might
have registered in Durham while he was at university, though
since his name did not appear anywhere else he might have
chosen not to be included in the open register – or simply not
bothered to register at all. After Geert's death Sarah's name
also dropped off the electoral roll for Felldyke, which could
mean she too had opted out of the open roll or else she had
moved and not re-registered.

In short, the family connection to Felldyke was the only
real lead I had to follow and by mid-morning the next day I
was driving towards that remote destination. It lay at the end
of a network of increasingly narrow roads, twisting through
the rugged moors and sphagnum bogs that filled the space
between dark millstone summits. Under a lowering sky that
threatened a heavy downpour, it was easy to understand how
the High Peaks gained their grimmer alternative name and
why so many aircraft had come down over the years on these
remote, brooding hills.

In the High Peak you couldn't get much higher than
Felldyke, though the actual title of highest village was
accorded to Flash, just across the border in Staffordshire.
Felldyke was north of Buxton, tucked away beyond Dove
Holes, where the gritstone of the Dark Peak morphed into the
softer limestone of the White Peak. According to what little
information I had been able to eke out it was, like many
villages in the Peak, founded on a remote hillside and often
obscurely swathed in mist and low cloud. It had a population
of just under four hundred and was distinguished by an
Anglo-Saxon church dating back to the 9th century, and by its
single pub *The Cavendish Arms.*

I drove past the latter on my way to *Garth Palen,* which
according to Google Earth was off Blamire Road at the
northern extremity of the village. It was a dormer bungalow
that looked suspiciously modern in Street View, an
impression confirmed when I had negotiated the roughly
tarmacked approach road that ran between a small builder's
yard and a field full of lethargic looking sheep The house

was an L-shaped, gritstone, chalet bungalow with solar panels on the roof, lots of light grabbing windows and a wide glass frontage looking into an atrium–style hallway. Even as I rang the doorbell I was thinking that I wasn't going to find any lingering trace of Drommel in this place. The suspicion was soon verified by the heavily pregnant, ash blonde who eventually answered the door.

I spun her a line about being a family history enthusiast trying to track down a distant branch of my tribe, which turned her expression of mild suspicion into one of slightly bemused sympathy but otherwise produced no useful result. As I suspected the house was relatively new, built within the last ten years or so, and the family living there had only been in residence for a couple of those, having shipped in from Wolverhampton to be nearer the husband's new job at the wildlife park in Chapel-en-le-Frith. She recalled that the people who lived there previously had sold up to retire to the isle of Lewis. They were called McAllister, she thought. She knew nobody called Drommel in the village or of any past connection to whatever property had previously occupied *Garth Palen's* space.

I thanked her and wished her good luck with the imminent new arrival. She wished me well in my search and that was that. As I returned to the car a few heavy drops of rain fell from the dark clouds bunched overhead and thunder rumbled in the hills. The Felldyke lead had not got off to a very auspicious start but I wasn't too downhearted. When the going gets tough, the tough go to the pub.

The Cavendish was a medium-sized, whitewashed pub overlooking the village green at the front and a large car park at the rear backing onto a small, untenanted field hemmed by dry stone walls. Not that they were going to be dry for very much longer. The fat single drops of rain became a sibilant downpour as I parked up.

Although Felldyke was both isolated and sparsely populated the pub seemed to be doing a fair trade as there were several other cars in the car park already. I guessed that in season there would be many more as tourists flocked to this starkly beautiful region of the Peaks.

I fished my weatherproof jacket off the backseat and slipped it on before stepping out of the car and making rapid strides to the pub's side entrance. I found myself in a narrow corridor running between the Gents and Ladies toilets. A small flight of steps at the far end accessed a door marked Restaurant, Lounge and Family Area. I pushed open the door, found myself in a single large room on two levels. The lower of these was obviously the restaurant part, though there were people eating on the top level too. This extended to my left, where an arched doorway lead through to another area, currently unpopulated and much more basic in décor and furnishings. Probably where the locals who missed the old spittoon hung out.

I approached the curved bar and caught the eye of the youth of twenty summers and twice as many acne scars who was busy putting dirty glasses into the washer. He wore a black roll neck sweater, black trousers and a look of practiced bonhomie that seemed almost genuine. The shiny name badge he sported said "Luke".

"Afternoon, sir. Wet one, isn't it? Just a drink – or will you be eating?"

It hadn't been on my agenda, but the smell of food had stirred up my appetite. I parked myself at the bar and asked for a bottle of Becks Blue and a menu. By the time he'd served my drink I had settled on the beef and ale pie.

"Good choice." the barman approved as he punched my choice into the till.

"It was a close thing between that and the ostrich steak with gooseberry coulis." I said.

"A perennial favourite." he said with a grin.

The pie was very good and so was the sticky toffee pudding that I couldn't resist chucking on top of it. I finished my meal with a coffee bought to me by a waitress called Sally, who smiled at me and asked if there was anything else I needed. I enquired if she knew anyone amongst the pub's regulars who might help me find somebody who had once lived in the village. The family history line worked well again, and she happily told me that she was from the village herself and would be pleased to help if she could. We very quickly established that she couldn't but without much further thought she came up with the name of someone who might be able to.

"'Brose Mozley!" she declared. "He's the one. He must be, like, really ancient. He saw the Beatles and everything. Alive!"

I didn't bother telling her that two of them still were. I guessed 'Old Brose' probably wasn't nearly as ancient as she thought he was but if he'd been around in the Sixties there was a good chance he'd have known the Drommels, or at least known of them.

"I don't suppose he's here now, is he?"

She shook her head, then glanced at her watch.

"Too early. He comes in most days and sits through in the public bar for a bite to eat around five o'clock then sits on his own reading the paper or some book until his cronies start to roll in. Nice old chap, he is – and he loves to tell a yarn!"

That sounded even more hopeful. I thanked her, and she cleared off my table and was striding off towards the bar when a thought struck me.

"Excuse me again but what does Brose drink?

She stopped and turned to answer in a throaty growl that I supposed must be her Brose Mosley voice.

"Pint o' the black stuff and a Jameson's, me duck."

"Not a cheap date then." I mused.

She chuckled fetchingly and went on her way.

I checked the time and noted that it was the best part of three hours before I could expect to see Brose. A glance out of the window told me it was still raining heavily. Despite all the practice I got I didn't much care for driving in wet conditions, especially on unfamiliar minor roads, or I might have considered a run into Buxton, where I knew there was an excellent second-hand bookshop. That narrowed my options to sitting in the car park for three hours or staying where I was. The non-alcoholic beer was not to my taste, but I thought I could safely risk a proper drink if I then stuck to coffee for the rest of the afternoon. Before going to the bar, I made a quick detour to the car to collect the Shakespeare book. On my return I ordered a pint of Amstel and took my time working my way through the lager and my book in that pleasant country bar.

In the event it was closer to half past five before the man I was waiting for turned up. By then the original bar staff had gone off shift to be replaced by an older man and a petite blonde girl. I had moved through to the public bar some time earlier and was sitting at the bar nursing a cup of coffee when a grizzled figure bundled in, cursing the rain that dripped from the brim of his grey newsboy cap and the hem of his long, waxed jacket. He stomped over to the bar, still muttering to himself and fumbling in his pocket for a well-worn wallet. The blonde greeted him with a smile that seemed genuine enough to suggest that perhaps he wasn't as curmudgeonly as first impressions suggested.

"Usual me duck?", she enquired chirpily.

"Aye, that'd be grand, Nettie. It's siling it down out theer." he said, shaking off his cap.

"You surprise me." the barmaid deadpanned, and he chuckled throatily.

Nettie smiled and busied herself drawing a pint of Guinness. When she placed it on the bar and turned towards the optics to measure out a shot of Jameson's, I spoke up.

"Mr Mozley is it?"

He turned his head to look at me. It was difficult to assess his age, though it was probably well north of sixty, I guessed. He had a strong face; a well-used but carefully folded map of his life from which a pair of sharp blue eyes regarded me warily.

"That would be me. Who's askin'?"

"Somebody who'd like to buy you a drink and pick your brains about bygone Felldyke." I said.

He studied me thoughtfully, rubbing one hand across his faintly stubbled chin.

"Not a journalist – you've not got the sly look. I'd've said 'copper' but tha' feet aren't big enough."

"I think they've reduced the entry criteria." I smiled. "But you're right, I'm not police, though I was once." I added, sensing that it would serve me best to be as honest as possible with this old man, whose age did not seem to have dimmed his eye or his intelligence.

"Well, nobody's perfect." he concluded. "I'll take a drink with you, though I don't know as there's much brain left to pick! I'll give you till my dinner comes."

He turned to the barmaid, who had been listening with an amused smile.

"I'll have the cod and chips with mushy peas." he said. "This young chap'll be payin'"

With that he picked up his drinks and wandered over to a table near the big, open fireplace, where a log fire blazed cheerily.

"Man drives a hard bargain." I said, handing the barmaid a twenty-pound note.

"He must've taken a shine to you." she smiled "He didn't order pudding."

I collected my change and followed Brose Mozley to his cosy fireside spot. He had shed his cap and waxed jacket, which he had been wearing over a dark brown Mechanic's sweater and a red and black plaid shirt. As I joined him he was just swallowing the first generous mouthful of his pint, which left the glass half empty.

"Harry Webster." I said, offering my hand as I sat down across from him. He had a firm, dry handshake, which came with a small nod of acknowledgement/

"Not from here 'bouts, are tha? A Yorkie by the sound of it."

"I am." I agreed. "But I come in peace."

He made a noise, part-laugh, part-snort, and reached for his pint again.

"Well, ge'rron wi'it then. Am fair clammed and I 'ate talkin' when am eatin'."

I took the hint and quickly explained. I told him the truth, mostly, confessing that I was a private detective trying to trace a family that had once lived in the village.

"Name of Drommel? Does that strike a chord, Mr Mozley?"

He considered the question for only a few seconds before nodding an affirmative.

346

"I mind 'em." he admitted cautiously. "Never knew 'em well. They weren't what you'd call the sociable kind. Been gone from 'Dyke a long while, I reckon. Twenty years or more. Missus, anyway. T'owd feller were dead by then. They had a son as went doolally, I recollect. Now, what were their names…?"

"Geert and Sarah." I prompted. "And their son was called Marius."

"Aye, aye – that's them. He were a little swine when he were a kid – the lad. Allus in bother round the village. Nasty, sneaky, little shit. Though maybe it weren't surprising. Summat off about the whole family. God-botherers, but not your common or garden kind. Church of Three Weeks Last Tuesday or some such nonsense! You'd see her around the village from time to time shovin' their pamphlets through folks's letterboxes. Pretty, she were, but thin as a wisp, worn to the bone. He were a beast, the father, did labourin' work for Caskey – him as 'ad the farm topside."

I nodded politely, as if Caskey from Topside Farm was a name on everybody's lips.

"'Course, tha'll not know him." Busted. Bose ploughed on. "Well, he's gone now too. No great loss. Miserable as sin and twice as ugly, I mind once -"

"I'd love to hear more about him." I interrupted hastily. "But it's really the Drommel's I'm interested in. Particularly the son? You said he had mental problems?"

"Eh? Oh aye, that's right. Well, he were always a bit strange, I suppose. Clever, mind you. Never got caught doing owt he shouldn't have been doing, though his name was usually the first one that got mentioned when owt went off. I heard it said more than once that it didn't pay to get the wrong side of young Drommel."

"That sounds ominous." I said. "What kind of thing are we talking about?"

"You name it: windows gettin' smashed, pets goin' missin', a bit of vandalism at the church, an allotment being trashed here, a bus shelter goin' up in smoke there. Anything that smacked of vindictiveness, you might say. He had that sort of reputation, though as I say, nobody ever pinned

anything on him for definite. Maybe it was just talk. 'Dyke's
a small place. Ingrown some might say. Anybody a bit
different is fair game for small minds."

He paused for breath and another pull at his rapidly
diminishing pint. Calm and unhurried in his movements and
his speech, he seemed as rugged and ancient as the Dark
Peak itself, stories in his bones.

"I understand he was very intelligent, though." I said.
"Didn't he go to university?"

"Oh, he was smart, all right! Smart enough to get out of this
place, at least, though not smart enough to stay away."

"Did he come back to the village then? I know that he
dropped out of university before he took his degree."

"Aye, that would be because of what happened to his
father. That was a bad do, right enough."

"What happened?"

"He topped hi 'self. They found him hangin' from a tree up
in Cleyton Woods. Summer of 91 – no – 92, it'd be!"

"That must've been hard on Marius." I said. "Was he close
to his father?"

"Close to his fists, maybe." Brose said distastefully. "Bit
free with them altogether was what they said about Geert.
The lad and his mam both had the bruises to prove it. Now,
they were close, and I don't reckon either of them was too
cut up about t'owd feller. She certainly didn't hang around
long after he hung himself. By Christmas she'd sold up and
left – and the boy was in Gatewood by then."

"He was sectioned? Why? What happened?"

"Don't know any details, son, though there was some
conjecture, as you'd expect. Rumour was he suffered a
breakdown because of what happened to his dad. Always
doubted that, m'self. Whatever sent him over the edge, I'd be
surprised if it was grief."

I nodded, assimilating everything that Brose had imparted.
None of it had in any way diminished my suspicion that
Marius Drommel was Killdevil.

"Do you know anything of what happened to them after
they left the village?"

He shook his head.

"Not a clue. I don't think anybody really cared to be honest. When you live here it seems like everybody in the village wants to know your business – but once you're gone that's it for most folk. You might as well have moved to the moon. Until you come asking I bet I haven't given that family a moment's thought – oh – since the old house went up in smoke."

"It burnt down?"

"Aye, it did that! Oh, must've been ten years or more since. Lit the village up proper, it did. Arson, they reckoned, though they never pinned it on anybody. I expect you can guess who the favourite suspect were though?"

"Marius?"

"Correct card." he chuckled. "The village bogey man."

"Why would he burn down his old house?"

"Nay, don't ask me. Just tellin' you what was whispered. Probably nothing to do with him – unless you put stock in all that curse nonsense." he added with an impressively sanguine expression.

"Who doesn't love a good curse story?" I said. "Tell me more."

"Nay, I've no patience for it and I see my dinner's on the way I'd like to eat it in peace if that's all right with you, young man?"

The barmaid was coming towards us bearing a steaming tray of food that made me feel hungry all over again. I thought about pressing Brose to overcome his scepticism but somehow, I thought I would just be wasting my breath. It probably wasn't relevant anyway, I told myself, so I thanked the old man for his time and prepared to leave him to his meal. I offered him my hand and he shook it firmly, fixing me with those clear grey eyes.

"Have you got a pen and a bit o' paper?" he asked.

I nodded, reaching into my jacket and handing him my pen and notebook. He opened the latter to a clean page and scribbled something down. The barmaid set down his food. He thanked her politely and ordered another pint and another whiskey. He drained the last few drops of Guinness from his current glass, then downed the Jameson's in one quick gulp.

I looked at the notebook, He had written a telephone number and a name: Arliss Gale.

"Who's this?" I asked, gesturing to him with the open notebook.

"Just ring her." he said. "Ask her."

"About what?"

"Ask her about the Remnant of Goodman's Acre. She'll tell thee."

34.

It was now nearly seven o'clock and prematurely dark. The
rain was still coming down remorselessly and showing no
inclination to stop. It was a night to be curled up by a fireside
somewhere with a good book – or a good woman – and my
strongest impulse was to head back to the city to pursue that
notion.

I scurried to the car, almost blown off my feet by a sudden
blast of wind hurtling off the High Peaks and driving the rain
almost horizontally across my path. I climbed behind the
wheel but made no move to drive off. I sat for a while
reviewing what I'd learned from Brose Mosley, who had
certainly provided enough background to firm up my
suspicions of Marius Drommel. However, none of what
Brose had told me took me any closer to learning where, or
who, he was these days.

The trail went cold in 1992 when Drommel and his mother
both disappeared from Felldyke. Marius's immediate
destination had been Gatewood Hospital, which at the time
had been one of the leading psychiatric units in the North.
Somewhere there would be a record of his stay there, the
reasons for it and maybe even some indication of what
became of him next. Gatewood had been closed at the turn of
the century. Its patient files would be archived and
inaccessible without a court order.

The fate of Drommel's mother was even more uncertain,
which left me in an investigative cul-de-sac. I took out my
notebook and opened it to the page where Brose had written
Arliss Gale's details. What was he'd said? The Remnant of
Goodman's Acre? What, if anything, did that have to do with
Drommel? I wondered. There was only one way to find out. I
reached for my phone to call Arliss Gale. To avoid any

interruptions, I'd turned it off while I spoke to Brose Mozley. When it came back to life I saw at once that there was a missed call from Molly. A warm rush of pleasure at the thought of hearing her voice drove everything else momentarily from my mind.

"Hey, you!" she said lightly. "What's up detective?"

"The Bronx, I believe, whilst the Battery is apparently down. And the people ride in a hole in the ground, so I'm told."

"You're mad, has anybody ever told you?" she laughed. "Don't tell me you're in New York!"

"A sodden pub car park in Derbyshire, actually."

"Ah, the exotic life of the gumshoe!"

"More like a gumboot in this weather." I said. "Are you okay? Is there a problem?"

"No, everything's fine. Just wanted to year your voice. Is that soppy, or what?"

"Soppy's okay between friends – and my voice is pretty great."

"Ha! I bet you even said that with a straight face!"

"My deadpan delivery is also awesome." I said. "Your voice is pretty cool too. See? I can do 'soppy'"

"Being soppy together would be nice." she said huskily.

"That it would." I agreed. "I'm just a little out of your way at the moment."

"That sucks but it's okay – good things are worth waiting for. When will you get back?"

"I have to see someone. I'm not sure how long it will take or even if it's worth it. Say the word and I'll forget about it and come back now."

"I want to – I really do. This person you're supposed to see – is it to do with Jen?"

"No – yes – maybe."

"It wasn't a multiple-choice question, Harry." she laughed.

"Sorry. Short answer: it may be connected."

"Then you must stay and see it through. Come round tomorrow?"

"*I'll fly to thee not charioted by Bacchus and his pards but on the viewless wings of poesy.*" I said.

"Well, just be careful of drones and low flying birds." she laughed. Oh bugger…"

"What?"

"Somebody at the door. Got to go. Wish it was you. Get those poetical wings flapping, Harry."

Then she was gone, though the smile on my face lingered even as I dialled the number that Brose Mosley had given me. The voice that answered was female, polite and vaguely accented. A brief enquiry confirmed that it belonged to Arliss Gale. I explained who I was and how I'd obtained her number. She responded warmly to Brose's name.

"The redoubtable Ambrose! How is the old curmudgeon?"

I assured her that he was still redoubtably curmudgeonly then hesitantly broached the reason for my call.

"This may not mean anything to you – and apologies if Brose was just pulling my leg – but he suggested that you might be able to give me some information about-" I consulted my notebook hastily. "– the Remnant of Goodman's Acre? Would that be right?"

"Oh yes, Mr Webster! That's a subject I know quite a lot about. Tell me, are you still in the area?"

I confirmed that I was.

"My husband and I were about to eat dinner and it's perhaps too long a tale to be told over the phone. Perhaps you'd like to pop round a little later? Say about half past eight? I'll be happy to satisfy your curiosity on that matter. From where it stems, might I ask?"

"I'm a private investigator looking for a missing person." I said. "Name of Drommel?"

"The devil you say!" she said with a knowing laugh.

"You're familiar with the name?"

"I am indeed – as Ambrose knows very well. Can I expect you?"

I agreed that I could and after reeling off details of her address she hung up. I punched the post code into my GPS, which confirmed that she lived about ten miles away, just outside Buxton. Despite lingering thoughts of Molly, my brief conversation with Arliss Gale had energised me again. Even with the narrow roads and driving rain I could be there in less than half an hour, which would still leave an hour to kill. I briefly debated going back into the pub, but more coffee or soft drinks didn't appeal. Instead I stayed in the car and rummaged in the glove compartment for my tablet to do a little background research on Arliss Gale.

She was on Facebook and Linkedin and between the two sites I soon built up a good picture of the woman I was going to see. **Dr** Arliss Gale was a graduate of Lady Hilda's College, Oxford and the University of Oregon, where she had picked up a PhD in Cultural Anthropology and her husband Mark, who was an architect. She had taught for several years at the University of Aberdeen, the only British University that offered a post-graduate course in Ethnology and Folklore. During that time, she had written several books that had apparently been successful enough that she had been able to take early retirement in 2010, moving back to her native Derbyshire in 2012. Her current social media profiles described her as a full-time writer, though she also taught an online course in Folklore Studies for the Midland Open College Network and occasional evening classes for the WEA. I guessed it was on one of these that she had got to know Ambrose Mozley. He was pure gold to anyone interested in the history and people of liminal communities like Felldyke.

I did a quick search of Amazon and found a list of the books Dr Gale had written, several of which focused on aspects of Derbyshire life and folklore. Amongst the titles were *T'Owd Lad of the Peaks, Mystery Lights of the Pennines, Phantom Eagles: the Ghost Planes of Bleaklow* and *Haunted Waters: Meetings with Mermaids and Water Spirits in the Dark Peak.* Maybe it was just the atrocious weather and the sense of the brooding hills bulking in the darkness beyond the small oasis of the pub, but I felt a distinct frisson as I studied the list and decided I'd done enough research for the moment.

Dr Gale lived in a detached house of weathered stone about three miles outside Buxton It stood back from the main road and probably afforded a stunning view of the Goyt Valley when it wasn't pitch black and coming down stair rods. A drive-thru portico stood at the top of the short driveway, leading into a broad forecourt. I pulled up in front of a double garage that was attached to the main house and stepped quickly out of the rain through a Doric archway onto the covered porch. I rang the doorbell that glowed in the centre of the solid oak front door and it was opened a few seconds later by a genial-looking man in a maroon sweater and grey chinos. He was, I estimated, somewhere in his fifties, with longish silver-grey hair and a salt and pepper beard. He offered me his hand and introduced himself as Dr Gale's husband, Isaac.

Isaac led me through to what I presumed was his wife's study, a cosy room with a living flame gas fire blazing in an antique fireplace surround. There were built in shelves on three sides of the room, packed floor to ceiling with books, magazines, DVDs, CDs and even some VHS videos. A walnut desk was pushed up against the fourth wall. On it sat a top of the range PC and a printer scanner.

The woman I had come to see sat at the desk engrossed in typing something up from a wad of written notes spread across its surface. She stood to greet me with a friendly smile; a trim, athletic-looking woman with brown hair cut in a pixie style that showed off large, black enamelled earrings shaped like crescent moons. She looked a few years younger than her husband, with pleasant, open features untroubled by make-up. She wore a light green merino sweater over a plain white blouse and blue jeans so faded they were almost white. As she shook my hand I caught the scent of her perfume, something light and floral, like rain on fresh cut flowers.

Isaac departed with a quick smile for his wife and a benevolent nod in my direction.

"I hope I'm not interrupting anything important?" I said, nodding towards the computer.

"Please, don't apologise. I'm afraid I'm the kind of writer who relishes almost any excuse not to write. Now, before we settle down. Coffee?"

"That would be appreciated." I said, feeling a hint of tiredness working its way into my bones.

When she'd had gone I wandered around the room, checking out the bookshelves. As I would have expected the collection showed a preponderance of books and other material on folklore, myths and legends, both popular and scholarly. Copies of her own books were prominent amongst them. There were also titles covering ethnology, social anthropology, a surprisingly large section of what seemed to be books about UFOs and a big section containing titles dealing with the history, geography and social customs of Derbyshire and the Peaks. One whole bay held bound copies of Folklore Magazine, Fortean Times and copies of less well-known publications in neatly labelled magazine boxes,

The wall space between the shelves was occupied by framed prints and photographs but, before I had chance to inspect them, Dr Gale returned. She was carrying a tray ladened with a cafetiere and the necessary accoutrements, including a plate of what looked like homemade chocolate chip cookies. That reminded me that lunch had been a long time ago. When she had served us both and I had gladly accepted the invitation to snaffle a cookie, I retreated to a comfortable looking Chesterfield.

Dr Gale settled herself once more in her office chair, swinging it round to face me. We chatted briefly about Brose Mozley who, as I had surmised, she had met during a short course on the Lore and Legends of Derbyshire Miners that she had run for the WEA. Brose himself was a former miner and she remembered him for his keen intelligence and a tongue-in-cheek sense of humour that had no doubt been finely honed by his years down the pit.

"I'm surprised that he showed any interest in that particular topic." I said. "He seems to have a healthy scepticism about such things."

"Indeed, Ambrose is very much a rationalist – as am I – but he has a keen interest in what makes people behave the way they do. On that level the old stories can tell us all sorts of things about the sociological and cultural pressures that act on closed-in or isolated communities. Not to mention giving a shrewd idea of the psychological framework that draws from the endless well of superstition, half-remembered history and mischievous fancy.

"Most of the stories I record and analyse have seeped into these hills and dales from one or other of these source springs, I believe. In a sense they're an outgrowth of the personality of the community from which they develop and are perpetuated, something that binds them tightly to each other, preserves the sense of collective identity and acts as a wall against outsiders. The lore of the land defines it and its people, and we will be the poorer if the old tales ever disappear completely. Something that is in danger of happening, I fear. As the world shrinks it's a fact that the ties that bind communities to each other and their domain are growing weaker. It will be a sad day indeed when all the old tales cease to haunt these hills."

She spoke with a passion for her subject that was both sincere and somehow sexy. It was a passion, which I suspected, extended to those like Brose who were, in a sense, the guardians of the ancient stories and country lore that were grist to her mill. I realised that what she had said went some way to explaining why Brose had not wanted to speak to me about the supposed 'curse' he had fleetingly referred to. Perhaps it was less a dismissal of such superstition than a reluctance to share something with an outsider that was an intrinsic part of the genius loci.

Then again, perhaps after all he had just been hungry and wanted to eat his dinner in peace.

"Sorry." Dr Gale said. "I tend to be rather voluble about my passion, don't I?"

"No need to apologise." I assured her. "I admire anybody with a genuine passion for what they do."

Except for serial killers, rapists, paedophiles, Arsenal fans, etc. Maybe I also envied people like Arliss Gale to some extent. A niggling thought that I nudged aside swiftly.

"Still, you really came her to learn about the Remnant, didn't you?"

I nodded in agreement and, rising decisively from her chair, she walked across the room and removed one of the framed prints that hung on the walls. She passed it to me with a smile but made no comment as she returned to her desk.

The print seemed to be a copy of a woodcut. The ink was faded and the paper showing signs of foxing and other blemishes of ageing. None of this detracted from the impact of the image I was looking at, in which a man dressed like the stereotypical passenger on the Mayflower was shaking hands with a naked figure sporting curved horns, a long, barbed tail and a mocking Satanic grin. Over the pair of them loomed the top half of a dark, hooded figure wielding a scythe in one hand and an almost emptied hourglass in the other.

Across the top of the woodcut in heavy, black type was the legend:

The True Tragical History of the Remnants of Goodman's Acre

In smaller print, across the bottom, were the words:

Printed by Robert Cartwright, 1673

"A play?" I hazarded.

"Possibly – but more probably a pamphlet. Such cautionary tales were popular from late Elizabethan times until well into the 17th century. There's no way to be sure. That's just a photocopy. I came across the original a few years ago in a box of miscellaneous documents. It was amongst a collection deposited in Derby Local History Library by the family of some local luminary who passed away back in the 1980s. Nobody at the library could tell me anything about it but they did point me towards the old lady who donated the papers. She was able to put a little flesh on the bones of that rather lurid print you're holding in your hands."

"It was her late husband who unearthed it. He was a GP by profession, with a real passion for Derbyshire history and folklore– and a wide constituency of patients. The story is a fascinating one, though how much actual truth lies at its heart is not discernible. Still, I'll give you the gist of it as it was originally told me – with a few additional details I've eked from my excavations of the memories of folks like Brose Mozley."

Before she started she insisted on topping up my coffee and I helped myself unashamedly to another cookie. Settling back in my seat I took out my phone and started the voice recorder.

"Where to begin?" she said sitting back in her chair. "Well, you'll have heard of Eyam, I suppose?"

"The plague village? Deliberately isolated itself so the disease wouldn't spread?"

"That's right. It's a truly humbling and moving story and, of course, an absolute matter of historical fact! It's a tale that should never be forgotten. In all two hundred and sixty-five villagers died in the outbreak, which is twice the number of fatalities that London suffered in that year!"

"That's a staggering statistic." I acknowledged.

"Indeed, though most people aren't aware of it. What is also not widely known is that, purportedly, Eyam was not the only Derbyshire village to be visited by the plague in 1665. Which brings me to the fate of Goodman's Acre or, at least, it's supposed fate. The village itself no longer exists – and indeed there is little or no evidence that it ever did! Not that I've been able to discover, at any rate. That isn't conclusive, of course. There are upwards of 3,000 documented lost medieval villages in England alone. Goodman's Acre doesn't feature in any such list I've studied or appear on any map I've consulted – and believe me I've consulted quite a few! Nonetheless, traces of the village do apparently linger in the deep folk memory of the Derbyshire Dales. Perhaps they're simple garbled echoes of real events or the oral memory of some fantasy spun by some forgotten country skald.

"Either way they make for a thrilling tale that begins, like the tragedy of Eyam, with an outbreak of bubonic plague in the small, isolated community of Goodman's Acre, a pandemic perhaps even more lethal as that which struck Eyam. The version of events that I have managed to piece together suggests that the rate of fatalities was as high as seventy per cent! Almost every household in the village was stricken so the story goes, apart from six families who miraculously survived the outbreak without losing a single member. They themselves allegedly attributed this to their pious devotion to God – though there were muttering amongst many of their less fortunate neighbours that God had little to do with it. They spoke of a darker allegiance and pointed the finger in particular at a man called Henk Drommel, who had a certain reputation as a herb master or hedge witch. Regarded by some as a healer – and by others as a dangerous practitioner of the dark arts. As such he would probably have lived somewhat apart from the rest of the village, at its outer edge or even a little beyond, which, together with his healing skills, might well explain why he himself did not succumb to the ravages of the plague.

"There were, inevitably, some who sought a different explanation. Henk, it was said, spent many hours scouring the countryside and woodlands for his treatments, the demand for which naturally increased with the onset of the disease. According to the legend, on one such foray he encountered a mysterious stranger in the woods who claimed to be an emissary of the Dark Lad – that's the devil to you or me – and offered Henk a deal to keep he and his chosen friends safe from infection in return for pledging his soul to Lucifer.

"In at least one variation of the tale I've come across, Henk's wife was sickening with the pestilence at the time and so, in desperation, he accepted the stranger's offer. When he returned to Goodman's Acre, to his astonishment, Henk found his wife had fully recovered and the household remained free of any further infection for the duration of the outbreak. As did the homes of his closest friends and relatives. These are the six families that became known as The Remnants: Drommel, Hatman, Reynot, Woodbead, Nithercott and Jarsdel."

"What about Cuthbert, Dibble and Grubb?" I ventured.

She shook a finger at me playfully.

"Mock if you will." she said with a smile. "To modern urban sensibilities it naturally sounds faintly ludicrous, but we must never forget that such stories originate amongst communities that were both closed and isolated and at a time when a belief in all aspects of the supernatural was every bit as powerful an influence in their lives as their belief in God.

Four hundred years ago the Devil was viewed as a very real presence in people's lives."

"Some might say he still is." I said.

"Indeed." she said soberly, frowning at me thoughtfully for a moment before picking up the threads of her story. "But to return to Goodman's Acre. The plague inevitably ran its course and it was only after all the dead were buried that the rumours about Drommel and the other Remnants really gathered pace. These were fuelled by the grief of the many who had lost loved ones to the disease and the vengeful sermonising of the village priest – a man called Righteous Fretwell who had lost his wife and two daughters to the plague. I imagine him as a fiery orator in whom grief and intolerance mingled in equal parts and shrieked for retribution. In no time at all the six families found themselves ostracised and reviled by the rest of the village until, one by one, they took the hint and left Goodman's Acre rather than live with their neighbour's rancour.

"Henk was, it's generally believed, the last to leave – an event that sparked a mood of celebration in the stricken community that very soon turned to horror when the plague returned more virulently than ever, winnowing the villagers down to a mere handful of survivors. Amongst the last to succumb was Righteous Fretwell, who it is said, in his death throes, continued to rant about the Remnant and Henk's unholy pact. With his dying breath he supposedly drew down a curse on all their heads, asking God to damn their souls and wipe their names from existence. The fate of their soul's is unknown though – and this is the only incontestable fact I have been able to confirm – the names of all of the Remnants, except for the Drommels, have indeed fallen from the written record of extant surnames!"

"Drommels are pretty scarce too." I said. "And none of those I've contacted seem to be related to the Drommels who lived in Felldyke."

"It's never been a common name in this country, so I expect that they are – they just don't know it!"

She was probably right, I recognised, though it didn't help much.

"Well, thank you for agreeing to talk to me." I said. "Whatever its origins it's a great story. It would make an interesting book.

"Oh, it will, Harry! It will!" she smiled. "A sizeable chunk of my next project, at least. I'm calling it: The Dark Lad: Peakland encounters with the Devil."

"Catchy." I said. "Shame you can't work "Girl" into the title somehow. That seems to sell well these days."

"I never thought of that!" she laughed. "Damn."

"Seriously though. You say there's no such place as Goodman's Acre?"

"Not exactly. What I said was that I've never been able to locate it with any certainty or met anyone else who could. That said, the version of the legend I've just told is a synthesis of various oral accounts that I've collected within a very narrow geographical area, beyond which the tale is unknown as far as I've been able to determine. That may mean that it's simply a very localised piece of fiction, perhaps an imaginative mangling of the Eyam tragedy by some village yarn-spinner, or then again, perhaps there is truth at the heart of it based on the travails of a real village whose name has been altered either for dramatic effect or in deference to local sensibilities."

"You mean, the names have been changed to protect the innocent?"

"Or the guilty. I tend to favour the first option myself. Internal evidence does support it. The name of Goodman's Acre is perhaps the biggest clue. You probably aren't aware but in many country areas Goodman was a popular euphemism for the Devil himself – which of course also happens to be the meaning of the surname of the legend's chief protagonist, Henk Drommel, which I suspect you did know?"

I agreed that was the case.

"So, you're saying that the names were deliberately chosen to add savour to the story or spare the real village's blushes?"

"The name of the village is almost certainly a fabrication, yes, though I'm less confident that Drommel is a similar kind of obfuscation. As I've mentioned it's of Dutch origin, as is

the Christian name, Henk. There was quite an influx of
Dutch protestant refugees at the time of the Reformation.
Chiefly in London, it's true, but there was a limited diaspora
to other parts of the country that could certainly account for
the presence of a Dutchman called Henk Drommel in a
remote Derbyshire village. Then, as now, a great deal of
hostility against refugees came from certain quarters. Henk's
status as an outsider may well have made him an object of
suspicion that would have been greatly multiplied amongst
his neighbours if they had happened to discover the meaning
of his name – the very oddity of which seems to me to make
it unlikely that it is purely a fabrication. The same goes for
the other names. They were all genuine surnames and
unusual enough to make it unlikely that they have been
slotted into the story at random. If that were the case I would
expect to find a few more mundane surnames amongst the
company."

"That seems a logical assumption to make." I agreed. "So,
you think the people involved are real, but the name of the
village has been changed?"

"I think that's possible – but who knows? Perhaps
Goodman's Acre's haunted ruins really do lie buried in the
deep undergrowth of Cleyton Woods – which I've found to
be the most popular putative site."

The name resonated immediately. I'd heard it just recently,
from the lips of Broze Mosley.

"That's where Marius Drommel's father, Geert killed
himself!"

"So, I understand. It may just be a tragic coincidence, of
course, but it's possible that the place held some significance
for him. If Goodman's Acre, or whatever it was called, did
indeed lay in that area then it's possible that knowledge was
passed down through Henk's descendants. How does it go: *I
the Lord your God am a jealous God visiting the iniquity of
the fathers on the children unto the third and fourth
generation of those who hate me.?"*

"That would please Righteous Fretwell, I'm sure."

"Indeed – though I think he may be an example of a later
accretion to the tale. The name just seems too delightfully

appropriate for a narrow-minded Puritan preacher. It's a fact, though, that Cleyton Woods had acquired a somewhat eerie reputation long before the ill-fated Geert Drommel came along. It isn't popular with walkers or locals, even though it's right in the heart of some of the county's most spectacular countryside. It is in fact a remnant itself, the dark and gloomy remains of what was once vast primeval woodland – and then there's the matter of the Devil's Tower!"

"Of course, there is."

"That's just the local name for it." she laughed. "It's a Victorian folly thrown up at the edge of the woods by some minor aristocrat to celebrate the quashing of the Indian Mutiny. Its official name is Topley's Wonder, though the real cause for astonishment is why he bothered building it in the first place. It's a grim, ugly place. It's been derelict for years and it's supposedly haunted, of course, which is how it got its nickname. Rumours arise from time to time that it's been bought for a weekend retreat by some eccentric millionaire, or by a brewery chain that wants to turn it into a family pub. They never come to fruition, though. I can't say I'm surprised. The wood is one of those liminal spaces where something seems off kilter, as if reality is ever so-slightly tilted. The sort of place that exudes a sense of high strangeness and nourishes the darker side of the imagination. Walk through places like Cleyton Woods and tales such as at of the Remnants seem just that little bit less fanciful somehow."

Just as she finished speaking a sudden spurt of wind drove a sharp tattoo of rain against the window. It reminded me that there was a world outside this pleasant room and that I ought to be making tracks for home. I thanked Dr Gale for her time and hospitality and we exchanged telephone numbers in case I had any questions. She also asked that I let her know if I succeeded in finding Marius. She relished the chance of speaking to someone who might be able to add fresh detail to the Remnants legend.

"At the moment that's looking unlikely." I admitted. "I suspect that he's rather keen not to be found. You probably wouldn't want to meet him anyway. I think that he may well be a very bad, very dangerous man."

"Then please be careful." she said, offering me her hand. "You obviously have a story of your own to tell. I hope to hear it one day."

"I hope to be around to tell it." I said.

35.

Driving back over the tops in the driving rain and wind I tried to process what I had learned about Marius Drommel from Arliss Gayle and Brose Mozley. The idea that he was Killdevil no longer seemed such a long shot. All the tell-tale indicators of psychopathy were there.

- Abusive childhood in a repressive familial and socio-religious environment
- Domineering father and ineffectual mother
- Difficulty in building and maintaining relationships
- Suspected of harming animals and committing acts of vandalism but practised in covering his tracks
- Intelligent but psychologically damaged enough to have spent time in a psychiatric hospital

Then there was this weird matter of the Remnants and his families link with a supposed four-hundred-year-old curse. From the outside looking in it was easy to dismiss it all as so much nonsense but, as Arliss had suggested, isolated and ingrown places like Felldyke bred a totally different perspective. The old stories assumed a potency that a city dweller like me could barely comprehend. In the context of his home life and upbringing it wasn't hard to believe that the story of his distant ancestor's alleged pact with the Devil might have taken a lasting grip on the imagination of a clever but isolated and mentally unstable boy. Or that this fascination had grown into a chilling obsession and identification with that powerful figure of evil.

Add to the mix the question of his father's suicide, which so obviously foreshadowed the manner and location of Glenn Wood's murder: strung up from a tree in a lonely, wooded space of ill- repute. If, of course, it really was suicide. Was it possible that his father was Marius's first victim? And did that death factor into the subsequent breakdown and hospitalisation that effectively marked the place where Marius Drommel vanished from history so far as I could ascertain?

If I could have accessed his medical records that would have at least told me how long he had been in care and when he had re-joined the world. They may even have provided a clue as to where he had relocated. More likely, though, he had taken on a completely new identity. Perhaps more than one given his Protean ability to change his appearance so convincingly.

His mother's trail had also gone cold after she left Felldyke in 1991 but perhaps there was a faint chance of picking it up again. Given the abusive nature of her marriage and the sensational nature of her husband's death it was possible that she also might have wanted to shed the ill-fated family name. It certainly wasn't unheard of for a woman coming out of a traumatic relationship to revert to her maiden name and I had nothing to lose by checking it out. If the idea came to nothing then I'd take what I had to Swanson, including the Killdevil journal, and hope it was enough to persuade him to treat Drommel as a genuine suspect.

It was a prospect as cheerless as the weather, which was not showing any sign of improvement as I crossed back into Yorkshire. The rain was coming down harder than ever and my wipers were having trouble keeping up with the downpour. It got so bad that when I hit the motorway for the last stretch home I pulled off at the first services to give the storm a chance to abate a little.

I was feeling hungry again, but motorway food was never my idea of a good meal, so I settled for coffee and a slice of banoffee cake. I carried them over to a seat by the window and stared out at the rain swept forecourt while I ate. The cake was hardly food for thought but the coffee was good. I was thinking about getting another to go when I noticed a poster behind the counter advertising free wi-fi. I got the coffee but took it back to my table and woke up my tablet. A few seconds later I was logged on to the network but suddenly found myself hesitating.

It was a Schrödinger's cat moment, freighted with the knowledge that if my search came up empty I was out of options. I stared at the screen for a few seconds longer and then began to type. I navigated to the home page of *Ancestry* and with fingers firmly crossed I typed in the maiden name of Marius Drommel's mother: Sarah Ruane. The name was not uncommon and there were plenty of hits but only one with the unusual middle name of Abra, who I discovered after a few seconds impatient scrolling had married a man called Graham Arthur Frewin of Scargill, South Yorkshire, in March1997.

Feeling elated I switched to a popular people finding website and searched for Frewins in the most recent electoral roll. I found no trace of Graham Arthur but there was a Sarah A. Frewin registered at *Buena Vista,* Gawmley, which was the next village down the Don Valley from Scargill.

It was a part of the county I knew quite well, about a three quarter of an hour drive from the city, and part of me was tempted to head there tonight. Common sense told me that wouldn't be a good idea. It would be the wrong side of ten o'clock by the time I got there, and I didn't think a widow, possibly quite an elderly one at that, would be too keen on opening her door to a complete stranger at that time of night. I also had no wish to frighten or intimidate her, whatever her son may or may not have done. The wise option was to wait until morning, by which time I might even be able to come up with a convincing, harmless-seeming reason why I was trying to find Marius.

I finished my coffee and returned to the car. I'd felt tired when I pulled off the motorway but now I felt wide awake and buzzing with a renewed sense of purpose. In another half hour I was home and after a hot shower and a change of clothes I ended the evening watching *Bad Day At Black Rock* in the company of a large pepperoni pizza and a couple of bottles of *Moosehead.* Once the credits began to roll, I followed suit and took myself off to bed a little after one in the morning.

I slept well, untroubled by nightmares. It was a Saturday and with no alarm to drag me back to the waking world I slept late, only roused by the jangling ringtone of my mobile. I reached for it groggily, noticing with surprise that it was almost eleven o'clock. Caller ID showed Molly's number and I felt the by now familiar kick of pleasure that her name evoked.

Who knew it would be the last good thought I would have for the rest of that weekend?

The voice at the other end of the line was feminine but it wasn't Molly. As the caller apologetically explained, she was Molly's housemate, Kelly

"I'm sorry to bother you-" she said hesitantly. "- but, well, first of all - I don't suppose Molly is there with you, is she?"

"No, regrettably not." I said warily. "Is there a problem?"

"Oh, well, I'm not sure – only we're supposed to be going to Manchester today? We've got tickets for Ed Sheeran?"

"Right. Well, I suppose it's best to find out these things early in a relationship."

"Sorry?"

"Doesn't matter. You were saying?"

"What? Oh yes, it's just, well, I was clubbing last night and didn't get in until the early hours. I got up late and when I realised Molly wasn't around I didn't think anything about it. I just thought she'd nipped into town or something but then I rang her mobile and - well - the thing is – her phone, it's still here in the house. It rang in the living room and I found it sitting on a chair arm there. It didn't bother me at first. Moll's not the sort who's always glued to their mobile and I thought, okay, well she's probably just slipped out to the Tesco Express around the corner."

"But -?"

"But that was almost an hour and a half ago and she still hasn't got back. That's when I started to get a bit worried and checked out her bedroom. Her handbag is in there with her car keys and her purse. I mean she might leave her phone but where would she go without money and her car?"

"Unless she'd been swept away for a night of passion by yours truly?", I joked.

"The reasoning does sound a bit lame, doesn't it?" she sighed.

Cheers, I thought.

"To be honest, that was just me clutching at straws." That made me feel a whole lot better. "I'm seriously concerned, Harry. That's really why I phoned. Moll says you're some kind of investigator?"

"It has been said."

"What should I do, is why I rang you, I suppose. Is it too early to contact the police?"

"They normally won't do anything unless an adult has been missing for twenty-four-hours, though they'll act if there's evidence that the person has been taken against their will. What you've told me concerns me that's a possibility. Is there any reason you can think of why she might slip out without her phone and handbag? Does she have any other friends or family in the area, for instance. Somewhere she might be able to walk to in a few minutes, get chatting, lose track of time?"

"I thought about that." Kelly said. "Her parents and sisters live in Cumbria and she doesn't have any other relatives in the city. Neither of us socialises in the area, so no she doesn't have any 'drop-in' friends around here. She isn't one for taking long walks around the neighbourhood, either. If she needs to clear her head, she'll take a drive out of the city."

Okay. Then – what else? Could she have slipped out to post a letter and bumped into somebody she knew who was out of their usual sphere of contact? Or, not a comforting thought, could she have been in an accident or encountered some wandering head case down the nearby high street? I was pulled back from such dire speculations by an awareness that Kelly was speaking again.

"It might be nothing but when I looked in her bedroom there was something odd – a card – just lying there on her pillow. "

Up to that moment, I realised, I had been half convinced that there would be some simple explanation for Kelly's concern, something all three of us would laugh about some day. Her last words changed all that. The central heating was still on and had kicked in as usual for the weekend about nine o'clock. The flat was comfortably warm and yet, suddenly, it felt like Iceland in February.

"A card?" I repeated, the words strangled by the ball of dread that had suddenly formed in my throat. "What sort of card?"

"I think – yes – I think it's a tarot card?"

As calmly as I could manage I asked Kelly to describe the card then brought our conversation to a close as smoothly as I could, not wishing to alarm her any more than necessary. I instructed her to take the tarot card and Molly's phone immediately to Rain Hill police station and ask to speak to Chief Inspector Swanson or some other member of the team working the Glenn Wood murder. I knew that as soon as Kelly mentioned my name and my connection to Molly Swanson's first thought would be to drag me in for questioning again. It was the natural response from the official point of view but that would only lead to a delay in mounting an investigation into Molly's abduction and hamper my own efforts in that direction. Even if Swanson accepted my theory that Drommel was the man he should be looking for he wasn't going to let me be party to the investigation, and I wouldn't put it past him to put me in a cell for twenty-four hours to stop me from pursuing my own enquiries.

I wasn't going to give him the opportunity. Molly was in the hands of a psychopath and I knew that it was partly my fault. By taking our relationship to the personal level I'd made her a part of the sick game Drommel was playing with me – and I intended to do whatever it took to find Molly and make him pay for snatching her and for his other crimes. That meant staying out of Swanson's way and off the police radar and I wasted no time in throwing my clothes on and getting away from my apartment. I left behind my phone, so the police couldn't use it to locate me, so my first move was to pick up a pay as you go mobile from a backstreet phone shop just off the market place. I left the car in the 24-hour car park a couple of streets away and walked to my next port of call: the city library, where I booked an hour's session on public PC in one of the private study rooms.

From Kelly's brief description I had no difficulty identifying the tarot card she had found on Molly's pillow and was soon looking at the Rider-Waite version of it on the computer screen. A crowned woman dressed in blood red robes sits upright between two stone pillars. In her left hand she holds a perfectly balanced scale, in her right an upright sword. Above her head is the Roman numeral XI, beneath her feet a single word: Justice.

When you draw that card your course is set, the outcome as finely balanced as the scales and dependent on what possibilities are open to you and the choices that you make. Within a spread there are shades of meaning dependent on the position it appears: Past, Present or Future. It might, therefore, refer to: a decision that you have already taken about situation, a decision taken on how to address that situation, or events yet to unfold that will force a decision upon you.

As I stared at the image of the card it seemed that in some way all three meanings might apply. One thing I knew for certain: Marius Drommel had Molly Grayson. He had taken her because he had realised she meant something to me, because I had made the decision to invite her to become a meaningful part of my life. The card, as seemed to be his habit, was both a challenge and a taunt.

How would I react? What choices did I have? What possible outcomes might those choices bring about?

For the moment I deferred any decision and turned my attention back to the main reason I was there. Over the next three quarters of an hour I crafted a document outlining everything I knew or suspected about Marius Drommel's history, his responsibility for Glenn Wood's murder, his efforts to frame me for his crime and the abduction of Molly Grayson.

Well, almost everything. Naturally, I kept back the detail of his mother's address, since that was my next destination and I didn't want to turn up there to find a posse of local plod waiting to escort me back to Rain Hill. In any case there was a strong possibility that it was just another dead end. If Drommel and his mother had never reconnected after they went their separate ways from Felldyke I was simply chasing shadows.

It was a possible outcome I did my best not to dwell on.

I was coming to the end of my session on the PC when I finished. I did a quick read through, changing the odd word or phrase here or there but generally satisfied that I had made my case succinctly and convincingly. I closed the document and attached it to a brief email to Raphael's personal account. It instructed him to pass the document on to Swanson, along with a copy of the Killdevil journal and the computer drive I'd lodged with him. I also explained why I didn't want to come forward to make my case in person. As an afterthought I blind copied it to Clegg and Eddie, then hit send. I waited just long enough to ensure that the mail had been sent without hitch then shut down the computer, grabbed my bag and left as unobtrusively as I could.

36.

Gawmley was a medium sized town that lay between the
rivers Don and Dearne in what had once been the heartland
of the South Yorkshire coalfield. Though it had never
boasted a colliery of its own it was at the hub of half a dozen
surrounding pit villages and had once been a thriving service
centre for those communities. Improved transport and living
standards had eroded that status in the latter part of the 20th
century when larger centres like Doncaster and Sheffield
became more accessible and the Socialist Republic of South
Yorkshire had pegged bus fares at a nominal level. It was
long gone now, as were the cheap bus fares and the old
communities, fractured beyond repair by the 1984 strike and
the triumph of Thatcherism that had sounded the death knell
for the coal industry. These days, a once thriving high street
was the usual desultory collection of charity shops, bargain
stores and bookmakers, with here and there a moribund pub,
battered to its knees by the Weatherspoon's that now
occupied the old market hall.

Gawmley was the town where my mother had been born
and raised until she met and married my father when she had
just turned twenty-one. In later years she brought myself and
my elder brother Jack on frequent visits to the immaculately
kept terraced house that our grandparents had proudly moved
into on the day after they were married; where they had lived
for fifty years and where they had died within six months of
each other in the last year of the old century.

The address I had for Drommel's mother was on Low Gate,
the long street that ran from the western edge of town almost
to its eastern extremity. It terminated at the old market
square, which was now a car park for the pub. If Gawmley

would be said to have a 'posh' part the western end of Low Gate was it.

The house I was looking for was one of a collection of detached houses with big gardens that sloped down towards a stretch of the Don, the river that formed the southern boundary of the town. *Buena Vista* was the last in the row of well-kept properties, separated by a high wall from the vicarage. This was itself adjacent to the small, attractive Anglo-Saxon church. Cars lined both sides of the street for most of its length but there was a pub, *The Towpath,* across from the church and its minuscule car park was empty.

After yesterday's downpour it was a bright, sunny afternoon but the street was quiet. There was nothing at this end of town to draw a crowd on a Saturday apart from the pub – and from what I could tell from a quick glance through the window business wasn't exactly booming.

I crossed over the road and approached *Buena Vista.* It was a nice house, well maintained, with a neatly trimmed square of grass at the front and a gravelled drive that ran around the side of the house, where it broadened out in front of a small garage with Air Force Blue doors. It wasn't at all the kind of place that fitted easily with the image that I'd built of Sarah. Whatever hardship she might have suffered in her first marriage it looked as if she'd hit the jackpot with her second. It was only when I pushed open the front gate and stepped through that I noticed the estate agents sign lying on the lawn, their name obscured by the large 'Sold' sticker pasted over it.

"Can I help you?"

The voice came from behind me and was accompanied by the breathy whining of a sleek, grey Weimaraner. It was being held on a short leash by a pleasant looking middle-aged blonde in a maroon Barbour jacket. She regarded me with a mixture of curiosity and mild suspicion.

"Hi. I'm not sure. Am I right in thinking Mrs Lewin lives here?

"Sadly, not any longer. The old lady died last autumn. You're not family, are you?" the woman asked, in a voice that clearly dared me to say 'Yes'

"Mrs Lewin's was my mother's cousin – but to be honest they haven't spoken in years. Mum didn't approve of her second husband. Thought he was a waster and told Cousin Sarah so - though it looks to me as if he must have done all right for himself."

I nodded towards the house. The dog looked at me, then looked up at her and whined plaintively.

"Sit!" she commanded. The dog looked back at me as if to say, "She means you".

"I never knew Mr Lewin – her husband, I mean. She was widowed when we moved in here. There is a son. He's been staying there quite a lot since she passed. Getting her affairs in order, I expect. The 'Sold' sign only went up last week."

"I've never met him." I admitted. "I don't suppose you have any contact details for him?"

"Sorry, no. He wasn't the most communicative of people. Neither was his mother for that matter. The longest conversation I had with her was a couple of years ago, during that bad winter? She had a fall on the icy pavement outside Sainsbury's. I happened to be passing and took her to the hospital. She was shaken up but not seriously hurt and I waited with her there and brought her home. She was quite chatty for once. Something to do with the shock of the fall, I expect. She asked me to call Marius and let him know. I'd often seen him visiting but I never even knew his name until that day!"

There it was! No doubt now that I was looking in the right place.

"You say he's been staying here?"

"At the weekends mostly. He stayed the odd night during the week when someone came to view. The last couple of weeks he's been here most of the time."

"When did you see him last, if you don't mind me asking.?"

"It must be three or four days ago." she said promptly. "He came around to finish clearing out the last few things from the house. We exchanged a few words about the weather, I think, oh, and he asked if we wouldn't mind putting out his black bin this coming Monday as he wouldn't be coming back. The estate agent came along the day after to put the sold sign up. Very friendly he was, the estate agent, I mean. Well, I suppose they have to be, don't they? He was very taken with Salome." she said nodding at the dog, adding proudly. "Many people are."

"Yes, I bet they lose their heads over her." I said. The dog appeared to sneer at me. It's owner simply ploughed on as if I hadn't spoken.

"If it's any help he mentioned that this Marius chap was planning on leaving the country. What with all this ghastly Brexit business, who can blame him? One wishes one could afford to do the same. Ah well, better press on. Sorry you seem to have had a wasted journey."

She moved off, the beautiful Salome panting appreciatively at her side. I let myself out through the gate and walked back to my car. The news that Drommel's mother was out of the picture was a real blow but at least I now knew for certain who he was, for all the use it was. Marius might have used his real name when he was at his mother's house, but I still had no idea what he actually looked like or where he might be holding Molly. If he was planning to leave the country imminently it must mean that his endgame had started, and the clock was running down.

Pushing down my rising anxiety I returned to the car. Not sure what to do next I switched on my tablet to check if Raphael or anyone else had responded to the mail I'd sent earlier from the library using a little used Gmail account. There was no new mail from anyone in the Inbox, which didn't particularly surprise me. It was barely an hour ago when I'd sent it, so Raphael was probably still tied up with Swanson, while there was every possibility that Eddie was still in bed after a heavy Friday night session. As for Clegg, he was no Silver Surfer and rarely used a computer outside office hours.

Just to be thorough I checked my usual email account. This was the first time that day I'd accessed it and it was, as usual, backed up. I cast a quick eye down my Inbox, more out of habit than from any sense of interest, and one immediately caught my attention. Sent at ten o'clock that morning, almost two hours ago, it was from someone identifying themselves simply as 'The Adversary'.

I opened the mail, which was blank but for a single attachment. When I activated it a video began to play. It showed a blindfolded and gagged female figure lashed to a kitchen chair. The figure's tousled head of red hair left no doubt about who I was looking at. Molly sat motionless, not struggling in any way, her head slumped to one side. Drugged or (please, no!) worse. My heart caught in my throat, colliding with an inarticulate groan of mingled dismay and rage that drowned out the first view words of a voice over.

"...your attention at last. Don't worry, the delightful Molly is just having a little snooze. Quite a feisty girl, isn't she? I can see why the great Devil Slayer is so smitten – though you don't have a very good record where damsels in distress are concerned, do you? Poor Corinne, such a shame. To lose one red-haired slag may be regarded as misfortune, to lose two would be – well, more incompetent than careless, wouldn't you say? Still, she's not dead – yet. Perhaps you can save this one? We shall see, devil killer. *Be sober, be vigilant because your adversary, as a roaring lion, walketh about seeking who he might devour!* Watch this space, Harry. I'll be in touch."

The video ended, and I barely add chance to digest it or think about forwarding it to Swanson when the email and its attachment suddenly disappeared from my screen. A few minutes futile searching confirmed that it had also disappeared from my mailbox. There was no trace that I'd ever received it; probably sent via some website or application that automatically wiped it from existence within a brief period of the attachment being opened.

I pounded the steering wheel impotently, exorcising my frustration sufficiently to calm down and consider what the video could tell me. First and foremost, if Drommel was being truthful of course, Molly was still alive, though incapacitated. Heavily drugged no doubt, probably with the same substance that he had used to subdue Glenn Wood. In the circumstances the gag and blindfold seemed like overkill, though the latter provided a glimmer of hope. It was possible that Molly did not know who her abductor was and the fact he had blindfolded her might be to ensure that she wouldn't be able to identify him at some future date. If he really meant to harm her would he have bothered to keep her in the dark that way?

It was the only shred of comfort I could draw from what I'd just seen, and it took me no closer to tracking Molly and her kidnapper down. The video itself offered little or no clue, other than that it had been shot in a poorly lit environment, perhaps a cellar or an abandoned building, somewhere with a bare, concrete floor at any rate. Other than that, there had been nothing that hinted at a possible location.

That left the off-screen speech delivered by Drommel. It had been a male voice with a deep, mocking timbre and a faint digital edge. It had probably been strained through voice changing software or the kind of handheld device you could pick up for less than a tenner off eBay. The words themselves were clearly aimed to taunt and sting by linking Molly with Corinne Winfield, the former client I had been unable to save from the White Devil. The implication being that I would end up failing Molly too. Drommel had closed the clip with the Biblical quote relating to the Devil. It was both self-referential and an open, challenge to me that was confirmed by his parting words: I'll be in touch. In this context it was clear that Molly was meant to be the bait in whatever trap he was laying. Unless I could come up with some meaningful course of action all I could do was sit around and wait for him to spring it.

The neighbour and her dog were nowhere to be seen by this time and no one else was around as I walked back to *Donview*. Trying to look purposeful and not in the least bit shifty, I slipped through the front gate and walked round to the rear of the house. A short patio overlooked an immaculately coiffured lawn, flanked on one side by the garage and on the other by a high, wooden trellis fence. Pushed up against this at that end of the patio stood the property's black and green refuse bins.

According to the neighbour Drommel had asked her to put out the bin for the next collection, due on Monday. That meant that whatever he'd thrown out during his last visit would still be there, offering just the faintest hope that somewhere amongst it might be something to put me back on his trail. Rifling through somebody's rubbish was never an edifying experience but I'd done it before and got useful results, though never when the stakes for finding information where quite so high. Pushing that thought away I lifted the lid of the black bin. It contained a single bin liner, crudely knotted and when I hefted it out I could tell that it was scarcely half-full. I was debating whether it was even worth my time when I was startled by a sudden outbreak of barking on the other side of the fence. It sounded as if Salome was back from walkies and had caught a whiff of something she didn't like. That seemed like a timely cue to get out of there as fast as I could and, still clutching the bin bag, I hurried back to the car. The street was still deserted as I slung the bag onto the back seat and drove away, up onto the main road that joined the dual carriageway that took me out of town.

I drove out of Gawmley and headed down into a sparsely populated area of the Dearne valley where open fields and woodlands softened the industrial landscape. After I'd driven a couple of miles or so I spotted a lay-by and pulled off the road. I grabbed the rubbish bag and retrieved an old blanket that I kept in the boot of the car. I spread it out on the ground next to the car and, tipping the contents of the bin bag onto it, I squatted to inspect them.

There wasn't much to look at, just the last dregs of the house clearing process that had probably been ongoing since his mother had died. At first glance it was pretty much what you might expect: bits of junk mail, some of it not even opened, food scraps, empty packets and fast food containers that suggested he seemed to prefer curry to pizza, and a handful of confetti sized bits of paper clumped together by the remnants of curry sauce that lay in the bottom of the foil container they had landed in. I guessed they must be all that remained of documents that had been passed through a crosscut shredder and were beyond any hope of reconstitution.

I took a biro from my jacket pocket and used the end of it to swat away the container. It had had been sitting on top of an upturned tin that I initially took for another piece of food waste. Something that probably contained sardines or salmon or something fishy that, layered with the stale curry smell, was making me feel decidedly queasy. I flicked the tin over with the pen and saw at once that, whatever else it was, it wasn't the source of the fish smell. It was not a food can at all but a closed metallic tin with a brightly painted figure on the lid. He was standing by the sea at the edge of a cliff, with a walker's stick and bag slung over his right shoulder. In his right hand he clutched a white rose and a small dog of similar colour pranced at his feet. I was more than familiar with that image from my recent researches. It was the Fool card from a tarot deck, which is exactly what I found inside when I prized open the lid. I tipped the cards out into my hand. The distinctive pattern of black and yellow lozenges on the rear of each one confirmed at once that the card I'd found at Wood's home was from the same pack – or one identical to it.

A tarot decks consists of seventy-eight cards. Fifty-two in the Minor Arcana in suits of fourteen - wands, coins, cups and swords and twenty-two trumps, known as the Major Arcana. All the cards Drommel had used to sign his work were from the latter: the Devil, left in Glenn Wood's house after his abduction, the Hanged Man, found on Wood's body at Hob's Tump, Judgement, sent to the police to taunt them and Justice, left on Molly's pillow to announce that he had taken her. If this was the same deck he had taken the other cards from there should have been seventy-four remaining. A quick count established that the deck was indeed short but by five rather than four cards. A miscount? Or maybe…? I counted again.

There were still only seventy-three.

Drommel had obviously discarded the pack because he no longer needed them for calling cards. Each card announced actions he had already taken but only four had shown up so far. That meant he had one card left to use in his insane game. If I could work out what the missing fifth card was then just maybe I could finesse his play.

I put the cards back into the tin and slipped it into my pocket. There was nothing else of interest in the pile of rubbish, so I bundled it all up in the blanket. I stuffed this in the bin bag and dumped the lot back into the boot to dispose of later.

Back in the car I went through the cards slowly, separating the Major Arcana from the rest, which I discarded. Each of the trumps had a number from 0 to 22 so I then sorted them in order and wrote down the numbers that were missing from the sequence: 11-12-15-16-20. After that it only took a few minutes to boot up my tablet and find a numbered list of tarot trumps. From this I was able to identify which was unaccounted for. The card that might well provide the key to finding Drommel and saving Molly.

The missing card was number 16. The Tower.

37.

The image on the card shows a tower standing on a rocky plinth. This is set against a black sky riven by a lightning bolt that had just struck the apex of the structure kindling flames that consume the roof and pour from the tower's black windows. Two figures, having jumped or been thrown from the blazing building, plummet towards earthly ruin. Not a cheerful picture and one which, unsurprisingly, represented nothing overtly good. It symbolised destruction on a physical scale, unexpected, catastrophic change, the revelation of unpalatable truths and ambition built on false perceptions.

It sounded like just another typical day at the office.

On a positive note, though it might also point squarely to the place Marius Drommel had set aside for his endgame. Where else but the Devil's Tower, the old folly in the woods where his father had left this world and Drommel's ancestor had supposedly made his pact with Satan?

Before I turned off my tablet I nervously checked so see if there was any further message from Drommel but there was nothing. I pulled up a search engine and did a map search to locate Topley's Wonder, which I recalled was the tower's actual name. Off the main road, about a mile outside Cleyton, a narrow lane called The Ramway dissected an area of open fields. These petered out on the fringe of the dense stretch of woods that took their name from the village in the valley beneath. The directions that accompanied the map suggested it would take about an hour and a half to get there from my current location.

I could be there well before nightfall but if Drommel really was holed up in the tower I would need to be careful how I approached the place. Molly was clearly the bait in a trap and I had no intention of blundering into it by charging in recklessly. A cool head was required – not easy in the circumstances – and a plan that didn't end with both of us tumbling from the top of Topley's Wonder like the figures in the tarot card.

I studied the map carefully in landscape and satellite mode to get as accurate an idea as possible of the tower and surrounding terrain. The folly was situated in a clearing near the eastern extremity of the woods, where the tree line stopped a few feet from a rough track coming off The Ramway at a right angle and running between the wood's edge and open terrain that swept down towards the main road. This presented the easiest – and most obvious – approach to the tower, which made it an instant non-starter. All other approaches entailed a passage through the surrounding woodland. This was good in so far as it offered plenty of cover, but it might prove difficult to navigate whilst also offering plenty of opportunities to get turned around and lost. Still, short of dropping in by parachute or helicopter, I had no other choice. The way through the woods it would have to be. At peace with that decision I switched off my device and set off for the Devil's Tower.

It was a little after three o'clock when I drove into Cleyton, a village of no more than five hundred people that had evolved to a familiar pattern. Four major roads converged on the centre of the village, where a few shops and houses, the village pub and the pretty, medieval church clustered around a small village green, complete with duck pond. In the shadow of the church I found a tight space on a cobbled parking area, between a 1990s Skoda and a Range Rover Sport that between them neatly summed up the socio-economic make-up of the village. It was not a tourist trap and I drew a few looks as I got out of the car. They seemed benign enough though, so I guessed they weren't thinking of trundling out the Wicker Man.

I went to the boot and took out the rucksack that I usually kept there. It contained all the basic kit I might have the need for on a surveillance job: camera, night vision glasses, high-powered binoculars, plus a first aid kit, a Swiss Tech multi-tool and a torch. From the village store I added a few bottles of water, several packs of sandwiches, crisps and a few energy bars.

I hadn't eaten anything at all since waking up that morning and the permanent feeling of sick anxiety in the pit of my stomach hadn't left much room for an appetite. I knew that I would need to stay hydrated and keep my energy levels up for what was to come, though, so back at the car I forced down a couple of sandwiches and an energy bar. I washed the food down with half of one of the small bottles of water while checking my emails again. There was still no word from Molly's abductor, but I now had messages from Eddie, Clegg and Raphael – all of which articulated the same basic message: we think you should come in and talk to the police, but we know you won't so just be careful. There was also one from Swanson, much terser in but with a certain restrained tone that suggested someone else, probably Mac, had drafted it.

I ignored them all and shut down the mail program. I brought up Google maps again to try and work out the best route to get me up into the woods. That seemed to lie via a footpath that wound its way up the hillside on the other side of the brook that meandered its way through the village at the rear of the church. The path veered away eastwards across the face of the hill some way short of the tree line. The terrain would be harder after that but not, I hoped, inaccessible.

Before I shut my tablet down altogether, I checked the weather, which looked set to remain fine and warm for the next few hours. The forecast for later was not so good though, with the temperature falling and more rain expected for late in the evening. With that in mind, I stripped off my leather jacket and swapped it for my weatherproof.

It was only a couple of minutes' walk down to the brook and across the small wooden bridge that spanned it. At the far end a weathered sign pointed up the hill, marking the start of the footpath. From there it was a steady hike of about twenty minutes to the point where the path dog-legged westwards. On the way I met a couple of hikers and a solitary man walking a chocolate Labrador. We exchanged nods and smiles in passing, though I'm sure they wondered why I was toiling up the hill in an Iceland jacket when they were in shirt sleeves.

I followed the footpath for as long as I could before it doglegged away from the woods. By this time, I was sweating freely and breathing hard as I contemplated the long slope that led to the tree line. Before proceeding. I paused to catch my breath, drink some water and swallow an energy bar. While I ate and drank I looked back down to the village, where normal life went on unthinkingly. Whatever 'normal' was. I realised that I no longer really knew – and hadn't done for a long time.

I finished the energy bar, took another long draught of water and set off on the last part of my hike with my calves and lower back protesting all the way. As I worked my way up the slope my rucksack seemed to grow heavier with every step until, eventually, I reached the top of the field and half-climbed, half-fell over the boundary wall.

The ground was still damp from yesterday's rain and I scrambled quickly to my feet just a few feet away from the edge of Cleyton Wood. After another brief pause for breath I moved forward under the threadbare canopy of the trees. It was a typical upland wood, mainly ash; late to leaf and scabbed with lichen; misshapen figures from a bad dream, skeletal amongst a coterie of wych elm, hazel and wild cherry. A mood of lingering winter clung to the shadows, despite the splash of colour from scattered beds of bluebells and primroses that bloomed amongst the muddy mulch of last year's leaf fall.

I passed out of the bright sunshine into the more suffused light that filtered through the trees. It felt like stepping into another world, gloomy and eerily silent in a way that recalled Arliss Gayle's comment about the unsettling atmosphere of the wood. It was as if it held its breath, though whether in anticipation or trepidation I couldn't say.

I readjusted my rucksack and began to work my way through the trees on a trajectory I calculated would eventually bring me to the clearing where the Devil's Tower stood. After about fifteen minutes I saw its domed cupola poking above the trees on top of the ridge where the northern and southern flanks of the wood converged. The ground rose steadily as I picked my way through the trees. There was no visible path to suggest that any regular human traffic passed that way, nor any trace of any transient hikers. Just the claustrophobic silence, broken only by the occasional crunch of a fallen twig or the scuffing of a tuft of sodden grass underfoot.

I had been walking for about twenty minutes when the trees ahead began to thin noticeably. Up ahead I now caught recurring glimpses of the green grass of the clearing and the brooding outline of the old folly at its centre. I moved now with greater caution and stopped as soon as I had a clear sight of the tower. Hunkering down behind the nearest tree I spent a few minutes drinking more water and calibrating my binoculars. That done, I checked my phone only to make the disquieting discovery that there was no signal in the wood. The realisation hit me like a short uppercut below the heart. Whatever Drommel had planned I was sure it must involve luring me to a place of his choosing. I was gambling on that being the Devil's Tower but if I was wrong there was no way I could now receive any message he might have sent about his true location.

It was disconcerting, but I still believed that I was right about the Devil's Tower, which gave me the advantage of second guessing Drommel and turning his trap against him. If I was wrong, well I would just have to find a place where I could get a signal and hope that my side trip to the woods hadn't blow any deadline Drommel might have set.

I brushed aside any lingering qualms and focused my Nikon Prostaff binoculars on the hundred-foot-tall pyramid of blackened sandstone up ahead. I had come up on the rear of the folly, whose grimy prospect was broken only by a solitary window about halfway down. The only other observable feature was the viewing platform that circled the tower behind a metal guard rail about fifteen feet below the cupola.

I lowered my glasses and moved off, tacking across the wooded slope until I reached a vantage point from which I

could focus on the front of the building. Settling myself
again, I tracked down from the dome, noting an access door
to the viewing platform, with a small, circular window on
each side. There were three larger windows at various
intervals down the front of the building and an arched
doorway at its foot. The door that had once occupied it was
long gone, along with the glass that had once filled the
frames of the ground floor windows to either side. As scruffy
and abandoned as it seemed, however, there was clear
evidence someone had been there recently in the tyre marks
of a vehicle that had crushed the sparse grass into the muddy
earth in front of the entrance.

I didn't let myself get too excited. If the tracks were recent
it meant that someone had obviously been there either during
or after yesterday's downpour – but the weather had been
unsettled for the last couple of weeks, so maybe they were
old tracks that had never got the chance to dry out. I debated
what to do next, resisting the temptation to take a closer look
at the tower for the moment. Better to stay where I was and
watch from a distance for a while, just in case Drommel and
Molly were already in there. He would have had to have
transported her in vehicle, which may indeed be what had
made the tracks, but its absence didn't necessarily mean the
coast was clear. He could have dropped Molly off, driven off
site to park up then walked back to his prisoner. I stayed
there for half an hour, watching for any indications that
Drommel was waiting and watching from inside the tower. In
that time nobody approached the folly and I saw no sign of
any presence within.

It was by now after five o'clock and, as predicted, the
weather was changing. Sun and blue sky had been swallowed
by an advancing phalanx of grey cloud. The temperature had
fallen noticeably, and a rising wind began to ruffle the
treetops. I was glad now of the heavy jacket and zipped it up
against the chill. It was time to find out one way or another if
I had guessed right about Drommel's intentions. I was as
sure as I could be that no one was currently inside the tower
and I needed to look around for solid evidence that I was on
the right track. If I didn't find it, then I would accept that I

was wrong and head back down to the village where I would be able to retrieve any message he had sent about his true intentions.

I worked my way back across the wooded slope to a point where I could not see the windows at the front or rear of the structure – and where I could not be seen by anyone looking out of them. From this blind spot I ran towards the door, scanning the viewing platform constantly to make sure no one was observing me from there. I reached the side of the tower, where I could no longer be seen by anyone on the platform. I paused there for a few minutes, eyes and ears straining to catch any out of place sights or sounds.

I heard nothing and resumed my approach, working my way round to the entrance. Up close, I inspected the tyre marks and noted that they seemed to have been made over several days. The older marks still held water from yesterday's downpour in the ruts but there was a set of tracks that was clear of any residual rain, suggesting that they were the most recent. Someone had certainly been here today.

I studied the ground carefully between the tyre marks and the entrance to the tower for other signs, but except where the vehicle had churned up the grassy surface it yielded no meaningful imprints. However, on the stone threshold of the door the passage of a least one pair of muddy feet was evident. This further boosted my confidence as I stepped cautiously across the doorsill and into the vestibule of the tower.

I unslung my rucksack and took out the torch, shone it around the entryway and the immediate are within. There was nothing much to see but dust, dried mud and bits of small rubble that had been kicked or blown in through the door to accumulate at the foot of a solid iron staircase that spiralled up in darkness towards the top of the tower.

I realised that my mouth and throat felt parched and I drank some more water before stepping over the threshold. My foot struck the bottom tread of the staircase with a faint clank and I trod more lightly after that. It was a slow ascent, broken frequently as I paused to listen for any noises from above or the approach of any vehicles outside. The higher I climbed, the faster my heartbeat became - and not just because of the physical exertion. I had no way of knowing what I was walking into and previous, mostly unpleasant experience, had bred in me a healthy apprehension of the unknown.

A few minutes later I reached a small landing from which another short flight of stairs climbed up into the cupola. There I paused for a final time to listen for any movement from above before switching off the torch and climbing the last few feet into the dark space beneath the tower's domed roof. As I reached the top of the final flight of stairs I stepped into a dim patch of light, bleeding through the broken shutters of one of the windows I'd observed from outside. If anyone was lurking in the shadows I made a perfect target in those few seconds, but they passed without incident and the still, slightly musty air held no sense of another presence.

I clicked the torch back on and found myself in a big, circular space with a concrete floor remarkably devoid of dust and debris; another sign perhaps that someone had spent time there recently. There were others, mostly notably an oil-fired portable generator over against one wall, hooked up to a site light on a metal stand. It sat on an old, wooden table, strewn with a miscellaneous jumble of objects. Beneath it was stashed a collapsible metal camp bed, a sleeping bag, and a plastic camping toilet.

Apart from the table, the only other items of furniture were a couple of chairs, one of which was pushed back against the wall alongside it. The other, curiously, stood alone in the middle of the room, facing towards the entrance to the cupola. I scanned the rest of the space with the torch but apart from in this small portion of it there was nothing else to see but shuttered windows, dusty floor and a few more heaps of the miscellaneous debris that seems to agglomerate over time in all derelict buildings.

I walked over to the doors that opened onto the viewing platform. At one time they had probably been locked but the lock, now bent and twisted, hung half off. The doors swung open easily at my touch and I stepped out onto the metal platform. It shifted slightly beneath my feet but seemed stable enough. Not so much the guard rail, which seemed more than a little rickety in places.

The view was quite stunning. From a hundred feet up above the ridge you could look out across the tops of the trees upon a vista of small villages and larger settlements scattered amongst open fields. The panorama drew your eye irresistibly across the valley floor between the wood and the distant line of the east Pennines on the Cheshire border, blue with the promise of the coming storm. Looking to my left I had clear line of sight down to the minor road called the Ramway, which was the only conventional approach to the tower. Anybody standing on the platform would get ample early warning of visitors coming from that direction. Similarly, any spectator on the platform could be seen at a distance, so I didn't linger for more than a couple of minutes before retreating into the cupola.

I checked out the table more thoroughly. It contained a disorderly jumble of waste – discarded food packaging, mainly – and an assortment of other items. These included a roll of duct tape, a plain black cotton bag, a couple of battered paperbacks, a kettle, tea bags and a jar of coffee, a couple of mugs, a half full bottle of milk, a bag of sugar, a plastic teaspoon, a couple of newspapers and a small, empty neoprene pouch of the kind that comes with some mobile phones and mini-digital cameras. There was nothing on or in it to hint at what it was for, however, so I put it aside and turned to the newspapers. Both were from dates earlier that week, confirming that someone had been staying there very recently. Any last lingering doubt about the identity of that person were banished when I came across one final item, which had been lying beneath the newspapers. It was the grotesque satanic mask that I had last seen Glenn Wood wearing in the recording of Jennifer Jensen's initiation into the Hellfire Club!

The mask was clearly of a standard of workmanship you didn't find in Poundland. It was made of soft, foam latex of a quality that suggested it might be worn in comfort for long periods whilst staying securely in place and ensuring maximum anonymity. I guessed Drommel must have taken it from Wood's house at some point. Either when he had abducted Wood, or after I had left following my encounter with his Donald Black persona. Just a souvenir? Or maybe something more to his sick mind; a reclamation of a personal identity that he felt Wood had usurped?

Whatever the reason, its presence here was unsettling and, as it leered back at me in the light of my torch, a sudden frisson slithered down my spine. At almost that exact moment, a deep growl of thunder reminded me that there was a world beyond the walls of this eerie sanctuary. The atmospheric noise had barely died away when I became aware of a more persistent sound, unmistakably marking the swift approach of a powerful engine

I clicked off the torch and moved closer to the viewing platform door. The noise of the approaching vehicle grew louder, then abruptly ceased. The temptation to step out onto the viewing platform to take a look was strong, though common sense held me back. If I could look down and see the driver of the vehicle he could just as easily glance up and see me, destroying any element of surprise.

After a few moments silence there was the sound of a car door slamming, engulfed by another rumble of thunder. As it died away I heard the indistinct sound of a male voice, then another door being slammed. The voice resumed, words still unintelligible but the tone cajoling, almost solicitous, as if an adult were speaking to a not very bright child. The patient monologue continued for a few seconds and then faded out of earshot.

From this I guessed that Drommel and a not entirely co-operative Molly – who else could it be? - had passed into the tower. It had taken me, alone and unencumbered, about three minutes to reach the cupola and it would probably take Drommel, with his not-so-co-operative prisoner a little longer. By my reckoning that gave me, at most, five minutes to decide on a course of action.

My options were limited. I could wait at the top of the steps and jump Drommel as he emerged into the cupola but there were a couple of obvious drawbacks to this idea. Firstly, I had no way of knowing whether he was armed. If he was using a gun to control Molly there was every chance he might get off a shot or that it would discharge accidentally, harming her or myself. Another consideration was my lack of information about his physical capabilities. I had only previously encountered him in heavy disguise. The general impression I had of him was of a man of roughly the same height and build as myself, a few years older perhaps but physically fit and mentally unstable. He wouldn't be easy to subdue and choosing the right moment for the inevitable confrontation was key to ending his madness.

A watch and wait strategy seemed best. The problem was the dearth of places to hide in the cupola itself. That left just one alternative. With fingers crossed that I was making the right call, I pushed open the door and stepped out onto the viewing platform once more.

38.

I pulled the door closed and waited, heard nothing for several minutes other than the odd drum roll of thunder and the steady sibilance of the rain. Then the indistinct mumble of that male voice made itself heard again, growing clearer by the second as its owner negotiated the last flight of steps to the cupola.

"Almost there now! That wasn't so bad was it?"

If there was any reply it didn't carry above the noise of the storm. I had a narrow view of the interior through one of the broken slats of the door but could see nothing other than the glow of a flashlight roaming quickly around the room.

"Welcome to your temporary palace your Mollyship! Your throne is this way. I apologise for the lack of amenities, but your stay will only be a short one. Your gallant Prince Charming is even now blundering his way through the tempest to the rescue – though I'd advise you not to get your hopes up. This is one tale of a damsel in distress that does not end in 'Happily ever after, I'm afraid – but then, that's so cliché don't you think?"

The brisk sound of footsteps scuffed the floor then bright light flooded the interior, briefly searing my eyes and forcing me to look away. Drommel must have turned on the standing light I'd seen. After a few seconds it grew dimmer and I cautiously looked through my peep hole again.

Drommel's back was towards the door as he faced the solitary chair where Molly was now slumped. The black bag that had been lying on the table was now over her head. Her hands, secured by a cable tie rested in her lap. She seemed barely conscious and would have slid to the floor but for the rope around her waist that secured her to the seat. Pinned in the spotlight of the site lamp, she was a silent, unresponsive audience, to whom Drommel began to address a rapid, stream of consciousness rant fuelled either by adrenalin, drugs, his psychosis, or a manic cocktail of all three.

"I hope you understand that I bear you no personal ill will? Indeed, I've grown rather fond of you in my way. No harm will come to you. You'll see nothing and remember little, if any of your experience – which is a sort of happy ending for you at least. Alas, not so for your prince. Ha! Ha! *Thou hast done much harm upon me, Hal. God forgive thee for it* – the devil will not! I will not! We will not! Oh, would it were dead time Hal and all well!"

He had started to pace manically back and forth as he rambled, strutting in the spotlight of the demented theatre of his imagination. I wondered again if he might be high on something other than himself or was his fragile shell of sanity simply cracking before my eyes? He came to rest suddenly, as if struck by an errant bolt of mental clarity. He seemed to compose himself, then turned again to address Molly in a more reasoned, less strident register.

"So – anyway, what do you make of the old place? A bit grim-dark, you think? It's true enough, though hardly surprising, I suppose. Years of neglect and casual abuse breeds a darkness in the soul of places too. There's something rotten here that goes deeper than its cold stones, a wickedness rooted in the very earth it stands on."

He giggled at the thought.

"It always feels like coming home! I was seven-years-old when my father first bought me here. That's nice, you're thinking. A lovely picnic in the woods! Well, think again, sweet Molly. Geert Drommel had not one ounce of compassion, or love in his miserly soul. A terrible, hard man, he was. His bones were moulded from the gritstone of the Peak, he used to say, which was as close to poetry as he ever got except when he was battering your ears with his hellfire bible verses!

"But, anyway, that's beside the point. Where was I, Molly dear? Oh yes, I was telling you about the day I first saw this place. The day I first began to understand why my father, that

fierce and pious man, feared Satan far more than he loved
God. The day I first learned about the Remnant."

Molly stirred slightly, mumbled something unintelligible
then fell silent again. Drommel continued his monologue
regardless.

"Who are the Remnant, you say? Oh, *I could a tale unfold!*
An everyday tale of evil country folk who did a deal with the
Devil to save themselves from the Plague. One of those spur
of the moment decisions, I expect. Something that seems like
a good bargain at the time – until the buy now pay later
period expires! If only they'd known their *Faustus*, eh? Oh –
and did I mention the curse? This is the tale that keeps on
giving! As if eternal damnation wasn't enough of a punch
line, it comes with added malediction. Not only do we
guarantee that your soul will burn in everlasting fire for
eternity, but we also promise that your names will become
anathema and perish from the earth! How's that for a hidden
bonus? A plague on all their houses, indeed." he added
meditatively.

"Well, that's just a brief synopsis, of course. The Cliff
Notes version if you will. My father made much more of it at
the time - indeed it was as well that he had the foresight to
pack spare underwear for me – and, as bedtime stories go it
missed the mark somewhat. I never slept a wink all that long,
dark night. Indeed, I lay awake for most of it thinking that I
probably wouldn't dare to ever fall asleep again, which was
really the reaction my father hoped for, I suppose. Oh, I don't
believe he actually took pleasure in scaring me half to death.
It was as they say: tough love. Fear is a great motivator and,
as I grew older, I came to understand that it was the very
foundation of my father's pious cruelty and that the tale he
told me was much more to him than a hoary family legend.
He actually lived each day of his life in the believe that his
immortal soul was imperilled. As if it could be bartered away
by some distant ancestor who may not even have existed at
all but, if he did, was probably just unfairly vilified for being
lucky enough to stay alive at a time when his neighbours
were dropping like flies.

"Well, he must have been crazy, you say and, though as a sometime occupant of a psychiatric ward myself, I tend to deplore such loose terminology, you could have a point. His intentions, however misguided, were good by his lights, at least. He lived each day in mortal fear of Satan's fiery hand and resisted through prayer and abstinence and a fierce determination to make his family's existence as miserable as his own. He was not about to go quietly into the flames, is what I am saying, and he tried his best to instil in me that same spirit of joyless resistance to the Old One – and when I say to instil I mean to beat. Oh, the love of God was fairly hammered into me from an early age! *Batter my heart,* the poet said. *O'er throw me and bend your force to break, blow, burn and make me new!* Well, dear old dad took that a little to literarily, I'm afraid and instead of beating God into me he beat him out of me and, in the hole God left… Well, I think we can all guess how that turned out, though the possibility seemed to elude my father to the very end. That first night, while I still trembled in fear and cried for my mother, he calmed me with a blow and we prayed together. Upon his bible then he made me swear with him a pact to resist all Satan's wiles and by a true devotion to the God of love – and broken bones – to finally break the curse that damned our family and the other Remnants."

He stopped pacing and swung again towards Molly.

"Every year on my birthday he would bring me here to renew our pact – and every year I grew to hate him and his cruel God a little more even as I grew to be a more accomplished dissembler."

There was something mesmerising about the performance – because that is what it was. Highlighted by the single spotlight he used the space with a player's ease and confidence to deliver a monologue that was compelling, theatrical and chillingly extempore. I couldn't help but feel a sense both of the genius that had so impressed the cynical likes of Ellis Thatcher, and the madness that resonated beneath it.

I puzzled again over his identity, willing him to turn around so I could finally see his face, his real face. Not fake Callum or Louis Sifer, or Donald Black, but the face of somebody I might know, the face of Marius Drommel or whatever he called himself now.

He was speaking again.

"Ah, but don't I rattle on once I get started? I hope you'll forgive me such self-indulgence and that you'll overlook the paucity of my hospitality. Please believe me when I say again that I have always liked you sweet Molly and it genuinely grieves me to see you in such straits. Of course, I take comfort in the fact that you are barely aware of your predicament and will be able to recall very little of this unpleasant interlude! There will be some tears, I'm sure, because you are a kind and compassionate young woman and, regrettably, I suspect that you nurture a genuine *tendresse* for a certain clueless detective. Let me assure you, however, that he is not worthy of either your respect or your affection. After tonight he will only be remembered as a deranged killer, whose obsession with another beautiful woman fuelled his mission to save her and wreak punishment on the men who corrupted her. His body will be found here at the foot of the tower, a broken marionette who never knew who was jerking his strings! You will be found on the platform outside, a little dishevelled, physically abused and with little trustworthy memory remaining of these last two days thanks to the drugs that are now paralysing your central nervous system. They will wear off in time but one of the regrettable side effects is a dimming of the memory. You will remember next to nothing since the moment last evening when you opened your front door to the man you thought was Harry Webster. The man who drugged you and kept you here against your will, for motives known only to himself. No one will be able to say with certainty what was in his mind but the evidence of your torn clothes and bruised body will suggest that you resisted with all your might and that, after fleeing out onto the viewing platform, you wrestled with him for your life and, against the odds, saved yourself when he lost his balance and fell to his death through a broken guard rail."

Molly again showed a brief reaction to his words, straining for a few futile seconds against the tape that held her so securely to her chair. Drommel reached out and calmed her with a surprisingly gentle touch.

"I suppose that for a while you will be unhappy, there will be an inevitable period of denial and that's only to be expected. Believe me when I say how hard it is to accept the truth when the heart has deceived us. I am one, after all, who has loved not wisely but too well. Oh, a sorry tale I could tell you, a tale *whose lightest word would harrow up thy soul, freeze thy young blood* – well, you get the picture, I'm sure. *It was in another country – and besides the wench is dead."*

He continued in this rambling and self-referential vein while he stalked the cupola, growing more manic and bombastic by the minute. He crackled with a dangerous energy that was building in him with the same implacable purpose as the storm that rumbled ever closer and finally burst overhead. It announced itself with a great crack of lightning that split the purple sky with such a noise that it struck him dumb. It was at that moment he turned, at last, towards the doors with a look of awestruck glee on his face.

It was a face that seemed both alien and familiar as he stalked towards the viewing platform, bland and commonplace, as pasty and malleable as putty it seemed. A face so unremarkable that it took me long seconds to remember where I had seen it before. A face that had on those occasions been obscured by a hipster beard and thin-rimmed spectacles, the longish, dirty blond hair that framed it scraped back into an outmoded pony tail. A face that belonged to Gareth, the amiable IT guru from *Stentor Alarms!*

He was heading straight for the doors and I drew back hastily, moving round the back of the cupola, out of sight. I heard the doors creak open as he stepped out onto the viewing platform, which shook ominously in a sudden, vicious burst of wind that brought with it the first fat drops of the promised downpour. I moved to zip up my jacket and flip the hood, which is when I realised for the first time that I still clutched the eerie face mask in one hand. I made to throw it from me in disgust, but something held me back, the glimmering of an idea. Sooner or later I would have to make a move and bring things to their conclusion and when the inevitable confrontation happened any slight edge I could gain might tip the balance. With that in mind and hesitating only for a moment, I pulled the mask over my head and edged forward until Gareth came into sight. With his back towards the cupola doors he reached out his arms, spread wide as if to embrace the storm that suddenly split the darkness with another brilliant flash of lightning.

Precisely what happened next, I am not clear about. Perhaps he heard my feet scraping on the wet metal surface of the platform or felt the infinitesimal vibrations that they sent through it. Or maybe he simply caught a glimpse of me in his peripheral vision when that last bolt of lightning pierced the dark. By whatever means it occurred, he seemed to sense my presence and he turned towards me, his hands raised defensively, just as another bright whiplash of lightning cracked across the sky. As I lunged towards him such a look of horror passed across his face that it froze my heart. He gave a half-cry and, waving his arms in a frantic effort to fend me off, he reeled back against a section of the safety rail. Weakened by a century and more of harsh weather and neglect, it couldn't resist the shock of his full weight upon it. With a creak of tortured metal it tore from its moorings and pitched him screaming into the rain-swept darkness. Above the raging storm it was difficult to make out the final words he shrieked in his terror, but it sounded very much like: "Too soon!"

39.

When I reached the foot of the tower I found Drommel lying on his back, a discarded sack of skin full of broken bones. His eyes were open but there was nobody there. They were just two black mirrors reflecting back the glare of my torch – except, just for a second, I thought I glimpsed something slithering swiftly away from the light.

I didn't need a medical degree to tell me he was dead, but I went through the motions and checked for a pulse anyway. Just then lightning danced above the summit of the tower and shook loose uneasy memories of too many old horror films. Despite my atavistic response Marius was beyond mortal aid. Molly, on the other hand, was in urgent need of medical assistance. Now I was certain his threat was neutralised her health and safety were my immediate concern.

I checked all his pockets quickly for his car keys and found them in his blue cagoule, along with what I at first took to be his mobile phone. On closer inspection, I realised that it was in fact a pocket taser, intended no doubt to render me insensate so he could more easily drop me off the Devil's Tower. Angered by this realisation I was seriously tempted to shoot a few million volts through his corpse as a 'Fuck you' – but then I remembered Boris Karloff again and decided not to risk it.

At this point I became aware of the lights and sounds of an approaching cavalcade of vehicles. I looked up from Drommel's body as the forerunners drew to a halt in an intimidating half-circle about twenty feet beyond the rear end of the SUV. I didn't need the flashing lights to tell me it was the police, who never could do stealth. Behind them were the lights of a couple of larger vehicles, one of which, I was relieved to see, was an ambulance. The other was probably a fire engine, I thought, though my attention was more focused on the darkly clad Armed Response Team that spilled out of the side of one of the nearest vehicles. Not to mention the large guns that they all seemed to be pointing in my direction.

It was about then that I realised I was still wearing that damned mask.

From somewhere in the ranks an authoritative voice shouted out the stock protocol the ART are obliged to follow before they're allowed to kill you. Careful to keep my hands in the air and well clear of my body, I sank obligingly to my knees as directed. One of the officers slung his weapon over one shoulder and stepped forwards to dispossess me of the stun gun and keys before cuffing my hands behind me and pulling me roughly to my feet. Only then did a familiar, bulky figure step forward from behind the ranks of armed officers to snatch the latex mask from my face.

"Fucking hell, Harry!" Swanson swore. "What have you done now?"

"Well – you'll laugh!" I said.

Well, he didn't, not in my hearing anyway. His reaction was a lot more restrained than I would have expected, though. No doubt down to the fact that he was off his own turf and obliged to defer to the local plod, in whose care I spent the rest of Saturday night and most of Sunday. The officer in charge was DCI Lombard, a tall, slim, middle-aged woman of quiet but efficient demeanour. She wore an air of competence that fitted as snugly as her black trouser suit and seemed equally disinclined to crack a smile in my company. The same went for her understudy, a ginger-haired scouser called Chalmers who was anything but.

You couldn't blame them, really. After all, they'd just caught me wearing a Halloween fright mask, clutching a completely illegal stun gun and bending over the still warm corpse of a man who appeared to have died in abject terror. Of course, that might have had as much to do with the last second realisation that he was falling one hundred feet to almost certain death as with the grotesque image that was the last thing he'd seen in life. On the other hand, I couldn't help wondering about those two words "Too soon" and to whom they were really addressed as Marius Drommel toppled backwards out of this world.

From the point of view of the police things certainly didn't look good for me. Molly was rushed to hospital, where she remained in an almost comatose state, unable to give her version of the events of the last twenty-four hours. With Drommel permanently beyond their reach that just left me and my story wasn't helped by the fact that I had no way of proving that Drommel had sent the email in which he confessed to kidnapping Molly. Luckily, as I had expected, Drommel had sent a further message around half past five that evening in which he gave clear directions on how to get to the Devil's Tower – along with a stark warning of what it would mean for Molly if I failed to show up.

By that time, I was in the wireless dead zone and couldn't receive his message, but Swanson's team had picked it up, having by this time recovered my phone from my apartment. It was this that had brought Swanson and the locals to the Tower, too late to be of any help to me but a blessing for Molly. Of course, there was an argument to be made that I had simply sent the email to myself to deflect suspicion – and Lombard was prepared to make it, if only to give me grief for the mess that had landed on her manor. I didn't hold it against her. Swanson would have done the same.

They drove me to the Buxton station and, after I'd been allowed to make my phone call, they put me in a cell to wait for Raphael to arrive. In the meantime, they were busy searching a caravan site about three miles from the Devil's Tower, led there by a fob found on Drommel's keyring. He had apparently been staying there since leaving his flat in the city and completing the sale of his mother's house. In his rented chalet the police discovered a ticket for a one-way flight to Amsterdam scheduled to leave East Midland's Airport at seven o'clock on Sunday morning. It was tucked inside a European passport in the name of Nicholas Old.

More crucially, from my point of view, they also recovered Drommel's laptop from which they were eventually able to retrieve information that included a copy of the fake Killdevil diary and the very real personal journal that he had kept assiduously over the last three years and sporadically during the previous fifteen following his release from the psych unit. That being the point when Marius Drommel had dropped off the grid and assumed the Gareth identity. The surname he adopted was Ruffin, yet another antique euphemism for the Devil

None of this was made clear to me until late on Sunday, by which time the tech's had cracked the laptop's security and Lambert and her team, along with Swanson had digested its contents. By this time, I'd repeated my version of events more times than I cared to remember and was sick to death of police-issue coffee. The first couple of times they went at me hard and I was grateful for Raphael's cool, professional presence at my side. Things quieted down a bit after that. The questioning became less aggressive and Lambert and Chalmers' expression less sceptical. With hindsight I suspect that Drommel's computer had by this time begun to yield its secrets and I was released around ten o'clock with a brief summary of what the police had learned in so far as it impacted on me.

The recent pages of Drommel's personal journal laid out in full the details of how he had tricked me into identifying Glenn Wood as the leader of the Hellfire Club and then planned to implicate me in his murder. I was always meant to end up cooling in the cold morning air at the foot of the Devil's Tower, it seemed. That way I wouldn't be around to refute the evidence he had planted against me. He had identified Molly as the means of drawing me to the Tower from the start. The fact that we had become close was an added bonus from his point of view, but he had been confident I would take the bait even if we had remained strangers. I was supposed to climb the tower and find Molly bound and helpless there. While I was distracted trying to help her Drommel, hiding on the viewing platform, would quickly rush in incapacitate me with the stun gun and push my inert body off the viewing platform, knocking out a section of the rickety guard rail to add a touch more veracity to the scene. Molly would remain unharmed but so out of it from the drugs he'd fed her that she would be unable to remember anything meaningful about her ordeal.

Once my body was found the police would assume I was the one who had kidnapped her and start to pull my life apart. That's when they were meant to discover the Killdevil journal on my computer. This would confirm that I was a violent, obsessive stalker of women with a particular grudge against an individual who could easily be identified as the recently deceased Glenn Wood. The various items I'd found in the tower – the sleeping bag, the tea-making things, the hood, etc - were all part of the set-up. Window dressing to make it seems as if I had spent time there setting up Molly's kidnapping. Glenn Wood's mask was the clincher, the macabre souvenir that identified Molly's abductor and Wood's killer as the same person and closing the circle of circumstantial evidence around me.

It had all been worked out in meticulous detail but what Drommel couldn't plan for was the fortunate and premature discovery of the Killdevil journal on my old PC. If not for that there was every chance he might have pulled off his plan, which was a sobering thought on which I didn't dwell. Of course, the fact that I had been twenty-five miles away in Derbyshire talking to Molly on the phone just minutes before her abduction might have tripped him up in the subsequent investigation but that wouldn't have been much use to me in the mortuary. Luck had been on my side and Drommel was the one lying in the morgue.

Bloody instructions being taught return to plague the inventor.

When they let me go I was surprised that Swanson offered to drive me to Clifton to collect my car. Raphael was still there but I figured he'd done enough for me over the last couple of days, so I told him to head off home and accepted Swanson's proposal. He was his usual blunt, uncomplimentary self on the short drive, but I found I didn't mind his bluster at all.

It meant he loved me, right?

Whatever else he might be, Swanson was a good detective. After the police had retrieved my phone from my flat they had played back the recording I had made of my interview with Arliss Gayle. After listening to it a few times Swanson had made the connection, as I had, between the tarot card Drommel had left in Molly's bedroom and the Devil's Tower. Drommel's second email had arrived shortly afterwards to confirm it.

"If you'd come to us straight away when you made the connection yon bugger Drommel might still be alive to answer for his twisted, bloody antics!" Swanson pointed out.

"And Molly Grayson might be the one lying in the morgue instead." I said. "He warned me he'd kill her if he got any hint that I'd contacted the police. I believe he would have too – and probably himself as well. Somehow I don't think he was the type to just shrug his shoulders philosophically and come out with his hands up."

"Huh. Well, we'll never find out now, will we?" he huffed.

He didn't labour the point though. Glenn Wood's killer might not have to stand trial but Drommel's death would do no harm to his clear up rate and all the tiresome paperwork over his demise was DCI Lambert's problem.

"You've read Drommel's journal, haven't you?" I said when we'd driven a little further down the road in silence."

"Aye – but don't be expecting me to talk about it! I know Lambert gave you the gist of what affected you. You'll have to settle for that for now. The rest'll get out eventually."

"I just wanted to ask about Jennifer Jensen. Does it say anything about what happened to her? Can you tell me that much?"

He sighed but not in exasperation. He shook his head.

"No – but you needn't poke about any more. We'll be opening an official missing persons enquiry. In the meantime, I want you in tomorrow to give us a full statement about this weekend's hi-jinks."

"I expect tea and biscuits this time." I asked.

Swanson snorted but didn't bite and we drove the rest of the way to Cleyton in silence. Swanson dropped me off by my car and pulled away with a gruff good night. I stood for a moment watching his tail lights disappear into the darkness then climbed wearily behind the wheel of my own car and headed home

It was about half past midnight when I got back and the first thing I did was to message Raphael to ask him to accompany me to Rain Hill in the morning. Though I didn't expect to sleep much I wasted no time tumbling into bed after that was done and, in the event, I was so physically and emotionally drained by the events of the weekend that I crashed on landing. I slept for almost ten hours and only woke when I received a phone call from Raphael reminding me of my appointment with the police.

After a hurried shower I threw on some clean clothes and headed into town. What followed was an enthralling couple of hours during which I was interviewed about Molly's kidnapping, my subsequent activities and events arising, and other matters mainly concerning the Killdevil Document and my reasons for not bringing it to the attention of the police when it had first been drawn to my attention. With Wood's killer chilling in a mortuary drawer away there was no great sense of urgency or censure about the questioning, as evidenced by the fact that Swanson apparently couldn't be bothered to waste his vocabulary on me and left it up to Mac and a DC Thurston, who I'd never seen before and who looked about twelve.

There were no questions about Jennifer and Callum Jensen as no investigation into their possible fates had yet been officially opened. Mac assured me that when it was I would be invited back for further questioning. He then brought the current interview to an end with the obligatory noises about possible charges for obstructing an inquiry and wasting police time. These caveats were delivered with no great enthusiasm behind them. As Raphael pointed out with an admirably straight face:, the fake diary plainly pointed the finger in my direction and so, by keeping it from them, I had actually saved the police valuable time that they might have wasted in trying to pin Wood's murder on me. At that point I almost wished Swanson had been there just to hear his reaction. Mac just shook his head and gave his junior a pained look that clearly said: "You'll get used to this."

When we were done I wrote and signed a statement.
Outside in the pallid, uncertain sunshine Raphael shook my
hand and took his leave with one last aside.

"Is there any point in me telling you to try and keep out of
trouble, Harry?" he said.

"Where's the fun in that?"

"Until the next time then." he said with a grin and we went
our separate ways.

40.

As Swanson had predicted the full extent of Marius Drommel's twisted personality and actions was soon laid bare by the contents of his journal and the records of his time in Gatewood. Between them these sources fleshed out the history of a man who, in Eddie's words, was stuck at the end of Crazy Street without a ride home.

I knew the bare bones of it from what I could piece together from Marius's ranting monologue in the cupola of the Devil's Tower. He had been born into a family gripped by a powerful religious fanaticism. This was rooted in an absolute acceptance of the bizarre tale of the Remnant families and fuelled a fierce familial determination to resist the fate mandated by the supposed curse laid by Righteous Fretwell. Geert Drommel made the annual pilgrimage to the Devil's Tower for the first time when he was himself a boy, praying all night with his father to defy Satan and repudiate the covenant made by their ancestor. When Marius came along his birth, seemed to validate this process, his arrival ensuring that another generation of the family would grow up to defy the bane of annihilation laid upon them.

That was the plan, at least. From the moment he was old enough to understand this Marius was indoctrinated by his domineering father through a combination of verbal and physical abuse and a rigid regimen of prayer. Continuing his own father's example, Geert's regime incorporated regular trips to the Devil's Tower, which family tradition situated on or near the very spot where their ancestor Henk had made the original pact with Satan. The long nights of prayer and abstinence that ensued were intended to reinforce a righteous fear of God and strengthen the boy's will to resist the foretold damnation of the family name.

What Geert did not allow for was the fact that not everyone responds well to attempts to beat God into them. Nor do they always end up loving their abuser, which was it seemed the case with Marius. The boy grew up fearing both God and his father but never surrendered to the will of either. Instead of love his heart nurtured only hatred; a tiny, flickering flame of silent defiance at first that grew over the years into an all-consuming blaze. This became to Marius a kind of balefire that, ironically, drew him to the very darkness his father hoped to vanquish. In short, at some point during one of those long, bleak, interminable nights in Cleyton Woods, he cried out to God and the Devil himself answered.

That at least, was his own perception of the experience he had undergone. The numerous therapists who encountered him during his time in Gatewood spoke rather of acute schizophrenia or dissociative identity disorder, though neither diagnosis ever seems to have achieved a consensus. All Marius knew was that on the occasion of his tenth birthday a change came over him during the annual vigil in the Devil's Tower. After that night he was filled with a renewed disdain for his father's narrow and repressive world view and found within himself an unfamiliar self-confidence that gave him the courage to reject it.

At home Marius continued to play the dutiful, submissive son but outside the Drommel's front door he became a different animal altogether: the disruptive but elusive village nemesis that Brose Mozley had described to me. People who had previously scorned or ignored him suddenly began to grudgingly respect and even fear him, without ever really knowing why.

His father too eventually come to a stricken understanding of the change in his son. As Marius grew older, taller and stronger the dark side of his character - as his father insisted upon calling it - became more dominant and he no longer left it on the doorstep when he came home. His father began to fade. Worn down by prayer, Marius liked to think, though the truth was that Geert was many years older than his wife and his health was broken by years of manual labour and a weakness for the cheap whisky with which he tried to drown his existential terror.

Despite, or perhaps because of his new born self-confidence and increasingly unnerving reputation, Marius had no friends except for his mother. His journal painted a picture of a downtrodden beauty, who did what she could to deflect his father's righteous anger when it flared and to console him in his darker, early years with the hope of eventual escape from his petty hell. It was her encouragement that drove Marius to do well at school despite his outcast status. A quick brain made study easy; a quick tongue and quick fists kept the bullies at bay and a Protean gift for the theatrical art even earned him a modicum of genuine admiration in his senior years.

By this time his father's declining health and his own physical development had rendered a sea change in their relationship. The last time Geert ever struck his son was on the occasion of Marius's sixteenth birthday, during their annual pilgrimage to Barad Dur (Marius was in his brief Tolkien phase). Geert had worked himself into a zealous frenzy, lost in an interminable, rambling monologue against Lucifer and all his works, when he suddenly faltered, mid-flow and, looking at Marius with a sort of uncomprehending horror, began to flail his fists at him in a distracted, ineffectual fury, screaming: *Ye are of your father, the devil and the lusts of your father ye will do.* He was by this time merely the shadow of the shadow of the man who had so terrified and brutalised his wife and son for so many years and Marius had little difficulty in fending off his blows and restraining his hands. Locked like this, they strained for physical dominance and stared into each other's eyes. Marius saw just two black holes of hatred looking back at him. What his father saw is not recorded.

Drawing on the rage born of sixteen years of oppression and abuse Marius had pushed his father away with an ease that surprised them both. Geert stumbled backwards like a tired, old drunk, bewildered by his body's betrayal then, slowly slumping to his knees, he threw back his grizzled head and howled in wordless grief.

That had been the end of those cosy father-son outings, though from then on Marius came to the tower often on his own. It became a sanctuary, his refuge from his father's hateful, if impotent, looks and the glowering suspicion with which the elders of the village and most of his peers regarded him. Their disdain was merely a pale shadow of the contempt he felt for Felldyke's ingrown, constrictive community. Marius wished only to leave it and them far behind, an ambition ultimately made possible by the seismic shift in his relationship with his father.

With his power corroded, his body and his iron will failing, Geert no longer wished to keep Marius at home. He had become a constant reminder of the older man's decline and his failure to mould his son to his fanatical purpose. Any objections he may have had to Marius ever leaving Felldyke had apparently vanished that day in the cupola, where he knelt in the rubble at his son's feet and realised that Marius was the master of his own soul. When Marius eventually announced that he had been accepted at Durham University something shone in his father's eyes that was neither fear nor hate but a savage, almost joyful relief that more than matched the young man's own elation.

Throughout his school days, regardless of his home life, Marius had been a good student. He particularly excelled in computer studies, for which he seemed to have a natural gift. Once he had thrown off the shackles of his overbearing father he had used that ability to secure a Saturday job in a computer store in Buxton. It was with money earned from this that he paid for the startling tattoo that Ellis Thatcher had described to me.

His early months at university had been, by his own admission, unremarkable. Solitary by nature and past circumstance he spent most of the first term immersed in his course work, honing his already impressive computer skills. He was not a drinker and had no interest in sports. His only concession to the teeming social life on campus was the drama society, where his obvious talent soon earned him the respect, if not the affection, of his peers.

It was through his other passion, however, that he first made a meaningful connection with another human being other than his mother. Callum Jensen was a young man whose technical brilliance was accompanied by a facility for charming people and making friends that Marius had never possessed. They were on the same course, had rooms on the same corridor and, as they discovered, shared a real passion for the growing video game scene that helped the two to form a genuine bond. A bond so close, in fact, that Marius had enough trust in their friendship to share with Callum another emotion he was encountering for the first time.

Marius was in love. Jennifer Morgan was her name, a blonde-haired girl from the Welsh valleys, who Marius had met through their membership of the drama society. Jennifer's burgeoning talent and fresh beauty went hand in a hand with an open, friendly nature that embraced even a defiant loner like Marius in its glow. It was natural enough that he would share his new-found passion with his only friend.

What happened next laid the foundations of a tragedy that would take almost thirty years to come to fruition. Impressed by the enthusiasm shown by the normally cool and aloof Marius, Callum Jensen was intrigued to meet the woman who could generate such a reaction. To this end, Callum had promptly signed up for the drama club himself, where he duly succumbed to the *glamourie* cast by the blond-haired girl from the Rhondda.

Marius then discovered what many of us learn from bitter experience: when love walks in the door, friendship often flies out of the window. With complete disregard for his friend's feelings Callum pursued Jennifer relentlessly while Marius could only seethe from the side-lines. As his best friend and the woman he all but worshipped became an inseparable item, Marius's friendship with Callum withered, naturally enough. Despite this he continued his involvement in the drama society, where he continued to excel in every role he assumed. Perhaps, in this way, he managed to assuage some of the anger and disappointment he felt for missing out on the one part he most desired. That of Jennifer's lover and soul mate.

This much he poured into his journal, which may have provided a much-needed catharsis that diffused some of his darker impulses. These seem to have spilled harmlessly onto his computer screen rather than manifesting themselves in acts of physical or psychological retribution against Callum or Jennifer. It wasn't until he arrived home in Felldyke for the summer vacation of his second year at Durham that his fragile psyche finally reached snapping point. The catalyst was the discovery that his mother was in hospital, suffering from a broken arm, cracked ribs and a severe concussion. According to her the injuries were the result of an accidental fall down the cellar steps at home but, despite her tearful insistence, Marius was in no doubt of their true cause. It was not cold, concrete steps that had brutalised his mother's frail body but the fists and boots of his now frequently drunk and permanently bitter father.

In the confrontation that ensued Marius had expressed his own overflowing disappointment and frustration in the only language his father seemed to understand. Geert was no longer any kind of match for his wiry, rage-fuelled son, who pummelled him senseless before storming out to bring his mother home from the hospital. When they returned some hours later Geert was gone, his absence a cause of relief rather than concern. As the afternoon and evening wore on his wife Sarah, in her soft-hearted way, did begin to express some anxiety for her ageing spouse. When he had not returned by the following morning Marius had reluctantly agreed she should report Geert missing. The resulting police search ended late the following afternoon when his body was discovered hanging from a low branch of a venerable wych elm in the shadow of the sinister folly in Cleyton Woods.

The similarity to the murder of Glenn Wood was striking, even down to the type of tree involved, though at the time no one suggested that Geert may have been helped out of this world by his son. Perhaps it was simply that the manner of his father's suicide had imprinted itself so deeply on his subconscious that Wood's killing was a macabre echo of Geert's death.

There were grounds, indeed, for thinking that Marius had been more deeply traumatised by Geert's death than you might expect given his often-expressed loathing for that parent. Father and son relationships can be complex, of course, and it may be that his hatred for Geert had formed a twisted, emotional anchor that the latter's death brutally removed. Whatever the reason Marius became unmoored from reality in the aftermath of Geert's death. The psychic conflict that had raged in him since his fateful tenth birthday bloomed into full-blown mental illness. Within just a few weeks of his father's funeral he had been sectioned, his mind adrift on a whole raft of symptoms that included paranoia, depression, glossolalia and mild catalepsy.

Gatewood Psychiatric Hospital was to be his home for the next half-a-dozen years. His medical notes suggested his condition had seriously challenged his carers. No single, unified diagnosis had ever been agreed on. Schizophrenia, Schizoaffective Disorder, Catatonic Excitement, Multiple Personality Disorder (MPD), were all labels that had been thrown at him but, like barely cooked spaghetti, none seemed to stick very securely. He was a psychiatric jigsaw that nobody could quite put together.

During the period immediately following his admittance to hospital his clinician first noted that Marius was exhibiting symptoms of MPD. This is a mental disorder that presents in the manifestation of two or more distinct identities in an individual. In his case it seemed that Marius, the apparently normal side of his personality ('normal' being an entirely relative term in this context) co-existed with an altogether more disturbing 'alter' who referred to himself as Mr Ruffin. He was manipulative, cynical, swaggering and verbally and physically abusive to staff and other patients, particularly when challenged or otherwise thwarted.

MPD, also known as Dissociative Personality Disorder is the subject of much controversy. Psychiatrists have found it difficult to arrive at a universally accepted description of the condition or to satisfactorily explain its cause. Indeed, many therapists dispute its existent as anything other than a ploy used in legal cases to bolster an insanity plea. Given his acknowledged acting skills, some staff believed Mr Ruffin was merely a fabrication, created by Drommel for his own amusement and as a diversion from the boredom of life in a mental hospital.

Drommel himself offered a third explanation, which he clung to in the face of all efforts to wean him from it. Namely, that he was possessed by the Devil, for whom The Ruffin was just one of many old country names. Whether this claim was evidence of a genuine delusion or mere artifice was again a divisive issue in clinical discussions that ebbed and flowed for most of the years he was institutionalised. Throughout this period the 'Mr Ruffin' personality became increasingly more dominant and hostile, a progression only halted and controlled after a long regime of patient psychotherapy, ECT and hefty doses of anti-depressants, mood stabilisers and anti-psychotics.

Eventually, however, the treatment seemed to produce positive results. So much so that the 'Mr Ruffin' had not surfaced in almost a year when Greatwood finally closed its doors in 1998. It had been rendered an obsolete anachronism by the provisions of the 1990 Community Care Act and, after some debate, it was also decided that Marius had made sufficient progress to be deinstitutionalised. He was subsequently discharged into community outpatient care, a regime he diligently submitted to for the next six months before abruptly vanishing from all official or public records.

His mother had by this time re-located to South Yorkshire and re-married Graham Frewin, a wealthy undertaker. It's possible that Marius had lived with her and her new husband for a short period after his release, while he made plans to drop off the radar and become Gareth Ruffin. Despite his assumption of a name so clearly echoing his well-documented psychiatric history, Marius/Gareth seemed to have lived a normal life for the next twenty years or so, In this time he lived variously in Newcastle, Bristol and Manchester, working worked for a variety of tech companies. He had the reputation of being a hardworking and genial member of a staff, a role strikingly at odds with the natural inclination of his character that he maintained, on a superficial level at least, until the last days of his life.

What went on beneath the surface during these years can only be guessed at as he had abandoned the daily record of his inner life when he was sectioned. He did still retain his former interest in amateur dramatics, featuring in amateur productions in all the cities where he made his home. However, he formed no close personal relationships outside the workplace or none that could be traced. By this time of course, Jennifer Morgan, now Jennifer Jensen, was beyond his reach three thousand miles away in America.

Marius was working and living in Manchester when the Jensens returned to England, a development he discovered purely by accident when he saw Jennifer again at *The Lowery*. The play, ironically, was an RSC touring production of *Dr Faustus*; an eerie synchronicity that no doubt had added significance for Drommel. Seeing his 'golden-haired Gwynhevar' again was a sufficient enough jolt to re-awaken his former passion. He resumed his long-abandoned journal entries within hours of arriving home from the theatre and he had maintained the daily record of his renewed obsession from then until shortly before she had last been seen alive.

He did not stop there. He had soon managed to trace her address and making full use of his technical skills he had soon managed to piece together a picture of her life, including her job with *Stentor* and her separation from her husband. From then on Drommel began to make regular short trips across the Pennine to keep track of Jennifer, assuming a variety of disguises to do so. He also kept a close eye on the job scene in the city and when a vacancy had opened for an IT specialist at *Stentor* it seemed like a sign that he was destined to become a part of Jennifer's life again. His obvious professional skills and his ability to assume a suitably engaging personality had helped him charm himself into the job and from then on, he had begun to stalk her in earnest.

At no point did Jennifer ever suspect that amiable Gareth Ruffin was the man she had known as Marius Drommel all those years before. The transformation from wiry, dark-haired Goth to slightly overweight, blonde hippy had been child's play for someone of his talents. Hair dye and a fake ponytail, plain glass spectacles worn over tinted contact lenses and expert use of facial putty and other cosmetic flourishes were enough to render him unrecognisable from the neck up. Lifts in his shoes and some body padding had added a couple of inches to his height and his body shape, completing the transformation. His own mother would not have recognised him.

Over the next year or so Marius began to insert himself in Jennifer's life with an increasing sense of purpose. Apart from their interactions in the office environment, however, he did so invisibly, assuming a variety of casual identities to follow her around. Only occasionally, as suggested by Dorian Wilde's reminiscences, did she have even the vaguest presentiment of something amiss.

Unlike many stalkers Drommel never indulged in open harassment. Jennifer received no pleading or threatening emails or letters, no menacing phone calls or tweets or secretive break-ins of her home. Except of course, for the small matter of installing the hidden camera in the West Bretton bungalow once he discovered that it was the base for Jennifer's casual sexual adventures.

Marius wrote often in the beginning about the purity of his feelings for Jennifer, which had rapidly developed into an almost fanatical protectiveness. She may not have been recognisable as the pure and innocent Celtic beauty of their student days, but he was still in thrall to that youthful ideal. Her unconventional sex life filled him with angry disappointment but the rage he felt was aimed squarely at the procession of anonymous men who passed before his artfully hidden camera lens. This eventually spilled over into violence when he had followed one of Jennifer's pick-ups home one night and administered a beating that had left his victim with severe concussion and a broken arm.

This event seems to mark the re-emergence of Drommel's long buried Ruffin alter-ego, the first of several such attacks over the coming months. After the initial incident, he had been careful to allow a reasonable passage of time between cause and effect, ensuring that no one had ever linked any of the attacks to the victim's brief involvement with Jennifer. The assaults began at around the time that Drommel had learned that his mother, Sarah, was terminally ill; the kind of stressor event known to act as a trigger for psychopathic behaviour. It was also around the time that Jennifer had met Dorian and been inducted into Wood's *Hellfire Club*. The description of these events he had lifted word for word from his own journal when concocting the Killdevil document. As his mother's condition worsened so did Drommel's mental state. The journal showed a spike in the number of assaults against Jennifer's casual lovers and a growing pre-occupation with saving her from the Hellfire Club and the 'fake' devil who had drawn her into his orbit.

Sarah had died about a month before Christmas, a further stressor compounded by the sudden re-appearance of Callum Jensen on the scene. If he had loved Jennifer for nearly thirty years, Drommel had loathed Jensen for the same period. He believed Jensen had stolen more from him during their friendship than just Jennifer's affections. Whilst Drommel had been shut up in Gatewood, Callum Jensen had also prospered from the development and subsequent success of the *Dungeons of Spite* video game. This was an added cause of grievance for Drommel, who claimed that the game had been jointly-conceived with Jensen during the days of their flourishing, pre-Jennifer friendship and collaboration. Whether it was true or merely another facet of his disintegrating personality would remain unknown but, fact or delusion, it fired further resentment against the man who was now poised to steal Jennifer away a second time.

At what point the toxic mixture of unrequited love and hate finally bubbled over into unrestrained rage can only be guessed at, though it was probably sometime over the Christmas period. Drommel's journal entry for the 23rd was symptomatic of his disintegrating state of mind. He poured out over twenty years of bitterness and emotional disappointment in terms that approached an epiphany; a recognition of the futility of his feelings for Jennifer and a lament for his failure to be the protector she deserved. Less coherently, the narrative veered at times into a defiant diatribe that wreaked of his amoral Mr Ruffin identify. There was no trace of doubt in these passages, merely a chilling, immovable certainty that Jennifer was meant to be his – or else she was nobody's. He had waited long enough, suffered so many casual betrayals to give up now and surrender her back into the embrace of his hated former friend. He could not, would not, allow that to happen.

At this point a few, increasingly incoherent paragraphs of his private record showed the warring sides of Drommel's personality wrestling for supremacy. It was a long dormant conflict, now fully rekindled, that seemed incapable of resolution. The anguish of his psychological torment was perfectly expressed in the borrowed words that climaxed this disturbing entry:

Which way shall I fly
Infinite wrath and infinite despair?
Which way I fly is hell; myself am hell;
And in the lowest deep a lower deep,
Still threat'ning to devour me, opens wide,
To which the hell I suffer seems a heaven

Swanson had not lied when he told me that Drommel never revealed the fates of Jennifer and Callum Jensen but the shape of it was there, beneath all the gloating, scheming and self-justification. The shadow of an unspeakable thing. What exactly happened cannot ever be definitively known. However, I imagine a sequence of events that began when Jennifer agreed to reunite with her estranged husband and return with him to America. I believed that the 'Dear Dorian' email and her sudden resignation from Stentor testified to this. I suspected that the latter of these may also have been what finally alerted Drommel that he was about to be separated once more, and probably finally, from the object of his twisted adoration. Whether he was moved by this realisation to a sudden, uncontrollable burst of violence, or a more measured, chilling but equally irrevocable response, I believed the result was the same. At some point between Christmas and New Year 2016, Marius Drommel, aka Gareth Ruffin, had murdered Callum and Jennifer Jensen. It was therefore Drommel who had sent the dismissal letters to Janet Lazenby and Jennifer's real gardener as the first steps in covering his tracks by fostering the impression that their employer had taken an extended holiday.

The journal did not resume until almost two months later, at which point, the author's voice was again calm and in control. The entries were markedly different in so far as they rarely mentioned Jennifer, and Callum not at all. His rage, now presenting very much like grief, was almost entirely focused on identifying the mystery man behind the devil mask who he now seemed to hold responsible for the corruption of his adored Gwynhevar. It was the kind of scapegoating typically associated with antisocial, borderline, narcissistic, and paranoid personality disorders. It is also one of the characteristic behaviours of a psychopath.

As I had originally learned from DCI Lambert, Drommel wrote in great detail about his evolving plan to identify the man in the mask. These machinations also confirmed much of what I suspected about his motives for choosing me as the unwitting instrument of his imagined revenge and the elaborate frame up that was supposed to complete the cycle of retribution.

I suspect myself that the roots of his plan went somewhat deeper. Drommel was too intelligent not to have considered that the Jensen's disappearance would eventually become a cause for concern. Other than Molly there was nobody who might begin to wonder about Jennifer's fate, but Callum had friends and business contacts in America who might eventually raise the alarm. With that in mind, I believe Drommel's plan was elegantly designed to frame me not only for killing Wood but also for those others murders he could not bring himself to openly acknowledge.

In the days immediately following Drommel's death there was the usual media furore that I avoided by refusing all interviews, issuing a brief statement on my involvement then taking myself off to the Dales to walk the green ways of

Yorkshire in my usual way. Molly had awoken and was well on the way to a full physical recovery. What the psychological effects of her ordeal would be were not yet clear. As expected she recalled very little of what had happened after she had opened the door to Drommel on Friday evening. All she saw was a figure wearing dark glasses and a hoodie before he hit her with the taser and she passed out. She seemed pleased to see me when I visited, and I hoped that we could eventually pick up the threads of our relationship somewhere down the road. I knew that I would make every effort in that direction in the coming days and weeks but for now she needed space. She had been released from hospital after a couple of days and was now recuperating in her parents' home in Cumbria.

Eddie and Clegg were their usual supportive selves once they had aired their recriminations about me going after Drommel alone. That apart, they were full of concern for Molly and relieved that I had managed to take Glenn Wood's killer off the streets without ending up in hospital or worse. I took any praise for that with due modesty because, truth be told, I had a lot to be modest about. I'd been taken in from the start by Marius, sucked into the elaborate little masquerade that had cost Glenn Wood his life, endangered Molly and could well have cost me my own life and reputation – such as it was. It could be me lying on the slab right now, damned as a kidnapper and possible multiple murderer while Marius flew off to a new life in the sun.

More than simply feeling sheepish, however, I felt a hollowness inside me that even the clean air and fair skies of the Dales could not banish. I was relieved and thankful that Molly was safe and that Drommel was dead and could do no more harm. However, I had to confess that there could be no real closure for me while the fates of Jennifer and the real Callum Jensen where unequivocally resolved. This was still on my mind as I drove back to the city a few days later and, almost without realising it, I found myself meandering through country lanes back to *Moorside.*

It was another bright, spring afternoon, with blue skies only marred by a few, wispy clouds, and the distant drone of a light aircraft heading over the Pennines. On another day I would have wound down a window and savoured the clean air of the countryside and the sheer pleasure of being alive to enjoy it. Instead I felt only a nagging sense of dissatisfaction that no amount of sunshine and fresh air could soften.

The house was much as it had been on my previous visits, just a little more so. More silent, more dusty, more abandoned. A few items of post lay on the floor behind the front door and I skimmed through them absently. It was all junk mail, though, and I dropped it into the drawer of the hall table with all the rest.

I wandered around the house with no real idea what I was doing there, other than a vague feeling that I was saying goodbye to Jennifer Jensen, a beautiful woman I had known all too briefly and somehow failed. There was still a faint hint of her in the rooms I passed through, some essence that had seeped into the bones of the house and lingered stubbornly in the dusty air. It was fading though. Irrevocably and remorselessly, the last quiddity of something beautiful was vanishing from the earth.

I found myself at last in the living room. Little had changed from the last time I'd been there, though the raunchy DVDs had gone, and one or two drawers had not been closed properly when the police had trampled through. The sun was at that side of the house, pouring through the French windows and striking the print on the opposite wall so the flat colours of Van Gogh's *Irises* flared with unfamiliar light. I was drawn towards it by the turmoil beneath the beauty, which seemed an apt metaphor for the Jennifer Jensen I had come to know. She had carried a bunch of blue irises at her mock wedding with Glenn Wood and I recalled that they were supposedly her favourite flowers.

Now who was it had told me that?

With a mental jolt, I remembered that it was Marius Drommel, in the guise of Louis Sifer, who had drawn it to my attention on the day I spoke to him in the garden. Gripped by a sudden icy feeling of dread in the pit of my stomach, I turned from the painting and walked over to the French window overlooking the flower bed where Drommel had been working while I had searched the house. That bare bed was now a riot of blue and as I watched their tall stems swaying slightly in the gentle spring breeze, I thought how quickly and how brilliantly they had bloomed and realised what horror had nourished them.

Proof

Made in the USA
Columbia, SC
03 September 2018